CRYSTAL VISION

CRYSTAL MAGIC, BOOK 3

PATRICIA RICE

Book View
Café

Crystal Vision
Patricia Rice

Published by Rice Enterprises, Dana Point, CA, an affiliate of Book View Café Publishing
Cooperative
Cover design by Kim Killion
Book View Café Publishing Cooperative
P.O. Box 1624, Cedar Crest, NM 87008-1624
http://bookviewcafe.com
ISBN 978-1-61138-739-1 ebook
ISBN 978-1-61138-738-4 print

AUTHOR'S NOTE

Spoiler Alert!

This is the third book of a trilogy. The romance and mystery stand alone, but there are on-going plot threads about the town which will be tied up (I hope!) in this book. If you like to read the ending first, then this volume is for you. Otherwise, you might want to start with SAPPHIRE NIGHTS (Book One) or TOPAZ DREAMS (Book Two).

I hope those of you who have been with me since the beginning of the series are enjoying the eccentric town of Hillvale and its inhabitants. Time moves quickly in Hillvale, maybe to make up for all the lost years of abandonment. But I want the romantic relationships to simmer a little longer. I may end up with an anthology called SIX GROOMS AND A WEDDING if I don't juggle all these stories right! But you will see more of these couples in the future.

ACKNOWLEDGMENTS

I know I'm negligent in acknowledging the universe of wonderful people who help me turn my fantasies into real books. There are just so many people who come to my aid, I'm afraid I'll forget to mention one. And yeah, I'm one of those people who never read the acknowledgements page!

But I really want to thank the guardian angels who have steered me in the right direction for my Crystal Magic books. Mindy Klasky brilliantly points out my flaws, of which there are soooo many! Phyllis Radford brings a fine tooth comb and laser vision to the final drafts. Kim Killion comes up with cover designs well beyond my wildest dreams. And I cannot even begin to list all the ways my tremendously patient and talented husband helps to bring these books to the market.

And as always, I am grateful to all the fine members of Book View Café Publishing who work behind the scenes, answering questions, promoting, and handling technical details that would be far beyond my capability.

Last but not least, I thank my readers for their enthusiasm and encouragement, without which I'd no doubt give up in despair.

My universe is immensely widened by your existence, thank you!

ONE

Soaring on air currents, sensing movement and energy patterns, she floated high above the earth. Sunlight heated her wingtips. The sensual awareness of wind through her feathers soothed her jagged nerves, offering freedom from her self-imposed cage.

Floating from the bluff heights to the valley below, she encountered a void, a dead spot in the sea of energy, a danger to her survival.

A flash of blinding light followed by an *explosion* of life forces shattered the tranquil breeze. With the piercing cry of an eagle, she plunged back to earth—

And tumbled off the damned ledge she'd been sitting on.

With the breath knocked out of her, she couldn't even swear. Mariah —as she called herself these days—shifted her bruised body, gingerly checking for broken bones.

What the hell had that been?

She lay there, trying to summon the sensation again, but it had been fleeting, simply a disturbance in the energies she detected when she meditated.

Flexing her wrists and scraped hands, she scanned the horizon for smoke or a sign of explosion. After a greedy Null had bombed Bald Rock last month, bringing down half a mountain side, she was understandably nervous about explosions—real or imagined. Earthquake?

No rocks rattled. No ground shuddered. The valley below appeared undisturbed, but Mariah felt as if a rip had been torn in her universe.

The Void, however, was still approaching. *Damn.*

"Miss Mariah, are you hurt?" A deep, Brit-accented voice called with masculine concern.

The Null of all Nulls. She hadn't thought anyone could be more Null than the Kennedy brothers who pretty much owned Hillvale, but Keegan Ives equaled the two brothers put together, in more ways than one. He had to have run up that hill where she'd last seen him, but he didn't sound out of breath.

"I'm fine, Keegan," she said, hiding her impatience and the fact that she probably wasn't fine. Her knee hurt like hell.

But she didn't trust an intrusive Brit who walked the land like a giant black hole. Not being able to sense his energies made her exceedingly nervous.

"You fell off a twenty-foot ledge," he protested in his elegant Oxford English. "I doubt that you are fine, Miss. . . Forgive me, but I never learned your family name. Let me assist you to your feet."

If only he had snaggleteeth or even a broken nose, she might tolerate His Voidness. But no, even his nerdy reading spectacles didn't detract from his sheer masculine perfection. Keegan's hair was softer and more blue-black than hers, with a hint of curl. He had amber eyes that had darkened to a polished chocolate gleam of concern. Well over six feet, he topped her by a head, which most men didn't. And worst of all—he had to be twice her not-slight weight and it was all pure male muscle.

She despised him just for existing. If she meant to survive—probably an unachievable goal—strangers were to be avoided at all cost.

"I'm simply Mariah, like the wind. And if I tell you I'm fine, then I am." Although she winced when he clasped her bruised hand in his big paw to haul her up.

"The wind?" he asked in confusion.

"They call the wind Mariah? Never mind." She reluctantly accepted his aid and tried to hide her wince when her knee rebelled at her weight. "What was that explosion? Did you see anything?"

"Explosion?" He frowned, puzzled. "Did you hurt your head? I don't see blood. How many fingers do you see?"

She should punch him, except he was so damned earnest. If she could find just one single ulterior motive in His Voidness's actions, she'd rip him to shreds. So far, unfortunately or not, he had been an open book.

A mourning cry split the stillness of the air, and a chill shivered her bones despite the July heat. Their local goddess of death was never wrong. Someone had died—someone she knew if she'd felt the rip.

"*Valdis*," Mariah muttered as the mournful wail continued, echoing off the hills. Had it been Val she'd sensed earlier? No, the blinding light had been accompanied by what she could only call a joyful cry, one of discovery.

There was nothing supernatural about Valerie Ingersson performing her operatic moans in her chosen role of death goddess. It was just damned eerie to experience.

There wouldn't be any resuming the freedom of her eagle spirit now. Returned to her earthly prison, Mariah hobbled on her aching knee down the path.

She almost fell flat on her face.

"You're injured." There wasn't an ounce of male told-you-so in his voice, only concern. "Is it only the one leg? Take my arm, and see if you can walk using your stick."

Her staff was so much a part of her that she'd picked it up without thought. She leaned on it now and eyed his offered arm in suspicion. "I'm only a little bruised." She tested swinging the bruised leg and leaning on her stick in its place. Awkward.

The cries from below were more insistent. Now there were more than one, and the weeping raised her hackles.

"Are they holding some kind of prayer circle?" he asked, studying the valley in bafflement.

"That's Val's death watch cry." Which was why Mariah's bones were cold and her hackles raised. *Who*? Who would have torn a hole in her universe? She didn't have enough friends to spare even one. Panic crept in and she hobbled forward.

"I would go down to see, but I can't leave you here." Without a hint of warning, Keegan grabbed her waist and swung her up in his massive arms.

Mariah nearly dropped her staff in shock. "Damn you, put me down! I'm fine, I tell you. You go do whatever it is you do and leave me be!"

He was already striding down the hill in big loping gaits, covering ground faster than she could even if her leg had been functioning, which it clearly was not. He didn't waste breath replying.

She considered beating him with her walking stick, but the wails below were so grief-stricken that she didn't want to spend the next hour hobbling down. *Someone had died.* And the only person regularly down on the abandoned farm was *Daisy.* Mariah had to clench her teeth to keep them from chattering.

She couldn't plead with the universe that it not be Daisy, because that would mean a younger friend had died—but Daisy was the closest thing to family Mariah had these days. Her birth family had disowned her, moved and left no forwarding address. She couldn't really blame them for not wanting to be hounded into eternity.

So she had returned to the home of her ancestors, to where she'd remembered sunny summers of her childhood spent with her Nana. Daisy had been there then. Daisy had always been present—physically if not mentally.

A world without Daisy—would be a cosmic explosion, *a rip in her universe.* Recognizing what she'd experienced earlier, Mariah closed her eyes and forced back the tears, already knowing what they would find when they reached the bottom.

Closing her eyes was a mistake. It made her far too aware of the faintly erotic aroma of Keegan's skin, the rough calluses on his broad hands, the power of the muscle carrying her like a piece of lumber.

It had been a very long time since she'd had a man's arms around her. And none had ever dared *carry* her.

She opened her eyes again, only to notice the dark bristles emerging on his square jaw. Damn, but she despised helplessness with all her heart and soul. She turned to see where they were.

The Lucys were gathering from all across the mountain, up from the town, down from the resort, even Harvey was striding down from Menendez land, drawn by the cry of death. Mariah shivered and sent prayers winging to the universe.

The universe seldom listened—but Val did briefly shut up when she caught sight of Mountain Man Keegan loping down the path carrying Mariah. The silence was almost as haunting as the wail.

With a passel of eccentric kooks turning to watch their progress, even Keegan faltered. That cheered her considerably. "Put me down and give me your arm, but I advise disappearing quickly once we're there."

He snorted. "I wish."

Given his size and looks, he had a point. But he set her down just outside Daisy's circle of foot-high stone guardians surrounding the old farm house foundation. Perversely, Mariah missed the strength of Keegan's embrace once she balanced on one leg, his arm, and her stick.

Cass wasn't here yet, but Samantha was striding up the path from behind the town hall. Standing on the remains of a stone chimney, Valdis returned to her wailing. Mariah waited for Sam before hobbling over to join the circle of women forming at the long-gone farmhouse. Afraid of what she would find, she needed a sensible head to keep her grounded.

Samantha Moon was the most sensible head Hillvale had produced in ages—probably because she hadn't grown up here. Slender, with wild platinum-blond hair and classic Nordic features, Sam was physically everything that dark, mixed-heritage Mariah was not. But Sam was young and not entrenched in Hillvale's superstitions and grudges, and she was a pragmatic scientist—so Mariah considered them sisters under the skin. Of course, Sam had no notion of who Mariah was, so there was that.

Sam eyed Super-Null Keegan with Mariah hanging on his arm. "I don't think I'll even ask." She proceeded onward, keeping pace with Mariah and Keegan so they arrived together.

Daisy's shabby, red-feathered cloak lay at an awkward angle across the sticks and stones of her artistic inventory. Wind lovingly lifted her long, graying hair, but the body hidden in feathers didn't move.

Mariah clutched Keegan's arm to keep her knees from buckling under her.

~

KEEGAN IVES FELT MARIAH SAG AND SYMPATHETICALLY COVERED HER BROWN hand with his. As fascinated as he might be by the black-braided female on his arm, he recognized that the eerie lament of the veiled banshee suggested an occurrence beyond his ken. He didn't know the person on the ground, but she was uncannily drawing people, even in death.

He'd only been in Hillvale a few days, but it was a small town. He recognized many of the faces weeping or looking stoic. But tall, mysterious Mariah had been the one intriguing constant these past days—always at the café, ready with his tea, showing up when he inspected the pottery the town meant to auction, even hiking the mountain when he thought he was alone.

Dark-eyed, seldom smiling, Mariah was as mysterious as the ghosts she claimed to catch in the colorful nets she hung on the ceilings around town. He'd thought her strong and unsentimental, but he could tell she was battling tears now.

He studied the feathered cloak spread on the dusty ground, recalling seeing it upon occasion whizzing by in a golf cart. He assumed there was a woman under it. "Shouldn't someone test her pulse?" he murmured to the two women at his side. They both served in the café, but he knew they were far more than waitresses. It would take time to unearth the town secrets.

He had a responsibility to his family and their livelihood to rip Hillvale wide open, if necessary, to prove his father's innocence. It all had to tie back to the books and crystals stolen from his ancient library, because he knew his father hadn't faked those diamonds. He hoped the women in this town weren't part of the problem, but his sorry experience at home led him to believe otherwise. He didn't trust anyone these days.

"We're waiting for Cass," Sam admitted. "But you're right, we're being superstitious. Daisy was old, but she always seemed healthy." She stepped past the curious circle of stone men and stooped down beside the cloak, pushing it aside to find a withered arm and look for a pulse.

Shaking her head in a gesture of sorrow, Samantha was about to return the cloak to cover the fallen woman when Mariah gasped. She released Keegan's arm and hobbled with the aid of her stick across the guardian circle to push the cloak back farther.

A puddle of blood was congealing and soaking into the dust.

Escalating to a high pitch, the banshee's wail would have shattered cathedral windows had there been any. Standing above the crowd in a long black veil and flowing black gown, she even gave Keegan cold shivers, and he didn't have a superstitious bone in his body.

"I'll get Walker." Samantha stood and hurried toward the path she'd arrived on.

Mariah's hawk-like features turned to stone as she gazed around the circle and finally focused on him. *"Who are you?"* she demanded in hostility.

That stabbed his innards. Did she think *he* was responsible for this crime? He'd been regarding her with admiration, while she was thinking he was a cad who would harm an old lady? "Keegan Ives," he replied coldly. "Would you like my passport?"

"That's Walker's job, but you're the only stranger here. We don't know how long she's been here, but you were in the vicinity recently." She hobbled back to the cloaked corpse.

The lanky male dressed in black who Keegan knew as a street musician shifted from behind the women to amble over. "Don't mind Mariah. She's grieving. Daisy was family of some sort. But shooting a harmless old bat seems a particularly senseless act. Did you see anyone up here?"

Harvey. The musician's name was Harvey. Keegan didn't relax, but he did apply his formidable brain to the subject. "I was studying the bluff and looking for the source of the potters' clay. My eyes were on dirt. I was not aware of anyone until I noticed Mariah. I heard no shot."

Harvey wrinkled his brow. "Neither did I. Sound tends to echo out here."

"Mariah claimed to have heard an explosion. I thought she'd hurt her head." Whatever she'd heard, it had caused her to fall off a ledge, but Keegan didn't see the need to explain that, or that he'd been so fascinated with the native goddess perched like an eagle in its eyrie that he wouldn't have noticed the sun falling from the sky.

"I figured you'd knocked her down in a fist fight. That's the only way I can imagine Mariah allowing anyone to carry her," Harvey said. "Here comes Cass. She'll try to send us home and carry Daisy off before the police chief arrives."

Wearing her gray hair in a tight bun, the tall, slender, professorial woman who marched down from the roadway bore a striking likeness to Samantha. Keegan knew from experience that small towns were filled with related families, so he assumed there was some connection. The woman Harvey called Cass lived in a Victorian mansion out by the cemetery, Keegan knew, but she seldom appeared in town.

She didn't bother acknowledging the crowd but stepped over the stone border everyone else was respecting to kneel beside Mariah. "You felt her spirit depart. You know she's happier where she is now. Let's send her off properly, shall we?"

"This is where I'd normally bug out," Harvey said with a set look to his shadowed jaw. "But Walker will want us all in place when he arrives. Unless you're into chanting, let's wait up by the road."

"Native customs are educational, but I fear this is a private ceremony," Keegan acknowledged. "Perhaps we could find a seat where we can view the area?"

"And see if anyone is hiding among the rocks? Good thought." Harvey considered the dirt and boulders cascading down the bluff, apparently the result of an earlier avalanche. "We'll have to watch out for rattlers, but that's probably the best view up there."

His intention had been to watch the women, not look for concealed enemies, but Keegan accepted any rationale that took him up the bluff.

Not noticing their departure, the women gathered outside the stone circle, hugging, crying, and one by one, following Cass's strong alto in what would have been an uplifting hymn in any church Keegan knew. He just didn't recognize the words.

"Why are you looking for potters' clay?" Harvey wielded a carved walking stick to poke the rubble they climbed. "The kiln burned long ago."

Keegan offered his prepared spiel. "The works of Hillvale's famed potters are a fascination to those who study ceramic art. Despite their often crude eccentricity, their work is mysteriously compelling and has become highly collectible. Critics claim the colors are the cause of the allure to the masses, much as the illuminated mall art was for a while. But I have a theory that it's the clay which enhances the glaze."

Keeping an eye out for vipers, Keegan strode across the slippery rock rubble. He'd been accused of seeing only the ground instead of the people around him. He no longer had any reason to change.

"Or the crystals in the glaze," Harvey said dryly. "You haven't stayed here for nearly a week without hearing all the crystal theories. Have you been talking to Teddy?"

"Teddy?" Keegan glanced back down the mountain to the chanting circle of women. Mariah stood as tall as Cass, but she was like a powerful Friesian filly next to a delicate Arabian. "Which one is Teddy?"

"She's not here. She's new to town and hasn't learned to come when called. She's the redhead who owns the crystal shop." Harvey poked his stick around a wide, flat boulder half way up the cliff, then satisfied no snakes lurked, took a seat in the shadow of sagebrush.

"Ah, yes, we've had a few discussions on the source of the Ingersson crystals." Keegan took a seat and forced himself to look away from Mariah and at the surrounding countryside.

He preferred not to mention that the crystals were one of the reasons he was here. He needed to study the situation before reaching any conclusions.

The rubble had once been a verdant, active hippie commune, he knew, one that had produced startling artwork forty or fifty years ago. Daisy lay inside the remains of the farmhouse below this now-barren bluff. To his left, in an uncleared area of trees and brambles, would be the vortex, and above that, Cass's landscaped yard and the cemetery. To his right was undeveloped, pine-studded mountainside, and below that, the famed resort for the wealthy that brought tourists up here in summer.

But the immediate area was scarred by boulders, dead trees, brush, and erosion deep enough to hide armies. A deer could run across it and not be noticed.

He had his work cut out for him. He didn't have a lifetime to waste sitting on boulders. He needed to talk with those people below—not exactly his forte.

Not seeing any lurking killers, Keegan returned his attention to the gathering of women. "Could she not have harmed herself? Why are we assuming she was murdered?"

"She wore that cloak and built the guardian circle in fear of bullets," Harvey said with a shrug. "Daisy saw her own death."

TWO

The instant Chief Walker—Hillvale's only policeman—arrived, Mariah dropped out of the chanting circle. She might be banned from her chosen career, but she was still a computer engineer by trade, not a superstitious spiritualist. Yes, she believed in the passing of spirits—she released their earthly ectoplasm, after all. She simply didn't believe songs would send Daisy to a better place.

What she did believe in was finding justice. She knew it wouldn't bring Daisy back, just as justice had not returned her best friend from death. But those who would harm a frail old lady had to be stopped. . .

That attitude, of course, was the reason she'd been banished to the town the world had forgotten.

She waited with Samantha while Walker took photos and examined the hardened ground. It felt callous to abandon Daisy, but the body beneath that cloak was no longer her friend. Daisy's spirit had departed the moment Mariah had felt the hole rip in her universe. She simply had to twist her heart around to accept that Daisy would never confide in her again.

"She was ready to go," Mariah admitted to Sam, who had tears running down her cheeks. "She'd seen this coming. I wish she'd seen *who* though."

"Or *why*," Sam murmured. "She was harmless."

Mariah snorted, relieved to praise her eccentric friend. "No, she wasn't. Daisy was the reason all the corroded art disappeared. Daisy was the reason no one ever dared explore the bunker unless she allowed it. She trusted you more than she trusted anyone else when she took you down there. I fear you may be our new Daisy."

"I can't be a new Daisy. She stopped an avalanche," Sam said, gazing up at the cascade of rocks ending just at the portal to the farmhouse foundation. "I wish she'd imparted the knowledge."

"You were there when she did it! You could have been part of whatever she did. You don't know what you can do until you try. Daisy kept her secrets because she understood that knowledge is dangerous in the wrong hands," Mariah said, speaking from experience, although Sam didn't know that.

But saying that, she glanced at Keegan perched up the bluff with Harvey. She'd really love to research that dude.

But she couldn't trust herself with computers anymore. She needed to learn new ways to protect those she called friends.

"Knowledge is power," Sam argued. "If we knew what Daisy knew, we might even stop earthquakes. Hiding art doesn't help us learn what caused it to corrode or if there's any truth about the crystals being evil or revealing evil."

"It's not that simple," Mariah said with a regretful sigh, feeling the loss of her old friend's certainty. "Daisy may have known how to stop a landslide here, but the same earth energy might not apply up the coast or inland. We could train people on Hillvale's energy, send them to Oklahoma to stop the fracking earthquakes, and they could make it worse. And then the government would start hounding us and the freaks would show up. . . No, Daisy did what was right."

Sam looked at her with curiosity. "You need to tell me your story sometime."

Mariah shrugged. "It's not pretty. Just accept that I know whereof I speak."

Apparently satisfied that he'd gathered what little evidence existed, Chief Walker turned Daisy's body over. The Lucys stopped chanting. A collective gasp followed.

And Mariah abruptly sat down and put her head between her knees.

A feathered arrow protruded from Daisy's chest.

THE MOMENT MARIAH COLLAPSED, KEEGAN RACED DOWN TO HER. HE didn't question his reasoning, simply accepted the instinct to aid a woman in distress.

He nearly slid to a halt as he came closer and saw the arrow protruding from the old lady's chest. He knew archery. Only a trained and experienced big game hunter, one with good upper body strength and the proper equipment could have pulled off a shot like that. He glanced around, estimating the distance and coverage. Had she seen her assailant?

By the time he reached Mariah, she had recovered enough to bat him away. "Don't, just don't." She hit at his helping hand. "Leave me be."

He was a large man who made most women uncomfortable. He liked that he didn't intimidate her. He stepped back and waited. This time, at least, she was surrounded by others who could look after her—although the golf cart was probably the only way she could leave. One needed the nimbleness of a goat to reach this forsaken spot.

Walker approached, looking grim. "Who found her?"

When Mariah refused to speak, Keegan did so. "No one was around when Mariah and I started down, but the lady in black was keening. I don't know from where."

"And then all the Lucys arrived?" Walker asked, not questioning the keening.

"Lucys?" He'd heard the term, but he preferred clarity before he replied.

"Lucent Ladies," Sam explained with a tight laugh. "Those of us who accept the unproven paranormal."

"I have not been here long enough to know who believes in the paranormal," Keegan said, studying the chanting women, unsurprised by the weird. "But all these women and Harvey arrived soon after the keening started. One assumes they were closest."

"A killer isn't likely to return to the scene of the crime and prove he was nearby," Mariah said in scorn. She took Keegan's arm and hauled herself up as if he were no more than a convenient lamppost. "I was on the ledge and saw no one but Keegan, but I was meditating and not looking for anyone."

He rather enjoyed her independent stubborn attitude. At least she wasn't clinging and weeping and expecting him to console her, preferably with diamond bracelets. "How many archers live here?" Keegan asked. "It is a dying sport."

"Bow hunters," Walker said curtly. "It's not deer season, though, so they had no reason to be armed. I can look for licenses, but I'd have to find out who was in the vicinity and what weight they're capable of taking down. Why would anyone kill a harmless old lady?"

"Because Daisy knew who was naughty or nice," Mariah said belligerently. "Guard the bunker. I need to put ice on this knee before I can make a plan. Do you need the golf cart as evidence? If not, I'll take it to town, and you can pick it up there."

Chief Walker shook his head. "You'll have to wait until after forensics is done with it, I'm sorry. We have no idea when this happened. Daisy may have brought someone with her. We'll need to test for fingerprints. I have to cordon off the area. I have a list of everyone present and can talk to you later. Keegan, if you can help Mariah to my car, Sam can drive her down to town."

Mariah didn't even look at him. She simply picked up her carved walking stick, gripped his arm, and began hopping toward the road, apparently expecting him to keep up.

Amused, Keegan strolled along at her pace. "What bunker did Daisy guard?"

Mariah ignored his question, turning to Sam, who walked with them. "Can Val guard on her own?"

"No one ever secured it regularly," Sam protested. "No one cares except Daisy. Collecting bad art was an eccentric habit and not reason for murder."

"Daisy lived here as long as Cass. She knew the infamous Lucinda Malcolm and more than we'll ever guess," Mariah corrected. "Now that the art walk is attracting attention, we've lured strangers to Hillvale. That may have been a bad idea. We need to heed the warning." She sent Keegan a dirty look.

"I had no reason to kill an old lady I didn't know," he said with equanimity. "I should think only the people of Hillvale knew she had any value at all."

"You're large enough to draw the kind of weight that arrow needed," she said accusingly.

"I didn't haul hunting equipment on a plane," he snapped. He understood her accusation was made in anguish, but the senselessness annoyed him.

"We need to know more about Daisy," Sam suggested.

"Or the killer could have thought she was Val and will come after you next." Mariah grudgingly allowed Keegan to help her into the front seat of Walker's official SUV.

"Why would anyone wish the shrieking Valkyrie or Miss Moon dead?" he asked, reasonably enough.

"Because they own that land and the Nulls want it. How do we know you're not here to design a ski slope?" She nodded at the pine-studded mountainside looming over the town.

"I am a geologist and mineralogist, not an architect." Keegan closed the door once she was safely inside.

"And a ceramics expert," Miss Moon reminded him, before climbing behind the steering wheel.

Yes, he knew ceramics, because his mother dabbled in them. They were only an excuse to be here. Keegan watched the SUV drive off in a cloud of dust.

If he'd never known Brianna, he would never have done more than analyze the molecular structure of the clay his mother used. But from childhood, Bri had been fascinated with his family's library. She'd been the one to read the journals, to tell him that dirt and crystals had more purposes than fertilizer and building materials.

He hadn't listened, but someone had. It wasn't as if the family firm had originally been set up to manufacture synthetic gems. He couldn't believe his father or brother had committed fraud. But whoever had those damned books had set them up to go to jail for their dirty deeds.

It was his task to find the scoundrel who had those dangerous crystal books and prove his family's innocence.

Keegan jogged down the road in the dust left by the SUV. He didn't need a career. He could live frugally off his savings for years. What he wanted was information, if he had to scour the planet to find it.

Mariah knew Daisy. Daisy knew crystals. Ergo, he needed to know Mariah.

The possibility that someone was killing for crystals was an ugly twist, but given the pain and suffering his family had already endured, not entirely out of the question.

~

JULY 8: SUNDAY, LUNCHTIME

Seated on a stool at the café's cash register, Mariah propped her ice-wrapped leg on a shelf and fought her pain and grief by eavesdropping. She rang up receipts when someone had to return to work, but mostly, the café was full of town inhabitants with no job to go to.

That had been the reason they had started opening art galleries and encouraging tourists to visit. Now Mariah had to study each newcomer with suspicion, but so far, Keegan had been the only one to try to get close. She had to ask herself *why*.

"Unless Daisy's spirit returns and warns us that artwork is dangerous, I'm not buying into paranoia." Auburn-haired Theodosia Devine-Baker owned the jewelry and gift shop down the street. She sat in a booth with her sister and her sister's kids, arguing with the aptly-named Amber, the orange-haired tarot reader wearing amber rings and bracelets. "The galleries have been good for business, and it will only get better as word spreads."

"But the cards are ominous," Amber insisted.

Since Amber was more of an agreeable teddy bear than a person who argued, Mariah kept one ear tuned to that discussion. She didn't particularly believe tarot cards could predict the future, but Amber was capable of picking up on vibrations, maybe even mental images, and translating them through the deck. If she was sensing danger, then it was wise to listen.

"Given the state this country is in, the cards should be ominous all the time," Teddy said cynically, scooping up a spoonful of her niece's ice-cream cake. "Or the cards could simply be warning that with increased business, we need to lock our doors more often."

Teddy was a fire sign, a rebel, and a fighter—pretty much Amber's opposite. Petite Teddy had been furious enough to momentarily paralyze a rapist a week or so ago, and she'd helped bring down a killer. One did not cross the jewelry designer the wrong way. Mariah liked that Teddy was upfront about how she felt—unlike the Nulls of this town, one of whom had just entered.

Kurt Kennedy, the bespoke-suit resort manager, slid onto the bench seat beside Teddy.

Mariah had no understanding of romantic relationships so she couldn't comprehend what the creative jeweler saw in the non-talkative, insensitive Kurt. Admittedly, he'd quit wearing ties, looked happier than she'd ever seen him, and was actually trying to communicate lately. So maybe Teddy—or good sex—had a little magic.

Keegan Ives had arrived in Kurt's company, but the large Brit took a stool at the counter. Looking sinfully handsome in a black-Irish sort of way, despite his dust-covered clothes, he took out his reading glasses and picked up a menu. "What does Dinah think I should eat today?"

Mariah had no reason to believe he had anything to do with Daisy's death. She wasn't psychic. She didn't read emotions as Teddy did. She couldn't read his cards. But in self-defense, she'd learned to read people. He was here for more than evaluating old pots. His interest in *her* rang clarion alarms. Her survival required that strangers dismiss her as a 404 kook. Like Daisy.

"Dinah, are you ready to poison the Brit yet?" she called back to the kitchen.

"Scot, actually," he corrected. "Although I lost much of my accent in my years at Oxford."

Before Mariah could form a snotty reply, Sam interfered by filling his glass from her water pitcher. Samantha had a Masters degree in Environmental Science and a gift for making plants grow. She'd only been in Hillvale a month, so Mariah hadn't worked out Sam's place in the scheme of all things, but she had her pegged as a peacemaker. Well, sometimes, she was a smartass, but only when justified.

"Cass isn't ready to contact Daisy yet," Sam said, filling Mariah's glass along with Keegan's. "It's impossible to tell if she's grieving. Want to go see her after lunch?"

Mariah grimaced at her still-swollen knee and called over to Kurt. "The lodge unhaunted for the moment? I don't think I can reach my nets." She kept the resort's ghostcatchers clear of wriggling ectoplasm, which reduced their poltergeist disturbances to a sustainable level—not that Kurt believed that she was doing anything except taking his cash.

Instead of making fun of her nets, Kurt shrugged. "I'll just move people to a different room if the ghosts start howling. We have space."

Which meant business was still down. She almost felt sorry for the Null and his brother, the mayor, but not sorry enough to bicycle up there and clean out her nets if it wasn't necessary.

She turned back to Sam. "If you can ferry me up to Cass's, I'll go with you. What about Val? She has to be lost."

"She's staying with Cass for now. It's hard to tell what my aunt is thinking."

Since Valdis was Sam's maternal aunt, and Cass her paternal great-aunt, Sam could have been talking about either. Her family communicated, but not necessarily in a fashion meant to be understood. The psychically gifted tended to be almost autistic in their need to shield themselves from forces the rest of the world didn't understand.

Sam reached through the delivery window to take the order Dinah passed through.

"Spam and eggs!" Mariah crowed as Sam set the dish in front of Keegan. "Our prescient cook has done it again. Junk food for the Brit."

Keegan didn't look puzzled at her outburst or perturbed by his lunch. He forked the boiled tomato and kale that accompanied the eggs onto his meat and munched contentedly. "This almost reminds me of haggis. Dinah, you are very good," he shouted at the kitchen.

A dark hand waved through the window.

"Don't taunt the paying customers," Sam warned, before rushing off to take another order and clear a table—jobs Mariah should have been helping with.

Keegan pointed his toast at the mural behind the coffee counter. "Has Dinah hired anyone to clean and repair that piece yet?"

"We're waiting for Sam's mother to arrive. She cleaned it last time." And then Susannah had run away from Hillvale and given up Sam for adoption—not precisely a reliable sort. "I wonder if she knew Daisy?"

"Susannah and Valerie were both good bow hunters at one time." Xavier, the Kennedys' recovering drug-addict lawyer, wiped his mouth on a napkin and stood. "Quite a few of the commune members hunted. It was their main source of protein in the early days."

Heads around the room swiveled to stare at Xavier. He looked bewildered at the attention.

"Xavier has memory issues," Mariah whispered at Keegan. "He's an unreliable witness, but if we could pry more names from him. . ."

Keegan took the hint. His pretty face hid a few brains—always a dangerous combination, but Mariah didn't mind putting them to good use. He stood and guided the muddled older man back to his stool. Kurt Kennedy seemed prepared to come to the lawyer's defense, but Teddy clasped his arm and shook her head silently at him.

Mariah reached for the coffee carafe and poured Xavier another cup. "Do you think you can remember the names of any other bow hunters who might still be around?"

He looked confused, but he screwed up his forehead in thought. "I was only a college frat boy when I was introduced to the commune, and most of the members had already left. The Ingerssons were still there. Lars was the one who taught his daughters to use the bow. I know they had competitions. But most of the women hated hunting. They complained about killing Bambi and Thumper. The girls mostly used targets."

"What about my parents and their families?" Teddy asked when Xavier seemed to go blank.

"I don't remember them," he admitted. "I only went for the drugs and psychedelics. I just remember the target practice mostly. Susannah should know more."

Mariah filed Sam's mother under her suspect list. Would anyone even recognize her now? Val was Susannah's sister, but under no circumstances could she imagine the death goddess killing Daisy, her only friend.

Outside the big front window a procession of county cars cruised down the main drag. Walker's official SUV pulled out of the parade and into the parking lot. The sheriff's car and the coroner's van traveled on down the county road out of town—taking Daisy away forever.

"We'll need to plan a funeral," Mariah said, pulling off her apron and throwing the ice bag at the sink, keeping her grief hidden behind action. "We need to see Cass."

As if that were a signal, half the café's customers stood to pay their bills.

Keegan rose, too, but he came around the counter to appropriate her place at the register. "Go, Chief Walker can assist you into his vehicle. I worked a store in my youth and can handle cash. I cannot say the same for serving dishes though."

He began taking receipts and cash like a pro, taking only minutes to assess the machine and the scrawled prices on order tickets. Mariah wanted to protest, but Dinah came out, gauged the situation, and waved her on.

"I'll fry his gizzard for lunch if he messes with me," Dinah declared, pointing her wooden spoon like a gun at her new employee.

Keegan didn't appear deterred. Given that he was twice Dinah's diminutive stature but possessed half her fierceness, the contest was equal Mariah decided.

She really wanted her computer to track this man. Was this justification enough to break her vow to never touch a machine again?

She'd broken her vow for less, but she really didn't need to invite more trouble to Hillvale—or she'd have nowhere left to go.

THREE

With the lunch rush ended and the Lucys congregating at the mysterious Cass's house, Dinah sent Keegan away from the empty cafe with enough leftover food to feed a few armies.

Tucking his glasses in his pocket and stepping outside, Keegan heard a deep voice speak in scorn. "The whole damned country's going to pot if real men have to work with little faggots like that."

Unaccustomed to hearing such talk in Hillvale's diverse community, Keegan studied the overall-clad, checked-shirt stranger spitting at the street. The man was almost as tall as he was, but given to paunch more than muscle. Keegan figured he could walk on his face, but there was little satisfaction in clocking bigots.

"Are you talking to me?" he asked in an even tone concealing his disdain.

"She ain't a she," the man responded without answering the question. He nodded his head at the café where Dinah, wearing her red fifties-style shirt dress, was cleaning up the counter. "Them queers are ruining this town. Shouldn't be allowed."

Arguing with a narrow mind was futile. Keegan knew he should just walk away, but the clod seemed out of place. "Do you live here?"

The older man sneered. "Longer than a furriner like you. Maybe you're one of them faggots too."

"Perhaps you just stepped out of a time machine?" Keegan asked, unable to resist. "If so, you will find much changed since the 1950s. Perhaps you should learn more about your surroundings before you disparage the inhabitants of the modern world."

The older man narrowed his eyes. "You makin' fun of me? I could punch your lights out."

Keegan was large—he always had been. He'd learned long ago that he didn't need to test his strength on the feeble-minded, and fortunately, he was given to more intellectual pursuits than pugilism. The automatic childish taunt of *you want to try* still came to mind because it would be ever so pleasant watching the bully hit the dust.

A female voice called from down the street. "George, come help me with these packages, will ya? Don't make me do all the work."

George blinked and turned to answer. Keegan chose the high road and walked away. One shouldn't taunt tourists, although Americans were a strange lot if the rich dressed like a character in *The Grapes of Wrath*.

He headed for Aaron's Antiques at the end of town. Aaron Townsend had known of Keegan's expertise and asked him to examine the Hillvale pottery that had been recently unearthed from storage. Aaron had been a strange one when they'd met at Oxford and hadn't changed much, except he was apparently wealthier. Surely there were other experts who lived closer, but Keegan suspected his school acquaintance had ulterior motives in bringing him here—just as he had ulterior motives in accepting the invitation.

Passing under one of Sam's colorful flower baskets, Keegan entered the warehouse that was gradually morphing into a ceramics gallery. The goateed antique expert arranging pottery on shelves glanced up at Keegan's entrance. "I smell Dinah's Reuben sandwich."

Keegan held out the bag. "Lunch leftovers. Help yourself. Has there been any decision on the best way to dispose of all these valuable pieces?" He gestured at the colorful display.

Aaron rummaged in the lunch bag. Attired in a black turtleneck, black jeans, and camel-colored blazer, Keegan's landlord would look more at home in the great auction houses and galleries of London than in this dusty California town.

"We're waiting for approval of a plan to set up an educational non-profit for artists in Hillvale. In the meantime, I've sent out feelers to several museums that still have a budget for ceramics. We probably should decide what pieces ought to stay in Hillvale, though. Tourists bring money into town. Starving artists don't."

Keegan circled the structure, looking for the pieces that intrigued him most. He settled on a mottled red and green dragon with an expectant gleam in its crystal eyes, lifting it from the shelf to examine it again. "Some of these pieces are worth fortunes. You need more security."

"We would have to sell them to *afford* security," Aaron reminded him. "I've set up some basic precautions, but I don't think we're a target of thieves yet."

"Just killers?" Keegan asked casually.

Aaron finished chewing before responding. "If any killers have come to town, they're archers, like you and me. But to pull a bow that force-fully, they'd have to have the right equipment. I can think of a dozen easier ways to get rid of a frail old lady besides an arrow. Admittedly, I'm eager to see what she concealed in the bunker, but killing her for that reason was unnecessary."

Keegan nodded. "That's my assessment. She owned nothing. She must have *known* something that the killer did not want revealed. I've not lived here long enough to know the inhabitants. Is there an element of. . ." He hesitated, looking for an inoffensive description, but how did one describe bigots without offense? "An element of narrow-mindedness that might not appreciate the value of a homeless, half-mad old lady?"

Aaron considered this. "Not just the narrow minded, although we have a few of those. But that land is valuable. We've already had one developer kill to keep it. If someone saw Daisy as a deterrent to the Ingerssons selling it. . ."

"That's foolish if she didn't actually own it." Keegan knew he shouldn't become involved in the local troubles. He had a purpose here, and while book thieves were his target, so far, they hadn't killed anyone. Still, because of the book contents, he was as interested in that land as any developer.

"As long as Daisy was guarding her treasure trove, Val and Sam weren't likely to sell," Aaron admitted. "Watch. Now that Daisy isn't stopping them, the Lucys will start pillaging the bunker, looking for the source of evil, for villains, for who-knows-what. Even I am eager to see what she concealed. But once we've done that, it's just a rocky hillside developers covet."

"What about protecting the vortex?" Keegan suggested, since he'd heard Mariah mention it.

"Cass owns the vortex. That's her excuse to keep out developers. The younger generation is less likely to accept it in the name of progress." Aaron swigged from a bottle of water and eyed the inventory with appreciation. "I like it up here. With the internet, I have the world at my fingertips. Outside my door, I have an eccentric community that accepts me as I am."

"If Hillvale becomes a ski resort and another Vail?" Keegan asked, returning the dragon to its place.

"Like the other Lucys, I may have to leave," Aaron said in regret. "Does your snowy mountain town need an antique dealer?"

They'd only been casual acquaintances at school, but Aaron knew who he was. Keegan shrugged. "Eccentricity *is* my family. You'd feel right at home, except it's colder."

"But the British Isles have so many antiques, that it would be hard for me to make a living there. It took a lot of research to find this place. I'd rather not leave."

"I have a crumbling castle full of aging journals written by my witchy ancestors. The village is full of our descendants. Eccentricity, as we call it, abounds. The same cannot be said of most places. Like seeks like." Which left him wondering about Aaron, but he was too polite to ask *Which kind of weird are you?*

"Will you be going back to your castle after you leave here?" Aaron returned to his inventory labeling.

"I was hoping you would lease out your small room a little longer. I am intrigued by the notion of crystals in a ground that shouldn't bear them. The dragon here—" Keegan stroked the ceramic piece, "—contains a diorite found only in India. Yet I've been told the commune used all natural materials found on the farm."

"I would take that with a large dose of salt. The Ingerssons used any substance they could lay their hands on. If they found a pirate's treasure buried in a cave, they would consider that all natural. They tried making their own paints but ended up buying much of what they needed. Do you think Daisy hid the secrets of those crystals?"

"I have no idea. I know these ceramics are laced with ingredients not encountered in normal clay. I am inclined to accidently break a few of the fraudulent pieces and analyze them." He'd already identified the fake pieces fired in imitation of the more valuable ones. Visually, the clay was similar, as was the glaze, but the crystalline structure was different—which was why he'd been hunting clay deposits.

Aaron picked up an ugly green frog and flung it in Keegan's direction. Frogs couldn't fly. It landed on the wood floor and broke a ceramic limb. "Oops."

"That was a particularly amateurish fake," Keegan said, stooping to pick up the pieces. "Not one of the pieces I need to study. Still we require a base to work from. I need my equipment. I could send part of this back to my lab, but I'd like to look for someplace more local that might be faster. Have I permission to use your internet?"

Besides, he could no longer trust his family's lab or personnel.

Aaron waved his hand. "Go for it. Our cable is reasonably reliable, unlike cell phones. But keep Mariah out of your laptop."

Keegan raised his eyebrows. "May I ask why?"

Aaron shrugged. "Just passing on the mayor's warning. You'll have to ask him."

"And you've never investigated this curiosity?" Keegan was ready to hit the keyboard as soon as he could reach it.

Aaron snorted. "You really think her name is Mariah?"

July 8: Sunday afternoon

"Daisy's spirit was Ohlone," Mariah explained, remembering with tears the day Daisy had gone into one of her trances and spoken of ancient tribal rituals. Outsiders thought her crazy—but Daisy's was an ancient spirit. The killer had truly ripped a hole in the universe. Mariah wiped angrily at her eyes. "We would need to gather all her belongings, wrap her in feathers and beads, and say farewell to her body on a funeral pyre. I doubt the county will approve."

Mariah sat on Cass's front porch stairs, letting others choose Daisy's funeral. Ceremonies were for the living—except ritual didn't work for her.

She needed *action* to ease her pain and helplessness. If she didn't have Daisy to talk her down—Her fingers itched for her keyboard.

The last time she'd acted in rage and grief, she'd unleashed a media holocaust and a personal catastrophe that had ended life as she knew it. A second episode like that would land her in jail.

If Daisy didn't need her anymore. . . What difference would it make if her prison was here or behind bars?

Well, she liked it here better than behind bars.

Teddy sat down next to her. Although the jeweler's parents were from Hillvale, Teddy was essentially a newcomer and not part of Cass's inner circle. Like Sam, Teddy had a more prosaic businesswoman's outlook.

"What do you know about the crystals Daisy used in her stone sculptures?" Teddy asked. "And do you know if she had any family? I think I can sell those statues and earn enough to pay for the cremation and more. But I hate letting those crystals loose in the world without knowing more about them."

Recalling the effort Daisy had made to give everyone she knew an object of beauty, love, and protection, Mariah answered that with assurance. "Daisy only used what she called *safe* crystals. The ones she made for us personally might vary in power, but the ones on the foundation were basic guardian stones. If she had access to evil ones, I never heard about it. It would be against her nature to deal with evil."

Samantha joined them, taking a seat on a higher step so she could stretch her long legs. "Daisy acquainted greed with evil. She created art for beauty, not money, which was why she was essentially homeless."

"And why she buried the art she considered evil," Mariah added.

Teddy drew lines in the dust with her toe. "Many of her guardians used black tourmaline and smoky quartz. Both have strong grounding elements to repel negative energy. But I'm still learning about crystal energies and don't feel comfortable being a judge of what's safe and what isn't. I wish Daisy had kept a book."

"She might have," Mariah said. Recalling Daisy and her secretive ways held her friend closer and offset her helpless rage. "No one has ever inventoried the bunker. And we know from your cousin's notes that Lucinda Malcolm left a crystal compendium. Is there any chance that Daisy may have stolen the book the way she did the art?"

Teddy's topaz eyes nearly gleamed gold in anticipation. "The police took apart my thieving cousin's house and didn't find anything that might be Lucinda's book. We're tearing down half the walls in the remodel, and it hasn't turned up yet. So if it ever existed. . ."

"We should look." Mariah's spirits lifted, and she glared at her still-swollen knee. Nurse Brenda had worked miracles on it, but even a gifted practitioner wasn't God. "I just need Daisy's cart to get around."

"I heard you used Mr. Ives as transport earlier," Samantha said with a laugh. "Maybe we could enlist him. I'm not sure why he's still around now that he's appraised the ceramics."

"He claims he's a geologist and mineralogist. Maybe he's hoping for a gem mine." Mariah ignored the reference to Keegan carrying her. She'd never been a delicate flower men liked to haul around. She was the sturdy sort who beat them at volleyball and who carried her own surf-board. Men were more likely to expect her to change their tires. Working in a man's world, she had preferred it that way.

She was just feeling a bit. . . vulnerable. . . with Daisy's death. Phys-ical action in the company of others shouldn't get her into trouble the way her computer vengeance had.

"Gems are unlikely," Samantha said, taking her seriously about Keegan's goal. "Gold, maybe. But with that fault line running through here, not a particularly safe venture. I looked Keegan up the other night. The most I can find is some relation to a mining family in Scotland—although there was one reference to a Malcolm library in his castle. Do you think he's related to Lucinda Malcolm?"

Thank goodness someone had the smarts to look him up! She didn't know if he was one of the people she'd harmed in her reprisal for Adera's death, but she needed to stay far away from him, just in case.

A little while later, Mariah stiffly climbed into the front seat of Sam's Subaru. "I need to be back at the café before the dinner rush," she insisted.

"You need to stay off that leg," Sam protested. "I can handle the café for a few days."

"We ought to make the Kennedys set up an urgent care office and put

Brenda in charge." Mariah diverted the topic from her injury. "She gets bored."

"Don't put me in a position between the town's needs and Kurt's business," Teddy protested from the back seat as Sam drove through town. "Kurt and I are still learning this living together thing. He's more wounded than you realize, and the weight of keeping all his employees while tourism is down is a heavy burden. It's up to us to make things happen."

"If *making things happen* got Daisy killed, I'm not certain I'm on board with that. Maybe the town needs to die." Mariah knew that was selfish. Just because she needed isolation didn't mean it was good for anyone else.

"You don't have enough bills to pay if you think we should stifle tourists," Teddy said with a laugh. "I need the business if I'm spending my spare time studying crystal energy instead of designing high-end jewelry. The art walk really made a difference at the cash register."

"And the town needs the income to keep Walker here. He's only playing police chief because I want to stay and because he thinks there's a need. If Hillvale turns into a ghost town again. . . He'll grow bored and go back to LA," Sam said.

"Then you and Val better come up with a good use for that land of yours before someone else does," Mariah said grumpily. "Without Daisy out there guarding it. . ."

Sam pointed out the windshield. "The vultures will prey," she finished for her. "That's not the sheriff's crew."

Trucks were lined up alongside the dirt lane and men were walking down the path to the farmhouse.

FOUR

JULY 8: SUNDAY, LATE AFTERNOON

At a loud, feminine, "*Ahem*" from the road, Keegan elbowed Aaron. "We didn't move fast enough."

Aaron snorted. "Not a chance we could have. I just wanted to be here when they showed up."

Ahead of them, Walker and the mayor halted to wait for the women. "Official police business," Walker yelled back at the trio of females.

Mariah was hurriedly hobbling along on her walking stick. Keegan winced just watching her. He jogged back up the path to offer his arm.

He'd come to expect her suspicious glare and wondered if it was men in general or just him that stirred her animosity.

"You're not police. You're not even a citizen." Since the others were striding ahead of them, she grudgingly accepted his arm.

Her strong fingers gripping his bare arm created a pleasurable thrill that balanced her crankiness. "Walker didn't want to disturb Sam or Val," he explained. "But if someone killed Daisy to get into that vault, then we need to know what's in there. Aaron and I are the only experts around, and Monty thought he ought to represent the town's interests."

"Aside from the fact that our mayor is a Kennedy and represents the *resort's* interests as much as the town, what about them?" She gestured at the other men. "Harvey's a musician. Orval's a veterinarian. What are they doing here?"

"They just kind of materialized," Keegan admitted. "Walker says it happens. He figured he could use them to guard the entrance while we were inside."

As they descended the path, Keegan did his damnedest not to notice the sway of Mariah's breasts, but he was pretty sure she wasn't wearing much under the embroidered cotton tunic. He concentrated on admiring her sleek black braid adorned with feathers and beads and. . . *crystals*. Not plastic trinkets. Where the devil did those things come from? These didn't look like more than glassy diorite, but crystals didn't lie around on the ground in bead form. Someone had to manufacture them from their rock origins.

"Why did *you* decide to come up here?" he asked when she only frowned in response.

"Not your business," she said.

"Mariah, behave yourself," Sam called back. "Remember, Keegan's the one with the Malcolm library."

Damn and hellfire. How far had the snoopy women dug into his background? He tried to lay low. Living in an isolated area as he did those rare times he was home, he was pretty much invisible to the rest of the world, and he preferred it that way. He wasn't good at lying or pretending. . .

As Mariah was. Aaron had hinted that she wasn't who she seemed to be—although it was pretty obvious that being a waitress wasn't her aptitude.

"He's not telling us everything, so I don't see any reason we shouldn't return the favor," Mariah shouted back. "It's not as if we have any real evidence about a book except the scribblings of a vengeful drug addict."

"A book?" Keegan asked, now very interested. "What book?"

"Not your business," she repeated, before calling to the men ahead, "Hey, Walker, is it okay if we take Val's golf cart back to her?"

They couldn't possibly be hunting the same book, could they? It would seem unlikely in any other context. Unfortunately, in Hillvale, everything always came down to crystals, even the art. And the books that had gone missing were all about crystals.

Ahead, Walker and Aaron were pulling aging shrubbery away from the door to the bunker.

Walker gestured at the abandoned cart. "Sheriff is done here. Help yourself."

Mariah shouted her relief at having her transportation back.

"Does the sheriff know about the bunker?" Sam asked.

"I have no way of knowing if the bunker is relevant to the investigation until I take a look at it," Police Chief Walker said. "The sheriff's team is only good for forensics. We're the ones who know who and what's up here."

"That's my man." Sam kissed his cheek.

Keegan admired the easy camaraderie between the platinum-blond scientist and the half-Chinese lawman. Once upon a time, he'd tried that kind of relationship. But Brianna had claimed he was a robot, then found someone new, proving he was better off keeping his nose in dirt.

He might be emotionally crippled, as Bri claimed, but he could still manage physical relations. He had hopes that Mariah might be the same.

Abandoning his arm, she hobbled across the farmhouse foundation to lay a feather and a daisy on the ground where Daisy had died. For a brief second, she looked so forlorn, that Keegan forgot she was a stubborn termagant.

And then she donned her resolute mask again as Aaron and Walker dragged open what appeared to be a steel door.

"Bomb shelter?" Keegan guessed.

"Got it in one," Mariah said. "It may have originally been an old root cellar. I don't know who decided to add the concrete, but the Ingerssons and their stoned crew had fun with it. They probably had pot parties or LSD orgies down there. I think they even lived in it after the farmhouse burned."

"So you've been inside?" Keegan asked, helping her over the rough terrain and the stone foundation.

"Only once. There's way too much to take in for one trip to be enough."

"Maybe we could turn it into a tourist attraction," Sam said before following Walker's flashlight down the stairs.

"What, for tourists into creepy crawlies?" Teddy yelled from the top of the stairs. "There better be no skeletons. I'm done with skeletons."

"No spiders or snakes," Sam called up. "A cobweb or two but Daisy took pretty good care of it."

"Did Daisy live here?" Keegan asked.

"Some of the time. She didn't have a place of her own. She usually stayed with Val if it was cold or rainy, but she liked it here." Sorrow tinged Mariah's voice. She released his arm and braced her hand on the wall inside the bunker, using her stick for balance.

Seeing that Harvey and Orval were roaming the foundation, and the surfer-dude mayor was keeping watch, Keegan followed after her. Aaron brought up the rear.

The stairs may have been tiled at one time. Keegan could make out pieces of colorful ceramics in the eroded concrete. Sam and Walker were lighting lanterns below that illuminated mirrors, colored glass—and crystals?—along the stairwell. At the bottom, Keegan assisted Mariah to a carved wooden bench situated in front of stacks of canvases. The wall above the stacks was covered in small portraits of people from a decidedly different era. Long hair flowed. Beaded headbands, scarves, furry vests. . .

"Very seventies," Aaron said dryly, studying the works. "Pretty amateurish, some of this."

"We need a way of identifying these people." Sam turned a light on the paintings. "They may all be dead by now, but the ones still living might give us some insights."

"Not if they're evil," Mariah argued. "Do we really want them back in Hillvale?"

"Evil?" The artwork didn't hold Keegan's interest. He left Teddy and Aaron working their way through the oils while he studied the construction of the bunker. Walker obligingly beamed his powerful flashlight along the walls.

"Daisy only collected the portraits that corroded—the ones she called evil," Sam explained. "Portraits of my grandparents and the Kennedys' father are down here, as well as the criminal who blew up our mountain. I suspect the mural at the café was doctored to cover up any corrosion, but we don't know for certain if those faces had red eyes like the ones Daisy collected."

"Evil, huh." Keegan poked at a crack in the concrete but nothing moved.

He sensed interesting structures all through the cellar, but other than the few crystals glued to the walls, he couldn't find the mother lode, if it existed.

Sitting on the bench, Mariah was riffling through the stacked canvases. "There are several paintings of the Ingerssons and Geoff Kennedy in this stack. If they are any example, the unfamiliar faces may be dead people also. There's a chance that Daisy knew who was living and who wasn't."

Teddy and Aaron joined Mariah in studying the canvases, while Sam and Walker continued in Keegan's path, examining the walls.

"The energy here is different," Sam said, running her hands under one of the paintings. "The further back I go, the stronger the effect."

"Energy?" Keegan had sensed crystalline structures, but *energy*? Just how eccentric were Hillvale inhabitants?

"I can't explain it," Sam admitted. "I never studied energy beyond what's good for plants. Mariah, can you toddle down here and see if you feel it too? Aaron?"

The antique dealer picked up his walking stick and began running it along the wall.

Curious, Keegan returned to the front of the shelter to assist Mariah to her feet. He enjoyed her weight at his side, and she seemed to be accepting his assistance more readily. He wondered if that meant anything. Not enough to trust him, he figured.

She poked her walking stick along the base of the wall as she hobbled along. "Not negative or positive."

"Maybe pushing at each other?" Aaron suggested. "What on earth did they build this thing in? Radioactive material?"

"Not radioactive," Keegan said, then regretted it. If they could sense *earth energy* in a manner few people could, then he should be allowed to speak of his extra sense, but he wasn't certain he was ready to.

Mariah poked his shoe with her stick. "Speak, Oh Great One, lend us your knowledge."

She was jesting, he was certain. He glared down at her. "Rocks hold natural radioactivity. Concrete doesn't. So unless they were storing uranium, the energy isn't radioactive. Not that I understand how one *feels* energy."

"Most people don't," she said smugly, without further explanation.

He wasn't a violent man, but he could easily see how one might wish to wring the graceful curve of this woman's neck. She deliberately set out to be provocative, and not in a good way.

But to put people off, he realized in surprise. This native princess didn't want anyone getting close. Why? Now his scientific mind was fully engaged.

"You have to accept the supernatural or the paranormal or whatever," Walker explained. "The women won't talk to you otherwise."

"Women don't talk because they're devious," Keegan argued. "If they'd just state their positions upfront, we wouldn't have such difficulty communicating. I grew up surrounded by females who declare they are descendants of Druids. My mother claims to have second sight." Vague warnings certainly hadn't saved his family from disaster. "Who am I to dispute them? But I know nothing of imaginary *energy*."

Mariah actually turned to *look* at him. The gleam behind her opaque brown gaze sent shivers down his spine, or maybe straight to his groin. She was a striking woman when she wasn't even trying. It would be a battle royal if she decided to really take him on.

"You are related to Lucy Wainwright, otherwise known as Lucinda Malcolm?" she demanded.

"That was a high-flying leap of logic," he muttered. "Are you claiming second sight as well?"

Knowing who Keegan was, Aaron merely smirked and returned to testing *energy*.

"I was simply using basic math by putting two and two together," Mariah said. "A few weeks back, we discovered Lucinda *Malcolm* visited Hillvale, painted a futuristic painting for us, and left a book on crystals here. The Null of all Nulls, owner of a *Malcolm* library, shows up later, claiming his family is descended from Druids. What are the chances of that adding up?"

"I need a good stout before I attempt explaining any of that," he grumbled.

"Unless anyone sees anything valuable in this dungeon, hitting the bar sounds like an excellent idea." Walker headed for the front. "It's been a damned long day."

Studying the wall crystals, Teddy, the jeweler, shook her head. "It's interesting, and I'd like to explore more, but I'm not finding diamonds and rubies. I need to get back to my shop."

"No books, no treasure trove." Sam returned from the end of the bunker. "Just a lot of old art we'd need an expert to evaluate. Or Daisy. I'm afraid any secrets died with her."

Mariah continued to stare at Keegan expectantly. Aaron leaned against the wall and waited. Keegan had never really explained himself to Aaron. They were acquaintances—who in a different time and place had acknowledged that they were *different.*

Here was where he either gained Mariah's trust or sent her rolling on the floor with laughter.

Keegan rubbed his nose while he formulated his words. "Unless you understand the physical structure of crystals, I cannot begin to explain what I sense. Put very crudely, I can tell you if there are diamonds behind this bunker. There are not. There is however possibly magnetite, which is of the same octahedron structure as diamonds."

They all stared at him. They wanted beer, not a lecture on molecular structures.

"You want us to believe you can *sense* what kind of rocks are around us?" Mariah asked in obvious disbelief. "You could make up anything you liked, and we'd have no way of proving it without blowing up the bunker."

Keegan shrugged. He'd expected disbelief.

"*Magnetite*—iron ore, ferrous oxide," Teddy said with interest, not questioning his statement as the annoying waitress did. "Not useful for jewelry but fairly common to California. I've been studying up on the power of crystals. Magnetite is pretty interesting. It can be found in the human brain. They think it may be related to memory, but magnetite is what creates magnets."

"Which possess *positive and negative* energy," Sam crowed, taking the ball and running with it.

Keegan rubbed his brow. These women were as seriously weird as his family.

"Iron rusts," Mariah said disparagingly, using Keegan's arm as a crutch and heading for the door. "And I wouldn't believe a Null without proof."

He let her lead him out, still amazed that no one had laughed. They were each processing his information through their own strange perspectives. He could comprehend Mariah's rejection easier than the acceptance of the others.

Mariah continued without his asking, "Not that I believe Keegan can sense such things, but in theory, if the artists used magnetite in their paint, then could that cause the corrosion in the paintings?"

"If they only used it on the eyes, maybe," Sam suggested.

"I don't think magnetite on its own actually rusts," Keegan argued. But he knew nothing of what went into paint.

Aaron removed a painting from the wall depicting a number of people in what appeared to be a costume drama. The eyes of some of them seemed red in the low gleam of the flashlight. "Let's take one of these to be analyzed."

Mariah increased her grip on Keegan's arm. She halted before they climbed the stairs. "Maybe we shouldn't be too quick to unleash these things on the world. We should probably ask Cass and Val first."

"What if someone steals in and sets the place on fire?" Sam demanded. "There's a killer out there, and he's after something! We could be sitting on evidence of what the killer wanted."

Walker cursed aloud. Keegan did so mentally. Aaron set the painting down.

Mariah returned to the bench and crossed her arms belligerently. "Bring me a shotgun. I'll take first watch."

"Don't be ridiculous." Like a red-headed fairy, Teddy flitted toward the stairs. "I'll have Kurt position resort security people here—if we can keep them from shooting Val and her cronies. No one is getting close to this place without our knowing it."

Mariah looked truculent. "I don't trust the Nulls not to strip the place bare while they're pretending to guard it."

Keegan knew Mariah thought he fell on the *Null* spectrum, but he wasn't leaving her down here alone with a killer on the loose.

"If you stay, I stay," he stated without inflection.

"Fine, we'll all have campfires and pow-wows all night, but I want a beer." Walker stamped toward the stairs.

Keegan wanted one too, but instinct wouldn't allow him to leave Mariah alone, shotgun or not. "We could start a bar down here," he jestingly suggested. "Call it the Bunker."

"I like that idea, but only if you make the drunks sleep it off before they go outside and fall off the bluff." Walker shoved open the outside door. "Until you have cots, I suggest we have Kurt's security pace the perimeter and let Daisy's guardians do their thing."

"I have paperwork to do and need to get home," Aaron admitted grudgingly. "These paintings appear to be exactly what they're said to be —bad examples of old art. All the pieces they couldn't sell, for good reason."

Keegan held out his hand to Mariah. "You don't have a shotgun, and you can't tackle a thief with a battered knee. I'll tell you my story if you'll tell me yours, but let's do it somewhere more comfortable."

He really wanted her to say yes, which meant he ought to stay down here on his own, far, far away from her.

She glared at the stack of paintings, then grudgingly took his hand. "Val has a key. I'll get her."

"Don't be silly. I need to help Dinah at the café. I'll tell Val to lock the door," Sam said.

"Or better yet, since Kurt has business down the mountain this evening, why don't I help Dinah and talk to Val while you share a nice dinner with our police chief?" Teddy suggested.

Keegan let the discussion flow without his input, unable to decide if it was a good thing he might be sharing a dark bar with other couples and a woman as dangerous and attractive as Mariah. He'd already been badly burned by a woman he'd trusted. He had no reason whatsoever to trust Mariah. Maybe he ought to run while he still could.

FIVE

Mariah disliked crowded public bars filled with strangers. She never knew if someone might recognize her. Her only hope was that if she stayed out of sight long enough, the world would forget her, and she could come out of hiding. But when Mayor Monty said he was buying, she grudgingly agreed to come along to keep an eye on the Nulls.

Besides, Keegan had offered to tell his story, attempting to ingratiate himself with the Lucys by pretending to be one of them, she assumed. She didn't know how to call him on it. When she'd had the internet to explore, she could prove someone was lying. Now, she writhed in frustration, knowing what she could do and fearing it at the same time.

She didn't even have Daisy for a sounding board. She missed Daisy's odd insights already.

Fighting off the emptiness, she chose to hear the Scot's story. The alternative was to go to her empty cottage and grieve.

The lounge at the Redwood Resort was one of those dark-paneled, masculine caves where the dads could hide while their families were out hiking and riding. Mariah only came here when it was empty, to check on her ghostcatchers.

Because she feared outsiders, she checked the bar. A trio of white guys in suits nursed whiskey glasses and argued vociferously under their breaths. At the arrival of the police chief and company, they shut up and threw back their drinks. Mariah fought an itch at her nape. They didn't look like reporters or the feds, and they weren't looking at her. That's all she normally cared about. But the itch forced her to study closer.

The one might be young and strong enough to pull a hunting bow. The other two were older but big enough.

Sliding into a black leather semi-circle booth, she studied her nets to see what the ghosts had to say. They quivered and jiggled unhappily— not a good sign.

"The spirits are restless," she told the group, just to raise a groan from the Nulls. She had no way of knowing if the old white guys disturbed anything but her.

"There's a storm moving in from the west and this place is drafty." Monty deliberately contradicted her.

"Watch what Mariah does sometime, and you'll think twice when she tries to tell you about restless spirits." Sam slid in beside her.

Aaron had gone back to his shop. Orval and Harvey had gone their own ways, too, but Monty, Keegan, and Walker remained. Walker slid in to claim Sam. While Monty put in an order at the bar, Keegan took the space on Mariah's other side.

She liked that he made her feel almost dainty, but she hated sitting beside him as if they were a perfectly matched couple.

Physically, she could see that they were, which made her squirm. With his symmetrical features and square jaw, he was much prettier than she was. She fingered her hawk nose and was glad of the relative darkness.

"Nulls can't see what I do," Mariah said disparagingly in reply to Sam's pacifying remark. "And they can't believe what they don't see."

Monty returned with their drink orders—ice tea for Mariah, a frou-frou drink for Sam, and beer for the men. "Mariah runs her fingers over string, and it straightens out," the mayor said. "I figure she has glue in her fingernails."

She didn't even bother rolling her eyes. She and Monty had gone to college together and argued these points into infinity.

Keegan studied the shivering, swaying net near the ceiling. "I don't believe glue would make them stop moving, if that's what happens. They're hung so they would continue to sway in any draft. The beads and feathers are designed for that."

"They also act as weights," Mariah said, sipping her tea, waiting to see where he would go from there. The ghostcatchers were a minor trick she'd learned from her Nana, but most people didn't believe in them any more than they did dreamcatchers.

"So the nets should sway back and forth rhythmically if there's a breeze." Keegan studied the motion of the one in the corner. "That thing is almost thrashing."

"Score one for the potter," Sam said, lifting her drink in toast. "Are you really a ceramics expert?"

"It's only a hobby, because of my resonance with crystalline structure. With our affinity for the earth, most of my family is involved in mining of one sort or another, although clay is another outlet. Some of them are ceramic artists. I help them locate the materials that work best for their needs. One thing led to another. . ." He shrugged.

"An affinity with the earth?" Monty asked. "What does *that* mean?"

"Ignore Mayor Surfer Dude. He's a jock," Mariah said, wishing she could go on the internet and explore crystalline structure. She'd never met a man other than Aaron willing to speak about paranormal gifts— even if he was lying about them. Even Harvey denied he was gifted— because he didn't understand what he did and refused to learn. She sat back, prepared to be entertained. "You have to speak in simple terms for Monty, or footballese."

"Behave," Sam admonished, poking Mariah's muscled arm with her bony elbow. "We're here to help find a killer, which means we have to work together."

"I don't see how that's possible when our Null mayor is hoping an *affinity for the earth* means Keegan plans on putting in a mine. We speak different languages." Had she just assumed that Keegan, the Null of all Nulls, was talking *spiritual* affinity and not mines? Damn, maybe she ought to consume alcohol to blot the hunky Scot out of her head.

"Communication is essential," Walker said, surprisingly, since he usually listened rather than speak.

"Communication is not always the answer." Mariah slid down in her seat. "Take my word for it, okay?"

"Honest, open communication is," Keegan argued.

"Is *tough*." Mariah shot him a challenging glare. "You want to honestly, openly explain your reason for traveling half way around the earth to look at a bunch of pots?"

"Is there a reason I should start first?" He glared down at her.

"Because you could be the killer?" Mariah suggested, even knowing she was being malicious. That earned her a snort of disbelief.

"Explain." Walker intervened, probably keeping Keegan from punching her out.

"You haven't established an exact time of death. I saw Keegan come up from the direction of the commune where Daisy was killed." Although if anyone would believe she'd *felt* Daisy's death, she could probably exonerate him. But even she couldn't be sure. "He's strong enough to pull a bow the size needed. And we don't know why he's here."

Even in her old life, Mariah was accustomed to being a loner. She didn't like being questioned. She crossed her arms and waited. Slithering down cyber holes was simpler than direct confrontation.

"The same could be said of you," Keegan retorted.

Well, he had her there, except everyone knew she would never harm Daisy. "I don't know beans about archery," she countered.

"Aaron said he knew you at Oxford and you were on the archery team." Walker addressed Keegan. He sat back against the bench seat and drank his beer as if he were talking baseball.

"The coal miner's son attended Oxford?" Mariah taunted.

"My grandfather once owned *diamond* mines," he retorted. "I have a second cousin who is a marquess. Ives have attended Oxford for generations. And yes, I was on the archery team as well as the rowing team. I don't like hurting people in rough athletics. Targets and finish lines don't have breakable bones."

"If you're telling the truth, I applaud your integrity." Mariah threw a spiteful look at the mayor. "Monty enjoys cracking heads in contact sports."

"Would you like to tell the group what you enjoy doing, *Mariah*?" Monty glared over his beer. "I'm not a complete airhead."

He knew her real name. She shouldn't taunt him. But she didn't work well with others.

"This isn't helping Daisy," Sam said—Earth Mother to squabbling toddlers. "We're here to decide what to do about the art."

"I vote we wait for your birth mother to arrive," Mariah said. "She has to know more than any of us do."

"You'd better hope she's more informative than Cass then." Monty emptied his beer.

"Crystals." Keegan directed the conversation off emotional quicksand. "The ones I've seen are not natural to this area."

The itch at her nape intensified when she noticed one of the men at the bar was actively staring. The light was dim enough that she could hope he couldn't see much, but she lowered her voice to argue. "They can be purchased anywhere. We need Teddy for this conversation. She says the crystals she has with power are from her parents. Harvey says the same. Their grandparents were part of the commune."

Mariah poked Keegan with her elbow. He checked the bar, frowned, and spoke more softly. "I do not understand crystal *power*, beyond their use in manufacture."

He rolled his beer bottle between his big hands as he sought words. "My family's journals speak of crystals gathered from around the world by one of my ancestors. They were reported to have odd energies and structures, which was why he gathered them. Both my more scientific and gifted ancestors studied them for generations, but I never read much of their writings."

"Lucinda's book," Mariah said, grasping the situation immediately. "Your *family* created the compendium of usage."

Keegan frowned. "So my sources say. I have never seen this book. Or the crystals. They disappeared at the same time."

Walker sat up straight. "How long ago?"

"A few hundred years. It's a long story. My problem is that another of the journals written at the time of the compendium has recently disappeared from my library."

"And what was in that journal?" Mariah had a bad feeling just watching him crush his beer bottle.

"Experiments in how to use the crystals," he said gloomily. "We had thought the journal useless because the crystals were long gone. Apparently, someone else thinks differently."

"What does it matter if they're experimenting with pieces of rock?" Monty asked.

Keegan winced. "Diamonds and rubies are pieces of rock. So is uranium."

"Damn," Walker muttered, polishing off his beer. "Maybe this time they're after *rocks*. But I can't figure out how Daisy plays into this scenario."

"I can think of half a dozen ways," Mariah said. "But speculation won't help. We need to find the crystals, the journals, examine Daisy's art for clues, and see if any of Keegan's family has been hanging around. And look into Keegan while you're at it." She said the last out of meanness, and maybe wariness. She'd learned the hard way to be cautious, and she really needed to know he was safe.

"Dig up the mountain," Monty suggested, being as malicious as she was. "Build a ski slope while you're at it. Maybe that's the solution—heavy equipment."

"I can find crystalline structures faster than heavy equipment can." Keegan gestured to a waitress for more beer. "So far, I've found nothing."

Everyone turned to stare at him. He shrugged. "You wanted to know why I was here. That's it. I'm looking for crystalline rocks and our missing books. So far, all I've found is Harvey and Theodosia and their stashes. Perhaps that's all that's left of the ones we had. It's not as if I can prove ownership, although it seems unlikely that so many oddities would end in one place."

Mariah wanted to believe him, but life had taught her otherwise.

The waitress returned carrying another round of drinks and the wireless landline. "A call for Miss Moon from Miss Baker."

Miss Baker—Teddy was working at the café. Mariah waited expectantly.

Sam took the phone, listened, and turned pale. "My mother's there? *Now*? What am I supposed to do?"

Walker hugged her and kissed her temple. "You go meet her."

"We'll go with you," Mariah said, relieved for an excuse to escape. "We'll put a hex on her if she doesn't immediately hug you when she sees you."

"She doesn't know I'm here," Sam whispered. "She won't know me."

"Then we get to know her first." Mariah shoved at the mountain of man beside her. "Let us out, big boy. We're about to interrogate our first witness."

Finally, action she could understand.

SAMANTHA

Her mother! She was going to meet her mother—the one who had given her away at birth. She had so many questions. . .

Sam swallowed hard and tried to hold herself together as Walker drove down from the lodge to the café. She'd lost her adopted parents five years ago. Discovering Hillvale and pieces of her extended family over this past month had showed her how much she'd missed having family. But a real mother. . .

Walker reached over and squeezed her hand. "I wish I knew how to help."

She managed a feeble smile. "I don't know if I could do this if you weren't here, telling me I'm not a misbegotten aberrant deserving abandonment."

"You know better than that. She did it for herself, not because of an innocent baby. She's the one at fault, not you." He parked the car in a suspiciously full lot. "The Lucys have turned out for you. We've all got your back. I almost feel sorry for your mother."

"Val? Do you think Val is here?" Sam asked in panic. "She just lost her best friend, and now her sister has returned after deserting her all these years. This is going to be awful."

"If Val were standing on the roof, wailing, I'd be more worried," he said with humor. "At least they're not planning on killing each other."

"Maybe that's what I need to do—look at the world from the worst possible perspective. Thank you for your cynical wisdom," she said, knowing Walker's past and that he had a right to see through jaded eyes. She respected that place, but she didn't want to go there herself.

He gazed out the windshield at the crowd on the boardwalk. "What the hell are they doing? Forming a welcoming committee?"

Sam sighed and opened her door. "They're showing off my planters. That has to be my mother."

She studied the middle-aged, stout woman examining the lush garden of purple flowers in front of Dinah's café. The pansies and lobelias were growing in one of Daisy's colorfully decorated planters. Sam thought the pots more artistic than flowers, but if this was her mother. . .

The Lucys were showing her mother that she was gifted. That ought to scare the woman to hell and back—if they were also telling her that the flower genie who produced bountiful gardens from almost nothing was her daughter.

Walker put a hand at her back as they approached. "Not world ending," he whispered. "You've got us."

The reassurance helped. She'd spent these last years of being truly orphaned, feeling alone and wondering about her birth parents. Now, some of her questions were about to be answered—she hoped.

At their approach, the Lucys quit chattering, all but forcing the visitor to look up. The stranger's eyes were the same sapphire blue as Sam's. Her hair was the same champagne blond, although more silver than Sam's. There were shadows under her eyes and her jaw muscles had started to sag—but the bone structure was indistinguishable from Sam and Val's. Their Nordic ancestors had left their mark.

She was about to meet her mother. Sam swallowed hard.

"And here comes our botanist now," Amber declared proudly as Sam stepped up.

"Environmental scientist," Sam corrected. "Are we having a party out here? I haven't had dinner yet."

The newcomer continued to stare at her as the crowd returned inside the café. Sam was aware that Mariah and the Brit miner had arrived with the mayor and were literally at her back. She had friends. She could do this.

Inside, Teddy waved from behind the counter. "Dinah has gumbo waiting for you. Take a seat."

Sam slid onto the stool and leaned over to whisper, "Can you tell anything about her?" She hoped Teddy's empathic abilities might give her insight into how her mother was feeling.

Teddy shook her head. "Too many people in here, sorry. She seems sad and nervous, that's the best I can tell you."

Bless Walker's heart, he was the one to take charge. He approached the stranger, who was still looking for a seat. "I'm Chen Ling Walker. You wouldn't happen to be the Susannah Ingersson I spoke to on the phone?"

Looking relieved, Susannah offered her hand. "Chief Walker, yes, good to meet you. I'm a trifle overwhelmed by the warm welcome."

"You can't think you and your family have been forgotten, Suz, can you?" Cass's voice carried over the chatter.

Heart in throat, Sam swung around to watch her great-aunt enter behind Mariah.

Cass had raised Sam's father. When he'd overdosed after Sam's birth, Susannah had sent her child off for adoption, effectively stripping Cass's rights to infant Sam. Since Cass had no other children, she had good reason for animosity.

Walker squeezed Sam's hand as the two older women faced off.

"Cass," Susannah whispered. "I didn't dare hope you'd speak to me."

"Life goes on." Looking like an ascetic saint in her floor-length silver skirt, Cass commanded the room, emptying a booth with just a look. "Have a seat."

She gestured regally at the newly-emptied booth. "Sam, Walker, you should join us."

"Hang on to your walking stick," Mariah whispered as Sam stood up. "If the stick's energy doesn't work, you can always beat them with it."

Sam almost smiled at Mariah's grim humor. *Friends.* She had friends —and Walker. Love swelled in her, giving her confidence.

As Sam approached the booth, Cass gestured. "Susannah, I'd like you to meet Samantha Moon, the talent behind those flowers you were admiring. Sam, this is Susannah Ingersson, your mother."

Leave it to Cass to lay all the cards on the table at once. Twenty-five years of emotion smoldered beneath them.

Susannah paled as she studied Sam. "Samantha Moon? Jade and Wolf Moon. . . ?"

"Were my adopted parents, yes. I'm happy to finally meet you, Mother." Sam slid into the offered seat. She hadn't planned what she would say in this moment. She wished she had.

"*Samantha,*" her mother said the name wistfully. "They kept the name we chose. I hope they were as good as I thought they would be."

"They were exemplary parents." Her adopted parents had given her the freedom to be herself, even when Sam didn't fit neatly into the conservative community she'd been raised in.

Susannah appeared teary-eyed as Teddy delivered food no one had ordered. "I never hoped to find you here. I really wanted you to have a better life than Hillvale has to offer."

"How long are you planning to stay. . . Mrs. Ingersson?" Walker asked, heading off any argument over Hillvale. "We've arranged a room for you at the lodge and hope you'll be part of the art walk."

"Menendez," Susannah murmured. "I married Carlos Menendez after I left here."

The Menendez family who wanted to turn the mountain into a casino. . .

Teddy nearly dropped the soup bowl she was setting down. Walker cursed under his breath. And Cass looked as if she could order a beheading.

SIX

"She's scouting for the Menendez family, mark my words," Monty muttered as Mariah made change at the register.

"She knows archery," Mariah whispered back. She understood how fear led to distrust and suspicion, but sometimes it was right to be wary. *Someone* had killed Daisy, after all—why not the woman who knew that land inside-out, and who had just returned out of the blue, aligned with avaricious forces?

Digging into the mountain of food Dinah had made for him, Keegan sent them both a questioning look.

"The Menendez family owns the land above the lodge and next to the commune farm," Monty explained. "They've been wanting to put a casino up there. Their lawyer has been talking to ours because the easiest access is through the resort."

"Only government-approved tribes can open casinos. Have they established legality?" Mariah asked in scorn.

"They're claiming their grandmother was Ohlone, just like you." Monty kept an eye on the newcomer in the booth.

"*Daisy* said I was Ohlone. She didn't mention any Menendez. Neither did Nana."

"Daisy was crazy," Monty reminded her. "And your Nana had no reason to draw a family tree."

Mariah could—if she had a computer. She never had because the past was best left behind. Witness poor Sam over there, learning what kind of crap piece of goods her mother probably was—marrying a money-grubbing Null!

"What if Daisy could have proved that they *weren't* Ohlone?" Keegan asked, apparently following her thought process.

"Daisy was incompetent. That's what made her harmless," Monty countered.

"She was gifted and traveled time," Mariah corrected. "But it confused her if anyone questioned too deeply. Our gifts don't always play well with reality."

Across the aisle, Walker got up holding a car key. "She's brought art with her," he told them. "Monty, help me carry it in."

"Way to keep it in the family, Walker," Mariah taunted, but the chief barely acknowledged her existence. Mayor Monty had spilled her secrets to the police chief, so she liked to keep Walker at a distance.

"This Mrs. Menendez is the one who may know about the crystals or my book, correct?" Keegan asked, studying the mural behind the counter. "She is too young to be one of those people in that portrait."

Mariah finished her sandwich while studying the counter-length painting. "That's Lars Ingersson, Susannah's and Val's father, posing as Jesus. Looks like he was only in his twenties then, so unless there are toddlers hidden behind the coffee pot, Susanna and Val aren't in it. That's probably their mother, though, the one with the beads in her platinum hair."

The canvases Walker and Monty carried in were small, easily transportable in suitcases, Mariah noticed. If she had a computer she could trace Carlos Menendez. . . Not going there. Not her circus, not her monkeys.

Teddy showed the men where to hang the canvases on hooks along Dinah's walls where she'd lately been displaying photographs.

"Cass, is this you?" Teddy asked, indicating one of the paintings. "This is brilliant!"

Unwilling to climb off her stool and hobble over, Mariah studied the paintings from a distance. The oil Teddy was examining showed a tall, slender couple holding an infant. If the subject was Cass, she had brown hair rippling down her back—very hippy-seventies. The man with her—Cass's late husband?—had a dark ponytail, a huge mustache, and wore a paisley shirt. The infant was wrapped in a lacy white shawl—Sam's father, the nephew Cass had raised?

"Can you see if the eyes are corroded?" Mariah whispered to Keegan, who sat closer.

He shook his head. "No red," he murmured back.

"My father painted these," Susannah explained from the booth. "I kept the sentimental ones, but I thought maybe they'd be better shared with the town, if we're celebrating Dad's art."

"That's the Kennedys and Xavier, back when they were all in college." Cass studied a painting brimming with people. "I'd forgotten how talented Lars was at capturing faces in a few strokes. You and Val are the children playing in the corner, right? Who are the others?"

Mariah wanted to limp over and examine that one, but no one was exclaiming over anything unusual about it. The Kennedys' father should have red eyes, at the very least. The man had recklessly stolen homes and lives in pursuit of wealth. If their theories were correct about the corrosion, Susannah had either tampered with the crystal paint or Lars hadn't wasted it on friends and family.

"That was done about ten years before Dad died," Susannah said. "He probably painted it while on a coke high, so the details aren't as good as his earlier works. But that's Carl's father and Ralph Wainwright at the table too. I think Mrs. Kennedy must have brought him. That's when I first learned about Lucinda Malcolm."

Lucy Wainwright, who was actually *Lucinda Malcom*, the famed painter with a gift for painting the future. Mariah studied the painting after Teddy hung it. Legend said that way back in the thirties, Lucinda took her pseudonym to protect her wealthy East Coast family from her reputation as a painter of oddities.

Ralph must be her son or grandson, or maybe a nephew. He looked older and less comfortable than the others at the table. He wore a white dress shirt instead of the colorful tie-dyes and jeans on everyone else. Even snooty Carmel, now mother to Kurt and Monty, looked casual in a flowy dress that probably cost a fortune from some San Francisco boutique. This was a portrait of wealth—sitting in a crude farmhouse getting high, if the paraphernalia on the table was any indication.

"Wainwright?" Keegan whispered. "There are Wainwrights around here?"

Mariah narrowed her eyes and returned her attention to him. "Not that I know of. Why do you ask?"

"We have distant cousins of that name. I remember a Ralph Wainwright visiting when I was still in primary school. He was a dodgy pillock. If I'm guessing the lady's age correctly, that portrait is probably thirty-five or forty years ago, correct?"

Mariah shrugged, ignoring an itchy feeling that she should recognize Ralph. "Probably. So, he visited your family what, twenty years ago? So?"

"So, I don't like coincidences," Keegan stated. "I know Lucinda Malcolm was a Wainwright. Your legend says she brought a compendium on crystals here—one that vanished from my library generations ago according to our records. More recently, I'm missing two journals on crystal experiments, one that could have disappeared anytime in the last fifty years, the other more recently. Ralph shows up in my library *and* here in Hillvale for no good reason I can ascertain. . . I need to look into my family tree."

"Well, just about all the people in that painting are dodgy pillocks," Mariah said, enjoying the slang from the proper Oxford scholar.

"Back to your theory about evil eyes?" he asked. "They don't look corroded."

"Because Susannah apparently knows the formula for disguising the evil." Mariah nodded at the mural behind her. "We know that she and Teddy's cousin repaired the mural decades ago, and Teddy's cousin was the last person who admits to having the compendium. She was murdered by her husband, and no one's found it in her possession or his."

Keegan's fathomless dark eyes lit from within. "Susannah may have the book?"

"Hadn't thought about it, but possibly." Mariah studied Sam's newly-discovered mother. Susannah Menendez looked like any comfortable housewife who had kids and didn't watch her diet or exercise. She didn't look like a thief.

Right on cue, Sam picked up the dinner table painting. "Your father didn't use the crystal paint on these?" she asked. "The eyes didn't corrode like the ones did around here."

Susannah rubbed wearily at her cheek. "That's an old ugly story. Let's not get into it now. I just thought people might enjoy seeing the history behind this town."

Dinah chose that moment to sashay from the kitchen. She'd put on fresh lipstick and wore an apron over her sprigged shirtdress. She wore her kinky curls cut close but smoothed them nervously before she spoke. "Are you the artist who fixed this here mural behind the counter?"

Susannah's eyes widened as she studied the mural they'd been working hard to uncover from a mishmash of shelves and appliances. "You kept it! It's a sacrilegious conceit. My mother used to complain about it." She stood up and leaned over the counter to study the various figures. "I'd forgotten his disciples. I don't think I ever knew who they were. Yes, Thalia and I cleaned and fixed it while I was still in high school."

"Could you recommend someone who could fix it up again?" Dinah asked. "My customers like it."

"Is Thalia still around?" Susannah asked. "She had the formula in that ancient book she had about crystals."

Keegan covered Mariah's hand with his and squeezed. *The Book.* Lucinda's book—with the crystal formulas.

It really existed. And Susannah didn't have it.

SEVEN

Taking a chance on the headlight cutting through the darkness, Keegan stepped in front of the golf cart puttering up the lane to the commune farmhouse. A chilly wind blew in from the west, scuttling clouds across the stars. But after spending these past hours in the stuffy café, listening for clues, he was more than ready to clear his head.

Mariah cut off the cart's engine to glare at him without speaking. He'd like to pretend it was only sexual attraction, but his curiosity about this mysterious female was eating him alive.

He climbed onto the padded bench. "I figured you wouldn't leave the shelter unguarded. Did you get the key from Valdis?" He was uncomfortable calling the wailing banshee by the fandom name for a death goddess, but calling her Miss Ingersson in a town full of Ingerssons was too confusing.

Mariah turned the key in the ignition and set the cart up the lane again. "Why is it your business?"

"Because I don't think it is safe on this mountain, and two people are more likely to scare off predators better than one female with a bad knee." He squirmed, barely able to fit his legs into the ancient vehicle.

She was silent long enough to have him wriggling with more discomfort. He was an experienced engineer and man of business, confident of his place in the world. Yes, his inability to connect emotionally had caused problems in prior relationships. Still, he had no reason to be concerned about the opinion of a woman who appeared to have no past and no name—except she stirred his base desires and more.

"The killer's still out there," she finally said. "And you think it's the bunker he's after."

"Not necessarily. But since you're here, you must, and I can't completely disagree. Your police chief has his hands full with the arrival of his potential mother-in-law and dealing with the sheriff on this murder case, so it makes sense for someone else to stand in for him."

"I can't decide if you waited for me so I wouldn't suspect you of sneaking around unauthorized, or if you just plan on killing me the easy way." She steered the cart down an even rougher lane, at an unnecessary speed, nearly jouncing him out of the seat.

Since he'd stopped trusting people, he appreciated the way her mind worked. "I wrote my doctorate on crystalline structures. I taught for a few years as a graduate student. If you dig deep enough, you might find my photo in a few places. I don't live a public life, so there won't be much to convince you I am who I say am."

"I'll have to trust Aaron," she said grumpily, stopping the cart near the bushes concealing the farm foundation. "He's the one vouching for you."

"Ah, yes, you never explained why Aaron says you are not allowed near computers." He jumped out and crossed to her side to assist her from the cart. In the chilly air, he thought he detected a hint of salt on the ocean breeze.

She ignored his inquiry. "You're expecting me to believe you've traveled half way around the world to find a musty old journal on crystals. You have that much wealth you can waste time chasing down bunny trails?"

"I'm on sabbatical," he said, helping her unload a sleeping bag from the back of the cart. "The family business is foundering and might benefit from historical insight."

"Now we're getting somewhere." She shouldered a backpack and pulled out her walking stick. "The book means money. I respect that—to a degree."

"As I believe I've heard Aaron say, you are a piece of work. Take my arm so you don't fall from the weight of that backpack. Did you bring the kitchen sink?" He held back the prickly bushes so she could climb over the rock foundation.

"Not that it's any of your business, but I brought food, clothes, and my net-making supplies. Does your copious knowledge of crystalline structure tell you anything about Daisy's guardians? Teddy wants to sell them. I'm not sure it's a good idea." She actually took his arm without protest to hobble over to the line of rock creatures the artist had left as her legacy.

Keegan took the stack of wired-together stones she handed him. He could easily identify the crystals, although he knew she wouldn't believe him. "I assume you aren't interested in my analysis of the molecular structure, but that's how my gift works. Textbooks will tell you these black stones are schorl, often called black tourmaline. It's fairly common, although I haven't heard of any deposits in this part of California. They have some good ones further south, though. The stones in this other figure are a silicon dioxide crystal that jewelers call smoky quartz. It's also quite common."

"That's what Teddy said—this is all found in books." She almost sounded miffed, as if he'd failed some test.

He'd never before attempted to prove he was *gifted* in any way. But he sensed Mariah needed to be convinced before she would trust him. "I am familiar with this particular variety of smoky quartz, however. It is cairngorm—from Scotland. Teddy's textbooks might not tell you that. We often use it in the handles of *skean dhu*, presumably for the so-called protective qualities of the stones."

"*Skean dhu*, those nasty little daggers kept in socks?" She took the rocks back from him.

He shrugged, unable to find a way to make her believe. "Not in *my* socks, but yes, a traditional Scots dagger. May I suggest we retreat to the bunker? I feel like a walking target if our villain is hiding in the hills with a primed bow." Keegan stood between her and the bluff, hoping the killer had been a rogue deer hunter who was long gone.

She produced a key on a leather necklace and unlocked the bunker door. "You want me to believe that you can tell all that just by *feeling* Daisy's stones? And I suppose you expect me to believe that you can tell if they were found here or imported?"

"As I said, these are common. Teddy can probably order them online by the box. My gift is only useful in the world of science. It tells me precise structures, but only my knowledge of where I've *felt* those structures provide origin. I would have to travel the world, testing rocks, to determine the nuanced differences of origin." He held her steady as she turned on the flashlight, handed him the key, and started down the stairs.

He figured her silence was scorn. He yanked the door shut, locked it, and frowned. "This door opens outward. There is no means of barring it, and this key won't stop a determined criminal. How did you think you would be safe down here?" He examined the heavy steel for bolts.

"Outer doors open out. The bunker wasn't meant to be a fortress." Dropping the discussion of his gift, she rummaged through her backpack. "But I did bring an early warning system. There are hooks on either side of the door, presumably for coats. I just need to tie some of my netting on them."

Keegan eyed the slender threads skeptically. "I'd rather tie them at the bottom of the door and trip anyone who intrudes. Do you have bells?"

"Val wouldn't appreciate being tripped in her own bunker if she decided to visit. So, no tripping, just warnings. And of course I have bells, and crystals." She handed him the collection. "Or you can go your own way now. I appreciate the help, but I'm good on my own."

He grunted and began wrapping the crude warning system across the door. The twine she'd given him felt like tensile steel, only lighter and more flexible. "What is this stuff made from?"

"I weave it myself. It can fray, but it's pretty tough. I could wrap your wrists in it and it would take you all night to get out," she added, eyeing him thoughtfully.

"I appreciate you not doing that," he retorted. "I can't decide whether to hope someone will test your theory by coming through the door so we can catch him, or to pray there is no killer and we'll have time to explore this cavern. I'd like to see if I can determine the crystals used in the paints."

He'd like to do a lot more than that, but he was thankful that Mariah allowed him in. A night on a rocky floor was a small price to pay for her trust. He was fairly certain she was the key to the town's secrets.

"Knock yourself out. The lanterns are there by the stairs. If you'd pull out one of those cots behind the curtain, I'm sacking out. It's been a long day, and I need to be at the café in the morning." She rubbed at her knee.

Well, so much for thinking they'd spend some time getting to know each other.

After she lit a lantern, he found the curtain behind a stack of canvases and pulled out two cots. Well, he wouldn't have to sleep on the floor at least. "These things must be antiques," he grumbled. "Military surplus from the first world war, at best."

"And probably stolen," she agreed with a yawn. "The Ingerssons rolled that way."

She was untying her braid. Keegan set up her cot, surreptitiously watching as she untangled a glossy river of black hair that rippled down her back to her waist. To his disappointment, she unrolled her sleeping bag rather than take off any clothes.

He set up his bed while she arranged the covers on hers. "Are there any more hiding holes where a book might have been stashed?"

"I don't know. Val told me about the cots just tonight. They could have tunneled the entire mountain for all I know. I never had any reason to care until today." She pulled the covers up to her waist but continued sitting, watching him as he examined the walls.

"You never told me your story," he reminded her, aware of her gaze in this intimate setting. She was like a doe he might startle away if he wasn't careful. Or in Mariah's case, she was more likely to snarl and bite, he figured, so maybe not a doe.

"I don't believe yours and you'd not believe mine." She lay down and hauled the covers over her beautiful hair.

Well, at least she hadn't snarled. "The other Lucys claim to be gifted, so I assume you also have some ability that most people don't."

Out in the real world, he never discussed his strange abilities or that of his family. Here in Hillvale, where one debated evil over dinner, it seemed perfectly natural.

"My ability is not a *gift*. It is the reason I'm hiding up here making ghostcatchers instead of a living," she responded testily. "So it's not any better as a bedtime story. Good-night, Keegan. Happy hunting."

Damn, but she had shields he'd need an augur to burrow through. What had happened to her out in the real world that she was stashing her talent under these rocks? She had it all—striking looks, strong character, good friends, and a quick, creative mind that followed his everywhere. She was a rare gem buried beneath coal.

He worked a while testing the crystalline structure on the glowing red eyes in the portraits. He detected traces of almandine garnet, not terribly valuable, but mixed with quartz, the glitter would have caught light and originally given the eyes life. Almandine garnets came from Mozambique and weren't as common as Daisy's guardian stones. There was aquamarine beryl in here too, probably for the blue-green color as well as the crystalline glitter—another stone that might be found in California occasionally.

Keegan thought of crystals in terms of practical uses, but he knew Theodosia, the jeweler, believed they had metaphysical properties. He had no way of testing the paranormal. That's why he needed the missing books—as a starting place for experimentation.

He didn't need to see to know what was beneath his fingers, but he donned his glasses so he wouldn't miss any clue. He ran his hands from top to bottom on the walls, working his way to the back. He found nothing that might be a hiding place. He had hoped the missing crystals might be in the same place as the book, but that had been wishful thinking.

Tucking the glasses away, he resigned himself to a restless night's sleep on a cot much too small for his large frame. Then he heard scratching. He dimmed the lantern and stood still, listening.

Mariah sat up, doing the same. "The door," she whispered.

He nodded agreement. Someone was attempting to unlock the door. It was old and not really intended to keep anyone out, which was why Daisy had hidden it in bushes. "Could it be Valdis?" he asked. "How many people know the door is there?"

"Just a few Lucys, originally. But who knows what the sheriff's men discovered?" She shook off the sleeping bag.

Keegan pointed at the back of the bunker. "Move out of firing range. We don't know if they have guns."

She grasped her walking stick to stand. The crystal in the handle glowed, as did the ones on the wall. Keegan dimmed the lantern more, but the crystals still gave off light. He was fairly certain that wasn't normal.

"And you plan to do what? Go up and greet them? No way. Come back here with me. I'll see if I can connect with Cass." She grabbed his arm and tugged—as if her tug could move mountains.

Amused that she attempted to protect him, he followed her. "Cass? I thought cell phones didn't work in Hillvale."

"They don't," she said curtly. "Now shut up and let me focus."

She sank to the ground, propped her hands on her knees, palms up, walking stick across them, and closed her eyes. Keegan snorted and returned to listening to the door noises.

Someone hit the lock with a hard blow. Hammer and awl to break the rusty connection, he surmised.

He eyed Mariah's wooden staff as a potential weapon, but decided not to disturb her. Instead, he hefted a heavy frame from the floor, yanked off the canvas, twisted until the nails popped, and ripped off the longest length of thick wood. Then he flung the cots and bench into a zig zag pattern to make it difficult for anyone to reach Mariah.

The door slammed into their early warning system, jangling the bells.

EIGHT

July 8: Sunday, late evening

"What the hell?" A rough male voice cursed and slammed the bunker door against Mariah's twine again. The bells jangled eerily in the semi-dark, disturbing her psychic concentration.

Her mental warning had just reached Cass over the neural pathways they'd developed over years of practice. She flashed an image of the bunker and let Cass feel her fear, then clenched her fingers around her walking stick as Cass signaled she understood.

Psychic communication wasn't easy and often left Mariah blurry and disoriented. But danger forced her to focus. She hadn't survived by living off the grid all this time to die so ignobly.

Taking a deep breath to steady her confused senses, Mariah used the thick staff to push herself up. Keegan had closed the lantern panel, leaving only the crystals for illumination. She didn't think they had been glowing earlier. The one in her staff usually reacted to the presence of bad energy, but it had never done so without another Lucy around. The walls gleamed like a hundred Lucys.

In the dim light, she could see Keegan's massive form pressed into the cot niche, nearly out of sight. He held a stick of some sort like a cricket bat. Her fear ratcheted up a notch. Cricket bats didn't work against guns.

Bullets in this narrow cellar could ricochet badly. She shivered in trepidation.

"They'll have to duck under the twine," she whispered, preferring to plot than to fear. "It won't break by slamming a door into it."

He glanced at her and nodded. She didn't know if he believed her.

Surprise was their only hope.

Over Keegan's protest, she pushed past him for her backpack while the asshat at the door conferred with someone. She produced a jar of her favorite hot sauce, limped to the stairs, and smeared the thick liquid across the step below the twine.

Understanding, Keegan snickered and joined her at the bottom of the stairs. Sticks ready, they stood on either side of the spot where an intruder would slide once they hit the sauce.

"It's not effin' ghosts," the male voice growled, sounding brashly defiant. "It's just jammed. I can squeeze through."

Ghosts, nice. She would give him ghosts. Mariah grabbed a cotton shirt from her bag and flung it over the twine, where it would dangle and brush anyone trying to duck under it. Keegan chuckled loud enough to scare ghosts away. She liked a man who not only got it but laughed in the face of danger. Dammit.

"No, I didn't hear anything. Quit being such a girl. I'm going in." A shadow pushed the door as wide as it would go, then groped around, looking for the source of the blockage. Finally locating the threads, he attempted to yank them off.

As she'd predicted, the threads didn't break. Her twine was meant to catch ectoplasm. It wasn't ordinary material.

Swearing, the shadow grasped the threads and tugged to lift them. Mariah tightened her grip on her staff. How long would it take for Cass to drag Walker out of his bed and send him up here?

The intruder wasn't small. From his silhouette, he appeared to be overweight and belly heavy. He couldn't easily crouch under the thread without putting his foot on the lower step. . .

His foot hit the hot sauce and slipped to the next stair. Unbalanced, his large frame toppled backward. He yelped in pain as his considerable posterior hit the hard stone and bounced downward. Sliding under the t-shirt draped twine, he howled in terror as the cotton brushed his face. Freaking, he hit every step going down.

"He's not even worth head smashing," Keegan said in disgust, making no attempt to conceal his presence as he stomped the helpless man's wrist with his boot.

No weapon clattered from the thief's grip. Keeping a watch on the door above, Mariah set her staff down and opened the lantern. Keegan hauled the prowler to his feet, locking his wrists in a massive fist.

Keegan uttered a grunt of disgust as the light fell on the prisoner's face. "George, isn't it? Did you think to find your fellow bigots down here?"

"Just doing a little exploring," the thief protested. "I used to go spelunking when I was a kid. I didn't know anyone was here."

Mariah crept around them to head up the stairs and peer out the open door. George's accomplice was running for the woods. If her knee hadn't been bruised, she could have run after him, but it was easier to assume Georgie-Porgie would spill the beans.

Walker's headlights were already coming up the lane.

Avoiding the hot sauce smear, which was mostly on Georgie anyway, she limped back down to watch Keegan wrap her twine around his captive's wrist. Without any compunction, she lifted Georgie's wallet from his pocket and rifled through the contents.

"George Thompson from Monterey," she read from his license. "Any relation to Lonnie?"

"My brother," George spat. "He said he'd been robbed up here. I just came up to look around. No harm in that."

"Lonnie is the scum who murdered Thalia and left her remains in Teddy's attic," Mariah told Keegan, continuing to rifle through Georgie's battered wallet. "He specializes in fake pottery. Those are probably Lonnie's bad pieces in our collection. What's your specialty, Georgie? Forging paintings?"

Walker couldn't drive his SUV down to the farmhouse, but she could hear the engine cut off in the lane above. He'd be down in a few minutes.

"I'm a plumber," George replied indignantly. "I tell ya, I was just looking."

Mariah produced a folded color photograph from the clutter. She held it up in the light of the lantern. "A photo of the triptych." She showed it to Keegan, who merely sent her a questioning look. "The triptych was Lucinda Malcolm's gift to Hillvale. It's worth a fortune, but we don't want to sell it. Lonnie had one of the panels in his garage. The police confiscated it."

"They had no right," George said indignantly. "That painting belongs to Lonnie. He says it could pay for his defense."

"And you thought we'd hide a valuable painting underground?" she asked in scorn.

Walker's boots crunched across the gravel above. Keegan's eyes widened in surprise. He hadn't believed she was contacting Cass. That was okay. She didn't believe it too often either. Cass was just that good.

Mariah found a few hundred-dollar bills in the billfold, some receipts so old they crumbled, discount cards for groceries and drugstores, club cards from the discount mall, the detritus of a messy man who liked to pinch pennies and didn't believe in banks.

Walker's flashlight beam hit the threads blocking the door.

"You'll need a knife to cut them," Mariah called up. "Or you can duck, but then you have to watch for the hot sauce on the stairs."

Keegan's low rumbling chuckle tickled her insides. She objected to any man tickling her insides, but she could see the humor.

Walker calmly reached through, untangled the threads from one coat hook, and let them fall. His flashlight illuminated the stairs, and he stepped over the smeared one. "Do I want to ask?"

"Let's just say we were afraid of thieves and caught one," Keegan said in that male-to-male way that left everything important unsaid. "This is Lonnie Thompson's brother. Mariah thinks that's significant."

"Another killer in the family?" Walker asked, shining his light on Georgie's face. Georgie flinched.

"I'm no killer! Neither is Lonnie! His bitch of a wife fell!"

"Teddy can probably tell you if he's lying," Mariah suggested.

"He doesn't have the calluses of an archer," Keegan pointed out. "I don't think he's our killer. But he was most likely looking for his brother's share of the triptych." He held up the photograph Mariah had handed him.

Walker glanced at the photograph and began reading Georgie his rights while their prisoner whined and complained and agreed he understood and demanded to be released.

"He had an accomplice," Mariah warned. "I couldn't see anything but a dark figure running for the woods."

"You're imagining things," Georgie shouted. "Ain't no one here but me."

"And countless ghosts," Keegan said solemnly, repeating the welcome sign that stated *Hillvale, spiritual home of 325 lives and countless ghosts.*

"I'll tell Cass and Sam that the two of you are just fine and deserve each other," Walker said with a straight face, hauling his whining prisoner for the stairs. "In return, you won't tell me how you reached Cass or why thread doesn't break and why all these damn crystals gleam like beacons."

"You're a good man, Charlie Brown," Mariah called after him.

"I want security cameras in the parking lot," he shouted back. "We'd have your accomplice then."

"Bloody hell." Keegan rolled his shoulders as the door closed. "We'll have to set up guards at the door 24/7." He glared at Mariah. "And I don't promise not to ask how you reached Cass or why crystals gleam."

She shrugged and limped over to her cot. "Want to hang the threads back up and call it a night?"

His curse gave his opinion on that. Mariah didn't care. She was wiped. And she wasn't getting any more involved with a man who rang her chimes. She was over men—for so many reasons she could count them like sheep.

JULY 9: MONDAY, MORNING

Keegan declined Mariah's invitation to breakfast as they climbed out of the golf cart at Dinah's café the next morning. They'd barely spoken after their rough night's sleep. He had too many questions, and she offered no answers. No matter how much she intrigued him, he wasn't into the masochism of battering his head against stone walls.

He stopped at his room over Aaron's shop to shower and find fresh clothes, his mind racing. Hillvale hid secrets: futuristic triptychs, gleaming crystals, garnet eyes in valuable paintings, and villains who knew more than he did.

He was an engineer, not a detective. Had he really thought he could just waltz in here and find his missing books? Or ask and have them returned? Stress had turned his brain to mush, if so.

What if the crystals in the bunker walls were from his family's long-lost collection?

He looked at the time, added eight hours, and figured his father was home by now. He donned his glasses and opened his laptop. Connecting with Aaron's wi-fi, he sent a message. His father merely replied that all was well, and he didn't have time to Skype.

Which meant the old man was too depressed to talk. Keegan rubbed his forehead and swore, feeling the ache in his heart that this damnable catastrophe had created. What were the chances he could find answers to his questions in time to keep his father out of jail? The old man would die of humiliation, if nothing else.

Closing his laptop, Keegan found Aaron in his shop, selling a chandelier to a tourist wearing designer clothing. He waited until she was gone.

"What can you tell me about the triptych Lucinda Malcolm painted?"

Aaron shrugged. "Now that we have all the panels back, we're setting it up in the old meeting house. The Kennedys' uncle Lance has practically turned it into a shrine. We need security guards to protect it and don't have the money. I think we'd do better to auction it off."

"Except it belongs to the town, and the Kennedys would want to spend the money on a ski lift?" Keegan asked in amusement at his friend's priorities. "May I see it?"

"You catch on quickly. Let me lock up and I'll take you down there. Lance isn't always a communicator, and he's usually the one in charge. He never used to come out of his studio, but he has some bee in his bonnet about setting up a gallery in that barn of a place where he can display his own work."

Keegan knew where the meeting house was. It looked like an old chapel, right across from city hall, not far from Aaron's antique store. Of course, in Hillvale, nothing was very far. But he'd not yet met Lance, so he assumed it was preferable to be introduced to the Kennedys' eccentric uncle.

Sunshine cut a swathe of light across the planks of the meeting house when Aaron yanked open one of a pair of huge old wooden doors. Inside, chattering voices halted, until they saw Aaron.

Keegan recognized Theodosia Devine-Baker's voice hailing them. "Come in, Keegan, tell us all about your night with Mariah!"

He needed to learn American informality. He nodded in Theodosia's direction and noted the urbane resort owner, Kurt Kennedy, at her side. In contrast to Kennedy's tailored suit and styled hair, the tall, almost anorexic man Keegan assumed was the artist uncle looked like a homeless person in baggy, paint-stained clothes. The chief of police was also there.

"Educational," Keegan replied, not revealing anything about his night with Mariah before addressing the chief. "Did our would-be thief have anything interesting to say?"

The impassive police chief often sat in the café, but Keegan had seldom heard him offer his opinion, and he didn't expect one now.

Walker shrugged. "He lawyered up and will be out on bail in a few hours. It's not as if we caught him doing much more than trespassing. I need to get back to the office." Striding for the door, Walker waved and disappeared into the sunshine.

"I think he and Sam are getting serious," the petite jeweler murmured. "They've hardly known each other a month, but I've never seen a more perfect couple."

Kennedy rolled his eyes and rapped her on the head. "Which makes us what, chopped liver?"

"It makes us *interesting*." She hugged his waist and continued on with her thoughts. "George Thompson and his wife were in my shop the other day. They're not poor. They tried to negotiate the price of one my designer pieces, and when I wouldn't give in, their credit card worked just fine."

"I hope it was a piece with the honesty stones in it," her significant other said with a grim smile. "They stayed at the lodge Saturday night, were rude to my best desk clerk, complained our housekeeping staff didn't do their jobs, asked for a discount, and didn't leave tips even for the wait staff."

"Let me guess, your staff is mostly brown-skinned," Keegan suggested, remembering his encounter with George outside the café.

Kurt Kennedy's eyebrows shot up. "Most of them, yes, if you want to put it that way. We hire locally." He held up his tanned wrist. "Brown."

"Not talking color so much as bigotry," Keegan said. "I met George

Thompson outside Dinah's café where he warned me about Dinah. I believe they may have stepped out of a different century. Or a hole in the ground."

"That sounds about right," Kurt agreed. "We still have our fair share out here who hide their fear of change behind hatred."

Keegan's far-sightedness allowed him to study the triptych from this distance. A set of spotlights dangled from wires in front of it. Not all of the lights worked, but he could discern the details. "Maybe they stepped out of the century in which that was painted. The mid-twentieth was not a time of acceptance. As far as I'm aware, Lucinda Malcolm died in the 1970's, at a very old age. So a work that difficult had to have been painted by the 1950's, if it's truly hers."

"The gallery owner who sells Lucinda's work confirmed it's an original." Theodosia stood back to study the three four-by-eight panels. "Lucinda may have painted it fifty years in advance, but it reflects a specific day ten years ago. We've identified Kurt and his brother on the corner beside the building they turned into city hall. That's Thalia, my mother's cousin, coming down from the farm with the vase. Lonnie, her husband, is flirting with his girlfriend by the woodie wagon. Kurt and Monty weren't even *born* when Lucinda painted an entire town that barely existed in her time."

"The triptych shows the day when Monty and I were told we had to take over the resort," Kurt explained.

Keegan went closer to examine the detail. "I'd heard she painted the future for family. So, who is Lucinda's family in this work?"

"Cass." The silent artist spoke up, pointing to a tall figure striding down the street, carrying a large tote bag over her shoulder. "Her mother was a Wainwright."

Keegan snorted as the others searched for a resemblance in his face. There would be none, not after all these centuries. "The Wainwrights were descended from a younger branch of the original Malcolm family. I'm from the Ives side. The families often intermarried. So this might have been a significant day in Cass's life?"

"I can't see how," Kurt said with a frown.

Aaron spoke up. "Ten years ago, I wasn't here, but when I arrived, Cass was living alone, just as she is now. Kurt and Monty taking over the reins of the town was significant, but not to Cass. She owns property on the far side by the cemetery and vortex. She has nothing to do with the shops or resort."

Theodosia added, "We thought the main significance of this painting was Thalia coming down the hill, seeing her husband flirting with another woman. We think she died that night."

"But this Thalia was the one who knew about Lucinda Malcolm's book?" Keegan zeroed in on his main concern.

"You think Thalia gave it to *Cass*?" Theodosia asked in surprise. "Wouldn't Cass have told us if she had it?"

Both Kurt and Lance made grunts of doubt, but they refrained from commenting. Aaron frowned and crossed his arms.

Ah yes, the pragmatic Nulls didn't like Cass, while the metaphysical Lucys believed Cass could do no wrong. Small towns were like that. "Then what about Daisy? Didn't someone say she may have stolen Thalia's book? Is she in this painting? Would she be related to Lucinda or Cass?" Keegan studied the faded paint in the unfinished lighting.

Everyone else did the same.

"I never saw Daisy without her cloak," Theodosia said thoughtfully. "But I think Valdis was providing her with the costumes, and Val didn't return to town until some years after the date this depicts."

"So Daisy might not have been wearing a cloak then," Kurt said, following her thought. "She's been here from the beginnings of time, but I never paid much attention to her."

"Cass did," Lance, the artist, said, peering at the triptych as if it were the Holy Grail. "Cass probably gave her food and shelter when needed."

As the Kennedys hadn't went unsaid. Keegan got that. The wealthy often lived in towers separate from the mundane. His intellectual tower was little better.

Theodosia pulled up a stepstool to look closer. Wearing a tank top that revealed all her splendid cleavage, she left Kurt looking glassy-eyed. But Keegan was immune to diminutive red-haired sprites. He wanted tall, dark Mariah to give him her cynical version of events.

"There, under the window of the shop next to mine." The jeweler pointed at a long-haired figure working in the shadow of the covered boardwalk. "Did Daisy start decorating the planters about then?"

Keegan hadn't seen enough of the dead woman to recognize anything but the graying hair. The perspective of the painting was from the upper story of what he assumed was now the jeweler's shop. The figure on the boardwalk almost under the window wouldn't have been clear to the painter. He waited for the others to respond.

"There were rotten, wooden horse troughs back then," Monty said in disgust. "I bought the new clay planters with my own money not too long after this."

"Daisy was known to decorate rusted plows," Aaron said. "If she had paint, she would paint troughs. That could be what she's doing there."

"Right outside the window of my house," Theodosia said softly. "She may have overheard the knock-down, drag-out fight Thalia and Lonnie had right after this."

"A witness?" Aaron asked with doubt. "You think George killed the witness to his brother's crime?"

"Daisy's testimony would never be accepted in court. No, if anything at all, Daisy would have feared the loss of the book to the wrong hands and decided that was the moment to steal it," Theodosia said.

NINE

Mariah glared at Keegan's long form sprawled in the golf cart she'd parked behind the café. "You need a ride?" she asked dryly, waiting for him to sit up so she could climb in.

"To Cass's, if you don't mind. I need an introduction more than a ride." With lazy grace, he unfolded his massive frame from the bench seat to assist her into the cart.

"Cass only accepts visitors when she's so inclined. I can take you up there. We can knock. If she answers, I'll make the introduction. I wouldn't get your hopes up, so I trust your mission isn't important." She slid behind the wheel and started the ignition.

Her distrust of men had let her ignore her urges for a long time. The Scot's wide shoulders, narrow hips, and potent pheromones were wearing down her physical barriers. If she wanted to stay hidden, she needed to keep up her mental ones.

"Is there any chance that Cass might have Lucinda Malcolm's book on crystals?" he asked bluntly.

Mariah scowled. "If there was any chance at all of laying her hands on that book, sure. And she's perfectly capable of not telling us she has it. But she did seem rather surprised to learn Thalia had it, so I don't see the connection."

"Daisy," he said as she steered up the back lane, avoiding the main highway. "Did Theodosia not tell you?"

"Her name is Teddy. No one calls her Theodosia. Or Devine-Baker."

"I was brought up using titles. I will attempt to adapt."

"Titles," she said in derision. "Like Lord Chamberlain or whatever?"

"Like Earl of Ives and Wystan and the Marquess of Ashford, my English relations. Are you avoiding the subject of Daisy?"

"You're related to royalty?" she asked incredulously, avoiding the painful subject of Daisy.

"They are not royalty," he said with an unusual touch of impatience. "They're not even toplofty enough to be considered nobility as far as I'm concerned. I regularly beat Ash at archery and golf, and the earl is an infant. This is all irrelevant to the problem at hand. If there is any chance Daisy may have stolen the book, would she have taken it to Cass?"

Mariah tried not to think of the huge lists of wealthy people caught up in her scandal, including some high-flying Brits. She was pretty sure the British aristocracy was not a large world. And *Keegan* was one of them?

She concealed a shudder. She'd stupidly thought she was safe from a miner's son. Maybe she needed a new hiding place.

"What does this have to do with Teddy?" she demanded.

"Your mind is a wondrous place," he complained as they drove up Cass's driveway. "*Teddy* was the one who pointed out a figure that may be Daisy in the triptych. She claims Daisy may have overheard something the day a woman died in the shop, and that she might have stolen the book then. There was something about the day of the triptych being of importance to Cass."

"If so, you'll never see the book again unless Cass wants it so." Mariah turned off the ignition at the front porch of the sprawling faux-Victorian mansion the town's leading doyenne called home.

If Cass wanted to talk with Keegan, she'd be sitting in that rocking chair, waiting for them. Of course, if Cass wanted to knock Keegan's socks off, she'd invite him inside. It was worth hanging around to find out. Mariah used her staff as a cane to limp up to the porch.

"Are you sure you should not have a physician look at that leg?" he asked in what sounded like concern.

How long had it been since anyone had expressed concern for her?

Interesting intellectual puzzle. Since her Nana died, maybe? Mariah shrugged it off. "The swelling is going down. It will turn purple and green and be good as new in no time."

And she didn't have insurance and didn't dare access her accounts, so the answer was an unequivocal no. She knocked on the dark green front door.

It creaked open. Keegan frowned. The man did concern real well. Mariah simply marched in shouting "Cass?"

Cass had the draperies pulled back to let in the light today, so she'd been expecting them. Mariah never knew what she'd see when she walked through the halls. Teddy had once called Cass's house something out of a virtual reality program. She wasn't far from wrong. Mariah figured they were striding through different dimensions, since the house was stuffed to the rafter with ghosts. Cass's weirdness was nothing compared to Mariah's, so she accepted the oddities.

Today, the front parlor was appropriately decorated in Victorian oak, burgundy velvets, and gilded frames. The enormous mahogany dining table had been reduced to family size. The walls were covered in artwork from different eras, and even the empty spaces where Daisy had stolen the red-eyed canvases had been filled with pretty landscapes. Cass was making an effort. Why? For Keegan?

"In the sunroom, dear," Cass called.

As if Mariah had known there was a sunroom. Last time she'd been here, she'd seen no sign of one, but admittedly, it was usually dark. She walked past the sweeping staircase toward the back of the house. Apparently accustomed to grandeur, Keegan didn't even bother examining the artwork or the ornately sculpted woodwork on the banister. Mariah was pretty sure dragons, trolls, and gargoyles were involved.

About where a kitchen ought to be, a room filled with sunlight greeted them. The windows overlooked the downside of the mountain toward the west. If that was the ocean in the distance, it was concealed in a fogbank.

Cass sat like a queen on her throne-like wicker chair, sipping tea. Wearing what appeared to be a long, brown, velvet robe, she gestured at a wicker love seat. "Good morning, children. What brings you here?"

Cass was many things, including a mean bitch when she wanted. She'd infiltrated Sam's brain for nearly a week. Gracious hostess was not normally in Cass's repertoire. She had an agenda this morning, as always. Mariah settled on the cushioned seat and helped herself to a teacup without asking. She poured tea and offered it to Keegan.

"I'm just here to introduce a distant relative of yours, Keegan Ives," Mariah said. "Keegan, this is Cassandra Kennedy Tolliver."

Keegan didn't take a seat or a cup until Cass nodded her approval and gestured for him to sit. "Pleased to meet you, Mrs. Tolliver."

"Cass, please. Tolliver died decades ago. Ives? As in the earl of Ives?" She sipped her tea, her sharp blue eyes missing nothing.

Keegan held the delicate china in one big mitt, but he didn't sip from it. Mariah thought that pretty damned smart for a Null.

"The earl and his father the marquess are cousins. I'm of the Scots branch. You know my family?"

"I've met a few through my mother's family, but as in everything, it's been a long time. I don't travel much these days. What brings you here, Mr. Ives?"

"A book, ma'am. You are aware of the extensive Malcolm library?" At her regal nod, he continued. "Several valuable volumes from the 1700s are missing. I've learned one of them was in the possession of a lady who was murdered ten years ago. And the person who may have had opportunity to acquire it has just been killed. That volume was missing from the 1950 inventory. A second volume was gone in the 1980 inventory. The one that set me on this journey has only recently vanished. The three together could be. . . unsafe."

Mariah tried not to raise her eyebrows in surprise. She hadn't realized that. She'd been so busy trying not to get involved that she'd missed a few key points here. Daisy might have been killed for a *book*?

"I see. And this concerns me how?"

Mariah heard the hard edge in Cass's voice. She could step in now, explain about Daisy, but Cass knew all that. So she let Keegan blunder his way into maybe surprising her.

"We thought Daisy may have brought the volume to you for protection," he said, without apology. "Books that old do not survive long in the conditions in which she lived."

Oh, very good, Mr. Ives, Mariah murmured mentally, enjoying her tea. The handsome oaf could be a diplomat when he tried.

"And if she did, I would protect it accordingly," Cass said, giving away nothing and everything at once. Cass was a master of illusion.

"Daisy may have been murdered for that book," Keegan reminded her, keeping his voice soft. "It would be safer under lock and key in my castle."

"Not if it was stolen, along with other volumes," Cass pointed out, equally polite. "Do you still have a Malcolm librarian? Or has that ability passed on, possibly to American descendants?"

"Chinese, actually," he said, starting to look uncomfortable. He stretched out his long legs and studied his polished shoes. "That's my branch of the family. Several traveled as missionaries to China, produced families who have extended around the globe. There's a branch of the family here in San Francisco. One of them learned about my library and took her studies in Edinburgh. She's been updating the catalog ever since, which is how we became aware of the third missing crystal journal."

Mariah knew Cass would not give up a book if she'd decided it was needed in Hillvale. So, she took a different direction. "What sent us up here was Lucinda's triptych. We know that Lucinda generally painted scenes that were important to a member of her family. As far as we're aware, you're her only relation in Hillvale. So how was that day important to you?"

"And this has what to do with the missing journal?" Cass poured a second cup of tea and watched them through eyes that sparkled like sapphires—like Sam's.

"Since that was the day the woman last known to have the journal died, we thought acquiring the journal might have been important to you," Keegan said.

Mariah wished they'd brought Teddy with them to determine Cass's reaction. But Teddy said the spirits filling Cass's house made her afraid to open her extra sense. This conversation gave Mariah some inkling of why Cass might like to keep her ghosts around.

"I can't remember that day," Cass said remotely. "I've only briefly seen the painting. It didn't appear remarkable in any way, other than knowing when it was painted. I was probably headed for the new grocery store. One must eat."

There was little point in calling Cass a liar. She never went to the grocery. She had friends all over the mountain who saw that she ate and had supplies. Mariah wouldn't call them servants, exactly, but close enough. Money might not be exchanged, but favors almost certainly were.

"Cass, we need to find who killed Daisy before they kill again." Mariah stepped in, understanding how Cass's mind worked. Poor Keegan thought honesty and directness should do it. "If there's any chance there's a clue in those books, we need to know."

"I've read the odd diaries Thalia left on the backs of her paintings," Cass said stiffly. "Besides mentioning she stole Lucinda's compendium, she had nothing of any value to say. She complained that her husband was a fraud, a bad potter who disparaged her artwork—rightfully so, if I'm any judge—and she was afraid of his temper. The single mention of Lucinda's journal labels Thalia as thief in her own words. If she possessed the journal, she didn't mention its use except that once, with Susannah's help, on the café mural. It's quite possible that she passed it on to someone else."

"Like to Susannah," Mariah concluded, as Cass had wanted her to. "Sam says her mother writes children's books. She has no use for crystals."

"Susannah—Mrs. Menendez, the lady who brought her father's paintings with her and is now cleaning the mural in the café? The one who thought Thalia still has the volume?" Keegan's gaze burned with interest.

Mariah wanted to bathe in his masculine attention—or slap him away. "Sam's mother, yes. She lives on some Indonesian island now, completely off the grid, and wants nothing to do with Hillvale's paranormal inhabitants. I see no reason she would have lied about not having it. No, I'm pretty sure Daisy is our key." Mariah shot their hostess a glare. "And Cass."

Cass merely sipped her tea and met her gaze without flinching. "Do come again to tell me what you've found out."

"She knows," Mariah hissed as they let themselves out a few minutes later. "If she doesn't have the book herself, she knows where it is."

"How likely is it that our killer will figure that out?" Keegan asked worriedly, offering his hand to help her into the cart.

"If we're assuming the killer took out Daisy to access the bunker in search of it, it will take a while—if we keep the bunker secured. Kurt has his security out there, but they're human, not dragons." She turned the ignition but didn't know where she was taking him.

In pursuit of the truth, she'd forgotten that she was supposed to stay clear of Keegan. It seemed natural to work together—and maybe necessary. If she couldn't use computers to trace a thief and a killer, she needed to learn better methods of obtaining justice.

Had she learned better methods sooner, she might not be moldering in Hillvale, waiting for the distant day it might be safe to leave.

"We should talk to Mrs. Menendez," he said. "We could at least confirm that she saw my book and not some other."

"She was pretty immersed in cleaning the mural when I left." Mariah steered the cart down the lane, past Sam's flourishing garden house and her own tiny cottage. Traffic on the main highway had declined since the fire that had stripped the mountain, but she still preferred this backroad. The cart wasn't much safer than her bicycle—which led to another thought.

"Where is Val? She was Daisy's closest friend. She might have some knowledge of the book. This is her cart I'm driving around. I'd assumed she was with Cass, but I didn't see any sign of her."

"The wailing banshee?" he asked with interest. "Does she actually speak?"

"She can, when she wants. But I've not seen her speaking to her sister since Susannah arrived. This damned town has more secrets than I do." Mariah pulled the cart up behind the café without thinking. It wasn't time for the lunch rush, but she wasn't up to her usual rounds of checking her ghostcatchers.

Keegan assisted her from the cart. Out of habit, she opened the kitchen door.

The operatic argument hit them before they could enter.

"The land is *evil*," the banshee screeched. "We cannot sell it!"

"Uh oh, trouble in paradise," Mariah whispered.

A plate crashed and a woman screamed.

TEN

Keegan lifted Mariah and hauled her into the kitchen in his rush to reach the front of the diner. Her generous curves fit perfectly against him, even if she was trying to rip off his arm. He didn't think she wore perfume, but she had a natural scent of sage that reminded him of the heather at home.

Looking frightened, Dinah hovered by the server's window. She didn't look any happier when Keegan dropped Mariah at her side. "Keep her here," he ordered.

Mariah got in a good smack before he could escape to the front. It was little more than a bee sting to relieve her frustration, he understood. He just wasn't having any more women murdered in his vicinity.

Samantha, the tall slender blonde he knew as the police chief's girl-friend, stood between her mother on a ladder at the mural and the shrieking banshee on the other side of the counter. Sam yanked a second plate out of the banshee's hand and glanced up to Keegan with hope. He wasn't certain what he was supposed to do now that it was apparent it was a cat fight and not a murder, but he obligingly stepped in front of the plate thrower.

"Valerie, act your age," the woman perched on the stepladder scolded. "This isn't the opera, and you're too old to be a diva. It's just us now, and Sam. You don't have to perform." She eyed him skeptically. "Well, and now it's the Scot, but I doubt that's a problem."

Keegan held out both arms to prevent the tall, dark-haired woman from reaching around him for another plate. Her long black veil concealed her features, as it had every time he'd seen her. Keening over a murder demanded costume, perhaps, but a family fight, not so much.

"I will not sell that land," the veiled Valkyrie wailed—operatically. Keegan understood the diva reference better, along with the dramatic *Valdis* instead of sensible *Valerie* as a name.

"I just said you could afford to return to the city if you sold that albatross hanging around your neck." Carrying her tray of paint, Susannah climbed down the stepladder now that attack didn't appear imminent. "I've never wanted the money, but I thought perhaps you and Sam might."

"It's not that easy," Samantha said with quiet authority. "Aunt Val, if you'd sit down, I could bring you one of Dinah's possets. You said they make the migraines go away."

Mariah was already limping out of the kitchen, carrying two large mugs. "Is the mural okay?"

"The mural is so plastered in varnish, it could withstand an earthquake," Susannah Menendez said dryly. "Mr. Ives, you may sit down. Sam has removed the rest of the ammunition. Thank you for stepping in."

The café was unusually empty, Keegan noted. He took the mugs from Mariah, set them on the booth table, and assisted her to a stool. She looked as if she wanted to shake him off, but curiosity burned in her eyes.

"The cowards all fled," she whispered. "They saw Val coming and didn't hang around."

"Cowards, indeed, if they feared a couple of fifty-year-old women. Did they expect bolts of lightning?" He sat down on the stool beside her while Samantha settled her family in the booth.

"Don't scoff. With Val, anything is possible. She walks on the other side of the veil, and I'm not talking about that rag she wears to conceal her scar. And no one really knows what Susannah is capable of. The family is multi-talented."

When Samantha signaled she was okay, Mariah spun the stool

around and whacked Keegan's biceps—hard. "Quit hauling me around. I'm not a helpless child."

He wouldn't ask questions about a woman who walked on the *other side of the veil*. There were women in his own family who said worse. He focused on the here and now. "You are currently lame, and I wished to move swiftly. I assume the coffee machine works normally? Shall I bring you a cup?" He nodded at the silver urn that had been moved while the mural was undergoing renovations.

She looked surprised at his offer and nodded with a hint of suspicion. "It may be empty at this hour."

"Give me instructions in filling it, if so." He got up and tested the spigot, filling two cups and setting one down in front of Mariah, while unabashedly listening to the family argument.

"This land they argue over, that's where the bunker is, correct?" Adrenaline still pumping, Keegan leaned against the counter to drink his coffee.

"The Ingersson farm, yes. It's been an ongoing thorn in the town's side for a thousand different reasons for decades, maybe longer. Sam thinks her mother sent her away to keep it from ever being sold, but it looks like that theory is wrong. It's in a trust, and Sam and Val are the executors."

"Not Mrs. Menendez? So she cannot actually sell it?" He listened to the murmurs in the booth, but Sam was mostly soothing her aunt and mother and urging them to drink their *possets*. Keegan wondered if they contained rum and if he could have some too.

"Not that I'm aware of. Sam and Walker have been looking into it. The land belonged to Sam's grandparents, Val and Susannah's parents. Foreclosures and lawsuits were still ongoing when the Ingerssons died. The court arranged for the land to go into a trust when the suit was settled. Sam was an infant at the time. Susannah sent her off for adoption, bolted, and Val couldn't sell until Sam came of age—and then no one knew where she was, until Sam found us. The Kennedys want it to expand their resort operations."

"Then there is little reason in killing Daisy to remove obstacles to selling," Keegan mused aloud.

"A developer murdered Walker's father and attempted to kill Daisy,

Val, and Sam for that land," Mariah reminded him. "This is California. Land is as precious as gold."

"This town is *evil*," Susannah shouted from the booth, as if emphasizing Mariah's point. "It's destroyed all of us. I never wanted Sam to come back here. I wanted her to have a normal life! This is all Cass's fault."

"Here's where I make an idiot of myself," Mariah whispered, standing. "You have permission to haul Val off me."

Keegan didn't know how seriously to take her, but he came out from behind the counter to be better prepared for action.

Tall and commanding, even in blue jeans, buckskin vest, and a braid laced with feathers and beads, Mariah stopped in front of the booth. *"Hillvale is not evil,"* she said without raising her voice, but with sufficient conviction to halt argument. "This is where people like us gather because like understands like. All we want is to be left in peace so we can employ our gifts for good, in whatever small way possible. And if we work together, we might accomplish a greater good."

"Yeah, we've heard all *that* before," Susannah replied in cynicism. "Listen to the voice of experience and get out before you're as corrupted as they are." She gestured at the mural.

"They didn't do this to me," Val howled, flinging back her veil.

A livid red and purple weal ran from her ear, down the strong line of her jaw to her mouth. Unimpressed, Keegan noted the death goddess had the same Nordic bone structure as Samantha. Susannah's face and figure were less sculpted and more rounded, pleasant while her sister must once have been striking. Samantha fell in between, not classically beautiful but easy to look at.

"Evil isn't a *place*," Mariah agreed. "Evil is in people, a much broader spectrum that can be found anywhere. Evil is selfishness, greed, and ambition without respect for others. It's possible the crystals your parents played with possessed qualities that enhanced evil, but we need to find them to understand. Selling the land would be criminal, if only because we don't know what's hidden up there."

Her dramatic gesture over, Val covered her face again. Keegan would have liked to know her story, but this was Mariah's moment, not his. He was impressed by her ardent plea. It seemed underneath her thick skin of cynicism boiled a vat of passion.

"Once the land is turned into another tourist hole, no one will care. Daisy was *killed* for what some greedy moron thinks is there," Mrs. Menendez protested. "Let them find out it's just dirt."

"Who put the land into trust for me and Aunt Val?" Sam demanded, unexpectedly.

"The lawyers Cass hired," her mother retorted. "Val was starting her career and was touring. I was newly widowed and not even twenty-one. Our parents had just died, leaving us confused and bereft. Cass had always handled your father's business, so I let her handle yours."

Val spoke normally, if rashly. "You *knew* what Cass's lawyers would do. Don't blame her! That land belongs to all the people who lost theirs because of the greed of the Kennedys and our father's obsessions."

Susannah rubbed her temple. "Our parents *died* because of that land. Sam's father died from the drugs they brought up here. I wanted nothing to do with it. Cass knew that, so the lawyers left me out and substituted Samantha instead, against my wishes. I was too stupid with grief at the time to care. I'd already decided I was leaving. If I thought anything at all, it was that the land could sit there and rot, but now I see it's still hurting people. Poor Daisy didn't deserve to die like that!"

"You denied Samantha her heritage!" Val roared. "She could have made a difference if she'd known her roots. You never cared about anyone but yourself."

Keegan bit his tongue, confident Mariah would take charge. Once the argument broke down to the personal, they'd learn nothing but old grievances.

"We all must take care of ourselves in the best way we know how," Mariah said, startling the older women into remembering her presence. "But once we're in a position to do so, we must look out for those who are still struggling. This town is full of people who are struggling. We have a chance to fix it, if we work together."

Keegan gained an inkling of understanding of why Mariah might be hiding in Hillvale. Those who fought for others often ended up in a world of trouble if they took on the wrong foes. Mariah was strong enough to conquer some opponents, but reckless enough to bite off more than she could chew. Now he was really worrying about her.

"Is Daisy in the mural?" Samantha unexpectedly asked, diverting hostilities. "If we could label the mural, we might know who else knew about the crystals."

Now they were getting somewhere. Keegan watched in satisfaction as the women emerged from the booth to direct their attention on the painting running the length of the café's counter. He eased to one side so as not to block their view.

"This was painted before we were born," Susannah reminded them. "I doubt most of these people, except our parents, hung around long enough to see us into adolescence. They'd be what, in their seventies by now? Or older."

"But they may have passed information to their children," Mariah said. "Teddy and Harvey's parents and grandparents left them crystals. How many others might have done the same?"

Susannah looked alarmed. "I thought all the crystals had been buried!"

"Don't be ridiculous, Suz." Val strode behind the counter. "They're just stones. These idiots up on the wall ground glass, stones, and anything that occurred to them into their so-called *natural* paints for texture and iridescence. Just because you preferred watercolors doesn't mean others gave up searching for the perfect formula. I think this is Daisy here on the end. She always had a fey look to her. The coffee urn concealed her before. I hadn't noticed."

Mariah sat on a stool at the end of the counter near Keegan. "She talks. She walks. Amazing."

Keegan assumed she referred to the operatic diva. "It's hard to be a death goddess around a sister who saw you playing in mud puddles." He studied the Daisy portrait. She'd been a plain girl with long brown hair, a vague look on her round face, and a tattoo of a rose on her cheek. "Did Daisy have a tattoo?"

"They used ink and henna," Susannah said, overhearing. "It's not permanent, so don't rely on identifying markers like that. But that is probably Daisy. She was always around somewhere, so I vaguely remember her. Apparently, she's the only one who stayed in Hillvale. I don't think she had anywhere to go."

"Walker says the sheriff has been looking for her family, but they haven't found anyone," Sam said with sorrow in her voice. "If she had children or siblings, we've not heard of them."

Val wrinkled her nose. "When we were little, she often had commune kids around her, but I don't remember any one in particular and few stayed for long."

Mariah climbed down to touch Daisy's portrait in the dark corner where it had been hidden all these years. Keegan thought her dark eyes might be shimmering with tears, but she expressed no emotion as she returned the discussion to the mural. "If Teddy and Harvey had grand-parents in the commune, would they be in this portrait?"

"We'd remember the children more than the parents. I don't know your Teddy and Harvey well enough to see facial similarities." Susannah gave up and returned to her mug.

"Did all of them have red eyes when you and Thalia fixed the mural?" Mariah asked while Sam studied the faces with more care than her mother had.

The interaction between the women fascinated Keegan. He watched as Susannah Menendez sighed and shook her head. The woman was hiding far more than she admitted.

"Our parents' eyes were the reason I took on the project. That was maybe twenty years after it was painted. Several of the others were degrading but as far as I remember, Daisy was fine. We just applied the acrylic formula to everyone to prevent further corrosion."

"How did you know to use acrylic?" Sam asked, picking at the varnish over Daisy's eyes with her fingernail.

"That old journal of Lucinda's. Thalia found a description in it with Lucinda's notes in the margins. The original description of garnets was centuries old, but Lucinda's more modern notes suggested an acrylic formula as a means of controlling the substance. We had to varnish the entire project to hold it together later, but Lucinda's suggestion worked."

"Did you use the formula on those oils?" Mariah asked, nodding at the old paintings Susannah had brought with her.

Susannah shrugged. "I did it as a preventive to corrosion."

So, she didn't know if the people in the portraits had red eyes. Keegan turned his attention back to the mural.

"The paintings Daisy collected were all ones using crystals that turned red." Sam scraped off a piece of dark brown paint on Daisy's portrait, revealing a more faded brown beneath. "Daisy's eyes didn't corrode."

Beside him, Mariah inhaled sharply. Keegan covered her hands with his, recognizing the itch to scratch out eyes. "We could ruin it," he murmured.

She balled her fingers into fists but nodded. He enjoyed a woman who understood without him having to explain. He liked it even better that she didn't jerk her hands away. They weren't manicured hands, but soft, unlike his, as if she regularly used lotion. That was unexpected of a woman who hid her sexuality beneath shapeless shirts and vests.

"I don't suppose you have any idea where Thalia kept Lucinda's journal?" Keegan asked, finally interrupting when they reached the point of his concern.

"Thalia was a lazy slut," Susannah said dismissively. "She left the book sitting around. I was just a kid and knew it was supposed to be valuable. So I peeked in it to see if there was anything I could use. But it was in ancient handwriting, and I couldn't read most of it. She only did the mural because Dad paid her."

"The varnish is pretty thick, so it's hard to get at the acrylic," Sam reported, peeling at another set of eyes, this time in the man next to Daisy. "This thing must have been really eerie when it was first done, if all the eyes were crystalline."

Now that he'd intruded, Keegan followed through by going around the counter to test the molecular structure of the painting. The women watched him with curiosity, but he felt oddly safe in their company. Had the Kennedys or any of the others they referred to as Nulls been here, he would have thought twice before performing this trick.

"Yes, the same crystal dust was used here as in the oils. It's not as thick," he reported.

"Tempera is a weak paint and probably wouldn't support it," Susannah said, sounding more interested. "So the eyes on this early attempt may not have been as distinctive as their later experiments with oil."

"If they were testing the use of natural substances like egg tempera, they would have used plant materials and not chemicals. And sapphires would have seemed natural." Sam picked at another figure, one where the finish seemed to be peeling.

"Who on earth grinds sapphires into paint?" Mariah asked in disgust. "They could have earned more money selling them."

"Not sapphires," Keegan corrected. "These blues are azurite, a much softer mineral. They did not use particularly precious gems, which adds to the curiosity. Why would so many different kinds of rocks be gathered in this one place?"

"I thought you said they used garnets and that's why the eyes turned red?"

"There are many types of garnet. The transparent red ones used in jewelry are the ones most people know. These appear to be the more opaque stones, the ones we use in the industry as abrasives. The structures are similar enough that it's difficult to say once they're ground to dust and in trace amounts, so I cannot be positive."

Dinah finally emerged from her kitchen to swat at Sam's hand with a wooden spoon. "I don't want that pretty picture ruined!"

She was a second too late. The paint beneath Sam's fingernails popped off, revealing red eyes beneath.

"We really need to identify these people," Sam told the room at large. "One of them could be a killer."

ELEVEN

JULY 9: MONDAY, LUNCH

The lunch customers began to arrive as Sam scratched eyes, and Dinah scolded and wrung her gnarled hands. Knee aching, Mariah didn't get up. She hoped Sam's mother would repair the mural, but at the moment, Susannah was protesting the destruction along with Dinah. Val joined in the scratching.

The painting was so smoke-and grease-coated that the subjects were barely distinguishable. It needed a good repair and cleaning anyway.

"That's not helping identify them," Mariah complained so only Keegan could hear. "And all those hippies have to be in their seventies by now. How many seventy-year-old archers are still able to bring down big game?"

He finished off his coffee while apparently considering her question. She thought they worked well as a team—because he actually listened. She winced as she realized she was enjoying Keegan's company. That didn't mean she could trust him not to expose her.

"Daisy was an easy target," Keegan said, leaving open the possibility of seventy-year-old assassins. "But if we're assuming it is a *descendant* of these people who is hunting the crystals, we would then have to ask if evil or greed or whatever is inherited from the parent. I fear this is a dead end. We need the book."

Damn, but it was hard to keep someone of his formidable concentration at a distance. If he would just once poke fun at her friends, she might be able to wipe him out of her head. But he was taking them as seriously as she presumed he might one of his own projects.

"Find the book, or the *crystals*," she reminded him. "Have you asked to examine Teddy's and Harvey's stones? If we knew *why* someone might want crystals, we might know *who* wants them."

As if conjured by her suggestion, Kurt Kennedy and Teddy entered together. Both stopped to gawk at the wanton destruction of the mural. Mariah used her staff to nudge Teddy's arm. "I'll bring you one of Dinah's creations later if you'll take Keegan over to examine your stones. And bonus points if you can persuade Harvey to reveal his."

"What is going on here?" Kurt asked before Teddy could agree.

"Family feud. You should know all about those. I have to get Dinah back into the kitchen before one of the Ingerssons goes ballistic. I can feel the power building as we stand here." Mariah dragged herself up, leaving Keegan to his bewilderment. She just couldn't manage the entire world at once. She'd already learned that lesson.

"They'll fix it," Mariah promised, going behind the counter to wrap her arm around the diminutive chef. "Cook something special, raise your prices, and call it a party."

Dinah frowned as expressively as any woman Mariah had ever known. "Only because you're asking," she said. "I'm trusting you, girl."

"That's a slippery slope. Trust Sam. The mural will be better than new when she's done."

Dinah shook her head. "There's a cloud forming in here. Wave your wand and make it go away." She trotted back to her kitchen, probably plotting a banquet.

Mariah watched wistfully as Keegan escorted the lovers out. She'd never found a man interesting enough to consider for more than sex, but she was feeling just the tiniest bit jealous that Teddy and Sam now had men who understood them. She was feeling left out, she supposed, which was why she'd been enjoying Keegan's company too much.

"I'll pop eyeballs if you'll start delivering water," Mariah whispered to Sam. "You're attracting attention."

Sam glanced over her shoulder at the lunch customers filling the counter and watching in fascination. "Damn."

With efficient haste, Sam ushered Val back to the booth with Susannah. Left studying peeling eyeballs, Mariah felt the first hint of unease. Did she really want the glare of evil staring back at her from all these young, smiling faces? Did she even want to know their fate? They'd been potters and artists and maybe even a musician or writer or two. The commune had attracted the lost and dispossessed, just as Hillvale still did.

Maybe only the rich and famous became infused with greed and evil. She could hope the rest escaped it. She looked at her thick fingernails. She kept them neat so they didn't snag on her weaving. A knife would work better. It was concrete masonry behind the paint, so she couldn't gouge canvas—just eyeballs.

With a sigh, she began attacking Dinah's prized mural with cheap silverware. Absorbed in the task, she ignored the gossipy guessing going on at the counter. She'd worked in the café long enough to let the voices go by without mentally processing. Not until a loud thump hit the counter did she jerk her attention from her task to glare over her shoulder.

Aaron stood there with an encyclopedic volume, flipping pages. "Josiah Peterson, born 1947," he stated solemnly. "Famous for multi-colored ceramics developed during his stay in the Ingersson commune in the late 60s and early 70s."

"That's him," Amber cried excitedly, looking from the page to the murky mural. "Can we label him?" Her bracelets jangled on her plump arms as she pointed to the figure in question.

Mariah swiveled on the aluminum counter she was using as stool and examined the book the antique dealer held up. The photo was later in Peterson's life, after time had sculpted long wrinkles down the sides of his angular jaw and thinned his mousy brown hair. But the image was immediately recognizable. She rummaged in a drawer beneath the counter, found the markers they'd used when labeling photos of the town, and wrote Josiah Peterson on a sticky pad page.

When she pinned it to the man sitting next to Lars Ingersson in the mural, a cheer went up around the room.

The town had found a new game to play.

With a sigh of regret, Mariah reached up to the famous potter's eyes and dug in her knife. The crowd waited expectantly. She only needed to flip one eyeball. *Red*.

"Damn," Aaron said. "We have two really good examples of his work in Teddy's collection."

Mariah's fingers itched for her keyboard. She could find out so much more if she could just slither down the interwebs. . .

Books. Aaron had found answers in *books*. That seemed almost medieval.

If she could find Peterson's descendants. . . "Does your book give date of death?"

Aaron flipped pages. "The book is twenty years old. He was still alive then. There are more ceramic artists in here. Peterson and Simmons are the only ones mentioned who I recognize from the commune. Simmons was younger, born 1955. I'm guessing he wouldn't have been here at the time the mural was painted. That's the original gang on the wall."

Mariah looked at the page he showed her, then up at the mural. "Nope, not seeing him."

Beside him, Amber tugged on the book. "Let me see. Are you picking up vibrations from these photos? Maybe if we had an astrologer, she could work charts based on their birthdates?"

Mariah wanted to shout that wouldn't find a killer, but this crowd thought they were playing a game. They might clam up if she mentioned their real purpose in identifying the figures. "A good chart takes too long. Maybe we should have a contest."

The things that came out of her mouth. . . She bit her tongue, but it was too late. The idea was out there and growing faster than a snowball rolling downhill in January.

By the time Sam had served lunches all around and Mariah was back at the cash register, the town had made the mural contest part of their weekend art walk extravaganza. People were snapping pictures to upload once they got off the mountain. Aaron passed around his book so they could snap pictures of Peterson the Potter.

Mariah had a very bad feeling about all of it. She didn't need more strangers snooping around.

She was relieved when Keegan returned with Harvey in tow. They looked around at the excited residents mapping out poster boards promising prizes no one had approved, then up at Tullah, who had taken to popping eyes in Mariah's place. As tall as Mariah, the thrift shop owner moved with lazy grace, as if popping out *real* eyeballs was an art she'd practiced. Sam wiped up behind her as Tullah progressed across the wall.

"Man, we can't leave you alone for a second, can we?" Harvey slung a leg over a stool.

Keegan narrowed his eyes and studied the results. "Only one of the women other than Mrs. Ingersson has a hint of red, but there are only three women out of the thirteen figures. The original founders of the commune were not very diverse in culture, were they?"

"Wealthy white men," Mariah agreed.

"It became more diverse over time," Susannah Menendez explained from her booth. She and Val hadn't stirred from the table while they watched the destruction of their father's work. "The original founders were just our father's friends from the university. The artists weren't wealthy at that point. As their reputation grew, they attracted all sorts. He never turned anyone away."

"So basically, we're barely scratching the surface here," Mariah said in discouragement.

Others hooted at the pun. She rolled her eyes at the warped humor and continued, "We'd have to bring out *all* Daisy's paintings and identify them."

That suggestion didn't stir the imaginations of people already wrapped up in their current project. Since they had no notion of the broader picture, they didn't have her incentive to do more.

Keegan understood however. The big engineer frowned. "It might be easier to identify arrows. Has your chief started hunting for local archers yet?"

Sam boxed up an enormous chef's salad and a stack of sandwiches. "He has his own investigators working on it. Hillvale is costing him a lot of money. His company doesn't come cheap."

Police Chief Walker owned a corporate investigation and security firm in Los Angeles. Hillvale didn't have the cash to pay for their services. Mariah knew Walker and Monty had worked out some kind of trade of favor deals—the only economy the town knew. But she figured Walker was coming out on the short end of that stick.

"Why don't you and Kurt take these up to Walker and the mayor at city hall?" Sam handed the box to Keegan. "You can talk archery over lunch. While you're at it, ask when the sheriff will release the crystals from Teddy's attic. I need to monitor mural mutilation as long as my family is here." Sam nodded at the women now surrounded by other Lucys.

"I'll show you my crystals when Teddy shows you hers," Harvey promised as Keegan frowned. "This evening?"

They were treating an Oxford scholar, a doctor of engineering, and quite possibly some sort of Scots nobility as an errand boy. He had a right to frown. Mariah kept a straight face at Keegan's hesitation. Then he marched out, evidently deciding he'd get more information out of Nulls than the Lucys. Urged on by Teddy and Sam, Kurt reluctantly followed. The resort owner had a right to be suspicious, since his jeweler girlfriend was teaching him that all was not as it seemed in this town.

"Now," Harvey murmured, focusing his attention on Tullah's destroyed eyeballs. "Beneath the crud and the villainous mustache, doesn't that one beside Mrs. Ingersson resemble our fine Scot?"

Sam and Mariah turned to study the figure Tullah was working on.

"Dark curly hair," Sam said dubiously. "It's hard to picture Keegan with hair down to his shoulders, especially hair that's prettier than any woman's. Did they have curling irons back then?"

"Broad square shoulders, cleft chin, brownish amber eyes, high cheekbones, five o'clock shadow before everyone else. . ." Mariah felt sick to her stomach, not just at the resemblance, but at her perfect recall of Keegan's good looks. She never bothered remembering faces.

"Signet ring," Harvey added helpfully.

They all stared at the gold ring on the curly-haired man's finger. Keegan wore an identical one—with a unicorn and what might have been a thistle carved into it.

Underneath the brown acrylic, his look-alike had red eyes.

Crap damn. Without a word to the others, Mariah slammed her walking stick to the floor, got up, and stormed out.

Keegan had gone to city hall. She couldn't steal that ancient computer as she usually did when she couldn't resist her obsession. But Aaron had cable internet. He had computers. She didn't think there was an engineer alive who didn't have a computer, so Keegan would have one as well. And he was living above Aaron's store.

Obsession overcoming sense, Mariah limped down the boardwalk.

Carrying his encyclopedic volume, the antique dealer caught up with her just as she tried his shop door. Pulling out a key, Aaron unlocked a series of locks and let her in. "After something?" he asked casually.

He wasn't fooling her with his nonchalance. Everyone in town knew to keep her away from computers, and she never visited his store.

Aaron had a vaguely foreign accent and a European sophistication that did not fit Hillvale. But his psychometric powers made him right at home, even if he resented being called a Lucy. Despite the sophisticated goatee and tailored suits he affected, he was still just a man. Mariah glared at him.

"A family tree. Keegan isn't here just for an old family diary."

"Even if he had some evil family member here half a century ago, that doesn't mean Keegan is polluted," Aaron argued, flinging the volume to an oak stand by the door. "You've met the man. He's as straight, uncomplicated, and honest as any man in existence."

"Saints don't exist," she countered, stomping for the stairway at the back of the store, making her knee ache more. "He was *right there* when Daisy died. He didn't tell us the truth about his damned family. What else isn't he telling us?"

"Probably as much as you aren't." Aaron grabbed her stick, stopping her. "Don't underestimate everyone simply because they don't reflect your expectations. I can't swipe ghosts the way you do but don't dismiss me. I can almost literally read you like a book, just by touching this staff. You're angry, hurt, and the pain all ties back to a memory you crush even in your own head." He released the stick. "Keegan conceals nothing compared to you."

Mariah glared at her walking stick. She *had* forgotten Aaron's ability to read objects. That he could read *her* didn't make her any less furious. "Keegan is a black hole in the universe. I doubt anyone can read him."

Aaron nodded acknowledgment. "I met him at Oxford. He was only sixteen and already in his third year of engineering studies and captain of the archery team. He was young and not easy to read even then. I was older, but as you said, like attracts like. I knew he was gifted. I gave him the usual parlor trick, picked up his pen, and read his anger at a cheating teammate. He accepted my reading and took my advice regarding the teammate after I advised him that he was correct about the cheating. In the year that I knew him, he was inevitably honest. I helped him to learn more about blocking others like us."

"I can still sense *your* energy—you don't create a black hole the way Keegan does," Mariah retorted. "And lacking your acuity, I need computers."

Aaron stepped back and shrugged. "Good luck. I doubt even you can open his programs. I'm not letting you near mine."

He had a point there, but she refused to acknowledge it. She could get into Monty's computer because he was a trusting soul and left his password where anyone could find it. She doubted Keegan would do the same.

She dragged her aching knee up the stairs to the room Keegan had adopted while here. She had expected an engineer's freaky order, but the place looked as if it had been ransacked. Drawers hung open. The bedcovers looked as if they'd been tossed. Papers on the desk were scattered. . .

Bed, dresser, desk. . . *computer*, a lovely advanced piece of titanium technology.

Gleefully, she carried the laptop to his messy bed, propped up pillows, and switched it on, luxuriating in the freedom from her self-imposed prison.

All she had to do was not remind the world that she existed.

TWELVE

Well-fed but armed with little more information than he already possessed, Keegan left City Hall feeling as if he'd been manipulated. When he saw Aaron in his doorway across the street, signaling to him, Keegan stomped across the parking lot.

He wanted to see what else had been uncovered on the mural, but even he had to admit that the mural was a distraction. What he really wanted to do was see what Mariah was up to, but accommodating his friend and landlord made more sense.

Aaron used his thumb to indicate the back of the store. "She's been up there for about ten minutes. She may have bombed Tokyo and evicted Congress by now. I thought you were smart enough to keep your computer password protected."

"It *is* protected," Keegan protested, pulling out his cell phone. And then he remembered there was no reception. He wouldn't receive a verification request without cell or wi-fi, and he wasn't connected to either. How in the name of all that was holy could she circumvent that? "Damn." Well, he'd wanted to see what she was up to.

"I don't think she's after your personal files, if that's any help," Aaron called as Keegan fumed through the store. "Mariah's not bent that way."

But she was bent. How much was the question.

She had to hear him coming. This old building with its creaky wooden steps protested his weight. When he flung open the door, she startled, as if he'd woken her.

Shocked at the state of his usually orderly room, he glared. "Did you have to toss the room? The computer wasn't enough?"

Sitting in the middle of his bed, pillows propped around her, she followed his gesture in puzzlement. "Toss the room? Why would I do that? I just figured you lived that way."

If she hadn't tossed it, someone else had. He flipped through the correspondence he'd been working on, finding nothing missing or of value to anyone but him. He had nothing anyone could want, but he hated the idea of strangers poking through his belongings. "I keep my travel kit in order so I may leave at a moment's notice. *Someone* has been in here."

She frowned. "I only touched the computer. I'm not much into men's underwear."

That created an awareness requiring adjustment of said garment. He cooled it by checking the dresser. "Aaron wouldn't do this. Besides, he was with us in the café."

"Someone thinks you're hiding diamonds?" she asked, rightfully dubious. "Or maybe. . ." She turned his laptop around so he could see the image she'd called up. "We're getting closer and someone's worried."

Images. She had half a dozen resembling him, if hair color and face structure counted.

Keegan swept the laptop from her clever hands, sat down in the cushioned chair, and pulled out his reading glasses.

"I labeled them for you," she said. "You have a few coyotes on the family tree."

"Coyotes?" He scowled and clicked on the image that looked like one he'd noticed in the mural. It brought up a short history of Trevor Gabriel.

"Tricksters, like Loki and Hermes, if you know your ancient myths. Coyote is Native American lore. Someone with godlike intellect or knowledge that he uses to trick others and who disobeys societal conventions and laws."

"My family isn't godlike," he growled, clicking his way through the images. "My father is a chemist. My grandfather was a miner. You would call them Nulls. Most Ives are Nulls."

"They may have stifled their gifts or not recognized them." She waved her hand in dismissal. "But your great-uncle Trevor, a few times removed, lived in the Ingersson commune. That picture on the computer is of him after he cut his hair and went into the guru business. His eyes in Dinah's mural are *red*."

"I'm guessing a ninety-year-old man didn't toss my drawers." But from this biography, he gathered Trevor Gabriel knew *crystals*.

"If you didn't have anything worth stealing, you may have just discouraged a thief," she acknowledged.

"Aaron is the one with the valuables," he countered. "They should have tossed him."

Keegan was having a hard time reading the website while trying not to look at the regal princess occupying his bed. She sat cross-legged, spine straight, as if practicing yoga. It was warm up here under the roof, and she'd discarded her vest. Her sleeveless cotton pullover emphasized the strength of her muscled brown arms and revealed more tempting curves. He forgot thieves. He wanted to untangle the long braid dangling over her breasts and see if it shimmered as it had the other night.

"How does pretending to be a guru make Gabriel evil?" he asked, not finding a list of crimes included in the biography.

Mariah smiled in a way that made him itch and held out her hand for the computer. "I thought you'd never ask."

Reluctantly, he handed it back. "I don't know that branch of the family any better than I know the Wainwrights. As far as I'm aware, they found their fortunes here a century or more ago and don't visit the ancestral home, probably for good reason. Scottish castles aren't very welcoming."

"The good reason is more likely that Great-Uncle Trevor of red-eyed mural fame conveniently had a heart attack at the age of eighty-two, after the children of his followers sued him for suckering their parents out of their inheritances. His half-dozen kids by his half-dozen wives and mistresses changed their names and melted into the night. Two of them have their own rap sheets. It will take me a little longer to locate all their offspring."

"How the devil did you. . . ?" Keegan backtracked to a more direct question. *How* didn't matter as much as *what* she'd discovered. "You think Uncle Trevor swindled the Ingerssons or their followers?" He took the laptop back, pushed his glasses up his nose, and started reading through the documents she'd pulled up.

"Teddy says crystals have power. If Trevor believed that, he would have helped himself to any he could lay his hands on. Crystals were part of his guru business. One of his sons was convicted of art fraud, like Lonnie Thompson, late of Hillvale notoriety. The less talented offspring imitating the fathers, maybe, although I don't see much evidence that Trevor was more than a half-assed artist."

"Another son went to jail for counterfeiting," Keegan read with a snort. "That still doesn't bring us back to Daisy, although his sons might be a better age for pulling a bow than Trevor's age group."

"Nothing I've found indicates his offspring spent much time in outdoor recreation. They had to have inherited millions. Trevor worked hard at his fraud and apparently had a talent for investing it. Junior and his brother just seemed to paddle around in hot water a lot."

"But they had another brother and three sisters who were never caught." Fascinated despite himself, Keegan kept reading about his distant American cousins. "How did you dig up so much, so fast?" he finally asked.

"Talent," she muttered. "I need food." She dropped back against the pillows propped on the headboard and closed her eyes. "Add fingerprint and eye identification to that flimsy piece of equipment if you want to keep me out. And you WANT to keep me out, I promise."

He shot her a curious look. She was warning him? After she'd already broken in? And didn't try to hide it.

"You are a strange woman," he muttered, continuing to read.

"You have no idea. That's a great big door of invitation you're holding. I want to track everyone on the commune and their families and see where they were the day Daisy died, and even I know that's insane."

"You might as well track every criminal in existence that day," he said, grasping the dilemma.

"Just the math makes my head hurt. Let's say a hundred people passed through Ingersson's commune. Then calculate each had 2.3 children who each had 2.3 children. . ."

"Over 500 offspring in two generations," he calculated without looking up.

She groaned.

"We have no reason to believe the sins of the father are passed on to the children," he reminded her.

"Unless they inherited evil crystals," she muttered.

He worked through the rest of the files she'd left open. Tired of handing the laptop back and forth, Keegan sat beside her on the bed. Mariah scooted aside to give him room. He plopped the computer in her lap and opened the next image that looked less like him. "Also in my family tree? Ian Dougal? Why are we looking into these people?"

"Facial recognition. I wasn't certain which one was in the mural. Yours comes up too. Nice to know you are who you say you are. But Trevor looks most like the painting and is the right age. Why does he have a ring like yours?"

All too aware of her sage scent and the curves pressed against him, Keegan had to yank his brain back to his head. He scrolled back to the image of Trevor Gabriel, older than in the mural but still a young man with sideburns. "The rings usually pass through the maternal side of our family, what my mother calls the Malcolm side— the ones with psychic abilities. Most generally, they go to the daughters who inherit Malcolm traits, but my mother had no daughters, and my brother is what you call a Null. I had to have this ring refitted."

"So Uncle Trevor here may have inherited a family trait and used it for *evil*?" she asked in horror.

"If you call fraud evil, then most likely. It's not exactly the first time. A family with weird mental abilities is bound to generate freaks every so often. I fail to see how this helps find Daisy's killer. I'd rather call Walker over here to look for fingerprints."

Looking stunned, she slapped the computer closed and handed it to him as if it were filthy garbage. "I don't want to know more. Lucys are supposed to be peaceful and help the world, not harm. The possibility of someone with my ability. . . No, not thinking about it."

She looked so shocked and horrified, that he needed to reassure her that it probably didn't happen often. But even after removing his glasses, he was too focused on the lushness of her moist lips, and his brain went south again. He leaned over and kissed her.

To his utter amazement and gratification, Mariah responded with enthusiasm. Apparently kissing was better than thinking of Lucys gone evil.

With a groan of sheer bliss, Keegan wrapped his arms around soft, giving woman and hauled her closer for more coffee-flavored kisses. She was perfect against him, digging her fingers into his arms, lifting herself into his embrace as if they'd known each other forever. The pressure in his aforementioned underwear increased.

With a vague reflection on reincarnation and soul mates, he stroked her unfettered, breast, felt her shudder with the same desire wracking him, and deepened his kiss.

Loud knocks battered the old oak door.

FLOATING DOWN FROM HEAVEN, MARIAH TOOK A MOMENT TO REGISTER THE reason why she had to leave her cloud. The banging and Harvey's shouts only partially registered. The loss of Keegan's embrace was as abrupt as falling off a ledge. At least this time she hadn't ruined her knee.

She gasped and shoved away. What the hell had she thought she was doing? Was craziness the result of sliding down internet holes? She'd thought Keegan had brought her back before she'd lost herself this time.

"Cass is circling the vortex," Harvey called. "Whatever you're up to, save it for later."

Damn. That brought her out of her sex-addled haze.

"Circling the vortex?" Keegan asked with a grumble, adjusting his jeans. "Is this some *Star Trek* speak with which I'm not acquainted?"

"Plain English." She pushed up from the bed, almost forgetting her knee until it reminded her. "The vortex draws spirits. Cass is psychic to a degree we can't measure. She lived inside Sam's head for days and had to be hospitalized."

Rather like the trance she could put herself into, Mariah knew. Human minds could only tolerate so much energy depletion, and not knowing how much was dangerous.

"And we are concerned why?" Keegan asked grumpily, setting his laptop on the chair.

"Do you really want to know what happens when a few centuries worth of ghosts begin to congregate? Or would you like to contemplate what Cass might do with them?" Mariah asked, grabbing her walking stick.

"Why can't Harvey stop her?" Keegan gave the musician a foul glare as he held the door for her.

"I write songs and carve sticks," Harvey said with a shrug. "I have no magic."

"None of us has magic," Mariah corrected, hobbling down the stairs. "And Cass won't listen to men. Where's Sam? Why didn't you call her?"

"I did. She's up there with Teddy. But they're new and don't know how to approach her." Harvey took the stairs down two at a time. "They're the ones who sent me for you."

"Tullah?" Mariah asked. "I need back-up."

"She has a customer but says she'll be there shortly. Anyone else?" Harvey held the shop door open. "Keegan, you probably want to stay out of this."

Mariah didn't need to hear his officious Scots' snort to know he wouldn't. And this time, she didn't object. He had connections deeper than any man she'd ever met, and possibly knowledge she didn't possess. His family tree was downright eerie.

"While you're at it," Keegan added to her commands, "Ask Walker if he'll test my room for fingerprints. Someone rifled through my belongings."

Harvey grimaced but took off.

Mariah hobbled back to the golf cart Valdis still hadn't claimed. Keegan added his heavy weight to hers. The golf cart's tiny engine protested as it clunked up the hill toward the cemetery.

"What did Walker say about the arrows?" she demanded, trying not to imagine what trouble Cass might be instigating now.

He didn't sound surprised that she interrogated him about his visit to the town hall. "The arrows are common and can be bought in any sporting goods store. They found no fingerprints, but that's not unusual. Many people prefer to wear gloves when pulling a bow of that size. Your police chief has his minions working their way through bow-hunting licenses." Keegan shifted uncomfortably on the bench seat and bent his head to see beneath the tattered canopy.

"And the attic crystals?" Mariah tried to distract her fears. She didn't really believe the crystals would lead them to a killer, but the clues were few and far between.

"The sheriff isn't ready to release them."

"Then we'll just have to work with those that Teddy and Harvey own, although I can't figure out how you can identify them or how they're related to Daisy." Mariah parked the cart as close as she could to the steep path down to the vortex.

"Without the missing journals, I can do no more than identify what type of crystals they are," Keegan admitted, helping her out. "I cannot see how we will find any motivation for killing an old lady, whether she was harmless or not."

More than anything, Mariah hated being helpless. But the internet couldn't track the life of a woman who hadn't existed beyond these hills. The answers to Daisy's death were here, somewhere. Mariah grimaced, knowing she had to physically work out this problem, just like any Null. And do it while crippled, she acknowledged, hobbling down the rocky path on Keegan's arm and her staff.

She halted half way down, where she could get a good view. The vortex was at the bottom of a natural amphitheater. From here, she could see any lurking intruders. She saw no one but Teddy and Sam watching Cass from the rocky platform that had been cobbled together beside the vortex. Cass often used it as a stage to address the Lucys in times of joy and sorrow. But today, she walked the rocky spiral maze around the vortex.

"She is calling on spirit energy," Mariah whispered, easing down the path.

"Spirit energy?" Keegan inquired.

He gripped her arm tightly so she didn't stumble. The clasp of his strong fingers reminded her too well of what they'd been doing before they'd been interrupted. She supposed it made sense that she'd eventually find a man who attracted her enough to drive common sense out of her head. She simply wished it had been someone a little less intimidating, one she couldn't suspect capable of ruthlessly doing whatever he thought necessary.

Someone like her.

"Ghosts," she said, almost angrily, shaking him off. "Centuries of tattered energies that haven't passed on as they should. There's little to be learned from most of them, but if Cass can find one who can connect to those who have gone beyond, she'll seek information."

That silenced him. Mariah had the uneasy notion he wasn't quiet because he thought she was just another whacky Lucy, but because he was trying to work what she'd said through his own understanding.

"She loses sense of time, and she's not as strong as she once was." Mariah used her stick as crutch and swung down to the next step.

"What can you do?" he asked.

"Channel the energy. I have no psychic connection to ectoplasmic energy, only physical. All I can hope to do is find and direct it, as I do with my ghostcatchers. At some point, we'll have to bring Cass back to reality so she can eat and rest. I have no idea how long she's been out here." Because she'd been diving down internet rabbit holes, dammit. She should have known Cass would pull this stunt after they left.

Again, Keegan didn't question. With a family tree like his, she got that. Maybe that's why she'd let herself go a little nuts with him. Learning his family was steeped in woo-woo, she felt safe confiding in him—which she knew was stupid. She just couldn't seem to help herself. A man who didn't laugh when she spoke about the weird was such a rarity that she was soaking up the attention like the earth soaked up rain after a drought.

He helped her down to where Teddy and Sam hovered. "Go away now," Mariah told him. "You're this huge energy void and can only interfere."

Keegan drew down his formidable black brows in a frown but reluctantly hiked up the far side of the hill where he could keep an eye on anyone approaching from the road.

"Energy void?" Teddy whispered, watching him go. "A man like that has more energy than he knows what to do with."

"I can't explain it," Mariah said impatiently. "I need to channel the spirits circling Cass so she doesn't have to reach so far. I've never tried doing this with anyone else. But if our walking sticks can channel earth energy, maybe they can do the same with spirits. If you let me borrow some of your power, our chance of success should be greater."

"Daisy had us put the ends of our sticks together in a shallow bowl in the rock when we stopped the avalanche." Sam climbed up to the rock stage, running her stick along the surface. "Maybe we could do the same?"

"I wish she'd left us operating instructions," Mariah muttered. "But yes, we've learned to communicate by finding or creating bowls in the granite. They have a crystalline structure that apparently resonates with the vortex energy."

"So it's not necessarily magic, but some kind of vibration?" Teddy asked, lying down on the stone to sight irregularities.

"Magic defines the inexplicable, which this is," Mariah admitted. "We'd probably need Keegan to give us the scientific theory." She located an indentation on the center rock. "This looks the right size. Just hold the ends of your staffs here and let me reach out to Cass."

She closed her eyes, centered herself on the crystal energy in the wooden handle, then let it flow toward the ground and the energy coursing through the other carved staffs.

As she'd suspected, Teddy and Sam had power well beyond that of the crystals Harvey had chosen for them. She didn't have enough experience working with others to know exactly how to use that much power, so Mariah simply concentrated on her own abilities. Letting the life forces circling the vortex find her, she blasted them toward Cass.

"She's stopped pacing," Samantha whispered.

Mariah released her physical body and flew with the souls she gathered. Turmoil, confusion, anger, sorrow whipped through her. A hawk's mind was easier than the detritus of the human condition. The solid sensibility of Teddy and Sam held her steady as her ectoplasmic self whirled, spun, then gathered and formed a thin line aimed directly at the shining light she saw as Cass's soul.

She hadn't realized she sought Daisy until she felt the feather-light touch that had always been Daisy's life force. Tentative, ragged, as incomplete as Daisy, it brushed reassuringly along Mariah's senses. Mariah reached longingly for that feeling, but Daisy had never been fully attached to the earth or anyone in it. She vanished.

Mariah knew when Tullah joined them. Tullah's psychic force was strong but untutored. Still, she anchored Cass in ways Mariah could not. With relief, Mariah began to let go, to return to the women on the platform before she lost herself.

The heavy staff held her weak body in place until she could sit on solid earth. Mariah heard Teddy making Keegan back off and stay away. She was grateful for the understanding. He'd hauled her around the last time she'd been in this weakened state. She needed to rebuild her strength to shut him out.

"Do we stop now?" Sam whispered above her head.

"I'm not feeling the vibrations anymore," Teddy said. "What's Tullah doing?"

"Sustaining Cass," Mariah answered. "Go to Cass before she falls."

She felt their departure as a weakening of her energy, and it was all she could do to remain sitting. Oddly, she sensed Keegan out there as a solid wall of nothing—a wall she could lean on. Was using her ability this way any better than when she sent it sliding down the interwebs?

"Reporters," Harvey cried from a distance. "Hide!"

Oh crap, and she was in no condition to run.

KEEGAN COULDN'T STAND TO WATCH MARIAH STRUGGLE. HE DIDN'T KNOW what the blazes she had done to herself—or why one should run from reporters—but he couldn't sit idle. He jogged over the stones, past the women gathering around the gray-haired witch, and to Mariah before she slumped to the ground.

He scooped her up and headed for the cart until she whacked him with her stick. He would be bruised from head to toe if he put up with her much longer. Contemplating the cost of a good psychiatrist, he halted and glared at her. "I am not putting you down."

"Cass's house, by the path." She pointed her stick to a well-trampled dirt path on the far side of the amphitheater.

Since the tall African-American woman was leading Cass that way, Keegan adjusted his direction. "Why are Theodosia and Samantha not joining us?"

"Because they're smart," she grumbled. "They'll talk about art and galleries and contests and lead the intruders astray."

"Intruders?" He jogged up the path until he was right behind Tullah and Cass.

"Reporters," the thrift store owner explained, glancing back at him. "They ask the wrong questions."

If Keegan weren't the descendant of a long line of enigmatic females, he'd put Mariah down and leave now. But comfortable with waiting for explanation, he played his role of beast of burden until they trusted him.

"Did you feel Daisy?" Mariah called ahead, apparently feeling stronger.

He'd watch her go pale and frail before his eyes, as if the life force had been sucked out of her. She still wasn't her normal healthy self, but color was seeping back into her lovely brown cheeks. He admired her thick black lashes while contemplating her question. How did one *feel* the dead?

"She only passed on the image of that damned cart," Cass said wearily. "She's well past the veil already. The connection was nebulous at best."

"I felt her," Mariah said. "She's happy is all she conveyed to me." Amazingly, she closed her eyes and leaned her head against his shoulder.

"Do we need to take apart the cart?" Keegan asked, trying to keep his tone neutral.

"I will buy Valdis a new one," Cass said without answering directly.

"Drive it up to Cass's," Mariah whispered. "We can take it apart together."

"How will you get around then? As much as I enjoy carrying you, I don't think it's a practical solution."

She almost smiled. "I can be the albatross around your neck. We'll work it out."

"I will not allow you to mess with my mind," he warned. "So wipe that puss-and-cream look off your face."

She smiled even more. "Then use your molecular engineering abilities to deconstruct the cart without tools."

"I've never—" But he could. He glared down at her. "You believe me?"

"Not yet, but I'm getting there. Leave me on the porch steps. I just need to catch my breath, and I'll be fine."

"You don't look fine. You're as gray as death's door." He knew he sounded grumpy. He always did when he was terrified. And this woman terrified him in ways he couldn't count.

"Oh, thank you for that," she said, wrinkling her lovely lips into a pout. "They had to take me to the hospital the last time I went spatial, so count yourself fortunate."

Went spatial? What the hell?

"I didn't need your help," Cass said querulously—while leaning on Tullah's arm.

"You wouldn't have reached Daisy without Mariah," Tullah said in the firm tones of a teacher to an argumentative child. "When will you learn to call on us?"

Cass didn't answer, but even Keegan could sense what she didn't say. She'd been here all alone for decades and didn't know how to ask for help.

"United, we stand," Mariah whispered.

Divided, we fall. Keegan tried to work his mind around that as he set Mariah on Cass's porch and jogged off to find the cart. How did one know who to stand with? He'd always thought it was loved ones, until someone in his family had betrayed them. If he couldn't trust those close to him, how could he trust strangers?

THIRTEEN

Nursing Cass's weak sangria, Mariah watched as Keegan donned his spectacles and cautiously ran his hands over the dilapidated golf cart. Gorgeous hunk looking intellectual—her heart did a little dance of appreciation.

Samantha and Walker had followed behind the cart, carrying food from the diner. Mariah bit ravenously into an enormous po'boy sandwich, willing her energy to return.

How did Cass manage to ride astral currents on a regular basis at her age? She sat there now, like a queen on her throne, not appearing as feeble as Mariah felt.

"I took a look at your room, Keegan," Walker said. "Way too many prints. How much do you want me to dig?"

Keegan waved a dismissive hand. "I'll persuade Aaron to install cameras."

"Maybe one of the journalists decided to check you out. They think they have a story with Gump's death in the avalanche, combined with an old hippie wearing a feather cloak shot with an arrow." Walker swigged the beer he'd bought at Pasquale's. "Someone up here talked."

"Tourists," Mariah said through the last bite of sandwich. "Mistake to bring them here."

"Hillvale will die without fresh money," Samantha pointed out.

"Your uncles may lose their business. That is not the same as the town dying," Cass said coldly from her throne on the porch.

"If you can't agree on anything, then you will make no progress at all." Keegan came up from underneath the cart looking dusty, oily, disheveled, and victorious. "There is a non-metallic anomaly beneath the bench, where I cannot touch it."

Walker produced a set of screwdrivers from the toolkit he'd brought up and began prying at the torn vinyl bench seat. "I doubt Daisy had tools to take this apart. It must pry up or the object was so thin that she slid it between the seat and the support."

"I do love watching Nulls accept that we know things that are not possible," Mariah said in her most saccharine voice.

"At what point do you accept that Keegan isn't Null?" Sam asked in irony.

She probably already had, but she needed to keep him at a distance, so Mariah shrugged. "When I've seen him do more than poke around at a cart because we told him to?"

Keegan snorted and popped the panel open beneath the bench seat. "She slumps and turns pale, and I should believe that means she's speaking to spirits. Even fake spiritualists did better than that." He reached in and fumbled in the compartment while Walker stood over him as if he might produce a rattler.

"I don't ask anyone to believe anything," Mariah retorted.

"Children, behave," Cass said wearily. "Our job is to find who killed Daisy. Have the decency to stay on task."

"Found it." Keegan drew a piece of paper from beneath the cart seat. He handed it to Walker and returned to putting the panel back together.

Samantha leaned over the chief's shoulder. "It's a pencil sketch of a man."

"Looks old." Walker reached over Mariah's head to hand it up to Cass. "Any idea who it is?"

Cass frowned as she examined the sketch. "I wasn't involved with the commune except to speak to their guests if they appeared in town. He looks vaguely familiar, but this could have been done any time in the last century. There is no date or signature."

Mariah backed up a step so she could lean over and look. "Hairstyle is more modern than the long-haired guys in Dinah's mural. No side-burns or mustache. Why would Daisy hide it in the cart?" Realization smacked her, and she tugged the paper away from Cass to wave it at Walker. "Daisy saw her own death! She's telling us something."

"I can't arrest someone because his sketch is in the victim's cart." Walker took the sketch away. "I'll see if we can get a date on this paper, have copies made to pass around, and try facial recognition."

"Or someone may already have identified him if this face is in the mural," Keegan added. "The last I heard, there was a grand prize involved."

"If we took photos of each face on the wall and ran it through the software, we'd have most of them identified in no time," Mariah said.

"Only if the people in the mural are alive and on social media. Most older people don't flash their faces all over the internet, and this paper looks old." The chief of police produced a plastic bag from his toolkit and set the sketch inside.

"Let's talk to Valdis and Susannah first," Mariah suggested. "The guy in the sketch isn't bad looking. Maybe they remember him if he was in the commune."

"The question remains, why would any man kill Daisy?" Keegan stood and dusted himself off.

"Knowledge," Cass said. "Daisy saw everything that happened in this town. No one ever paid her any attention. Aside from stealing artwork, she never interfered. But she was everywhere gathering her sticks and stones, painting anything that sat still long enough, putting together her treasures and distributing them throughout the town. The question becomes—*why now*? What did she see or hear *recently* that may have caused her to put this sketch in the cart?"

They left on that sad note. Mariah let Keegan drive the cart into town.

Bumping across potholes into the parking lot, they arrived in time to watch a procession wind through the park Sam had been creating next to City Hall. Mariah's pulse quickened at the direction they were taking. "A memorial service! Up to the farm, please. No, wait a minute, Daisy loved Dinah's donuts."

"No one said anything about a memorial," Keegan protested, halting in the parking lot.

"Dinah may have said something. Tullah would have taken her up on it. That's how things happen here." Mariah pried herself out of the cart and hobbled inside—where Dinah waited with a pink box of donuts. "Send her my prayers too," the cook whispered, wiping the back of her hand over her eye.

"Thank you!" Mariah hugged her, then took Keegan's arm. Of course he'd followed her in. "I'm not a cripple, mind you," she warned.

"But I have this notion that I need to keep an eye on you every minute or you'll slid e down a bunny trail and never be seen again." He helped her back into the cart.

Did he know? Mariah jerked her head around to study his expression, but he appeared to be making a simple comment. "Prescience run in the family?" she asked grudgingly.

"Second sight, certainly, but not me. Does that mean you were planning on disappearing?" He shot her a glare of disapproval, then backed the cart out to follow the parade by road instead of walking path.

"It's what I do best." She kept her expression enigmatic as they drove up the lane. Someone had handed out candles, and now the procession was a line of flickering lights winding in and out of the pine trees and up the bluff.

"Not with that knee, you don't." He turned the cart down the dusty path toward the old farmhouse foundation. Below, Val, her veil and long black skirts blowing in the breeze, was standing on the chimney remains again. This time she was singing in a hauntingly beautiful voice instead of wailing.

Mariah hopped out with her box of donuts and walking stick. Keegan strode around to help her, but she insisted on stepping over Daisy's guardians on her own. She could swear the crystalline eyes of the little stone statues sparkled, as if with tears.

Inside the foundation, the memorial she'd begun with a daisy and a feather had built to a pyramid of shiny rocks, flowers, and other mementoes. Mariah took the donuts out of the box and scattered them around the bottom of the pyramid. "I love you, Daisy. Please brighten the world again someday," she whispered under her breath.

Stepping back, she let Keegan hold her arm this time. Her eyes were too blurred with moisture to see where she was going.

With Valdis singing hymns above them, the funeral marchers set out their candles and their gifts and sent Daisy on with their individual prayers and promises.

If nothing else, no intruders would attempt to enter the bunker this night. Mariah buried her face in Keegan's broad shoulder and wept.

~

JULY 10: TUESDAY, MORNING

Keegan sat at Dinah's counter, drinking his coffee and digging into his eggs while various Lucys and tourists snapped images of the murky mural. Nine of the thirteen subjects had red eyes, including the Jesus/Lars figure in the center. Daisy was one of the four exceptions. The Judas figure was another. Holding a wallet, he had his head turned away so his eyes couldn't be seen.

None of the images looked like Daisy's sketch. If Keegan squinted his eyes, the sketch vaguely resembled his curly-haired relation, except the hair was lighter and straighter and the face rounder. Perhaps a descendant or relation? Or imagination.

After having his room tossed, he needed to start studying these people with suspicion, but his mind just didn't work that way. He'd dusted the floor and desk to catch prints in case the intruder returned.

The contest to identify all the mural portraits had expanded to printed fill-in-the-blank lists with the most correct numbers claiming the grand prize, although no prize had been announced.

Lars, his wife, Daisy, and the famed potter, Josiah Peterson, had been dead giveaways from the first, so the contest was really only over the last nine. Keegan and Mariah knew the one wearing the signet ring was his distant relation, Trevor Gabriel, the fraudulent guru. Trevor definitely had an evil eye. Keegan nibbled his toast and wondered if Trevor had any psychic abilities that had warped with his use of crystals.

Theodosia, the jeweler, slid onto a stool beside him. "Harvey is ready to bring over his crystal stash this morning. Are you still interested?"

"I'm interested. I just wish I knew what to do with the information once I have it," he admitted. "I'm hoping their molecular structures will be so distinct, I can just walk out and find similar ones without digging up a mountain. Looking for coal and diamonds almost works that way."

"Knowledge is power. If the area is riddled with evil, we need to dig

it out. Although admittedly, that sounds ridiculous." She gave a depre-
cating shrug.

"Not ridiculous." Mariah slid a glass of water down to Teddy.

Nurse Brenda had given Mariah a knee brace, Keegan knew. In conse-
quence, the obstinate waitress had apparently decided to test her
strength by working on the counter. After Daisy's memorial service, she
had practically pushed Keegan out of the cart at Aaron's and sped away.
Guess that told him she wasn't ready to return to where they'd left off
yesterday.

She was probably right to keep her distance. That didn't mean he'd
slept any better.

"I'm interested in whether I can determine the powers of a stone by
testing its structure," Keegan admitted. "But powers of evil sounds a
little far-fetched."

"Why the fecking hell don't you have cell towers up here?" a young
man in a blue shirt shouted from the far end of the counter.

"Reporter," Theodosia murmured. "We'll have to talk elsewhere."

Keegan looked for Mariah—she'd disappeared, just as she'd said she
did. Dinah now stood at the register, taking cash. "We'll have to start
eating elsewhere as well, if Dinah has to work the counter instead of
the stove."

"One of these days, Dinah will have to hire real waitresses." With a
sigh, Theodosia climbed off her stool, went behind the counter, and
grabbed an apron.

From the booths where she was refilling coffee cups, Samantha gave
her a thumbs-up. Dinah returned to the kitchen. Mariah did not
reappear.

Keegan glared at the mural for a while. "Cell phones are not consis-
tent with the resort ambiance," he finally said, loud enough to be heard
over the murmurs of the other customers. "*Most* of us are here to escape
the rat race bustle."

The young man looked up, presumably with a retort. He shut up
when he realized it was Keegan talking. Keegan got that a lot. He rolled
his shoulder muscles under his shirt, sipped his coffee, and waited.

"If I had internet, I think I could identify that guy in the bear claw
necklace," the reporter finally said, moving over to take the seat Theodosia had vacated. "How the hell else are we supposed to identify them?

That hideosity must be fifty-years old. The odds are in favor of locals winning."

"It's a local contest," Keegan said mildly. "The point is to show off knowledge of local artists, not internet skills. Lars Ingersson and Josiah Peterson were two of the more famous occupants of the commune fifty years ago. The others shouldn't be so difficult to identify, if one knows the commune's history."

So, he embroidered the truth. Daisy wasn't exactly famous. And Trevor Gabriel might have been infamous, but not as an artist. Keegan studied the clean-shaven portrait of a man with long sideburns wearing a bear claw, but he wasn't familiar with artists, American or otherwise. Still, knowledge was power.

"I'll trade you the smarmy guy wearing the signet ring if you'll give me the bear-claw man," Keegan suggested.

The reporter frowned at the mural, glanced at Keegan again, and smiled. "I'm good with faces. That's how I got this job. I'm guessing from his looks, smarmy guy was a relation of yours?"

"Distant but probably. Smarmy apparently runs strong in the family." Not smarmy so much as greedy, he decided. He'd never understood that before, but after this past year, he'd believe almost anything except in his father's guilt. "Does that mean you've met bear-claw man and remember him?"

The reporter had been scrolling around on his phone while they talked. Now he held up a photograph of a man at a podium in front of an audience wearing graduation caps. "I thought that was him. He spoke at our commencement ceremony a few years back. Bradford Edison, old-time conservative politician with ties to most of Sacramento Valley, currently one of our dinosaur state representatives. What do you think?"

Keegan enlarged the photo and shrugged. "I'm not good with faces. You're right—we need the internet to look for younger photos. I don't have any pictures of smarmy guy, but we think he's Trevor Gabriel. He's not an artist, and as best as we can tell, he didn't live here long. Are you saying a conservative politician was once a promising artist?"

"Musician." The reporter typed the name Keegan had given him into the notebook on his phone. "He was in a folk group in college, back when that was the thing to do. So chances are, not all the people in that mural were actually artists. Thanks."

Chances were all the people in that mural were higher than kites, Keegan reflected as the reporter paid his bill at the register. Maybe the crystals reflected drug use, not evil.

The breakfast crowd finally cleared out. Theodosia took off her apron. Harvey paid his bill. And Mariah reappeared as if she'd been there all the time. Keegan dropped a bill behind the counter for his fare and rose from his stool. *Finally.* It had taken him over a week of gaining their trust. Now he could examine what he'd come here to see.

"My place?" Theodosia—Teddy—suggested.

He needed to remember informal names if he meant to blend in. It had always been hard for him to fit into groups, if only because of his size. Attending university while still young hadn't helped, nor had his *difference.* He was accustomed to being a detached observer and not a participant.

But here in Hillvale, he wasn't different. He almost felt at home as they ambled down the boardwalk to Teddy's Treasure Trove. It helped that Mariah came up past his shoulder. Petite Teddy alone would have made him feel like an ox.

"Does the name Bradford Edison mean anything to anyone?" He offered his arm to Mariah, who ignored it, choosing instead to shoot him a wide-eyed, thoughtful look. Remarkably, she held her tongue while they waited for the others to reply.

"My father's favorite politician," Harvey said, surprisingly. Harvey wasn't much inclined to actually adding information to a conversation, Keegan had noted. "He represents money more than voters."

"That's the way the world works," Teddy replied without rancor, leading them into her shop. "The rich get richer, the poor get poorer, so why represent losers who can't help you buy your office?" She waved at the striking strawberry-blond woman behind the counter. "Hey, Syd, thanks. You're off the hook now. Go beat up the kids or dunk them in a pool. I'll just close the shop at lunch."

"We're going down to see what Kurt's uncovered in the ice cream parlor and then heading over to Lance's gallery. I'll fix lunch if you want to stay open." The woman addressed as Syd gathered up her computer notebook, waved at everyone, and departed through the back.

"Teddy's sister," Mariah explained, pulling out a chair at an oak table displaying an assortment of crystals and Daisy's stone statues. "Syd is another good example of why Hillvale needs to stay out of the public eye."

"I'm torn about that," Teddy admitted, reaching under her counter and producing a metal box. "I love being a shopkeeper and seeing the tourists filling our registers with cash. But Syd and I came here for the privacy, so I get what you're saying."

"I don't think it's possible for anyone to have complete privacy without becoming a hermit," Keegan offered, roaming the shop rather than take a chair. "And with satellites and drones overhead, you'd have to be a hermit in a cave."

He waited with interest for Mariah's response. *She* was the one hiding from reporters.

Surprisingly, it was Harvey who answered. "Hiding in plain sight works fine. People see what they want to see." He dumped his sack of crystals on the table. "Tell us what these are, O Crystal Guru."

Setting her box on the table, Teddy gasped in awe and reached to touch the glittering collection catching sun from the front window.

Keegan nearly fell backward from the strong waves emanating from the conflicting crystalline structures. He swore and swept them back into Harvey's canvas bag. "Lead," he demanded. "We need a lead box."

FOURTEEN

Mariah dropped Harvey's bag of crystals into Teddy's metal box and slammed it shut. "That was less than helpful, Keegan." She'd been shaken by the urgency of his command. Mountain Man could have sent soldiers over a cliff with that level of authority.

Harvey growled and stalked around the room examining the staffs he'd left in the shop on consignment. "Are you saying all these are somehow polluting the air?"

They all watched as Keegan ran his fingers over the crystals Harvey embedded in the wood. "Basic quartz diorite. These didn't come from that collection."

The tension almost visibly left Harvey's shoulders. He swung a chair around and straddled it. "Okay, I bought the ones in the shop off the internet. So it's the crystals in my grandfather's collection that are polluted?"

"The ones you've been putting in *our* staffs?" Mariah asked edgily, swinging her own.

Keegan grabbed her swinging stick and stroked the gorgeous smoky quartz Harvey had inserted into the unicorn's horn on her staff. "Trigonal quartz oxide, commonly called cactus quartz for the secondary generations of crystals pointing away from the central one. I sense no radiation or *dangerous* vibrations, but it does seem to have a life of its own."

His professorial tone dropped, and he hesitated before continuing. "I've never noticed crystals vibrating before."

Teddy thumbed through her various reference books until she found the article she wanted. "Cactus quartz, transforms negative energy to positive, good for astral projection and shamanic journeying. Shamanic journeying?" She glanced at Mariah.

Damn, was that what she did? So maybe it was the staff and not just Cass helping her? Mariah held her staff up to the light to study the little protrusions on her unicorn's horn. "Cass is the one who astral projects," she said, not admitting anything. She was a programmer, dammit, not a hippie freak New Ager. "And maybe Val, a little."

Harvey glared at his own walking stick, then shoved it at Keegan. "I liked the dark purple."

Keegan stroked the purple stones in the bent guitar of Harvey's staff. "People call it ametrine," he said with a shrug. "It's just another quartz, this one mostly from Brazil. Amethyst and citrine are formed in the same crystal under the right conditions. I've held ametrine before. It's never vibrated like this. Again, it doesn't feel like whatever is in that bag."

They turned to Teddy, who was already flipping through her book. "Amethyst is pretty common in meditation, as are most purple stones. But ametrine. . ." She read from the book. "Good for those in the creative arts, helps to focus, energize, and amplify the creative talents."

Harvey nodded and stroked the crystals Keegan handed back to him. "These are the reason I started adding the crystals to my staff. It's hard to stroke a guitar holding a crystal, and I don't always have pockets, but having the staff nearby inspires me."

Mariah sat back and stared at the closed box on the table. "So how do we sort good from bad if we can't even open the box?"

"Harvey apparently can just by touching," Keegan suggested. "He's apparently chosen the correct stones for each of you."

"I just picked out colors to go with the wood," Harvey said grumpily.

"I do the same with my jewelry." Teddy removed several pieces from her display case. "I'm an empath. The crystals don't project feelings, so they're just objects to me. I only learned about their power in order to sell them to customers. I figure most everything is in the power of the mind, so it doesn't hurt to advise people on which crystals they need to use and why. But the jewelry—that's pure inspiration. I see the pieces forming in my mind as I work."

"The stones calling to each other?" Mariah suggested, while keeping an eye on Keegan sorting through the glittering gold and silver of Teddy's expensive jewelry. Her designs intermixed crystals with valuable gems.

"I can tell which stones come from the box." Keegan held up a pendant in varying shades from violet to black. "This is charoite, from Russia. It's a silicate and has only been found in one place. It's so rare that it wasn't even discovered until around World War II—which means it did not come from the collection of my ancestors. Still, it vibrates."

Mariah studied his expression, but Keegan looked like a chemist who had just discovered a new element, not an angry or disappointed heir.

He stroked the remaining gewgaws on the chain. "The other beads around the pendant do not vibrate the way the charoite does."

"Charoite," Teddy read from her book. "Helps in accepting difficult situations, recommended for people with nightmares." She slapped the book closed. "I made that while Syd was in the hospital after her ex tried to kill her. Bad dreams were hardly the tip of that awful iceberg."

Unhappy with this turn of events, Mariah slid down in her chair and tried to sense vibrations in her staff. Computers had destroyed life as she knew it, but she at least understood them. It was hard to imagine they might be safer than a piece of wood and a stone. "We've been using these things without any idea of what we're doing."

"You are fortunate that Harvey is good at choosing the ones with positive vibrations." Keegan stood thoughtfully over the metal box, holding his hands over it. "What happens to people who choose the ones with negative vibrations?"

"Daisy claimed the red crystals were negative and the blue ones were good," Teddy explained. "You told us some kind of garnet was used in the oil paintings in the storage bunker. We don't know if the garnets were chosen for the color or the vibrations."

"If Daisy was killed for her knowledge, could it be for her crystalline knowledge?" Keegan suggested.

"Or the sketch in her cart?" Mariah poked the box with her staff.

"My resident ghost told us the eyes in her paintings contained tourmaline." Teddy gestured at several ugly oils on the shop walls. "Did she know what she was talking about? The rubellite form of tourmaline, at least, is a pretty rare and pricey gem, but it's usually pinker than red."

Keegan studied the paintings in question, then stroked the eye areas with his fingertips. "Beryl in the blues, with a hint of garnet. More garnet in the browns, pretty much the same as in Daisy's stash. This last one might have a trace of rubellite mixed with the garnet, but the dust is too fine to be certain. Your ghost was duped if she thinks this is pure rubellite."

"I *hate* guessing," Mariah said in frustration. "Keegan, now that you know what the stones feel like, can you search the bunker again?"

"I would have noticed anything feeling like those in the box," he said dryly. "It isn't radiation as we know it, but I'd recommend lead sheathing for the container and lead gloves for handling until I can test them in a laboratory. Harvey, I hope you weren't in the habit of carrying those on you or you ought to see a physician."

Harvey shook his head. "I kept them in a locker." He twirled his staff, studying it. "You've been wandering our hills, and you've not felt anything like these?"

Keegan looked at the box with distaste. "Those aren't natural. What I need is my ancestors' missing journals to see what experiments they performed to create that weird energy. If someone like the Ingerssons acquired the old journals, they may have tried the formulas on new crystals. We have no idea what's been done to them."

"That may be where your Trevor fits in," Mariah said, frowning. "He may have had access to the journals and/or have some of your gift."

"I have no idea when the first journal disappeared, but you said your Lucinda Malcolm had one," Keegan said. "We haven't had a good librarian until recently. So Trevor stealing the second journal half a century ago is a possibility."

"How old are the journals and crystals that were stolen from your family?" Harvey asked, running his thumb over his staff.

"From the late 1700s, when experimentation first became popular." Keegan glanced at his useless phone. "I need to order the lead. Teddy, do you have a password for the internet I see in here?"

She retreated to her counter, pulled out a laptop, and set it up for him. "I don't remember passwords. Just use this."

Mariah sighed and wanted to admonish Teddy for her casualness with a dangerous weapon, but she couldn't yell at the world for existing. Keegan gave her the evil eye before he accepted the computer. She smirked in retaliation. He still had no idea what she could do and wouldn't believe it if she told him.

"So if Daisy was killed for knowledge, what did she know that we didn't?" Mariah said, thinking aloud while Keegan typed on the keyboard. "She had access to all of Hillvale from the resort to the cemetery."

"Which means she could have overheard anything from Kennedy business deals to ghosts weeping on a tombstone," Harvey said in disgust. "And what if it was something in the past, something from the commune?"

"Why would anyone worry about anything from half a century ago? My bet is on more recent information. What knowledge would someone kill for?" Mariah glowered at the sunny main street outside Teddy's front window. The tourists didn't usually wander around town much until after lunch, but she could see a gaggle of flowery dresses and fancy hats heading this way.

"And how would they know that Daisy knew it?" Teddy asked reasonably. "It's not as if she was in the habit of communicating."

Keegan pushed a button, closed the laptop, and returned to the conversation. "What if they were simply removing a *possible* witness? Or what if a news story like those from Expoleaks about corrupt corporations and politicians and international fraud—only something a little more local—made a villain worry that his past would be uncovered?"

"By a half crazy old lady?" Harvey scoffed. "That's more far-fetched than a country music song."

Mariah narrowed her eyes at Keegan, but Mountain Man wasn't even looking at her. She couldn't live with paranoia. She had to assume he was talking theory and not about her. "You think the killer's past was in the commune, and Daisy is the only remaining member who could identify him? That doesn't sound right."

"We should find the names of everyone who ever lived in the commune and see if they're being killed off?" Teddy suggested.

They all groaned. The shoppers shoved open the door and filled the room with chatter and light, dispelling the gloom.

"I still need to hunt my missing journals." Keegan headed for the door. "And I need to determine if there might be a stash of those crystals buried on the farm. I don't think I'm of much use with Daisy."

"Wait." Mariah used her staff to push to her feet. The knee throbbed, but the swelling had gone down. "I know those hills better than most. I'll go with you."

He looked as if he'd object, but she brushed past him and out the door before he could say a word.

She had an ugly vision of turning into Daisy: secretive, non-communicative, half-crazed, driving around the mountains hunting stones. Was that the way she wanted to spend the rest of her miserable life? No. She just hoped the world would eventually forget her existence so she might eventually return. . . under a new identity. Right.

"I'm not a geologist," she announced, deciding to share what little she knew. "But I've been poking around, trying to determine where the hippie crystals came from. I know a canyon further inland with rocks that look like ones I used to find on the coast down by the Channel Islands. They're out of place."

"The Channel Islands are volcanic rock," he said instantly. "They were formed by ancient volcanoes from the vicinity of the Santa Monica mountains. The Santa Cruz mountains around us have tectonic faults, but I had not heard of volcanoes."

"Volcanic rock glitters?" Relieved that he was taking her seriously, she led him toward the golf cart.

"Quartz glitters, and most volcanic rock contains a degree of quartz. What you call crystals are simply combinations of minerals in the soil forced together by pressure." He slowed his great strides to match her limping one.

"Keeping in mind that my rock hounding is only a recent hobby—is it possible an earthquake could have brought some form of old volcanic rock to the surface?" Deciding either her knee wasn't so bad this morning or the painkillers were doing the job, Mariah climbed behind the wheel of the cart.

Keegan shrugged his ox-sized shoulders and checked to see if she had water in the storage compartment, helping himself to a bottle. "Given what we know about our paranormal talents, we have to admit that anything is possible. I go into any situation with an open mind. So you're thinking there are natural crystals in these hills and not just the ones from my ancestors?"

"I'll let you be the judge of that. I don't go into the canyon often." And when she did, it was often in the mind of a hawk, which could see the glitter but not analyze it. "I'm just worried that the place might have gotten Daisy killed. She would have known of it."

"I trust this will not be a rugged hike." He glanced at her knee.

"The path to the edge of the canyon can take three-wheelers. This cart can get us there, if we don't take out the suspension and the engine doesn't croak."

He muttered an imprecation under his breath. Mariah figured that revealed Keegan's level of desperation when he didn't outright call her an idiot. He really wanted those rocks.

She really wanted Daisy's killer, but she lacked experience. She needed whatever help she could find.

She took the cart to the end of the dirt road up to the farm, then bounced it off road through dry chaparral along a path she'd carved out with her feet over the years. Daisy had used it, too. There were still wheel marks in the dried mud. "Do you feel vibrations in Daisy's stone guardians?"

Ever the gentleman, Keegan helped her out of the cart when she parked it in front of a stack of boulders at the end of the path. She grabbed bottles of water and stuck them in the pockets of her camping shorts.

"Not like those in Harvey's bag, which was why they surprised me. If he's been handling them for years, I shouldn't have reacted so strongly." He sounded disgusted with himself.

"Teddy and Samantha reacted just as strongly when they were doused in crystal dust. Cass called it evil. I'm guessing the red crystals, at the very least, have been infused with something that causes chemical reactions in oil paint and affects our paranormal senses." Mariah tested her knee as she led the way past the boulders into the inhospitable canyon. The northern-exposed slope had more scrub pines and cover. This western ridge had sandier soil and grew rocks better than vegetation.

"It would make more sense if someone experimented with *creating* the garnets," he said. "Heat and pressure break the chemical bonds of mineral structures, causing them to recrystallize into tougher substances like garnets. They may have used a solution in the process, but I cannot imagine what constitutes an *evil* solution."

"We'll have to hike around the resort property another day, see if you react to the vibrations over there. Samantha feels them through her staff and calls them negative. Cass calls them evil, but she's a trifle biased against the Kennedys." Mariah slid on a pebble, and Keegan grabbed her elbow to steady her.

"Perhaps we are human Geiger counters?" he asked in amusement.

"Well, if we are, we should start ticking shortly." She used her staff to point at the barren south wall. "There's the granite formation that marks the area where I've found odd crystals and geodes." To prevent sliding, she grasped a boulder and started down the dusty slope.

Keegan loped ahead of her, the better to catch her if she fell, Mariah thought wryly. Hiking with a bum knee wasn't one of her better ideas, but she'd do what it took to find Daisy's killer.

A shot rang out, splintering a rock at her feet.

The next report sent Keegan tumbling down the hillside, into the sage.

FIFTEEN

Flung off balance from the force of the bullet, Keegan dropped for cover and hit the ground with a thud and puff of dust. He'd only heard the two shots. He bit down on a cry of warning to Mariah. If she'd sensibly ducked, he didn't need to let the shooter know she was here. Perversely, her silence terrified him.

Pulse pumping, he slid toward the cover of prickly bushes while keeping an eye out for Mariah, praying she was hidden. He knew from bitter experience that his wound would hurt like the very devil once he recovered from the shock. He needed to take all precautions now, in case the damned bullet had hit anything vital.

Pebbles slid past his nose. No more shots rang out. A moment later, Mariah's booted foot connected with his hip. He grunted and grabbed her ankle.

"Stay down," he muttered, although she'd cleverly done that on her own, he gathered as she slid into the bushes with him. "Can you tell where they are?"

"They're shooting upward, from the canyon. If this is the only path in and out, we're in deep shit." She shoved aside a branch to peer downward. "I can't see a damned thing from here."

He muttered an expletive. She rolled over and tore off her vest, then the t-shirt she wore under it. "Good way to scare the crap out of me, Mountain Man."

Mountain Man? Nerdy professor, maybe, but not a rugged frontiersman. He must have really scared her. But his mind blanked and his tongue froze when confronted with the vision of lovely brown skin and full breasts barely covered by a spandex tank top. Keegan thought he might pass out from lust. He did pass out from the pain when she folded the t-shirt and jammed it against his bleeding shoulder.

He recovered as she used her bootlace to tie the padding over the wound. That unfroze his tongue. "Ow, damn, don't cut off the circulation!"

"We need to crawl into that crevasse over there." Brisk and businesslike, she ignored his complaint and nodded at the scrub brush. "I think there's enough cover if they're keeping their heads down."

"Me first. I've already got a hole in my hide—what's another?" He could only use one elbow for crawling, but he was pretty good at wriggling into tight places. He worked his way to the edge of the brush and saw the steep, narrow gully she meant them to use. He ran through his litany of curse words, turned around, and backed down.

Mariah clambered in after him. "Over there, in the shade, under that ledge."

She bumped his hip to indicate direction.

He'd wonder ten thousand things about Mariah and this situation, but the pain blooming in his shoulder warned he didn't have much time. He had to concentrate on staying upright—or what passed for upright while on his belly and sliding down ruts.

They lay silent, protected only by the ledge and chaparral overhead but out of sight of the canyon. Keegan clasped Mariah's fist and felt her pulse pound. A hawk screamed overhead. Sun beat down on the ledge and shimmered on the dust. He caught a glint of quartz in the rocks. He waited for shots, shouts, an engine, anything.

"I can't stand this. I'm rebooting. Give me a minute," she whispered. "Don't move. Don't say anything."

He was too woozy to figure out what she meant. He stayed still. Mariah didn't go anywhere. She lay beside him, motionless as a rock.

It took half a minute before he realized there was no *Mariah* pulsing through the fist he held. Her eyes were closed. She breathed shallowly. But he knew she wasn't there.

All right, so he must have passed out or was hallucinating. He bit his lip to keep from squeezing her hand tighter. The shadow of the hawk crossed the glitter of the rocks on his right. The air crackled with heat. He'd probably fry before he bled to death. Mariah's impromptu bandage seemed to be doing its job, as long as he didn't move.

How many hours to nightfall? Too many. He had only half a bottle of water. He didn't know how much Mariah had left. He'd heard that rattlers came out at night. Charming.

A quick, deep breath, and the woman beside him returned. Very definitely hallucinating.

She lay still another moment, then her fist unclenched beneath his. "They're gone. There's a plume of dust on the other side of the canyon. Must be another path out."

Keegan's heart pounded on the dust beneath him. His shoulder throbbed with pain. He wasn't hallucinating enough to believe her physical body had disappeared. She hadn't moved any more than he had. She had no way of seeing down the canyon from this angle.

"Keegan?" she asked in a voice finally reflecting her concern. "Keegan? You okay? It looked like the bullet just shot through muscle. You have an awful lot of that."

"I'm processing," he muttered, not acknowledging her comment about his muscles. "Do I stick my head back out there to see if anyone takes it off?"

"Unless you want to rot in this hole, that would be my suggestion." This time, her voice was laced with irony. He did love a woman who didn't get hysterical on him.

He had to trust her mad declaration that she'd *seen* the shooter leave.

Because he wanted out of this hole and saw no other choice, he nodded and began the painful crawl back up.

No one took off his head when he stuck it out. A breeze blew his hair. Using his one good arm, he pulled himself out, then instinctively held his hand down to help Mariah. She crawled up on her own, thankfully, or she might have pulled his arm off his torn shoulder.

He could believe she'd mysteriously *seen* the shooter leave or that she'd made a lucky guess. He might just have to start believing.

He rolled over on his back and stared up at the crystal blue sky. "I'm starting to hate this place."

"Can't blame you there." She stood—as if confident the shooter was gone—and studied the canyon. "Impossible to tell where they were hiding, but someone is using the canyon. I've not seen evidence of anyone growing weed out here. So what's with warning us off?"

Wincing, Keegan scrambled up, grabbed her waist with his good arm, and steered her in the direction of the cart. "I don't give a damn what they were doing. Let's not wait for them to return."

"Right. Brenda needs to clean that wound." She led the way as if they'd only been out for a jaunty hike.

Except Keegan noted Mariah was pale again and leaned on her staff more than she had earlier. "How did you see into that valley with your back to it?" he demanded, if only to distract from the pain.

"Magic," she retorted.

The damned woman never showed weakness, message received. He prodded her anyway. "Which leaves me to assume you were working with the shooters and knew they'd leave."

Her long black lashes lowered in a glare that perversely thrilled him instead of warning him. With that strong hawk-like nose and high cheekbones, her features reflected the power of the woman within. She'd make a formidable foe.

"You are free to assume anything you like, and you still wouldn't have it right," she informed him coldly.

"Shamanic journeying," he retorted, clasping the bandage tighter against the blood starting to flow. He hadn't missed her reaction to Teddy's crystal knowledge. "Explain."

They reached the cart, and she slid behind the wheel. This time when she narrowed her big, dark-lashed eyes, Keegan assumed it was in concern as he fumbled his grip sliding into the seat. She said nothing until he finally settled in.

"A shamanic journey is no different from astral projection. It just adds a New Age spin, or maybe Old Age, because various Native Americans have been using it for generations. It's as good an excuse as any to use hallucinogenic mushrooms—which are a lot easier than nearly killing yourself the way some tribes did." She pushed the cart button angrily. *"I don't use mushrooms."*

The cart didn't start.

Keegan leaned his head back, feeling the pain kicking in. "Battery," he muttered. "Did you charge it last night?"

She hit the ignition again. Nothing.

MUTTERING CURSES, MARIAH CLIMBED OUT. MOUNTAIN MAN WAS GETTING under her skin anyway. "I'll walk back. There's water if you need it."

Her unlaced boot was falling off, and she had the strength of a limp noodle. The sight of that big man sitting in the seat, pale and holding his shoulder, turned her insides to frozen tundra. She wanted to shriek and cry for help and hope the good guys came running and not the bad.

But it was her fault the ancient battery was dead. She should pay the price. Even with her bum knee, she figured she could walk the trail. She could walk it better if she hadn't been flying with the hawk. She stomped down the hill.

Keegan caught up with her. She'd yell at him, but she didn't want to waste her energy.

"How far to the farm entrance?" he asked curtly.

"No odometer on a golf cart," she snapped, slowing her stride, for which her knee was grateful. "I'm guessing less than two miles, easy half hour walk."

"When we're not the walking wounded," he corrected. "But it's closer than town and vehicles can reach it. There are security guards posted there, are there not?"

"At night." She shrugged. "We can hope Val is there. I don't have the strength left to mentally summon Cass. And you'll probably bleed to death if you don't lie down."

"I've been worse," he said grumpily, clomping along. "I need distraction. Tell me your story. I've told you mine."

"All you've told me is that you sense molecular structure. That could be a big whopping fairy tale told to earn our trust. I'm not inclined to believe men and certainly not strangers."

"Then tell me *that* story." Dust flew up from his scuffling boots.

She was terrified this very large, brave man would collapse on her watch, but she defiantly hid her concern.

"Why I don't trust men?" she asked. "It might be more interesting to hear why anyone would blindly believe in anyone else."

"True. But it's your turn, and we have a long walk ahead. Give me something."

"I don't like talking about it. It's not my story to tell." And it was ugly, and she preferred keeping it bottled up inside where she didn't have to take it out and examine her guilt and failure.

"Change the names to protect the innocent," he suggested. "Make everyone in it rabbits. Just keep talking."

She chuckled at the idea of rabbits. "I'm a computer engineer. I don't do imagination." She swigged her water and thought about it. "Okay, let's do it this way. Once, there was a lovely princess from a faraway country. She was smart, ambitious, and worked very hard."

He was probably thinking this was about her, but she would never in a thousand years describe herself like that. But Adera's story was too excruciating to be told any other way.

He stayed silent. It must be nearly noon and the sun was damned hot. She wasn't certain he'd last half an hour. If she had to tell this tale, she wasn't certain she would either.

"Miss Princess worked in a castle full of trolls."

He snorted. "It's usually dwarves."

"Trolls," she said with conviction, using her staff as brace. "The filthy-minded, egotistical trolls sat in their castle towers, casting covetous glances on the princesses below, making rude comments on their many or few assets. These trolls thought princesses were objects to be compared like hot cars, then bought, used, and cast aside when they were tired of them."

Mariah cast the Scot a glance to see if he was still upright. "We are not talking about me. The beautiful foreign princess was a Lamborghini to the trolls, which I am most obviously not."

"What do you think you are, a VW? Don't be stupid."

"A Jeep," she retorted. "Sturdy and reliable."

He groaned.

She wasn't certain in pain or at her story. "You want me to tell this or not?"

"Tell me. I'll hope there's a new spin on this old tale."

There was, but she wasn't telling him that part. "This kind of tale is always ugly and you asked for it," she reminded him.

When he saved his breath by not arguing, she continued. "This particular princess had worked long and hard and won many awards and fought many brave battles. But she was still paid worse than the lowliest of trolls. So, one day, she gathered her courage and went to the boss troll and asked for a promotion."

He said nothing. She continued coldly. "Boss Troll said she could have a raise, along with a new title, and a fancy new office—if she'd be his new play toy."

Mariah thought Keegan growled under his breath. That he wasn't defending his sex gave him extra points.

"And this is where you fully understand that I'm not talking about myself. Miss Princess was raised in a country where one does not sell one's body for anything less than marriage. She had earned that promotion with her hard work. She told the troll where to stuff it and said she would take her complaint to the public and to the Troll of all Trolls, and she slammed out."

"She should have recorded the creep," he muttered. "She'd have him on so many charges that she could use him for carpet."

"But Pious Princesses do not think that way," Mariah said. "They shouldn't *have* to think that way. You want all women to walk around with cameras on our collars like the cops? Although now that I think about it, that might be a good idea in Trolldom."

"So what did Boss Troll do, fire her?" he asked, staggering slightly on the incline they walked.

Awkwardly shifting her staff, Mariah placed his good arm over her shoulders. She was weak, but she would recover quickly. He would only get worse. And proof of that was that he didn't drag his arm away but leaned his weight on her. A man smart enough not to play the macho card—she'd have to start liking him if he kept that up.

Despite the heat and their sweat, he smelled like temptation, so she stuck to her story. "Oh no, trolls like to play games. He told everyone that he had slept with her, that she was easy, so all the trolls started hitting on her. That just made Miss Princess furious. She might have been raised differently, but she was still smart. So she started rumors about him."

"Some office you worked in," he said grudgingly. "Nothing better to do than gossip?"

"We're talking trolls here. They don't know how to communicate normally. It's like living in a frat house where farting is hilarious, getting high is normal, and civil discourse nonexistent. Geniuses but no social skills. They live in caves."

"Even princesses?" he asked with what almost sounded like interest.

"To some extent, yup, which is why Miss Princess lowered herself to their level. She didn't have the skill to retaliate any better. She did hire a lawyer, though. He told her that without proof, she had no case. If she'd been fired, then they would have more than *he said, she said*. So making fun of the troll's dick was her way of using his crap against him and getting fired."

"I'm no lawyer, but that doesn't sound feasible."

She shrugged, and he gripped her shoulder harder. It was like hauling a Buick around. "Miss Princess liked her job. There were very few places where she could do what she did best. She followed all the procedures in the employee manual and nothing worked against Boss Troll. He was male and had power. She was nothing. The rumor war escalated—until the day another princess brought our heroine evidence of fraud in Boss Troll's corner of the kingdom."

"Bloody hell," he muttered.

She ignored him. "Our heroine princess gave the evidence to her lawyer, sent copies of her complaints to every official in Trolldom and in the kingdom beyond. What neither princess quite realized is that trolls *like* games. If one has a big sword, the other gleefully finds a bigger ax. If one has a posse of three, the other summons four stooges and a hell-hound to do the dirty work."

"This sounds like a video game," he muttered.

Mariah would pat his hand in approval, but it was all she could do to stay balanced between her bad knee and his weight. "They can't sell video games as graphic as this one gets. Boss Troll took his posse to Miss Princess's apartment. They raped her. Repeatedly. And took videos doing so."

His fingers nearly crushed her shoulder. "I don't like this story. Tell me again that you're not talking about yourself."

"I am most assuredly *not* talking about myself. I would have shot them. I use sex the way other women use a glass of wine—to unwind. But Miss Princess was a *virgin*. And she was my friend. I don't have many friends. They took her from me. Not just the trolls, but her family as well."

This was where the knife twisted in Mariah's guts. She should have understood what would happen when she'd offered Adera an opportunity for revenge. She should have revealed the fraud on her own. Instead, she'd destroyed Adera instead of helping her.

And in her rage and grief, she'd gone even further, destroying herself and everyone around her. That part, he didn't need to hear.

"Her family?" he asked, apparently still not getting it.

"The videos were posted all over the internet. She had dishonored the family name, and they disowned her. She got in her car one night, and the next morning, she was found in a ravine. The cops called it an accident. I call it murder."

SIXTEEN

Sick to his heart and soul at her story, and staggering from loss of blood, Keegan didn't have to be persuaded when Mariah simply plopped down in the shade of a pine at the farm entrance.

No security vehicles waited—a pretty good sign no one was around. Mariah chugged her water. Keegan lay back, resting his head on his good arm. The other ached like hell, and blood seeped through the shirt bandage.

Her story bled worse.

His gut gnawed, and he wanted vengeance for Mariah and her friend. He knew that was ridiculous. He couldn't even have vengeance for the wrongs that had been done to his family. That was what the law was for.

"Tell me the pricks went to jail for something," he growled.

"Oh, they'll go to jail, all right, even if not for murder." She almost purred with satisfaction. "The feds are currently crawling all over them for multiple examples of trollish wrongdoing. The company's board of directors fired the lot of them and appointed a princess as CEO. They're facing serious jail time and fines that ought to bankrupt them. They'll never work again." She finished off her water and crushed the plastic bottle. "Nothing brings back Miss Princess."

"The world can be a horrible place," he concluded, too weak to run through news stories of the past few years to match against her fairy tale. Working in remote areas, he was often out of touch. "Hiding out in Hillvale almost makes sense."

"Which brings us to why *you're* really here. Your journals have been missing for decades or more. So why look for them now?" She poked at his bandage and frowned.

"The adult equivalent of needing to get out of the house," he suggested, wincing. "Curiosity, restlessness, inability to do anything while lawyers and authorities tear my family apart. Distance was required."

"So, you trotted half way around the globe to look at old pots and hunt for missing books? Why do I find that hard to believe?"

"Because you're a cynic who rightfully doesn't believe any man," he suggested, trying to hold on to consciousness.

"Look, we need to get you to the hospital, which is half an hour away from Hillvale. It could take me another half hour just to stumble down to town, and even longer before an ambulance arrives. You could bleed to death in those hours. But if I can sit and rest and regain my strength, I can attempt to reach Cass. She could call for help, and we'll be in good hands within the half hour. Tell me your story while I recover."

He'd been there when she'd *called* Cass and brought Walker to the bunker after the intruder. He didn't know if he believed Mariah had used mental telepathy or whatever, but Keegan supposed she deserved recompense for tearing out her heart and revealing the bleeding remains. He couldn't call her a fraud after her painful honesty.

"I can't get my story straight even when I'm coherent," he grumbled. "I've twisted it every which way and none of it makes sense."

She sat cross-legged, with her staff across her knees, looking like a native princess despite the tank top. The feathers in her braid fluttered in the breeze. "Mutter, then. I just need time. I may not even hear you, but your voice helps stimulate the part of my brain that needs it."

"You say things like that and it confuses me even more." He propped himself up enough to finish off his water before lying back down again. Facing him, she had her big brown eyes closed, so he thought he might be able to do this. He could just watch her breasts lift as she breathed and pretend she was asleep, and he was talking to himself.

"My home is a small town like this one," he said, looking for a starting place. "My family has been in mining forever, possibly because some of my ancestors had my ability to detect mineral structures. My brother didn't inherit the ability, so he runs the company office, along with my father, who's tired of traipsing around the globe. Traipsing is my job."

She didn't move, but the wind stirred a little more, blowing dust devils up the road. Keegan worked to formulate his thoughts. If nothing else, he'd like to remain conscious.

"My ex-fiancée's parents once worked for our company too. Brianna's mother died in an accident when we were kids, so her dad often left Bri with my mother. We grew up together, much like brother and sister. She loved exploring our library, the one with all the journals."

It hurt remembering golden-haired Bri climbing on the furniture to reach the highest volumes, the winter sun beaming through the medieval windows to illuminate her like a fairy from one of the storybooks. He hadn't been interested in cryptic scribbling in ancient books. He'd been reading through his father's geology texts at the time. Bri had been the laughing sprite to his nerdy. . . Keegan sighed. He was pretty much a *troll* in fantasy nomenclature—a large, mountain-dwelling humanoid, not the internet kind.

Mariah still breathed. Keegan couldn't tell if she was listening. Her hands were relaxed, palms up, soaking in the sun.

He skipped all the parts about university and youth and travel and coming home to Bri and deciding it was time to marry because his parents were getting old and wanted grandkids. No women of his acquaintance would want to live in that tiny cold town. Bri thrived on it. Decision made.

"Bri and I got engaged last year. I was working on a project in South Africa. She was working on the wedding. She has a business degree and works in the company too." Her enthusiasm and interest in his job had been another deciding factor.

Maybe that's why Mariah's disinterest in his occupation intrigued him—she was everything Bri was not. He couldn't imagine Mariah coveting diamonds and gold. He watched her expression, but she wore none.

"While I was out of the country, a computer hacker dumped boatloads of information on the internet, providing evidence of fraud, theft, and hidden bank accounts on dozens of large corporations. Our firm was one of them."

Keegan thought Mariah blinked, but she didn't move otherwise. His concentration was fading, so he stuck to gathering his thoughts. "It's taken me a while to piece together how our company could be involved. Bri had always insisted that we could do more than make fertilizer with minerals. But I had more work than I could handle and didn't listen. Apparently after she gave up persuading me to use my gift to hunt for diamonds, she told someone about the Malcolm journals."

Mariah's eyelids lifted. The color was starting to return to her cheeks, and she watched him wordlessly. Keegan figured he'd gone this far, he might as well finish. "One of our scientists apparently listened. My theory is that he used an old formula to create synthetic diamonds. I don't understand how the rest went down. But the records show that the company sold the synthetics as genuine and funneled the proceeds through my family's bank accounts using company invoices, and then into offshore accounts. My father and brother are currently being indicted for fraud, money laundering, and I'm not sure what else. And I *know* they are as bewildered as I am. I can only hope the lawyers come up with the paperwork to prove their innocence. But I need to find the real villain."

"And Bri?" she asked, finally breaking the silence.

He would have shrugged but his shoulder hurt too much. "She obviously profited from the proceeds, but she's just an office clerk who handled the invoices and claims my family told her to. They're still compiling evidence against my father. I feel as if I need to be doing something, anything, to make things right. Maybe the missing journals hold formulas that can be used for good. Maybe crystals can reveal truth. I don't know. I just want to smash everything open and see what falls out."

Mariah muttered a crude expletive, squeezed her eyes shut, clenched her staff, and—disappeared, just as she had earlier.

She was there, but she wasn't. Fascinated, Keegan watched her breasts stop moving. He didn't dare touch her to test her pulse. He could see her color fading again. If he'd been fully conscious, her stillness probably would have terrified him. But as long as she breathed, he didn't react.

She returned faster this time, taking a deep breath and flexing her fingers before opening her eyes. "Cass will send help. She's not fond of strangers, so it may only be Brenda or a truck instead of an ambulance, but it shouldn't be long."

Keegan nodded. "If someone shows up as you say, that's pretty creepy. Once could be a coincidence. Twice is hard to believe."

She shrugged. "I was unaware that I could do it until Cass showed me how. I belong here, the way your Bri belongs to your home. We're trapped by our need for the familiar."

"That's an odd way of putting it." Keegan struggled to grasp the concept. "I belong wherever I am."

She waved a dismissive hand. "If you're a baker, you bake. It's who you are, what you do, what you surround yourself with. If a baker tries to be a motorcycle mechanic, he's out of his element. It might pay better, take him better places, but the kitchen is his home." She removed another bottle of water from her pocket, edged closer, lifted his head, and helped him drink it.

Keegan swallowed gratefully. Her hands and thighs were as soft as a woman's should be, belying the hard carapace she displayed to the world. "But a baker can bake for kings or the homeless. He has choices. He's not *trapped*," he argued.

"And what does a shaman do?" Her voice was harsh. "Looking through the eyes of a hawk is not generally useful. It's not recognized as spirit-walking or even telepathy, which is the closest I can come to explaining what I do. Other than that, I remove blighted ectoplasm from this mortal plane, which is only slightly more useful, and only in Hillvale."

"You said you're a computer engineer. Is that not useful?" Keegan's head rested against her thigh, and he willed her to run her hands through his hair. He ached in too many places and needed physical distraction.

She examined his wound instead. "So useful that I'm now hiding up here, out of public sight, so the world can't hunt me down to perform more magic tricks, or rake me over the coals for being what I am. You really and truly do not want a shaman whose mind can leave her body messing with your computer. I know what I am now, and engineer is not it, no more than the baker can really be a mechanic."

An SUV roared up the road at high speed. Keegan wasn't conscious enough to decide if he was glad or not that she was forced to quit talking.

He'd been warned to keep Mariah out of his computer. She spoke of vengeance for her friend. He had painful reasons to remember the explosive news stories of the hacker who had uncovered the synthetic diamonds and worse. One of the corporations nearly destroyed by the Expoleaks info-dump had been an enormous computer company—one that only recently chose a female CEO to replace the arrested executives.

Passing out was the easiest thing to do as they loaded him into the back of the police chief's car.

~

July 10: Tuesday, evening

"Dinah, come here and sit down," Teddy commanded from a booth in the back of the café. "You can't keep dithering. You need to talk to Kurt."

Sitting on her stool in front of the register, knee raised in hopes the swelling would go down again, Mariah counted cash from one of the last lingering customers. Behind her, Sam and Susannah were repairing the tattered mural, arguing over colors. Samantha was an environmental scientist, not a painter, but that didn't stop her from arguing. It was nice to see the newly-reunited pair acting like a family.

Fretting over Keegan's injury, Mariah wondered if there were any way to connect the gunshot to whomever had trashed his room. Had someone not wanted Keegan in particular to see the crystals in the canyon? That seemed a little too organized for Hillvale inhabitants, but she kept an eye on strangers.

Walker had declared the canyon off limits until he'd sent the sheriff's department down there. Kurt Kennedy had declared the land didn't belong to the resort.

She was back to needing computers. Couldn't at least one of her talents be useful? If only the effing ectoplasm would convey information the way computers did!

Maybe she could call the hospital to see if Keegan was all right. . .

At the jeweler's command, Dinah took off her apron and hesitantly settled across from Teddy and the hunky resort owner. Kurt was still an aloof bastard, but at least he wasn't wearing suits and ties since laughing Teddy came along. Maybe that was an outer sign of inner improvement.

Maybe people needed connections with each other to become better human beings.

Mariah had revealed more to Keegan today than she'd revealed to herself over the last years. She hadn't realized that her means of survival had left her feeling *trapped*. Watching Sam with Walker, and Teddy with Kurt, she suspected she was only leading half a life, if that. Sam had found a family and a home and was expanding her gift for growing things. Teddy had saved her family, exorcised a ghost, given Kurt a new lease on life, and was learning how to use her gift for empowering crystal.

Mariah had done no more than tie her hands behind her back—probably good for the world but not necessarily for her.

"I own the building, you own the café business," Kurt was explaining to Dinah. "My lawyer has been looking into the liquor license laws, and I think we can get one in my name. You could expand your business into the building next door."

Which he also owned, Mariah mused. But Dinah had a criminal record and couldn't get a license. The town needed a decent restaurant that sold wine by the glass—besides the one at the resort. Kurt was setting up his own competition—

While wiggling out from under the burden of his family's business. Interesting.

Cass sauntered in, looking regal in her floor-length linen dress roped with turquoise beads. She took a seat beside Dinah. Teddy shot Mariah a look of amusement to show all was well. This had been planned. Cass working with a Kennedy—would wonders never cease?

Mariah watched the door, trying not to gnaw her fingernails to the bone. Brenda had insisted that Keegan be taken to the hospital. He'd lost too much blood for her to trust her healing abilities. No one ever admitted that Brenda was more than a nurse practitioner, but Mariah had experienced her healing touch. Her knee would have required a lot more rest and ice if Brenda hadn't looked at it. In Hillvale, it was easy to fool oneself into believing the impossible, but Mariah was jock enough to have sprained various body parts before. She knew she was doing far better than she deserved after overworking her knee today.

Glancing up at headlights flashing across the café's big front window, Mariah saw a flatbed truck pull into the parking lot. With most of the tourists gone back to the lodge, the street was empty enough for it to park across the parking spaces. In the twilight, the one lamp over the lot hadn't yet come on. Who would make deliveries at this hour?

Gradually sensing her interest, one-by-one, the other customers turned to watch. Outside, Walker pulled up in his SUV as if this meeting had been planned. He stepped out and walked over to consult with the truck's driver.

Behind the counter, Sam climbed down from her ladder to watch.

Glumly, Mariah realized that this was what her life had become—watching trucks in the parking lot. Well, she supposed she hadn't had much of a social life even before she'd blown up her career and her identity. But she'd *liked* computers, even if she'd hated the company.

Swinging her foot down from the shelf, she left Sam to manage the cash register and limped toward the door.

Outside, the truck's passenger got out. Mariah would recognize Mountain Man's silhouette in any dark alley. What the hell was he doing back here already? Shouldn't he be in the hospital having drugs pumped into him? *Brenda*, of course.

Realizing how worried she'd been, Mariah slowed her pace and waited so as not to reveal her anxiety. The truck driver got out, and along with Walker, the three men lowered the back of the flatbed and pulled down a ramp. Keegan strode up it. She thought he had one arm in a sling, but that didn't appear to slow him any.

A moment later, a motor rumbled.

Mariah had to snap her jaw closed when he roared down the ramp riding an enormous ATV and steering with one damned arm.

Half the café's remaining customers followed her out.

"Helmet?" Walker shouted over the noise of the motor.

Balancing on the seat, Keegan gestured with his good arm at the ATV's wide back. Walker rummaged inside and produced two helmets. Satisfied, he handed them to Keegan. Keegan chose one and held the other out.

It took Mariah a moment to understand he was handing it to her.

"We need to haul Val's cart back," Keegan shouted over the roar of the motor. "Walker will follow us as far as he can."

He wanted to go back to the canyon? At night? Was he crazed?

Mariah grinned in delight and took the helmet. Now they were getting somewhere.

SEVENTEEN

Keegan heaved a sigh of relief when Mariah took the rear seat and wrapped her arms around him. He had despised looking like a wet noodle today. He had hated worse that he'd had to disappoint her by leaving the job undone and any crystals unearthed.

To vent his frustration, he'd spent the afternoon with the blessed use of his cell phone while the hospital left him sitting around waiting for doctors and stitches. He'd called his family first—his father was being tested for heart trouble and had been unable to come to the phone. The upsetting news had him grinding his teeth in impatience to be home.

In the meantime, shooters in a crystal canyon needed investigation.

He started with finding an off-road vehicle to reach the canyon. He had some vague notion his action would clear a path to Mariah's bed. That she willingly clung to him now went a long way toward boosting his hopes.

After the ATV, he'd hunted down news stories about the info-dump from a few years back. Like Wikileaks, the media had given the explosion of documents a name—*Expoleaks*, after the website where the information had been parked. He'd already read and studied the material stripping the secrets of his family corporation, so this afternoon, he'd hunted out the sections on Macro Computers.

If Mariah had been the hacker, Keegan couldn't imagine how she'd ferreted out so many details without an army of help. She'd tracked bank accounts as well as inflammatory e-mails, insider corporate data, and embarrassingly personal information. She might as well have gone into every single hard drive in Macro and dumped the contents and entire lives on the internet. Didn't the executive trolls she'd scorned use passwords? Security?

If Mariah was the Expoleaks hacker, he ought to dump her off a mountainside for what she'd done to his family.

But just the possibility that she'd blasted light on the despicable Macro trolls increased his admiration. Was that perverse?

Rather than think too hard, he stuck to enjoying the experience of having Mariah's arms around his middle. She wasn't shy about leaning against his back. He could feel her unfettered breasts pressed against his bandages. After a day of lying around, he apparently still had enough blood in him to be aroused. He'd spent a lot of time pondering her comment that she used sex to release tension like other women used wine. That had probably infected his brain.

He halted the ATV at the end of the paved road near the farm entrance. Walker parked his SUV and got out, shouldering a rifle.

"Mariah, you want to wait in my car while we go up to get the cart?" Walker asked.

Keegan snorted and waited in expectation.

"Tell you what, Chief," she called back. "Why don't you give me the rifle, and you can sit here and write love notes to Sam."

Keegan smothered a laugh of appreciation.

"I ought to do just that," Walker grumbled, heading up the trail on foot. "Give me a head start, at least."

"He should have just given me the rifle," she grumbled.

"He's the cop, you're not," Keegan pointed out, starting up the engine again. He didn't need to mention that she probably didn't have a gun license—not under the name of Mariah, anyway.

The woman behind the Expoleaks website had been eventually identified as an engineer in Macro Computer's head office, *Zoe Ascension de Cervantes*—a perfect name for this defiant princess who tilted at windmills and won.

Of course, she'd killed her career and future in the process. Zoe had disappeared after the info-dump, relentlessly hounded by journalists, lawyers, and government officials—which pretty much explained everything about Mariah except how she did it. He'd save his profound admiration for her courage and defiance until he'd learned that tricky piece of the puzzle.

Since he heard no argument, Keegan rumbled the ATV off the road and down the dirt rut that they'd taken that morning. Walker stayed to one side and waved as they drove on.

The golf cart was still sitting forlornly where they'd left it. With his one arm in a sling, Keegan climbed off more awkwardly than he liked. Equally hampered by her knee, Mariah swung off to examine the cart, presumably for a place to hitch it to the ATV. He had to remember she had an engineer's mind, like his. That they were both slightly warped in different ways almost made sense.

"Do you think that machine of yours can go into the canyon?" she asked as he pulled the chains out of the storage container.

"You planning on wearing armor?" Together, they fastened the chain to the cart. "Men with guns aren't as harmless as suits with keyboards."

"Trolls don't wear suits, although they'd swagger in armor if you gave it to them," she said in scorn.

"Fine then, this isn't a video game. This is real life. For all we know, those are armed pot growers down there. Let the professionals handle them."

"I've been down in that canyon and no one has ever bothered me. There's no water for growing anything. Weed just doesn't make sense," she argued.

"I admire your willingness to tackle monsters, but our expertise lies elsewhere." He hooked the cable and carried the other end to the ATV.

She glared at him. "I'm not tackling monsters. I prefer to let them eat each other. I'm not admirable in any way."

"Fine then. You're a cuddly ball of feathers, and no one thought you were a danger when you were in the canyon on your own."

He couldn't see her glare but he felt it. They both knew she wasn't cuddly.

"Wouldn't it be a giant yawn if that's all Daisy's death meant? That she'd found an illegal weed patch?" she grumbled.

"If I'm to believe you and Cass, Daisy directed us to that sketch in the cart. It's about more than narcotics if someone local is involved. But I agree. I still need to see the volcanic rock in that canyon." He tested the connection between the two vehicles, then glanced down the hill. "No sign of Walker. It must be more than two miles. Let's go down and relieve him of his duty."

"And come back?" she proposed. "No one's shot at us."

"We're not on the edge of the canyon either," he said dryly, swinging back in the seat. "I want full use of my arm and an army before we come back. Maybe dogs and elephants."

He waited for her to call him a gutless boffin. Bri had flung such epithets at him since childhood. He preferred to think he was too smart to do dumb things—which made him boring and non-heroic, he knew.

"Will a posse of Lucys with staffs and Daisy's guardians suffice?" She climbed on behind him, not scoffing at his suggestion, to his relief.

So, maybe he had a chance?

"Invite me over tonight, and we'll draw battle plans," he suggested, preferring not to consider a posse of eccentrics carrying crystal staffs wandering these hills. He started the engine before she could answer. He'd give her time to think about it.

They waved at Walker as the ATV crawled down the hill tugging the golf cart. By jogging, the chief almost kept up with their slow pace back to the road.

Once they reached the ranch entrance and Walker's car, Keegan turned off the ATV and called back to the chief, "Go on back to Sam. We should be good from here."

Walker inspected the connection between the cart and their vehicle and nodded approval. "That should work. I've talked to the sheriff. He can't provide a helicopter until next week. I'm asking a few of the locals to go in with me tomorrow. If we arrive with enough vehicles and weapons, anyone there should think twice about shooting at us."

"We're going with you," Mariah insisted. "The locals will want to ride in on horses. You need noise."

"I can bring noise," Walker said, his tone a reminder that he had men and money at his command. "But if I invite locals, I guess Lucys get included, don't they?"

"You didn't think you could keep them out?" Keegan asked with humor. "Give us a time and place."

"Tomorrow, at dawn, in the parking lot. I've already lined up my posse. You're on your own with the Lucys." Walker swung into his vehicle and closed the door.

"Definitely a planning session tonight," Mariah said with decision. "It's early. Cass can call them."

Keegan had been hoping for just the two of them to do the planning —stupid thought.

MARIAH DIDN'T HAVE TO TACKLE CASS. BY THE TIME THEY RETURNED TO town, the Lucys were gathering in the meeting house where Kurt's uncle Lance had been setting up an art gallery.

"Walker must have told Sam," she murmured. They climbed off the ATV and watched the steady stream into the old steepled barn at the end of town. "If we're not meeting at the vortex, Sam really is taking over Cass's place."

"And this means what in Lucy World?" Keegan asked, draping his good arm over her shoulder.

She'd allowed that when he was weak. He was obviously recovering rapidly, but Mariah still permitted the embrace, trying on companionship to see how it fit. It felt scarily good. She had never been a girly-girl who needed men, so maybe it was just having someone who *understood*, who didn't run when she told horror stories. Plus animal magnetism, she had to admit.

"I can't say what it means other than that there's a pretty strong connection between Sam and Cass," she said. "They share genetics, and they've shared the same brain. The weird part is that Cass has fought the Kennedys for decades, but Sam is as much Kennedy as she is Lucy. Choosing Lance's gallery over the vortex may be her idea of finding a common ground."

"You speak in riddles," he griped. "I will observe and learn."

Mariah snorted. "Good luck with that. That's Val going in with Brenda. Hurry. I don't think Val has ever been inside. Sam has to be nuts to invite her aunt into Lance's domain."

Not showing any sign of pain or weakness after his encounter with a bullet, Keegan strolled along at her side, greeting Harvey standing guard at the door. She liked that he didn't get grumpy when she took the lead, but she had to wonder if he was hurting.

She really wasn't much used to thinking of others, she realized.

Had she thought about Adera's situation, she'd have recognized the potential for retaliation. But she'd only been thinking in terms of herself, and she'd always been able to fight back. Adera had been tied down by love and family that had never hampered Mariah.

So, she was as self-involved as the trolls and belonged in a cave. She cringed as ghosts of the past warned she could never touch a computer again.

She could change. Now that her nose wasn't buried in a keyboard, she could observe. Tonight, she'd practice being sociable—like Keegan.

She turned at a loud voice at the door. Harvey was blocking a tourist from entering. The barn had been a good idea if they meant to keep out strangers.

Track lighting illuminated the paintings and pottery on the walls of the meeting house. Lance and Teddy's sister had been working on the gallery for a week or more. In the empty center of the hall, where the lighting didn't reach, the mayor unfolded chairs.

Mariah felt everyone inside hush expectantly as Val entered in her long black veil and floor-length lace dress. Sam rushed up to greet her aunt, but she kept her voice to a whisper.

"I need super hearing," Mariah muttered, towing Keegan toward the artwork. "Val is likely to kill someone before the evening ends."

"She is dangerous? I thought she was Daisy's friend." Keegan peered at the first portrait displayed—an early depiction of the mayor and his brother as young boys.

Impatiently, Mariah urged him on. "Have you met Kurt and Monty's uncle? The tall, gray-haired man up at the front, by the triptych—that's Lance. He did most of the portraits in here. He used to be an architect until he blew his mind on drugs. He's been recovering for some years now. This gallery is the first time he's displayed his art. Val features preeminently in half of them."

Mariah strolled a little faster, hoping to be near when Val exploded. Sam had grown up sheltered and naïve and might be expecting a normal reaction to the surprise Lance had set up. Val did not do normal.

So, maybe she hadn't been completely unobservant these past years if she knew that much.

"Why do I feel as if we should be passing out shots of whiskey?" Keegan asked, finally noticing her tension.

"Whiskey might make things interesting if Kurt sets up a tavern in town. We could pick up our drinks on the way to watch the dramatics. You can import Scots malt for him."

"This happens often?" he asked in justifiable confusion.

"Only every time the Lucys get together. I used to think it was Cass who kept the nest stirred, but Sam has caught on quickly. Except without the vortex to raise psychic awareness, the meeting house might not be as magical. Lance isn't a Lucy. Neither is Monty, Kurt, or Walker. She's invited Nulls and is mixing it up."

As Val halted at a portrait, Mariah waited half way between the diva and the entrance. She could tell Keegan was picking out the Nulls in the crowd. Most of them were conversing at the front of the room with no understanding of the drama unfolding. That was fine. They needed to be out of range.

Val froze. In front, Lance stood equally frozen, watching her. Gradually, even the Nulls noticed and turned to watch.

In a dramatic arm gesture an opera diva might use to indicate great passion, Val silently marched to the next portrait. And the next. Her skirts whirled. Her veil blew in a nonexistent wind. Her silence was almost as dramatic as her voice. Mariah admired the performance. "I wish I'd seen her on stage."

"The town could produce Shakespeare, and she could play all the parts," Keegan agreed in what sounded like awe.

"Poor, shy Lance. He really doesn't have a chance of surviving unscathed." Mariah headed toward Sam, who waited nervously where her aunt had abandoned her.

The painting Val had condemned was one of a striking black-haired young woman in Shakespearian costume, her face contorted into shrewish anger.

"Why tonight?" Mariah asked Sam as Val continued her circuit of the room, blatantly ignoring the artist following her every move.

"I thought an audience would make the confrontation less. . . incendiary," Sam admitted. "Poor Lance has put his heart and soul out there for everyone to see. I don't want Val shooting him down and sending him back to drugs."

"What about poor Val?" Mariah gestured at the painting. "He's put her unscarred beauty all over the walls—the beauty she'll never be again. She's likely to go after his work and him with a knife."

Keegan straightened at the warning. If Mariah didn't know better, she'd fear he was going for his *dirk*. Abandoning her, he strode for the nervous artist. The Scot had only one damned usable arm, and he was riding to the rescue anyway. Because Keegan paid attention to others, and his sense of justice was as strong as hers, she was learning.

Sam touched another of the portraits of a costumed performer. "Val is still talented. Lance is right. She needs to quit hiding."

Keeping one eye on Val, Mariah checked the various portraits along this side of the hall. They'd been interspersed with other artwork and shelves of pottery, but Lance's inspired vision of Val on the stage dominated the display.

"I wish I'd seen her in those productions," Sam said, almost wistfully, indicating the portrait that looked like *Taming of the Shrew* and another that could only be *Hair*. "She must be tremendously talented."

"Well, she certainly knows how to command attention." Mariah took off across the room in Val's direction before the climax of the evening had a chance to start. She could feel Val's vibrations that intensely.

In front of a particularly large painting, Val emitted a low, almost musical shriek that built in a frenzied crescendo. It echoed off the high rafters and ended in Val melting into a puddle of lace on the floor.

"Well, that starts off this meeting with a dramatic performance," Sam said loudly as she reached the front of the room.

Designed as a church or meeting hall, the acoustics carried her voice over the rising murmurs of concern as the Nulls ran to Val. Understanding Sam's plan, Mariah almost grinned. She applauded instead.

"Let's all give a hand to Valerie Ingersson and her performance of *Tosca*," Mariah called, stepping up to the role of assistant that she usually shared with Cass. "Lance, if you'd carry the lady out, we'll continue with the business of this meeting—the crystal canyon."

Of course Lance couldn't carry Val out by himself. A middle-aged woman was no slender ingénue, and Lance was no longer a muscular young man. It took both Kennedys to help their uncle lift her. Sending a narrow-eyed warning to Mariah and Sam, Brenda hurried out after them.

From his place near Walker, Keegan studied the situation. But with his one arm in a sling, he couldn't be useful with Val. Instead of following the other Nulls, he chose to take a seat near Aaron off to one side, remaining with the Lucys.

"And Cass carried this show alone, how?" Sam whispered as Mariah approached.

"By slowly learning each one of her flock as we appeared. You start the meeting, I'll make the report, and then we'll let the men think they're organizing us," Mariah murmured back.

"Cynic." With her walking stick, Sam rapped the railing and waited for the buzzing to silence before speaking. "Mariah and Keegan have a problem to resolve. I'll let them explain."

"Mediator," Mariah whispered back as Sam stepped aside, and Keegan, looking surprised, got up from his seat.

Sam only chuckled as the roomful of Lucys sat up and took heed for a change.

Mariah outlined her hope of finding crystal deposits and using them to compare with the ones that had been inherited and possibly those used in the artwork. She admitted she had no idea how this might relate to finding Daisy's killer, unless someone else was after the crystals, and Daisy had discovered them.

Keegan explained the limitations of entering the canyon, the range of the shooters, and the dangers involved. He admitted he didn't see how they could go in safely, even with Walker's armed men providing official cover.

Sam stepped up. "I was hoping we could do what we did to prevent the avalanche—use our staffs as a vehicle of guiding the energy we feel. But I don't know how it works, and stopping men with guns isn't the same as stopping rocks."

Wearing her colorful African garb, Tullah stood. "We will need vehicles to transport us as far as possible. We all know our places around the Ingersson farm, but you say this canyon is two miles further out. That's more than many of us can walk. And once we arrive, we'll have to explore positions. I don't think we can do more than that on this first visit."

That's what Mariah had feared. They had a posse, but groups were never nimble. She suggested horses and several people agreed they could ride. The ATV could make multiple trips for those who couldn't walk far. There would be utterly no element of surprise—except in what they might be able to do. And even the Lucys didn't know that for certain. There was no encyclopedia or Google search to explain the vortex or the strong earth energy they all sensed and manipulated.

"We can hope we scare the shooters off with just our presence," Harvey suggested, adding with his usual cynicism, "We can wear magic hats and flourish batons and chant."

Sam stepped up and waved away the laughter. "You do just that, Harvey. The rest of us can bring the guardians Daisy created. We'll congregate in the parking lot at 5 AM tomorrow. That's when Walker's crew will be striking out. Those of us driving will park at the farm entrance. We can hike, ride horses, or take the ATV from there. Walker's men aren't any less conspicuous, so maybe they'll scare off the shooters first. That will clear the way so we can look for positions while his men go into the canyon. Walker believes this is Menendez land. He talked to the owners this afternoon, and they say they've not leased the land to anyone. So if nothing else, perhaps we can warn off trespassers, let them know we're watching, and they'll go away."

Teddy, the jeweler, was new to Hillvale and had never attended a Lucy meeting. She'd simply been listening, but now she stood to add, "If no one minds, I'd like to go down in the canyon to see the crystals. If they have power, we may need to be careful about removing them."

"Unless you're prepared to carry a weapon besides a staff, I'd suggest you stay on top with the others until we see what's there. I'll see that no one touches the crystals except me. Will that suffice for this first venture?" Keegan asked.

Teddy nodded and sat down. Teddy knew more about crystal powers than any person in this room. Keegan had one good arm and only knew molecular structure. Mariah would smack the man for his arrogance, but then she'd have to smack Teddy for being dense. *Observe*, she reminded herself.

After a few brief discussions of details, Sam dismissed the crowd. As they filed out, Keegan leaned over and whispered in Mariah's ear, "Now can we go to your place and discuss *our* plans?"

A frisson of fear and a shiver of excitement rushed through her. Was she ready for this?

EIGHTEEN

Even though he'd bought the ATV with the intention of giving it to the town—he certainly couldn't transport it back to Scotland—Keegan kept the keys as he escorted Mariah out of the meeting house. He could tell she was prepared to stalk straight up the back alley and lane to her cottage without speaking to anyone. He respected that. But he held her shoulder as he greeted the Nulls gathering in the parking lot. She didn't have to talk to them, but he did.

And he wanted to go wherever she did, so they needed to work it out.

"How is Miss Ingersson?" he asked of Kurt and Walker, who leaned against the chief's car waiting for their Lucy partners.

"Brenda says Val is fine. We took her back to Cass's place." Walker watched as Sam left the hall, chatting with animation. "I take it the Lucys are joining us in the morning?"

"It appears so, but only in the position of observers," Keegan said.

Beneath his hand, Mariah wriggled restlessly. She was like the hawk she claimed to use, not comfortable around others.

Keegan didn't linger to discuss the problem of meddling Lucys. He'd simply wanted to ensure that he was included in *Null* consultations. He didn't want to be written off as a *Lucy*. He didn't know why people insisted on using derogatory terms for people unlike themselves, even intelligent people like these. But as an outsider, he needed to engage both sides.

After saying his farewells, Keegan followed Mariah through the dark and up the hill toward the cemetery, grateful she didn't tell him to *stuff* it.

"I'd offer wine," he said as they traipsed up the path. "But the hospital gift shop didn't sell any. Would you rather go to the lodge?"

"I'd rather not think," she growled. "We aren't dating. We didn't meet in a bar. I've never gone to bed with a *friend*. So I need to think of you as a means to an end, and quit trying to put the friend hat on you. It's taking some mental rearranging."

He chuckled, relieved that she accepted where this evening would end, and that he hadn't been fooling himself that she shared his interest. "Your definition of *dating* is having someone to call when you need sex? You don't date men you talk to? Which makes your definition of *friend* just exactly what?"

"Until now, exclusively female or gay," she said, sounding surly. "I don't talk to Harvey and Aaron unless I have to. They're like fellow workers. But you. . . You're like a Heisenbug that's crept into my code and can't be dug out."

He feared she was calling him a virus, but with someone as thick-skinned as Mariah, maybe that's what he needed to be. "I'll admit, I'm new to dating as well. I travel. I don't have time to make friends. I find willing women who want what I want. Then Bri decided we should be partners, so I've been with her for a while. It severely curtailed my activities while traveling since I had some notion that engagement meant fidelity. But I never really *dated* her, not in the getting-to-know-each-other way. So this is an educational experience for both of us."

"We're not dating," she pointed out. "There is nowhere to *date* here. We're *encountering*."

"Suits me. Is this your place?" He studied the tiny cottage that looked no bigger than a hobbit hole, in a lane of equally tiny burrows. "It needs a thatched roof to match the fairy tale look."

"This is California. We're lucky there aren't wooden shakes. Someone had the sense to replace the old ones with fireproof shingles or you'd have the full quaint bungalow fantasy." She unlocked the door and let him in.

Inside, the interior was surprisingly spacious and modern. The ceiling had been lifted to the roof. The living room and kitchen occupied the entire front of the house. He guessed the bedroom and bath were behind the door on the rear wall. Mariah was tidy and apparently had no possessions. The furniture looked 20th century rental—faux suede couch and recliner in massive proportions and a TV over the fireplace. The coffee table stacked with magazines was the only personal touch he noted.

She crossed the Saltillo tile floor to the refrigerator and removed two cans of beer. "I think this evening justifies the calories. How's your shoulder? Do you need Tylenol?"

He produced a small container of pills from his pocket, accepted the beer, and swallowed gratefully. "The stitches hurt," he admitted. "I'll survive."

"It could have been worse." She sipped her beer and studied him worriedly. "You scared the hell out of me."

That she'd worried about him heated the lust factor to the nth degree. Keegan tried to roll it down a notch. "Could have fooled me. You performed like an experienced combat officer. Were you in the military?"

Without being invited, he took his beer to her overlarge couch and relaxed on it. Furniture his size was a luxury.

"I was pretty much raised in rural areas like this. We had to be self-sufficient." She settled cross-legged on the cushion next to him. "I learned to get things done. I've been called unfeminine for that attitude."

Keegan couldn't control the urge. He liked touching. He stroked the length of her silky, beaded braid. She didn't dodge away. "Trolls don't appreciate courageous women. You needed to be out of their cave."

She sent him a wary look, but he didn't admit he'd figured out who she was.

She relaxed and sipped her beer. "I'll probably never be a girly sort."

Keegan held the beer with the hand in a sling and wrapped the other around her shoulder, dragging her toward him. Just having her giving curves against his side made him feel at home for the first time in a long time. "You needn't be girly and worry over me. I've been shot, stung, bit, and knifed far from medical services and survived. I'll admit I tire of doing it alone. So it was a pleasant change to have you to take charge."

He loved the way she glowered at him, as if she thought he poked fun. He bent over and gave her a quick kiss, just to remember the flavor of her lips, and to reassure her that he meant it.

She tasted of beer. The way her mouth clung to his wiped out coherent thought. Setting his bottle on the coffee table, Keegan dragged her against him and lost himself in her welcome.

Mariah ran her hands under his shirt, but hesitated at his bandage. He wanted to rip off the gauze so she could touch freely. He unfastened the Velcro sling, and in sheer bliss, cupped her beautiful breasts, savoring the way the tips puckered under his touch. She met his challenge by tweaking his one exposed nipple.

Like teenagers, they pawed and sucked and ripped off clothes. The damned bandage hampered him, but Mariah yanked off his shirt and covered his neck with kisses so he forgot the pain. She straddled his lap so he could easily reach around her to remove her bra.

She was sturdy and strong, and he didn't have to worry he'd break her. He was the one who was weak here. The experience aroused him in new ways—he didn't want to take and plunder but touch and enjoy and *anticipate*.

She leaned over and licked his nipple. He yelped in surprise, then lifted both her breasts and took turns caressing and sucking. In moments, she had his jeans unfastened and was stroking him to the breaking point.

He muttered an obscenity when he couldn't lift her enough to yank off her camp shorts. She wriggled out of them without his aid.

He caressed her between her legs until she cried out and sank down on him with a moan of need to match his own.

"Condom," he muttered.

"Birth control," she replied. "No sex in two years, no STDs."

"Same here."

And that was their last moment of lucidity.

July 11: Wednesday, early morning

Mariah woke to the dawn song of a mockingbird and a massive block of warmth in her bed. It took all of half a minute to savor the languid aftereffects of fantastic sex, process the knowledge that she'd actually let a man sleep with her, and remember their task for the day.

She punched Keegan's ribs and shot out of bed.

He muttered and stirred as she dashed for the shower. A few minutes later, he joined her, already more than half aroused. He was a damned fine male animal, even with the bandage marring the upper part of his chest and shoulder.

"You can't get the bandage wet. Get out of here." She shut off the water.

"Good morning to you, too, Sunshine." He chuckled and leaned over to kiss her.

He actually had to *lean* to kiss her. He could *almost* make her feel small. And a man who didn't mind her bossiness. . . she couldn't contemplate at this hour.

"We need to be out there *now*," she protested, pulling away from the pleasure.

"I am going to take you to a tropical isle with no one on it but thee and me," he grumbled, flipping the shower back on but keeping his shoulder out of the spray.

"You let me know when you find one, and I'm all there. But with no airport, we'd have to sprout wings." She grabbed a towel and headed for her closet.

"Yacht," he called. "We'll go by yacht. Tropical nights in a blue lagoon."

Damn, but he awakened dreams she'd long forgotten. Or more likely, dreams she'd set on fire and let blow away like ashes.

Still totally naked and apparently more comfortable with it than she was, Keegan kissed her again when he emerged from the bathroom. She only had one arm through her shirt and almost fell over from the shock. He chuckled and picked up his clothes from yesterday. She had to sit on the edge of the bed to steady herself and pull on her hiking boots.

She'd loosened her braid to rinse out her hair. It fell nearly to her waist, so she didn't have time to rewrap but tied it off, top and bottom, with the twine she made for her nets. "Dinah usually doesn't come in until six. I'll see if I can find anything in her kitchen because there's nothing in mine." She shoved her keys in her jeans pocket and added her guardian statue to her backpack.

"I've been known to drink beer and eat cold pie for breakfast." He yanked his jeans over his fine long legs, then grabbed his shirt. "Good thing I put this on clean before the meeting last night."

"I daresay they had to cut the other off of you. How does your arm feel this morning?" She filled the rest of her backpack with her usual hiking supplies.

"Itchy. How do *you* feel this morning?"

"Not itchy." She checked the clock and marched for the door.

His chuckle did things to her insides she'd never experienced. She was brisk and cold, and he laughed and warmed her all the way through. If this was the kind of man available elsewhere, she'd spent way too much time among trolls.

Dinah wasn't there when Mariah unlocked the kitchen, but the diminutive cook had left covered trays of breads and pastries and bowls of fruit on the counter. In the enormous refrigerator, she'd stockpiled sliced meats and cheeses.

"It's not eggs and bacon, but I think we'll survive." Mariah emptied her pockets of the cash the Kennedys paid her for ghost catching, left it in the register, and began filling up boxes.

Keegan threw larger bills down with hers and did the same. "Coffee?"

The man was not only generous, but useful. Mariah appreciated that. Or maybe it was just the afterglow from the best sex she'd ever known.

By the time they left the diner, their arms loaded with boxes and trays of coffee carafes, the others had begun gathering in the parking lot. The more efficient had already eaten, but the bleary-eyed gratefully fell on the food while Walker organized his troops.

Mariah noticed Sam's mother was there, looking lost and wary in a blue hoodie over her graying blond hair. To her immense surprise, Val stood beside her, a long black cloak with a hood thrown over her usual veil and gown. Surreptitiously, Mariah scouted the crowd, finding Lance with his nephews over on the far side, with the other Nulls.

"Wow, impressive turn-out," she murmured. "We'll scare off half the county."

Keegan followed her look. "Or fill up the county emergency room with snake bites and broken legs. How often do these people hike?"

"Val, surprisingly, hikes all day and half the night. Looks like she's brought a box of Daisy's guardians to hand out to those who may have forgotten theirs. Maybe you should get one."

"I have one good hand," he muttered. "Should I wear it on my head?"

Ignoring his Nullness, Mariah nodded at a stranger inappropriately outfitted in Abercrombie & Fitch jacket and khakis. "Who's that over there?"

"No clue. Shall I ease over and find out?" Keegan tore into his meat-filled bagel and studied the scene as she did.

The stranger talking to Kurt was older than the resort manager but not old enough for silver to thread his dark, thick hair. His tanned face spoke of time outside, but this was California. That meant nothing. "Might be a good idea to know," she said warily. "I don't trust strangers."

As Keegan worked his way over to Kurt and the visitor, Mariah joined Sam and Teddy, great sources of information now that they were sleeping with two of the town's most influential men. "Do we know who the new guy is?"

"He was introduced as Caldwell Edison," Sam whispered. "Walker said he joined them over breakfast at the lodge, said he was interested in buying land here, and wanted to come along. Walker tried to get rid of him, but they couldn't tie him to a post."

"Kurt told me Edison is the son of a politician." Teddy looked worried. "He's a regular guest at the lodge, and his father represents this district, so Kurt can't tell him to mind his own business."

"*Edison*?" Mariah asked, coming alert. "Son of *Bradford* Edison? The musician wearing a bear claw in the mural? Can he be the man in Daisy's sketch?"

NINETEEN

"Put your lie detector hat on," Mariah ordered Teddy. "I don't like a mural guy showing up after Keegan just got shot."

Teddy wrinkled her nose. "He's *son* of Mural Guy. And he doesn't look like Skanky Man in the sketch. He looks perfectly respectable." Still, the petite jeweler fell into step with Mariah.

"Believe me when I tell you that respectable people can hide secrets, not all of them nice. You play the pretty smiling face, while I'll be the annoying one. I'll see you don't lose any potential customers."

Mariah walked up to the men as if she'd been invited. She'd survived in a man's world by mimicking their arrogance. She held out her hand. "Hi, I'm Mariah. Will you be joining our troop?"

She sensed Keegan smothering a smile and resisted her usual obnoxious reaction to any male noticing her. It might be time to grow up. Kurt hastily introduced the stranger as Caldwell Edison, a real estate marketer. The stranger looked bored and a little irritated at her interruption, but he shook her hand. His kind was the reason for her hostile reaction to men.

"I'm just an observer," he said stiffly.

"As are we all," petite Teddy said, possessively taking Kurt's arm and beaming. "It should be a lovely day for a hike, if you don't mind getting up at this hour."

Mariah didn't think the polished stranger looked like the type accustomed to watching the dawn, which made his presence even more suspicious.

"If you're looking at real estate in the canyon, have you talked with the Ingerssons yet?" she asked. "They own most of the road and the land back where we're going."

"I understood the canyon was Menendez land." Edison still didn't seem interested.

Warning alarms clamored. *Sam's mother was married to a Menendez.* How had she forgotten that?

Mariah touched Teddy, the human lie detector, to indicate that she switch on. Teddy didn't like being assaulted by other people's emotions, but at this hour, people were barely awake.

"Are you familiar with the Ingersson commune?" Mariah asked genially. "It's Hillvale's history. From here, we have to go through the commune to reach the canyon."

Caldwell's eyes hardened. "The commune is no longer there. It's just land."

"We're hoping to restore and re-enact that period of time," she said briskly, inventing the idea on the spot. "I believe your father participated at one time, didn't he? Perhaps he'd like to help us fund an arts and crafts center there."

Teddy pinched her. Mariah hoped that meant she was getting a reading.

Caldwell looked briefly startled, then hid behind his bored mask again. "My father may have visited. He played in a folk group in college. I'll ask him when I see him next."

His father was painted on Dinah's mural with the original commune members. He was more than a visitor.

Living with Teddy, Kurt was apparently more aware of Teddy's talents than the others and quickly caught onto the reason behind this meaningless discussion. "The ladies are planning a homecoming festival for the commune members and their families. We'll add you to the list," he said heartily. "Tell your father, ask if he knows some of the original members. Maybe we can enlist him on the committee."

The jeweler was smiling brightly, but her eyes had that far-away look she sometimes developed when consulting with whatever weird monitor she had in her head. Mariah wished Teddy would jump in here with some revelation, but the talented artist hadn't learned to manipulate her gift well enough to process two things at once.

Looking uncomfortable, Caldwell muttered what might have been agreement.

"Excellent. Would you happen to know Trevor Gabriel's family?" Mariah poked the nest more. "He's on the mural with your father. Once we identify everyone, we'd like to send special invitations to all of their descendants."

"I have no idea who you're talking about," Caldwell said, blatantly turning his back on her. "Looks like the sheriff is starting out. My car, gentlemen?"

"Cars can't go the last two miles. You'll need boots," Mariah warned. "Keegan discovered a nest of rattlers at the trail head. That's why most of us are going on horseback and carrying sticks. And Orval's been reporting some rabid foxes, so you'll need your gun as well."

She hid her delight at her meanness when Caldwell's lined brow drew down in a frown.

"Kennedy?" he asked, turning to Kurt.

Kurt shrugged. "Some of the hazards of canyons," he conceded, without lying.

"It seems I'm ill-prepared then," Caldwell admitted reluctantly. "I'll leave you to your search and come back another time." He stalked off.

Mariah whistled under her breath. With a lifted eyebrow meaning he'd want details later, Kurt followed his guest.

Keegan rested his hand on Mariah's shoulder and studied Teddy. "Explanations?"

"Seriously stressed and lying under pressure," Teddy announced in satisfaction. "And there was a guilt factor in there. He knows *of* Trevor Gabriel, if nothing else. The guilt played in mostly when you mentioned land."

"But we've not learned anything useful." Keegan frowned. "He doesn't appear to be the kind of man one wants as an enemy."

"Ruthless," Teddy agreed. "Greedy, ambitious, self-involved, I got all that. This is not a man one wants as friend either."

"We need to learn more about him, in other words." Mariah glared at the ATV they walked toward. "Bradford doesn't strike me as the type to know archery, but he'd have minions, like the guy who tried to break into the bunker. Did Walker ever find anything more about George Thompson?"

"Only that he lived on the commune as a child, along with the brother who has gone to jail," Keegan said. "He doesn't have a bow-hunting license. Whoever shot Daisy was no novice."

"Sorry, I've got to go. I'm carrying Lucys in my van. I need to round them up. I'll see you up there." Teddy abandoned them to head for Amber and several of the older women.

Mariah climbed onto the ATV seat, still puzzling out pieces. "Canyons are worthless. They burn. They flood. They turn into mud rivers. One does not build in canyons. Any idiot knows that."

"No one said he planned on *developing* the land, just that he's into real estate. Canyons are pathways into the interior. These hills are filled with minerals. Maybe they've located oil or gold. The possibilities are endless." He kicked the motor into gear, ending that line of speculation for the moment.

Gold? Or crystals? Crystals were far more likely, but they could be found anywhere, so it had to be these particular rocks if land was Edison's goal.

~

ONCE THEY REACHED THE CANYON, KEEGAN SWALLOWED ANOTHER painkiller and washed it down with bottled water while the unorthodox search party sorted itself out. Anyone down in the bottom had surely heard the assortment of ATVs and horses gathering on the ridge. Walker's posse wasn't trying to be surreptitious—the whole point being to drive out intruders, not catch anyone. He got that, he thought.

While the Lucys tried to find safe deer paths through the chaparral along the ridge, and the Nulls sorted out their equipment for descending into the canyon, Keegan studied the terrain.

Rejecting the Lucy regiment, Harvey joined him. "How much do you know of the geology here?"

Keegan shrugged. "It's a unique mixture of volcanic layers, ocean sediment, and the remnants left from glacier movement, in a terrain weathered by the coastal climate on one side and the desert interior on the other."

"Ideal for crystals?" Harvey asked.

He didn't know why the musician was interested, but Keegan nodded. "Shale and sandstone are predominate, but they've found limestone, marble, gold, iron, silver and quartz in this short range. Most of it isn't in amounts worth anyone's time."

He'd come here looking for journals and answers to impossible questions. He was unlikely to find either in this canyon.

But miraculously, this trip had enlightened him to the value of *compatible company*. He'd always felt out of place anywhere except in his hometown, where his family eccentricities were well known.

At university, he'd been younger than his fellow students, left out of their sexual exploits and scorned for his intellectual focus. He'd had to take up athletics to garner friends—but competition was not his natural milieu. Paraphrasing Mariah, a nerd would always be a nerd and not a jock.

In Hillvale, he could talk about minerals and their complex structures, and people *listened*. Despite his being a stranger, they accepted him and his oddities as one of their own.

Harvey absorbed his mini-lecture with interest. "So, maybe crystals." He grimaced at the women and reluctantly strolled off to join them.

Keegan watched Mariah organizing the Lucys. In her drab green linen and khaki camp shorts, she ought to blend into the environment, but to him, she was a shining vision of possibilities. She hadn't taken time to weave beads and feathers into her glossy hair this morning, but she still resembled an exotic bronzed princess who made his pulse pump an extra beat or two.

He really didn't have the heart left for a relationship, especially not with a mystery woman who kept secrets. So he forced himself to listen to Walker organize the canyon party. Keegan didn't need a horse. He'd hiked higher hills than these and made his way down them again without mishap. He'd rely on his own two feet—he'd be closer to the ground and better able to test the structure of the rocks he encountered.

While the horses searched for animal paths, Keegan used one of Harvey's walking sticks and his one good arm and started down. Samantha, the environmentalist, had explained the other night that the lack of evergreens in the canyon meant the original water source had found new outlets, and the soil was too sandy for anything but this vegetation that dried up every summer. So Mariah was correct that the land was effectively uninhabitable for anything but animals.

As he descended into the narrow canyon, he caught glimpses of the Lucys spreading out above. Val in her black cloak blended into the shadows of the south wall, but her blue-garbed sister could be spotted easily. The sun had already reached Mariah's north side. Amid the lifeless-looking shrubbery, he caught glimpses of sunlight reflecting from the crystals in their sticks.

That no one was shooting at them was a distinct relief. He'd prefer not to face an army, although he'd done so elsewhere. He was no adrenaline junky. He'd rather just take his pickaxe and examine rocks.

While the others took a more direct path, Keegan wandered among the boulders, testing for molecular structure, finding nothing more than the usual quartzes. He scooped up pebbles as he slid into the deeper recesses of the ravine and rolled them in his hand. Sensing quartz, he put them in his pocket for the jeweler to test with whatever obscure power she possessed.

The horses beat him down, but not by much. While Walker directed his posse, Keegan continued his survey. He didn't think Walker would catch whoever had shot at them yesterday, but he did think the shooter was here for a purpose. He wanted to know what it was.

With an understanding of the geological shifts reflected by the rock formations in the canyon walls, Keegan had a good idea what part was mostly granite and might conceal quartz. But the limestone layers also offered opportunities for caves and subterranean structures where the ocean might once have swirled, creating the more valuable crystals.

The tumble of boulders he had his eye on was on the southern wall, not too far into the canyon. It would be an excellent place for snipers as well. A good rifle could reach anyone on all three sides of the ridge. The police chief and his posse didn't appear to be interested in the walls of the canyon so much as the exit to the east. They rode straight down the middle.

Checking to see where Mariah was on the north ridge, Keegan ambled around to the south, trying to stay in her sight. It was always good to have someone know where he was in case of emergency. He could almost feel Mariah following him with those piercing eyes of hers. Hawk eyes, he decided.

Working his way around to the boulders that interested him, Keegan sifted more pebbles through his fingers. The ground was mostly sandy gravel, with a slightly higher concentration of diorite. He added the stones to his collection for Teddy. The jeweler's auburn hair stood out along the north ridge, some distance from Mariah. He suspected the jeweler was watching Kurt on his horse, so Keegan didn't bother signaling her.

He did lift Harvey's walking stick so the sun caught the crystal before he entered the shadows of the boulders. Mariah lifted her stick to indicate that she'd noticed. Oddly satisfied, Keegan poked into the crevasse, scaring off any snakes. Finally finding what he sought, he stepped beneath the shadow of a ledge, into a sandy cavern behind the rocks.

Before he could even rub his hand over the sandstone, he stumbled over a large—soft—obstacle.

Splayed just inside the entrance was the pudgy frame of the bigot he'd encountered just a few days back—George Thompson.

TWENTY

Mariah had found a hollow to plant her stick in if Lucy energy was required, but the canyon seemed peaceful. She'd put inexperienced Teddy on her side of the canyon. She could see Sam settling the last of her team on the far side, not too far from where Keegan was exploring. Below, Walker had sent his men down the middle of the valley, but their search was pretty futile. It was obvious there were no cultivated beds of marijuana, no barrels of water, nothing that would indicate drug dealers might have taken up residence. She supposed they might look for wheel tracks.

She was yawning when her staff vibrated with shock, catching her unprepared. Pulse jumping, she anxiously searched for Keegan. He'd disappeared into the shadows earlier, but he was emerging now, waving his stick and shouting. Her relief at seeing him whole and unhurt was superseded by his agitation.

Damn, but she was too far to help. If she broke rank now, so would everyone else, and their protective circle would fall apart—just when they might need it. She bit her lip in anxiety, unaccustomed to caring what happened to anyone but herself—unaccustomed to working with others.

She thought she'd shut down her ability to care after Adera's death.

But Daisy's loss had left a hole in her heart that Keegan had apparently sneaked through. She bit her lip in unusual indecision, wanting to go to him, while wanting to stand guard over her friends.

Feeling vulnerable, she gripped her stick, and held it high, indicating everyone remain where they were. Sam's staff glinted in the sun across the canyon, returning the signal. All along both ridges, Mariah could see Lucy crystals lifted in unity. She breathed deeply and tried to relax in this display of strength.

Below, the police chief motioned for his men to converge on Keegan. What the hell was happening down there?

She needed a better outlet than computers and hawks, Mariah concluded. She needed a human mind to enter—and Cass wasn't here.

What's wrong?

Keegan felt Mariah's demand inside his head. Was he so worried about her that he was imagining her fear?

Walker rode up and Keegan gestured at the cave. "I've already disturbed the scene, sorry. It's Thompson."

Thompson? the voice inside his head asked in shock.

That was going one shade too far. Keegan smacked his temple with his good hand and debated the wisdom of pain pills.

Descending from his horse as smoothly as if he were climbing out of his fancy BMW on a city street, Chief Walker removed a flashlight from the collection of tools on his utility belt. "George Thompson? The one who tried to break into Daisy's bunker?" He eased toward the crack between the boulders.

"The one and only. I didn't have a light to see how he was injured, but I could smell him. He's been here more than a few hours." Keegan glanced up at Mariah. She was sitting down and leaning against a large rock. The sight made him uneasy.

Crystals? The voice in his head demanded.

Damn, it was bad enough having a woman get under his skin, but in his head? Still, he understood the urgency of her question.

He ran his good hand over the boulders in his immediate vicinity. Nothing interesting. He followed Walker, blocking the entrance to the cavern with his breadth while the lawman examined the body and its surroundings. At the same time, Keegan surreptitiously tested any rock he could reach. Still nothing much.

I'll send Teddy.

The voice faded, and Keegan felt a distinct *absence*. Retreating from the dark cavern, he drank more of his water, wondering if he was light-headed from lack of blood and over-exertion. But even making those excuses, he knew he hadn't imagined Mariah's presence in his head.

And he knew it wasn't coincidence that Teddy started making her way down from her position on the ridge while everyone else stayed in place.

Keegan took a seat on a flat rock and guzzled his water. He was an engineer. He worked with minerals and formulas. The scene unfolding was better left to the professionals. He tried not to glance back at Mariah on the ridge for fear he'd see her slumped over while she raced around in a hawk's brain. He glanced uneasily overhead but they'd scared off the birds.

Monty Kennedy rode up with his posse. But Kurt Kennedy, the mayor's brother, rode in the opposite direction to meet the woman he was apparently cohabiting with. Watching Teddy accept Kurt's assist to the back of his horse, Keegan couldn't resist one glance above. Mariah was standing again, although she seemed to be leaning on her stick now instead of holding it up.

She'd gone limp like that after *calling* Cass. The fury that had been building rolled over him. He never got angry, and he didn't fully understand the response now. He hated having his brain invaded, but of more concern—*how much did the damned woman endanger herself with these impossible stunts?*

Looking as if he belonged on a beach and not a horse, the blond, long-haired mayor swung down to join his police chief.

"The coroner will have a heart attack if I call him down here," Walker complained from inside the cave. "Literally. The man likes his dinner too well."

"I'm not hirin' a younger coroner just for Hillvale," the mayor drawled, inching past Keegan to look inside. "Can you tell how the bastard died?"

"Gunshot to the chest, not close range. Even if I call it a hunting accident, we'll have to call the sheriff and have an autopsy. I can't see any Lucy magic changing that." Walker almost sounded aggrieved.

Keegan seriously hoped Mariah wasn't still in his head. She'd need her strength to keep the Lucys in check and get out of this canyon. "Is it safe for the Lucys to join us?"

Walker and Monty glanced up at the ridges where the heat had to be building.

"Can we just send them home?" the mayor asked. "We don't need the women down here."

"Too late." Keegan pointed at Kurt riding across the valley with Teddy.

"One's enough." Walker detached a small walkie-talkie from his tech belt. "Sam, send them all home. We're in no danger. Call the sheriff, tell him we have a body with a gunshot wound, and we'll need search and rescue to haul him out."

Walkie-talkies, imagine that, Keegan mused, watching Mariah. Shouldn't a tech geek have thought of that?

Although he supposed if Mariah was living on cash as a waitress, she probably didn't have money for gear. And it wasn't as if he'd given her time to plan this expedition. Maybe he should provide a supply of walkie-talkies so she wasn't walking around inside everyone's damned brain.

He'd build up another head of fury if he wasn't so totally out of his element. He ambled over to help Teddy down from Kurt's horse.

He had to force himself to ignore the ridge where he'd last seen Mariah.

"Do I want to go in there?" Kurt asked, watching Teddy slip in around Walker.

"Not unless you like rocks and dead bodies. I like rocks fine enough, but I'd rather not climb over a corpse to reach them. Think your girlfriend will?" Keegan watched with interest as Teddy disappeared from sight.

"Only if she senses something, and don't ask me what, because I have no understanding. And let's just pretend we're not having this conversation so I can sleep at night." Kurt crossed his arms over his chest and waited.

Keegan glanced overhead. Without need of walkie-talkies, the Lucys were leaving their various positions. Some were sensibly heading back to work. Others, like Sam and Mariah, were making their way down the valley on foot.

"Ignorance is bliss?" Keegan asked, doubting ignorance around Mariah was wise.

"In some cases, yes. I would like to spend my time building a better Hillvale, while forgetting dead bodies and corrupt politicians and that the woman I want to share my life with feels ghosts. Not *sees* them, but *feels their emotions*, like dead people can have emotions. Consulting with corpses might be useful, but feeling them, not so much." Kurt sounded almost insulted that Teddy couldn't be weirder than she was.

Somewhat relieved that he wasn't the only one aggrieved by the women and their inexplicable talents, Keegan chuckled. "Maybe she's in there having an emotional battle with Thompson's ghost. We probably ought to quit griping about the improbable and begin figuring out what in hell is happening."

"No sign of drug dealers," Kurt admitted. "But Caldwell Edison didn't want to come into this useless hole for a land deal. He knows something. We need to send a few people out the far end to see where the canyon goes. Walker said it looked as if there were old wheel tracks." As if in pursuit of that idea, he strode off to speak to a few of the locals.

With a sigh of resignation, Keegan strode across the rocky valley to meet Mariah. By the time he reached her and saw her pale cheeks, he couldn't shake her like she deserved. Instead, he dropped his good arm around her shoulders, squeezed, then bellowed, *"Don't do that again!"*

"I've never tried that before," she said, blithely limping across the rough terrain. "Cass invited me to try and we practiced. People are a lot more difficult than electrons. Do you think George's ghost might still be here, and we might talk to him?"

Since that's what he'd just been discussing with Kurt, Keegan rolled his eyes and tried not to imagine what she could do with electrons. "Isn't that Cass and Tullah's job? Where is Tullah?"

"I don't have the same kind of physical connection with her as I do with you and Cass, so I can't mentally communicate with her. It's up to her to decide whether she wants to join us. She's not much of a hiking sort, and it's a bit of a climb down here." Mariah glanced up at the walls. "Looks like she may be following Sam though."

"A man is dead, and we're more interested in talking to his spirit and looking for crystals than in who he was and why he was here," Keegan grumbled. "What is wrong with us?"

That caused her to look at him in surprise. "I expect that response from Teddy or Sam, but you're an engineer. You should be more interested in the whys and wherefores than in a bigot who tried to rob us. Don't tell me you harbor a soft heart under that pile of muscle."

"Hearts *are* muscles," he retorted. Since he'd been accused of softness in the past, he had built-in shields, but Mariah had the ability to pierce them. "And I'm only an engineer because I understand molecular structure. What else is there to do with that ability?"

Her eyes brightened with interest. "I don't know, but maybe you should find out. You only took geology because that's your family's business, but what if you'd studied medicine? Or become a veterinarian? Would you understand animal molecules?"

"Touch people and see how they're made? I don't think so." But she was right. Mining was what his family had done for generations, because of their peculiar abilities and because of the land they owned. What if he'd been born into a family of physicians?

They reached the cave just as Sam and Tullah scrambled down a narrow path nearby. Keegan helped them over the last boulders while Mariah tried to bully her way past the guards at the entrance. She was in a shouting match with Walker by the time Keegan arrived with the other women.

"If you don't let us in there, Walker, we'll hold a séance right now and raise the dead while you're standing over him!"

"That won't work on Walker," Sam whispered, covering Mariah's mouth with one finger. "Allow me." She peered around Monty and called into the cave, "Do you want to let Tullah see if there's any spirit lingering, or shall I wait for Cass to come and cleanse the canyon?"

Winking at Keegan, Monty stepped aside so Sam could see in. In practical khakis, Tullah took a position on a flat rock at the entrance, closed her eyes, and mentally departed the way Keegan had seen Mariah do. He wasn't certain how he knew the thrift shop owner was no longer mentally—or maybe spiritually—present. He just sensed it. Was that a Hillvale thing?

He wrapped his arm around Mariah's shoulders to make certain she didn't disappear on him too. "Walker has a job to do," he warned her. "There have to be parameters drawn between science and the paranormal. In the meantime, the law is on his side."

"Because men and the law are ignorant," she muttered. "Walker knows what we can do. He can bend the rules when he wants."

"But he's chief of police for a reason. If that man in there was killed by someone with money or power, Walker needs to prove in a court of law that he did everything by the book. Talking to Thompson's ghost will not convince a jury."

"Caldwell Edison," she said, understanding. "Damn. If he'd come down here with us like he wanted, what could he have done to cover this up?"

"Chosen this area to search and convinced the others there was nothing here?" Keegan thought about it. "Or maybe just verified that his minions had done their job. He didn't seem the type to climb down here and do it himself."

"Or maybe he was just concerned about a missing colleague," Sam added, gesturing at the cave. "We have no reason to believe he even knows of Thompson's existence. Walker says Tullah can enter if Teddy leaves. It's not a large area."

Tullah didn't respond. Dark face lifted to the sun, she communed with her own thoughts—or the spirit world.

Teddy trotted out, holding a handful of pebbles. "Not finding anything valuable, but I'm sensing. . ." She wrinkled her small nose in thought. "Discord? Warring factors? The crystal power is stronger than any spirit."

The women turned to Keegan expectantly. He really didn't want to slot his bulk into that narrow space with a decomposing body, but intellectually, he needed to. Glaring at them to express his disapproval, he inched around Monty. "Walker? Tullah is otherwise occupied. Might I take a look at the rock structure?"

"There's a ledge outside the roping. Stick to that. I didn't know I'd need to bring crime scene tape with me," Walker said in disgust.

Keegan found the rope laid in the dust and, with his back to the rock wall and his head bent, edged toward the rear of the narrow aperture. Unlike Teddy, he couldn't sense the power of crystals. He felt no discord, only unease at the sight of the decaying body. When he reached the far side of the roping, he stepped off the low ridge and straightened. Unfastening his sling, he stretched his arms out to either side, placing one hand on each wall.

The combination of geological layers was fascinating, far more complex than any other he'd ever encountered. He could lose himself in following the kaleidoscopic mix of molecules. . .

The orderly series of particles shifted into a new configuration at his touch.

Keegan yelped and yanked his hand back before the whole wall gave way.

TWENTY-ONE

"That's a whole mountain—it can't crash down," Teddy argued as they returned to the café to cool down and fuel up.

"And molecules can't shift either," Keegan retorted. "You want to see what happens if I put my hand through the wall?"

Mariah would have been amused by the Scot's acceptance of weirdness except his fear and anger were so unusual, she knew what he'd experienced was no laughing matter. She didn't need Teddy's empathy to know he'd been furious with her earlier. But she admired the restraint that had prevented him from strangling her for what she knew had been an unconscionable invasion of privacy.

At the time, she hadn't believed she could do it. That she'd been able to connect so easily. . . she didn't dare examine.

And now Keegan was seriously shaken by. . . What?

The potential for the gentle giant to turn into a raging berserker was a little scary in itself. The man had muscles on top of muscles. His abdomen could be used as a washboard and his pectorals. . .

She shook off that mouth-watering image and limped behind the counter to pour glasses of ice water to cool everyone off. "Let's put our rock samples on the table and see if Keegan finds any unusual pattern in them."

Apparently everyone in the party had collected pretty rocks. Keegan visibly calmed down when he saw the dirty loot piling up on Dinah's clean counter. He worked through the stack with the speed of experience.

Teddy and Harvey picked up the stones he discarded. From their usual booth, Cass and Tullah watched and waited. Tullah had been quiet about what she'd experienced in the canyon. The thrift shop owner had a history, like everyone else in town. Tullah might have the majestic presence of an African queen, but she never said much, especially in public.

Using both his good and injured arms, Keegan shuffled a few of the dusty pebbles into inexplicable patterns.

Dinah began shoving platters of sandwiches through the pass-through window. Sam joined Mariah in handing out plates. No one quibbled over the menu as they gulped water and watched Keegan.

Aware of strangers lurking in booths and at the end of the counter, Mariah kept an eye on them. The journalists had apparently given up on their story for the moment, but there were always visitors in the café. She understood their curiosity about the notorious Hillvale eccentrics, but sometimes, they weren't just tourists.

Like those in the furthest booth wearing brand-new, Hawaiian-style shirts. Journalists couldn't afford high end lines like that, not new. Lodge guests leaned more toward boutique casual, not mall clothes. Mariah would bet good money the flowered-shirt guys were wearing pressed chinos straight off a Macy's sales rack. Why should that raise her suspicion?

"There," Keegan said in satisfaction, arranging the remaining pebbles. "They react in conjunction with each other."

"I do admire a megalithic egghead." Mariah limped over to admire the pattern he'd created. She saw nothing more than rounded stones with glittery bits in them—just like on the coast.

Teddy cautiously reached her hand over the stones. "Discord," she concluded in satisfaction.

"Can you find a pattern that doesn't cause discord?" Mariah asked in fascination.

"With the book," Tullah said, surprisingly. "They have a book, with formulas."

The entire café hushed. Glancing back at the three men in the booth, Mariah tapped Teddy's hand. It took the jeweler a second to turn on her emotion monitor and read Mariah's fear and wariness, but she instantly slipped over to Cass and Tullah in their booth. "A meeting," she urged.

"We're tired," Amber complained. She looked longingly at the sandwich platter being passed around.

Surprisingly, Sam's mother stepped behind the counter. "I used to waitress when I was a teenager. Sam, why don't you take your friends someplace more comfortable? You've had an exhausting morning. Mariah, let's box up these sandwiches."

"Everyone needs a good mother," Mariah murmured in amusement, doing as told.

She'd rather pick Keegan's brain on her own, preferably somewhere with a bed. But that would have to wait until they cleared evil out of Hillvale. Two murders escalated the threat.

She hoped they'd find the killer soon or she'd live with constant paranoia. To that end, she followed orders and let the older women choose their gathering place.

With his sling still unfastened, Keegan carried a stack of boxes. Others grabbed drink trays. The Nulls had stayed in the canyon to guard the cave and watch for the sheriff. So it was strictly Lucys marching down the boardwalk to the meeting house.

Val balked at their choice, but Sam took her arm and whispered assurances in her aunt's ear. No one wanted to hike out to the vortex in the heat of noon, and the meeting house had a door that could be closed to outsiders. Mariah understood Cass's decision, but she worried about her mentor. Once upon a time, Cass would have dragged them up the hill to her place, where the Nulls never set foot.

"I'm wondering if ignorance might not be better for all," Keegan muttered.

"Not if the villains have knowledge," she murmured back. "What if the bad guys know something we don't?"

"What if the villains have my family journals?" He posed the question as if thinking aloud. "Does that mean they can conceivably have the family curse as well?"

"Curse? I wouldn't call molecular detection a curse. How many rural villages have you helped by discovering valuable minerals on their land?" Mariah steered him to a table to set the food on.

"The same number that have fallen to the greed and corruption of wealth and modern living," he said irascibly.

"Well, there's that. You're sounding like a true Lucy now. We're corrupting you."

Over the babble of a dozen voices choosing their lunch, Cass rapped the wooden railing for attention. "In case you haven't heard, there has been another murder," she said in a carrying voice of command.

"I don't want to be her," Mariah whispered, surprising herself. She'd vaguely accepted that she would eventually end up as a crazy lady who ran the town from behind the Screen of Oz.

"You belong in a larger world," Keegan replied, chowing down his sandwich.

What would happen if she told him who she really was? Given what she knew about him, he'd probably hate her.

Cass sent them a glare, and they quieted, along with the rest of the room.

"Tullah, would you like to tell us what you learned this morning?" Now that she had their attention, Cass took a seat.

Rather than move in front of the faded triptych on the back wall, Tullah simply stood where she'd been sitting.

"There is power in the stones," Tullah said in her ringing voice. "Thompson's spirit is trapped there. Mariah, I fear you will need to free it once the area is safe."

"Crap," she muttered. But she let Tullah continue rather than respond. Keegan squeezed her hand, and Mariah found that oddly comforting. She couldn't remember the last time anyone had tried to comfort her.

"His spirit is full of spite and anger, as well as a sense of despair and failure. In his mind, he had information he thought others wanted. His failure is related to that, I believe, but he's not coherent enough to speak, except to mention the book and the formulas."

"Did he leave any impression of who killed him?" Cass asked patiently—while Maria stewed in impatience.

"No, there is confusion. I received impressions of wealth and power and his desire for both. So it's possible he was meeting someone who had what he wanted."

Samantha stood to be acknowledged. At Cass's nod, she added, "Walker says Thompson was shot from a distance, so it's possible he didn't see his killer."

She glanced around the room until she located Keegan. "Walker found a newspaper article in Thompson's pocket. It was about a chemist in Scotland who created synthetic diamonds and sold them as real."

Mariah held her breath as Keegan stood and waited for permission to speak. He didn't seem the least concerned, but it seemed he grasped how the Lucys worked. Did they have a similar system in his home, which he'd said was inhabited by equally eccentric residents? Regretfully, she would never know.

At Cass's nod, Keegan reported, "A chemist in my family's company is in jail for that fraud. We believe he was using formulas from an old family journal. My family has worked with minerals for generations, using knowledge and abilities we've passed down. I will admit, I never read those unscientific books, but they may contain information others consider useful. I believe you have heard of the crystal compendium Lucinda Malcolm left here—that was once part of my library."

He sat down to the murmurs filling the high-ceilinged hall. Mariah caught his hand and returned his reassuring squeeze.

"Where is the journal your chemist used?" Cass asked.

"We don't know. He claims he only had the formula and not the journal. Any member of my family is free to access that library and copy anything of interest. Removing the journals isn't permitted, but it has happened."

Mariah stood. "Which means someone has the journals and may be looking for Lucinda's volume, which brought them here. Daisy and Thalia Thompson were the last people known to have seen Lucinda's crystal compendium, and they're both dead. Sam's mother verified its existence. George Thompson could very well have seen it in his sister-in-law's home. Since he lived in the commune, he would be familiar with crystals and quite possibly the cave. He did have knowledge—and whoever took the recent journal might have been after it."

Sam stood again. "If we think the search for the journals or the crystals is the reason for two deaths, we need to learn *why* they want them. That might point us to *who* might want them."

Before anyone could remark that the deaths had occurred after Keegan's arrival, Mariah popped up again. "We might not have the books, but we have crystals and two people who understand their composition. Possibly three, if Harvey will admit to it. I vote that we ask them to work together to see if they can find a use for our crystal inventory."

AMID THE ENSUING HYSTERICAL DISCUSSION OF EVIL AND GREED AND BURYING all the stones, Keegan squeezed Mariah's hand in gratitude. He was aware that she had diverted the suspicion which rightfully ought to fall on him.

She finished her sandwich and nodded in Teddy's direction. The jeweler was looking back. With some unseen signal, both women rose. Mariah tugged Keegan after her.

He feared others might object but apparently they were settled in for a brisk argument over a good lunch. Only Samantha got up to join them. As an environmental scientist, she might lend objectivity.

Outside, Keegan located the musician strumming his guitar on the boardwalk, collecting coins from passing tourists—and probably acting as guard to the meeting.

"Go on to Teddy's," Keegan murmured. "I'll bring our reluctant musician."

"He won't admit he's a Lucy," Mariah warned.

"Don't blame him," Keegan said with a snort. "I want to be called a Leo."

"You're a Capricorn goat." She laughed and added, "Not a trace of a lion in you."

He glared, then stomped down the boardwalk in pursuit of Harvey. Bri had called him a stubborn goat often enough. So, he'd live up to the name.

He grabbed Harvey by the arm and yanked him to his feet. "Come on. Don't leave me alone with the women. If nothing else, you can agree with everything I say."

"They've twisted your head around, too, have they?" Harvey hastily gathered his loot and shoved it into his pocket. "I can't tell you what to do with a box of rocks."

"You think early man knew what to do with fire? Or how to grow seeds or make knives?" Keegan gathered up the guitar and case. "Progress can't be had by sitting on our bums and watching the world go by."

"Progress gets us corrupt politicians and greedy financiers," Harvey grumbled. "Maybe we're better off in caves."

"Where the biggest ax wins? I like to think progress isn't about who has the biggest weapon, but about civilization, about working together to build a stronger community. A strong society has the ability to build a better ax if needed."

Harvey didn't have time to argue the point, Keegan shoved the more slender man through Teddy's open door into the jewelry shop where the others waited around the oak table.

The petite redhead gestured at her elegant sister behind the counter. "Syd says we've had an unusual number of customers inquiring about our crystals."

"A number of unusual customers," Syd corrected. "It's normally kids and women into the healing powers of smoky quartz. These were men in Tommy Bahama who looked like they belonged in suits. And they asked weird questions. I played dumb."

Spies? Keegan's gut ground, and he nodded at the door to the back of the shop. "Can we work back there, where we won't be noticed?"

"It's a galley kitchen with a tile counter and no table," Teddy warned.

Mariah grabbed a blank poster board from the stack Syd had been working on. "Write out something professional looking—'Rock club meets here on Wednesdays at 1 PM. Sign up online.' Make up a website or give Teddy's. We'll just pretend we're nutty spelunkers."

Keegan tapped her Roman nose in retaliation for the insult to his profession, but he was too eager to get the meeting underway to argue. He had no illusion that they'd uncover a murderer, but any step toward solving the mystery of the crystals would help him sleep at night.

So would Mariah in his bed. She bounced her hip against his to acknowledge his mild rebuke, then set about organizing the meeting. He liked the familiarity of the gesture and that she was as physical in her reactions as he was.

Mariah wanted them to work together to find a *use* for their crystal inventory, but the only uses Keegan knew were material. He didn't think she meant insulation.

Harvey wandered the room, examining the staffs he'd left on consignment and looking uncomfortable.

Rather than take a seat with the women and their dangerous box of crystals, Keegan poured his collection of pebbles on a shelf near Harvey. He could feel the molecular structure shift as he moved the stones, but he couldn't tell if it was from his touch or the position to one another.

"Tell me what you see or feel on these things," Keegan demanded.

Harvey glanced down at the motley assortment of rounded, mostly gray, pebbles. "Looks like you've been to the beach."

"Exactly, they're tumbled, as if they'd spent a lot of time in water. They came from all across the canyon. I suspect if I examined the topography more closely, I could see where it once broke through to the sea. A few hundred millennia ago, it was probably an inlet, possibly with a small volcano or earthquake fault at its furthest inland point."

As Keegan expected, Harvey couldn't resist playing with the pebbles. Behind them, the women were using the protective gloves he'd ordered to sort through Teddy's crystals, but he knew they were listening.

"No sea glass," Harvey said, mocking disappointment. "Why did you arrange them like this? Does it mess things up if I move them?"

He did so without waiting for permission. Keegan understood the temptation.

"They're hot," Harvey said in perplexity. "What did you do to them?"

Keegan held his hand over the newly re-arranged stones. "They weren't hot a minute ago."

The women pushed back their chairs, eager to see, but he held up his hand. "One at a time. Teddy, since you're sensitive, see what you feel."

The redhead studied the pattern of pebbles without touching. "I'm not feeling the discord."

She picked a pebble with strong quartz lines. "It *is* hot." She poked it closer to a bluish stone. "Still hot."

Harvey reached over and separated half a dozen of the pebbles from the rest, then stepped back.

Keegan let Teddy test them first. She frowned. "It's. . . resonating?. . . with the others."

Keegan pushed his big thumb into the blue stone and felt the weird shifting. This time, he didn't yank his hand away. When he was satisfied the molecules had stopped shifting, he lifted his hand.

He'd left a thumb print in the stone, one that glittered like polished crystal.

Both Teddy and Harvey gasped and backed away.

"Diamond," they said in unison.

TWENTY-TWO

"We're never going to solve any of this, are we?" Entering her cottage, Mariah climbed on a stool to clean a wisp of ectoplasm off her net. "I hate this. Why can't I make this goop talk? Or at least let me be a Grim Reaper so I could go around yanking out the souls of turds instead of just swiping leftover goop."

"I don't believe turds have souls," Keegan said in amusement. "And I don't think you get to choose your victims. What if you'd had to yank out Daisy's soul?"

"Gad, I hate rationality. Just let me rant. None of this is sane. You just made a *diamond*." She reached in the refrigerator and produced a bottle of beer and one of mineral water.

"I could recite an essay on diamond formation," he said, accepting the beer. "But essentially, it requires carbon, high pressure, high temperature, and takes thousands of years. It's hard to believe my finger produced sufficient pressure."

"I need a computer," she grumbled, pacing the floor, fighting her need for knowledge with her fear of losing her soul.

"Walker has computers and minions who wield them. There is no need for you to do so. You're exhausted. I want to know if sending ectoplasm to the Great Beyond feels as weird as creating a diamond." Keegan slumped his big body on her couch and chugged his beer.

"I don't even know if the goo goes up or down or just dissipates. I see the ectoplasmic remains, rub them, and they vanish. Nana never explained. If I could only learn from it as much as Tullah does. . ." She slumped on the cushion beside him.

Keegan's solidness and life blocked the slime of the afternoon's ordeal.

Keegan draped his good arm over her shoulder. She liked the way he was always touching her. It kept her grounded, and she seriously needed an anchor in reality. She had learned long ago to accept the weird, but today had stretched her limits.

"Do you think the killers really thought they could turn granite into diamonds if they had the right formula?" he asked in disgust.

"You did it. If the books say it's possible, and maybe they had some example to go by. . ." She let her voice trail off, too tired to follow that thought.

"Since no one else could turn hot pebbles into anything, I'm guessing it's just my family curse. Explaining that won't keep my family out of jail. But now I have to wonder if Bri or her chemist boyfriend don't have some of my ability. I should probably go home and start asking questions. The family has another library in Edinburgh, but I'm pretty sure I have all the geology tomes." He finished his beer and set the bottle down. "Bed?"

She had to remember he would be returning to Scotland, and the feds would never let her leave the country. She didn't jump on his welcome suggestion but continued sucking on her water bottle. "If you'd scanned your journals into a computer, you could search a lot easier."

"One of a kind, handwritten books, many in Latin," he reminded her. "We can't tear them apart to run through a scanner. It would have to be done by hand, one page at a time."

"Then create a bunch of diamonds and hire someone to do just that," she said querulously.

He sighed and leaned over to kiss her. She eagerly drank in the pleasure, knew she shouldn't succumb, but before she could push away, he backed off.

"You're being deliberately irrational," he told her. "One tiny pebble out of a sea of them does not equate to a fortune. None of the other stones responded in kind. And any way you look at it, it's a fake diamond. Do you want me to leave?"

"I want to apologize for invading your head," she said with a scowl. "I didn't know I could do it."

"Just don't ever do it again." He didn't release her but waited.

Edgy and uncomfortable, she thought about that, and shook her head. "I can't promise that. What if you're in danger?"

He growled and got up to stalk the room as she'd done earlier. "I grew up with women who kept warning me not to do this, that, or the other because their prescience saw disaster. If they'd had their way, I'd live in a cave and never leave. There's a *reason* mankind ignores weird abilities and sticks to what they can see for themselves."

"Diamonds aren't real enough for you?" she asked, uncertain how to take his reaction.

"It's an *artificial* diamond," he insisted. "No matter what a jeweler's loupe says. It might refract like a real diamond, have the density and thermal conductivity of a real stone, but I *made* it. It's not natural, therefore it's artificial. And I do not intend to end up in jail like the company's chemist. My family has enough problems without adding me to them."

"Fine then, you made an artificial diamond. It's still something you could see and hold in your hand. It's not woo-woo. It was *real*. Prescience is a little more difficult because it's in the eyes of the interpreter. And what you did relied on a particular stone. You can't turn *any* stone into a diamond. So that should be right down your alley, learning the properties of that particular stone."

"Waving a hand over pebbles and declaring them hot is not scientific," he said morosely. "And this is getting us no closer to the journals or the criminals."

"Yes, it is. We now know one journal has a formula for creating precious stones, that it's quite possible your ancestors were experimenting with what you call your curse, and that someone besides your chemist is probably trying to duplicate the results."

He stopped pacing to stare at her. "Do you think the commune's crystals may have been created that way—by someone with the family curse?"

"And Lucinda's compendium told them which crystals to use?" Mariah sat up excitedly. "And one of your family is in the café mural!"

"Trevor Gabriel, the guru fraud." Keegan dropped down beside her. "Expletive deleted," he muttered.

"He's dead," Mariah reminded him. "What are the chances that his descendants have the curse?"

"As far as I know, the genetic odds aren't good unless one of his wives, mistresses, whatever are also a descendant of my family. I've never studied a family tree. Our company chemist might have some family connection, but I wasn't aware of it." He gathered her against him. "Bed. We'll think clearer in the morning."

Mariah considered that a most excellent proposition. Otherwise, she would be compelled to find a computer and hunt down the formula his chemist claimed to have.

She could probably do it, if she didn't mind losing her soul or never leaving Hillvale again.

~

JULY 12: THURSDAY MORNING

Keegan glared at the newly cleaned mural on the café wall. All the young people in their long hair and hippie wardrobes looked bright and vibrant now that decades of grease and smoke had been painstakingly removed. He'd like to think Trevor Gabriel looked malevolent even with the red eyes recently repainted to brown, but he wasn't that imaginative. Trevor looked like any other college kid.

"Trevor could have brought the crystals with him," Keegan suggested. "Maybe his family stole them in the first place."

"The evil is old," Tullah intoned from her booth, where she sat with Amber and Brenda, the retired nurse. "It has seeped into the land and spread through the vortex. If anything, the land polluted the crystals."

"Not helpful," Keegan muttered.

Mariah patted his hand. "We all come from different places with different perspectives. Tullah comes from the land of voodoo. Teddy knows jewelry. You know minerals. Teddy and Harvey helped you identify the blue stone because of their different backgrounds, not because they're scientific."

He'd always thought he'd had both feet solidly on the ground, but Hillvale had upended him. Oddly, the most mystic of Hillvale's residents was grounding him now. He wrapped her braid around his hand and let memories of last night soothe his churning gut. Sex with Mariah was almost an out-of-body experience, but his body certainly appreciated it.

Walker took the empty counter stool on Keegan's other side. Sam slid him a coffee mug and the police chief gulped caffeine before speaking.

"Thompson was shot with a long-range rifle, approximately the evening of the same day you were shot. He'd been let out on bail the night before. The person paying his bond paid cash and used a fake ID. Thompson's wife claims to know nothing of his friends or who bailed him out." Walker sipped his coffee and scowled at the mural the same way Keegan had done.

"We need a mind reader," Mariah said, getting up to help Sam behind the counter.

"A circus clown and unicorn as well," Keegan retorted.

"Amber, read Keegan's cards and tell him how many ways he's an asshat," Mariah called to the tarot lady.

Looking like an orange-haired Gypsy in her flowing skirt, bracelets, and rings, Amber laughed. "I'd be happy to, but he hasn't asked."

Harvey took the seat Mariah had just abandoned. "Caldwell Edison checked out of the lodge yesterday. Kurt is looking at computer records to see if there are any others who regularly stay there when Edison does."

"We're pinpointing Edison why?" Walker asked as Sam slid him a plate of what appeared to be pancakes with eggs, pickles and onions on top.

Keegan thought it resembled an Asian dish he'd once sampled. Dinah aimed for comfort food for every nationality, apparently.

"Because Teddy says Edison is hiding guilt," Sam said cheerfully. "We don't like him, and his father used to live in the commune."

"All perfectly logical reasons," Walker said sourly. "I'm really glad I don't have to report to the sheriff anymore."

Sam leaned over and kissed his cheek. "What would you do without us?"

"Write nicely researched reports, complete with footnotes and annotations to real evidence," Walker said, but the chief's mood had lifted.

Keegan glanced over at Mariah taking cash at the register. As if she sensed his gaze—or his thoughts—on her, she looked his way and winked. Just that tiny gesture of recognition raised his spirits, and other parts. He was in serious trouble here. With his father's health at stake, he had to go home soon. Given what he suspected about Mariah, he doubted if she could leave this hiding place.

"Does the sheriff have everything he needs from the cave?" Keegan asked, finishing his coffee.

"Yeah, there's not much we can pry from stone and trampled dust. We have the bullet. We're tracking the gun. If we could match the make with someone who has a bow hunting license, we'd be getting somewhere."

"Except criminals generally don't bother with licenses." Keegan stood and laid his cash on the counter. "Since I'm the only one not working, I guess I'll be the one who goes back down there to examine rocks."

Mariah looked alarmed. "You can't go alone. What if the killers are back?"

Keegan gave her his blackest glare.

Apparently remembering their conversation about prescience and not taking warnings, she glared right back. Fair enough. She could threaten to invade his head all she liked. That wouldn't keep him from what needed to be done. And that crevasse had to be explored.

"Walker, is it safe?" Mariah demanded.

The police chief shrugged. "The shooter isn't likely to return to the scene of the crime."

"I have time. I can go with you. Tourists don't show up until afternoon." Harvey gulped down his poached egg and water.

"I'm not turning rocks to gems," Keegan warned. "When I want diamonds, I can look for real ones."

"Diamonds need provenance, just like art," Harvey said with a shrug. "I'm just curious. I didn't get to explore yesterday. I'll fetch my backpack and stock up on water."

"Radios," Walker said unclipping his. "I don't know if it transmits to town from the canyon, but it will from the farm. I'm counting on the two of you to be sensible and get the hell out if there's any evidence that the bad guys have returned."

Practical, Keegan could accept. He really didn't want Mariah inside his head again.

"I can still borrow Daisy's cart. It's charged up," Mariah called as Keegan followed Harvey out.

Of course she could. Her bruised knee was healing rapidly, but another day of hiking would hurt. He raised a hand in acknowledgment that the warning meant he'd better not take too long and tempt her to follow.

She didn't have to be inside his head for him to understand her. Weird.

Harvey met him at City Hall, where they'd parked the ATV. The musician climbed on the back with the ease of experience. "I used to have one of these, but they messed with my hearing. Maybe I should take up horses."

"Or put mufflers on your engine. Are you carrying weapons?" Unfastening the Velcro of his sling so he had two hands free, Keegan put the engine in gear.

"Staff and knife, as always. You expecting trouble? Because I'm not much of a fighter," Harvey shouted over the roar.

"Just being prepared." Keegan had learned to travel armed, but his weapons were close range too.

Once they drove off-road, Harvey directed him to a different path, one that didn't require traipsing across the valley. Keegan turned the ATV off behind the protection of a stack of boulders.

"You know this country pretty well?" Keegan hated suspecting everyone, but he no longer trusted his instincts.

"Spent the summers here with my granddad." Harvey adjusted his backpack and took the lead. "I've spent the last year or so relearning the old paths. This one would have been more accessible from the commune if Gump hadn't blown up Boulder Rock."

Keegan had heard the story of the mad land developer who'd rearranged the commune with explosives and nearly killed a lot of people. He had to wonder if *evil* wasn't in the water. "Do you think Samantha and her aunt will sell the land now that Daisy isn't living there?"

Harvey shrugged. "It's not as if they're receiving offers. Kurt had plans for it back when he thought the family trust owned it, but he doesn't have the cash to buy it on his own."

With a surprised whistle, Harvey abruptly halted. Keegan side-stepped him to look down the hillside.

Half hidden by a throne of boulders below was Val, long black veil rustling in the meager breeze.

"At least she's not moaning," Harvey muttered.

"Is she sane?"

"Sometimes. Let's see what surprise she has for us today."

Before Harvey could push past him, Keegan noted the book in Val's lap—a slender volume, faded black with crumbling binding. He recognized a family journal instantly.

TWENTY-THREE

The journalists were back, making bets on who could identify all the mural portraits, while asking questions about Thompson's death.

Not wanting to be noticed, Mariah removed her apron and slipped through the kitchen. "Sorry to desert you, Dinah, but the crowd is slowing down."

"I been handling that café for years before you got here," Dinah assured her. "Most of them out there now just want coffee. You go on and do what you need to do."

Sam followed her back, taking off her apron. "Teddy says Kurt has finished stripping the mural in the ice cream parlor. Let's check it out."

Mariah couldn't quite comprehend the suit-and-tie resort owner descending to the filthy work of stripping paint. Now that she knew Keegan wasn't a Null, she had to return the Null-of-all-Nulls prize to Kurt. She wasn't convinced he'd chosen to uncover the exuberantly cheerful mural just for Teddy. She had a notion he was flipping off his controlling mother in the process. Carmen certainly had been scarce in town since Kurt had moved out of the lodge and in with Teddy.

Teddy and Kurt were in the ice cream parlor, cleaning the mural that covered the entire back wall. To Mariah's surprise, so was Susannah, Sam's mother. The older woman was wiping away a surreptitious tear when they entered. Sam immediately crossed the room to hug her. Sam had grown up with loving parents and knew how to do that sort of thing.

Mariah didn't, so she stuck with what she knew. "Wow, that's some high-end graffiti." She admired the colorful rainbow adorned by a VW van, unicorns, dashing knights, and assorted figures apparently costumed as the artists thought of themselves. Lars Ingersson and his wife had been identified as the long-haired van driver and passenger. A very young Lance and Valdis on a unicorn followed the van at the center of the rainbow. Mariah studied the newly uncovered prone figure in a loose linen suit at the end of the rainbow holding a flower in his hand with a look of bliss on his face—the one apparently causing Susannah to cry. "That's one happy camper."

"That's Zachary, Samantha's dad," Susannah said, retreating to one of the small tables.

Stunned, Samantha choked and stared.

Mariah knew Sam had been adopted and knew next to nothing of her father, except that Cass had raised him. Apparently undemonstrative Cass hadn't thought to give Sam photos.

Finally unfreezing, Sam glanced at her mother, then circled behind the ice cream counter for a better look. "Was he tall, like me? We don't look much alike."

"He had your wavy hair and blue eyes, and yes, he was over six feet tall." Susannah produced a Kleenex. "I'd heard that wall had been painted over and thought I might be safe returning here without churning up too many memories. I'd not expected to find a daughter and see your father again."

Mariah exchanged glances with Teddy. How did they handle this? Susannah looked devastated. Sam was enthralled. Kurt was looking a little shaky as well. He'd only been acting in defiance and couldn't have expected any of this.

"Drinks all around?" Mariah whispered.

"I wish." Kurt leaned over the counter and ordered coffee for everyone while the poor clerk watched them in puzzlement.

Sam returned to her mother's table to sit down. "Why? I've been trying not to ask, but why did you give me up?"

Susannah dabbed at her face with the Kleenex. "That image is one of the many reasons. I painted it before we married. He's wearing his wedding suit. He always wore jeans and shorts but for that one day, he dressed up for me. The next time I saw him wearing it was in his casket. That was the only time your father ever looked peaceful."

Mariah bit her finger rather than speak out. The image did look particularly blissed out. Zachary had been an addict, she remembered. He'd died of an overdose.

Sam looked shaken but still puzzled. "That portrait is as good as any of the others on there. You're a talented artist. I don't understand. . ."

Susannah spoke bitterly. "I painted that portrait *years* before we married. Zach never looked peaceful, not even on our wedding day. He was always on edge, hyper. He'd play his electric guitar all night, working off that energy. Even on drugs, he couldn't sit still. I have no idea what made me paint it. I was probably only sixteen at the time, cocky with my talent and new love. He got a kick out of it, so maybe he bought the suit to match the painting, I don't know. But that isn't Zach on our wedding day. That's Zach at his funeral."

Mariah winced. Sam looked stunned.

"You painted your future husband at his funeral?" Sam finally asked. "A prescient painting, like Lucinda's?"

Susannah wiped fiercely at her face and straightened her shoulders. "I don't know. I don't want to find out. I quit painting after the funeral. My parents were dead. The farm was in default. I figured I was cracking up. Hillvale was cursed as far as I could tell. The Moons desperately wanted a baby. They were the most stable, sane people I knew. They were established teachers and artists, with a good income, so if you inherited the talent, they could guide you better than I could. And they promised to raise you somewhere so benign that you'd never have to suffer the horrors I did. And from what you've told me, they gave you the childhood you needed."

Sam leaned over to hug her mother. "They gave me a perfect child-hood. I never really wondered about my birth parents until Jade and Wolf died. I'm sure you did the right thing. But I don't understand. . . why would you give up painting?"

"What if I painted *your* death?" Susannah cried. "Or even Cass's? Lucinda painted pretty pictures. I painted *dead people!*"

Mariah sipped the coffee Kurt handed her and waited for someone else to state the obvious. When no one did, she thought maybe only people who dealt with the remains of dead people on a regular basis would understand.

She cleared her throat. "You painted a happy person," she pointed out. "You show that Sam's dad achieved the peace he never knew on this plane. From my point of view, that's not a bad thing." She bit her tongue on finishing with *if you'd painted him as a tortured soul. . .*

Both blond women turned to study the image again. But believing Susannah had painted Zach's soul in a better place was too far-fetched for either of them to comment. Mariah would have to think it on her own.

"Basically, it's a very happy, upbeat mural," Teddy said. "It makes me feel good looking at it. The Ingerssons look a little manic maybe, but there are no red eyes in the bunch."

"It was never meant to be serious, so they didn't use the crystal paints." Susannah smiled weakly. "Lance had the most awful crush on Val, but she was young and had her heart set on the stage. And then we lost everything, and it all just fell apart. There were rumors and accusations between my family and his, and it was all awful. Val ran off to the city. When Carl offered to send me to work in his uncle's South Pacific travel business, I grabbed the chance. It was like starting life all over, and it was what I needed. I'm sorry, Sam." She squeezed her daughter's hand.

"You were younger than all of those people up there," Sam said. "You deserved a chance. I remember Jade buying me books by a Susan Menendez. I had no idea that was you. They were lovely lessons for a child in handling uncertainty in a chaotic world—except mine wasn't chaotic, so I probably didn't properly appreciate them. You didn't do those wonderful illustrations?"

Susannah shook her head. "I did some brief sketches and let the editors find the illustrator. I haven't touched a paint brush until I came here."

"How did you know the Menendez family?" Mariah asked, ready to drag the conversation to less sensitive ground. "They're not in any of these murals. They don't live here. There was never any family homestead on their land."

"They live down the mountain mostly. I knew the younger ones from high school. Carl was already graduated from college when he sent me to his extended family. They used to grow grapes up there, until the water dried up. They still think of this area as home." Susannah looked a little more composed as she squeezed Sam's hand. "I have to go back to our island. I never meant to stay this long. We just popped over to say hi to Carl's family and bring those paintings. I'm so glad I had this chance to see you!"

That was a conversation she didn't want to hear. Mariah saluted them with her paper coffee cup and left.

Long distance families just didn't work. Keegan would have to return to his. She'd have to learn to enjoy the sex while she had it and not bother becoming any more involved.

She'd always been a free spirit. She would manage somehow. The tears in her eyes were just left over from Susannah's tragic story.

"You were supposed to come alone," Valdis whispered, hiding the black book in her long veil. "No one should know who has the book."

"That can be arranged." Keegan held up his hand to Harvey, halting him in his tracks. "Step back, old boy. Private conversation required."

"I'll take the goat path over there and head on down then." Harvey saluted with his staff and ambled off in a different direction.

Even when Harvey was out of sight, the black-garbed crone sat stiffly, hiding the journal. "I don't know if I'm doing the right thing. You said the books belonged in your library."

"Malcolm journals do. I don't know if that's what you have." He was almost certain it was, but he bolted down his excitement.

"Lucinda wasn't really a Malcolm," Val said, looking into the distance. "She just called herself that to protect her family."

"None of us are really Malcolms any longer. Names are irrelevant. Blood lines are what counts, and Lucinda's family is a direct descendant from the original Malcolms. I'm not sure why any of them would have removed a journal from the library, though. It's regarded as dangerous to do so." Rather than tower over the older woman, Keegan leaned back on a shorter boulder and waited, hiding his impatience. If she meant to hand him what he wanted, she deserved his attention.

"I had wondered." She produced the volume again, rubbing her hand over the faded leather. "I think, perhaps, the book is jinxed."

Her hands were not those of an old woman, and he remembered she was Sam's aunt, not old. The spooky drapery just made her seem ancient.

"I've not had experience with journals that have escaped the library. I can't imagine my ancestors deliberately jinxing the journals, though. Still, my family is pretty spooky. Things happen that we can't always explain." Like turning rocks to diamonds, he thought grimly.

She nodded. "Daisy didn't want it to ever see the light of day again, but I don't think I can protect it as she did. If you can return it to where it belongs, I will sleep easier."

Finally, she lifted the book and handed it over. Breathing deeply, Keegan clasped the slender volume in his large mitt. "Thank you. I hope you don't believe Daisy died because of this book."

He wanted to flip it open right then and there, but he slid it into an inside pocket of his hiking vest, one beneath his sling, completely concealing it even when the sling wasn't fastened.

"Daisy knew she would die, and she was ready. She tried to protect all of us before she left. She was always the heart of this land. I'm hoping Mariah will stay to take her place. Daisy believed she would."

Keegan gritted his molars, fearing this was a warning. He'd been vaguely considering ways of returning Mariah to the world of travel he lived in, but if she was needed here. . . "Why Mariah?"

"This land once belonged to her people. Mariah's ancestors lay beneath this ground, enslaved by missionaries, slaughtered by settlers. Her clan was a peaceful one. They had mystics long before your Malcolms did. Daisy was descended from them as well."

"How much of this does Mariah know?" Keegan asked out of curiosity.

"I can't say how much her grandmother told her. We've left her to find her own way, hoping she'd fly back when she was ready. And she did. That's enough, for now. With Daisy's departure, she's all we have left."

Ah, Keegan got it. She was giving him the book in hopes he'd go home and leave Mariah behind. He ought to. He needed to. He just wasn't ready.

"Do you really think Mariah should be condemned to the life that Daisy lived?" he asked. "Shouldn't she be free to fly as she wishes?"

Val clasped her hands in her lap. "What will be, will be."

"That's a hell of an attitude. What will be is what we make it be. I thank you for the return of the book. If there's anything I can do for you, I will be happy to do so. But I will not hold Mariah back from whatever she wants. She deserves our respect." He stomped off before he said anything worse.

He'd never had a volatile disposition until he'd met Mariah. She was ripping off his armor, and he didn't like it—but he had to admit that he was feeling more fully alive than he had in years.

Harvey was scanning the cavern's wall when Keegan arrived. "I didn't hear any wailing, so I assume our resident death goddess wasn't telling you the limits of your mortality?"

"No, she was trying to persuade me to make Mariah stay here, as if I had anything to say about it." Keegan headed straight for the narrow back of the crevasse where he'd found the most promising quartz earlier.

"The old ladies have a habit of being right, or at least, getting what they want. So be careful." Harvey tapped the crystal head of his staff along the wall as he followed Keegan.

"We have that at home. Women worry. It's what they do." Keegan stepped back and let Harvey proceed along the wall that had caught his interest.

Harvey halted in the same place Keegan had. "There's a streak of energy, right along here, isn't there?" He traced his staff along a line parallel to the ground.

"I don't sense energy the way you do, but the molecular structure through there is irregular. It's almost as if. . ." Keegan ran his hand along the broad line of vibrating crystals. "It's almost as if they're waiting for me to tell them what I want them to be. And that's just crazy."

"Can you use that little pick in your belt to pry out a few stones? Is there some way to compare them with the crystals we already have?"

"Normally, yes. With these. . . Do we want to chance a mountain tumbling on our heads? This is about where I felt as if I were putting my hand through a wall." Keegan warily pressed one hand against the long streak. Perhaps using both hands last time had caused the anomaly. Malleable, he concluded.

"The energy feels stable and neutral to me," Harvey reported. "Over by the lodge, there are whole fields of negative vibrations. This. . . seems benign. Not that I'm any expert, mind you. I never felt vibrations until I came to Hillvale."

"What brought you to Hillvale?" Keegan didn't really care. He just wanted to keep Harvey talking while he assessed the situation. The streak ran deeper into the mountain, but he was losing his sense of direction as he squeezed down the narrow crevasse.

"Back in the sixties, my grandfather used to live on the commune. His family owned land up here. The family tales say that the crystals are supposed to help us access our talents, so I came looking for someone to help me understand the ones I inherited."

"Only to find everyone else as puzzled as you," Keegan said. "I'm starting to recognize that feeling."

"Yeah, well, I'm thinking the crystals are what you make of them, but that's a bit hard to prove. Do you think they pried crystals from this cave?"

"Some of them, not all. I suspect the original stash came from my family, centuries ago. If they stayed with someone who has my ability, that person may have been looking for more like them. I have no way of determining if any that you or Teddy own are the originals or if they were created here or purchased elsewhere. A crystal is a crystal. The origins might be detected if they contain certain types of flaws, but my knowledge is limited." Keegan gestured at the *malleable* wall. "Find me the most stable area you can, and I'll risk prying loose some stones. Maybe if I don't touch them, they'll stay solid."

"I can't tell that any are more stable than others. I'd probably avoid anything that looked red and go for the blues but it's hard to see color here." Harvey ran a flashlight beam further into the crevasse. "It glitters, that's all I can say."

"All right, I have my sample boxes and markers. Let's do it this way —I'll take a sample about every ten inches along this streak." Keegan swung his pick, removed a fist-sized chunk, placed it in a box, marked it, and put a corresponding mark on the wall. "You keep track of the samples like this as I go."

They worked their way inward until they reached a narrow wedge neither of them could ease through and Keegan's bad arm ached like hell.

"I think we have enough samples for now," Keegan decided. Besides, the book was burning a hole in his vest. If this was Lucinda's compendium, it hadn't been in the family library for decades, maybe longer. It wasn't the one Bri had taken and wouldn't unlock the key to his father's innocence, but it might take him one step closer.

Keegan led the way to the opening, carrying a considerably heavier backpack. When a shadow blocked the exit, Keegan stepped in front of Harvey, shielding the slighter man with his bulk.

"Who gave you permission to take from my land?" a menacing voice asked.

TWENTY-FOUR

"Keegan told me to hide his computer," Aaron called from his desk in the antique store as Mariah entered.

Shit. Feeling useless and without anchor, she stopped at a display of the pottery Teddy's family had collected. "I just want as complete a list of people who lived at the commune as I can put together. I don't suppose any of your books has that?" She gestured at the shelves lining the walls. This was an antique store, but Aaron's real passion was books.

"No one has that." He set down an ornate silver urn he'd been polishing. "I can't imagine it can be googled either. It wasn't as if they kept records. How would a list help?"

Mariah grimaced, forced to put instincts into words. "Daisy was part of the original commune. Thompson's family was a more recent part of the commune. He tried to break into Daisy's vault for a reason, and now he's dead. We know the people with red eyes in the portraits often turn out to be criminals. It seems to make some weird sense that it all goes back to the commune."

"I thought Daisy's sketch vaguely resembled Keegan's relation. Go ask the reporters about Trevor Gabriel. Journalists love a good scam artist. Let them do your research." Aaron put down the urn, crossed his arms, and leaned back against a wall of drawers.

Mariah figured his position concealed Keegan's computer. She had been hoping if she didn't delve too far, she could handle a quick internet search, as she'd done in looking up Trevor's image. It wasn't as if she hadn't worked with computers for years before going off the ledge. But she wasn't explaining her limitations to Aaron. "I'm not hanging out with journalists. And focusing all suspicion on one person is bad policy. Don't you ever watch TV mysteries?"

"No, I don't. And you still can't have the computer. I don't know what it is with you and computers, but you have no right to invade other people's property."

She shouldn't. Like an addict, she knew she shouldn't. But she was restless and uneasy, and touching stones and talking to ghosts didn't work for her. Computers were all she had.

"You should have gone with Keegan," she said, roaming Aaron's shop, hoping for inspiration. "You could have felt the rocks, tried to understand what happened there."

"I did that," he said. "The killer didn't touch anything. Only Thompson left fresh impressions. And after everyone stomped through that area yesterday, there isn't a chance of my finding anything coherent. You might as well ask Cass to reach beyond the veil and talk to Daisy."

"Daisy was pure essence," Mariah said with certainty. "She moved on very quickly. She's with us in an incorporeal sense, but you'll not pry any more out of her in that state than you did in a corporeal one. It's hard to explain."

"But makes sense, in its own way. My mother used to call the mentally challenged the Blessed and the Innocent." Aaron returned to his polishing.

"Like evil and sin exists only in functional brains. I can buy that. It's hard for the mentally incapacitated to plan two murders, much less carry them out and not get caught." Mariah debated how much she dared say. Keegan needed to go home and help his family. She needed to crucify Daisy's murderer. Something had to give. It might as well be her.

"You can hold the keyboard, and I can just tell you how to search," she suggested. "I don't employ the usual browsers. I write programs for a living. I know how to work from inside your operating system."

Maybe if she did it this way, without touching the computer herself, she could stick to the straight and narrow and not be tempted down the rabbit hole. Maybe.

Aaron looked suspicious. "Do I need to call Walker?"

She waved a dismissive hand. "If you control the keyboard, I can't do anything dangerous. You want to find Daisy's killer, don't you?"

"Damned right, I do. But I also want to nail the creep who made that fake pottery, jeopardized our exhibition, and swindled Teddy's generous parents. I want a lot of things. That doesn't mean I'll do anything illegal to get them."

"I thought we'd decided Lonnie Thompson created the fraudulent pieces? Are these the ones Keegan said were fakes?" She circled back to the table of colorful, ugly ceramics. "I can check Lonnie's invoices, sales, and trace the ceramics he sold," she suggested, like an alcoholic promising only one little drink. "If you have some way of proving they're fakes, you can help the police nail them."

He finally looked interested. "I tried to persuade the sheriff to do that, but they're understaffed. He's more interested in nailing Lonnie Thompson for murdering his wife."

"He has a point. He doesn't care about rich fools buying fraudulent junk. But Lonnie is a fairly simple search compared to locating commune members. There were no computers, no records, back then. It will take researching every newspaper reference to every well known member, hoping for additional names and contacts. And then tracking families. Now that I think about it, I should probably take a chill pill and go home and sleep on it."

She really needed her hands on the computer for her inner hawk to flit down the electronic byways. She couldn't tell that to Aaron.

The door rattled and a customer entered, distracting Aaron from any reply. While he turned his attention to the newcomer, Mariah eyed the drawer he'd been guarding.

Why hunt for Keegan's computer when Aaron's was sitting there open, just waiting to be used? She inched in the direction of his desk, hearing the siren call of electrons whizzing over invisible airwaves. All she had to do was capture just one. . .

"Say, don't I know you from somewhere?" a woman's voice asked from the front of the store.

Mariah froze. She had no reason to believe the question was for her, but every reason to fear that it was. She eased toward the exit in back, hoping—

Aaron's voice murmured something reassuring. The woman insisted, "No, no, I'm certain. If you'll just excuse me. . . Miss de Cervantes?"

Behind Mariah, furniture scraped the old floor as the woman pushed past Aaron. Without need of more warning, Mariah bolted out the back.

She slipped past delivery entrances, passing the café, finally reaching the safety of Teddy's fenced backyard at the end of town. She only needed to cross the highway to run up the lane to her cottage—but she didn't want to lead anyone to her lair.

Inside the fencing, Syd's kids were chattering. *Teddy would have a computer.*

With any luck, Teddy should be in the shop at this time of day. Hoping for the best, Mariah shimmied up the pine tree leaning over the fence and dropped in on a tea party. The kids looked up expectantly from their plastic plates on a rotten stump. The furry monster they called a dog flapped his tail.

Breathing easier, Mariah added the granola bar from her pocket to the kids' feast and entered through the kitchen door, calling a greeting as she did.

The sooner she solved these murders, the faster the journalists would leave town—if they didn't think they had an even juicier story. If anyone discovered who she really was. . . The pain of losing all her hard-won friends and her only home would be too excruciating to bear.

"Who are we avoiding today?" Teddy called cheerfully from the front room.

The shop was blissfully empty of customers as Mariah passed the once-haunted stairs to enter the front room. "Damned journalists are everywhere. We need to solve murders so they'll all go home."

"I don't want them to go home!" Teddy held up one of her new creations—a brilliant sapphire bracelet. "They like mentioning that *famed jewelry artist Theodosia Devine has recently opened a shop in the trendy up-and-coming artist community of Hillvale.* They have a way with words, don't they? Business is building nicely."

Of course. The whole point of the weekend art walk was to attract media attention. Mariah scowled. "Then I may need to take a hike. My fame isn't salable, except maybe on the black market."

"Do tell," Teddy insisted, gesturing at a chair. "I'll fix coffee."

"What you don't know, can't hurt you." Mariah gestured at the open laptop behind Teddy's desk. "May I borrow your computer?"

"Chief Walker said you weren't allowed to touch them," Teddy said warily. "How much trouble will I be in?"

"Kurt won't let Walker yell at you. I want to start a search on commune members who knew Daisy. People have already identified three more of the mural disciples. I know it's an insane approach, but it's all I've got."

Teddy grimaced. "Anything to do with computers is insane. Can you fix my malfunctioning website while you're in there?"

Mariah beamed. "In the blink of an electron."

KEEGAN LET HIS EYES ADJUST TO THE SUNSHINE OUTSIDE THE CREVASSE. HE already had his hand on his knife, but he didn't have any need to use it if the other man wasn't armed.

The shadow blocking the entrance was shorter than he was, but stocky enough to have muscle. Given that Keegan had one injured arm, it would be a fair-enough fight.

"We have the sheriff's permission to search for evidence," he said slowly. "We were told he had the landowner's consent. Who are you?"

"This land does not belong to any one man," the shadow insisted with a growl. "You do not have *my* permission."

Harvey leaned around Keegan. "Hector? What the hell are you doing here?"

Keegan rolled his eyes. Identifying a potential killer was a certain path to the graveyard.

"Harvey? That you, son? What the hell are you doing back here risking your precious fingers?" The shadow stepped aside to let them pass.

"Don't give me that *son* business, and I'm not risking anything." Harvey stepped out from behind Keegan to pound the muscular older man on the back. "I thought you were in Montana."

"The family is having a powwow in Monterey. Why are you not

there?" The short man called Hector grabbed tall Harvey in a rough embrace. "Your *abuela* misses you."

Harvey twisted free. "They miss free concerts," he scoffed. "Keegan, this is my uncle, Hector Menendez. Hector, Keegan is a geologist helping the sheriff solve the murder up here."

Harvey was a Menendez? Keegan needed more time to process the knowledge, but when Hector stuck out his hand, Keegan had no choice but to shake it.

"I heard about that—one of the old communists got shot, right? Good riddance to the lot of them." Hector's grip was tough.

Keegan's was tougher. The shorter man broke first. Keegan generally disliked physical one-upmanship, but he could play as well as anyone.

"Not communists," Harvey said in scorn. "It's that kind of thick-headed ignorance that holds us back."

"It's lack of respect for your elders that holds you back," Hector retorted. "I went to college. I know what a communist is—doomed, just as those rich farts were. So how is a pianist helping a geologist?"

A pianist? Keegan glanced at Harvey's long, slender fingers and realized why the musician had said he wasn't a fighter. But what was he doing in Hillvale, where no piano existed?

"I'm just a guide," Harvey said dismissively, not mentioning his crystal affinity. "And a mule." He gestured at his back pack. "How did you get in here?"

Hector shrugged. "Horse. Borrowed from the resort stable. The north path is still sound. How can rocks solve a murder?"

Keegan figured this was where he stepped in with fabrication. "We're looking for bullet holes and hoping to discover a reason for Thompson and the killer to be down here."

Hector screwed up his broad brown visage until it wrinkled even more. "The hippies used to come down here, I'm told, probably prospecting. That's what everyone seeks—gold."

"The geology is all wrong for gold," Keegan said truthfully. "There are some trace minerals but not enough to mine."

"Good to know. I'll relay that to the family. They're hoping to decide this week whether to sell the land or keep it." Hector started walking toward a sturdy palomino cropping dried grass. "Harry, you come down, kiss your *abuela*. You would be nothing without her."

Harvey waved him off while muttering curses under his breath.

"*Abuela?*" Keegan asked. "You are avoiding your grandmother?"

"I am avoiding the whole damned family. Listen, don't let anyone know I'm related. The speculation about that freaking land is rampant enough and has nothing to do with me. I'm too far down the totem pole." Harvey started up the path to the ridge and the ATV.

"Isn't Sam's mother married to one of your family?" Keegan tried to piece the family puzzle, but it was impossible. "Or is that a different Menendez?"

"We're all related, one way or another. We're a huge clan, and we keep up with each other. The way the deed is set up, we all own infinitesimally small portions, not enough to be looking at dollar signs if we sold. Carl probably flew in because Numero Uno is feeling sickly and wanted a reunion before he dies. Hector usually lives in Sacramento, when he's not at his ranch in Montana, so it's not far for him. I try not to live anywhere they can find me."

"I'm starting to suspect this town is full of people who don't want to be found." Or seen—which niggled an idea at the back of Keegan's brain.

"No cell phone reception is an excellent start," Harvey agreed, hauling his heavy pack up the steep path without breathing hard. "No one lives here who might know you from elsewhere. It's kind of freeing."

"I can see that. But as annoying as my family can be, I never had any desire to hide from them." The conversation prevented Keegan from dredging up the thought nudging him. Harvey's secrets might be more important.

Harvey grunted. "I get that. My family worked hard to give me an education, but I paid them back. I just want to know who I *am* without them telling me who I *should* be."

"I would say that sounds like a sulky teenager, but as you say, I get it. In Hillvale, you don't have to be a pianist, and I don't have to be a miner. The slate is clean, without expectations. We can make different choices."

"Yeah, exactly. I can write songs all night and not have to perform if I'm not in the mood. I can carve walking sticks and not worry about my highly-insured fingers. We can find food and shelter in trade for our talents without Mammon breathing down our collars."

They threw their packs in the ATV carrier, swigged water, and rode back to town, comfortable with their own separate thoughts.

Keegan had always assumed he would work for his family's mining business. It was the only thing he knew how to do, and he did it well. Unlike Harvey, he wasn't giving up a good career to find himself. He was hunting for information to help his family. Back home, they needed lawyers and accountants, not him.

But this break in routine did leave him feeling the call of the wild, so to speak. Unhampered by specific obligations, he could explore *himself*, as he'd never done as a youth. Interesting.

Even more interesting—when they reached Hillvale, they discovered *CLOSED* signs on half the businesses.

"What now?" Harvey muttered, heaving his pack out of the ATV and watching the confused, milling tourists on the boardwalk and parking lot.

"Café's still open. Let's start there." Besides, Keegan hoped that's where Mariah would be. He needed to bounce a few ideas off her, get her feedback. She had a way of making him focus on angles he wouldn't see on his own.

"Your rocks?" Harvey glanced at the antique store. "Looks like even Aaron shut down."

"I have a key. We'll drop these off. We probably ought to shower but. . ." Keegan glanced at the unopened shops.

"Armageddon might be at hand?" Harvey suggested.

Which instantly returned Keegan's thoughts to Mariah. Whatever was happening, she was either behind it or on top of it. He felt it in his bones.

"Better go in the back," Keegan warned as they approached Aaron's and potential customers watched them expectantly.

They bypassed disappointed faces to go down the alley and drop the packs off in the storeroom. They jogged back toward the boardwalk, but the side door for the meeting house gallery was open. Inside, people milled about, studying the artwork under Lance's nervous supervision.

Harvey hesitated. "Maybe I should stay here, help look after the valuables."

The triptych alone was priceless. They weren't displaying the more expensive ceramics, but Keegan had no idea of the worth of the oil paintings. Glancing at the crowd, he nodded. "Good thought. I'll send someone back with food and help."

As he eased past the crowd toward the café, he tried to discern some commonality between the closed shops, but nothing in Hillvale was similar except basic utilities, and everyone seemed to have electricity. The boardwalk wasn't on fire. Those were the only elements he could imagine the closed shops shared.

Inside the café, it was business as usual for the lunch rush, except it was midafternoon. Standing room only at this hour—

Mariah wasn't at the register. Sam was there, looking harassed and worried. Her mother, and even Dinah, were waiting tables.

Where was Mariah?

TWENTY-FIVE

JULY 12: THURSDAY, AFTERNOON

Mariah had her hands on the keyboard and her essence spinning down the wormholes she'd programmed into the operating system. Each time she hit a node of information, she spun off more electrons to follow all the bunny trails.

She drew more energy, and her focus thinned as she dived deeper. Spirals of light grew fainter, faster, stretching the mental connection to the point of pain as she struggled to hold the shreds together. With bytes of her tunneling through decades of material, any attempt to pull back now—

A door banged in the distance, and she startled. Electrons crashed, spun, and slammed together.

A male voice shouted—and she collapsed into the Void.

"WHAT THE DEVIL DID YE THINK YE WERE ABOOT, WOMAN?" KEEGAN shouted as he entered the jewelry shop to the sight of Mariah, pale and stiff as a robot at the keyboard.

He addressed his ire at a mesmerized Teddy, but it was Mariah who toppled.

He winced as he caught her weight on his bad arm, but he'd dumped the sling while driving the ATV and had both hands free.

Mariah's lids fluttered. She breathed, faintly. But Keegan could swear she was as near to death as it was possible to be. Terrified, he lifted her and clutched her close, wondering if mouth-to-mouth resuscitation would help return her mind to her body. Because he was sure that's what she'd done—sent her mind winging elsewhere. Again.

Petite Teddy shook off her daze and rubbed her eyes. "I've never seen anything—" She glanced at Mariah's limp form in Keegan's arms and blanched. "Take her upstairs. I'll fetch Brenda."

Heart in throat, Keegan carried Mariah up the stairs. The jeweler's shop had sported a CLOSED sign like all the others, so maybe Teddy's sister had taken her children somewhere safe.

Safe—from whatever in hell Mariah had been doing? Or maybe that had been Zoe de Cervantes at the keyboard, computer hacker bar none.

He shivered, wondering what damage she may have caused this time. Her last episode had exploded his life and that of thousands of others.

Whoever he was holding, the woman in his arms was not the vibrant woman who'd been in his bed. She was as cold and lifeless as a piece of machinery, and she was scaring the crap out of him. He was new to this emotion thing and didn't know how to handle panic.

Laying her on a bed in the room not cluttered with toys, Keegan rubbed her wrist, hoping to increase her pulse. Would CPR help? He didn't want to break her rib cage. He leaned over and pressed gently, feeling the beat of her heart beneath his palm.

Come on, Mariah! he whispered inside his head. Don't you dare die!

He was a world traveler, but he'd never met a woman as fascinating as Mariah. He hadn't had a chance to know her the way she deserved to be known. He needed more time. . .

Deep breath, don't cock up this time. It had taken her a while to recuperate each time she'd used her mind to reach Cass. She had ordered him to tell stories while she recovered—just as he'd asked her to do to distract from pain. So maybe she was in there, and maybe like someone in a coma, needed to hear a voice to find her way out?

Hoping and praying he was doing the right thing, he removed the coveted journal from his pocket and donned his glasses. If anything would catch her interest, this should. "I have the journal, Mariah," he whispered. "Listen, the frontispiece says—'*This is the Compendium of Ian Macleod Dougal, dated this year of Our Lord, 1758.*'"

Did her breath come just a little faster?

"*For future generations, I hereby list the Nature of Stones as I have discovered them in my travels, in hopes that my descendants will continue with my endeavors.*"

Keegan glared at the page in the poor lighting. "His penmanship is atrocious. We may need a handwriting analyst."

Mariah's fingers moved—in impatience?

He wrapped her hand in his and struggled on with the reading. It was the most boring tripe in the world, but he had to admit that the case studies were painstakingly annotated.

He'd only reached the fourth page of excruciatingly concise script before he heard footsteps rushing up the stairs. He hastily shoved the book back in his pocket.

The first one through the door was the small older woman who had treated his shoulder—Brenda, the retired nurse.

"She's coming around, I think," Keegan told her, wanting to believe his own words. "She overexerts herself." That was the simplest explanation he could offer.

Teddy followed after, along with Amber, who remained in the doorway, anxiously twisting her rings and bracelets.

"I didn't know. . ." Teddy whispered in apology. "She said she would fix my website!"

Brenda took Mariah's pulse, checked under her eyelids, listened to her heart beat, then shook her head. "She's alive. If I had an office—" She cut herself off. "She could use electrolytes, but I don't have an IV. We either need to move her to the ER or hope she recovers on her own."

"It is not wise to take her to a hospital," Keegan said, suspecting who Mariah really was. "May I take her home? She responds to being read to."

Brenda placed her palms on either side of Mariah's head, hummed thoughtfully, then nodded in reluctance. "Given time and enough energy, our bodies are capable of regenerating what they need without the benefit of modern medicine. But if she does not wake to take liquids in an hour, we'll need to move her down the mountain."

"I'll have Kurt send for an IV," Teddy said, sounding desperate.

"You need Kurt to give Brenda an office," Amber corrected. "She can't practice medicine out of a suitcase. I think there are laws."

Brenda smiled ruefully and got up from the bed. "And the laws don't exactly cover what we need. Take her to the hospital if she doesn't wake in an hour."

"Thank you," Keegan said, although he wasn't entirely certain for what he was grateful—reassurance, maybe. "I will see that she's taken care of."

Brenda took a quick look at the bandage on his shoulder, pressed a hand there that should have hurt and didn't, and nodded. "Healing well, excellent." His shoulder felt warm where she'd touched it, the pain gone from his recent exertions.

Mariah's hand twitched in his. *Come back now, you damn fool woman!* he shouted in his head. But she wasn't in there to hear him.

When Brenda and Amber had departed, Keegan glanced at the red-headed jeweler. "What did you mean, she was to fix your website? She's not supposed to touch computers."

Teddy ran her hands through her thick hair. "She said it would only take a minute! Did you know she shut down every computer in town? I had no idea anyone could do that. We were only working for a few minutes!"

Well, that explained the closed shops, although he thought *a few minutes* might be a serious understatement. "How can you know Mariah did that? I found you sitting right there with her, as stoned looking as she was."

Teddy paced nervously. "Yeah, that was weird, like being hypnotized while watching all that information spin past. But the rest is simple deduction. When I found Brenda in the café, Amber rushed in to say her computer was working again. I didn't even know she had one. Why does a tarot reader need a computer?"

Keegan shook his head. Teddy was talking in circles. He shifted Mariah into his arms again. Oddly, the pain didn't return. So, yes, it seemed Brenda was another Lucy, one with a healing talent. "So you think Mariah did something to shut down the internet, and when I interrupted, she somehow set it free again?"

"Put like that. . ." Teddy grimaced. "It doesn't make much sense. But playing with a computer shouldn't make anyone catatonic either."

"Maybe she's like a faulty wire that blows a fuse," he suggested.

"I've heard of people who fry electronics, but my *computer* was still working. Mariah was the one who fried," Teddy protested, leading the way down the narrow dark stairs.

Gritting his teeth against fear, Keegan carried Mariah across the narrow two-lane highway and up the deserted path to her bungalow. With difficulty, he fished her key ring from her belt. It was awkward, but he got the door open.

She stirred as he carried her back to the bed they'd left surely a hundred hours ago.

She snuggled into her pillow as if conscious that she was home. He ought to let her sleep, but the nurse had seemed to think hydration was important. Besides, he was too agitated to sit idle. The book was boring as hell, but he had to read it, and if it helped wake Mariah—even better. He pulled out his glasses again.

Sitting on the bed beside her, he watched her eyelids for movement while reading through descriptions of each stone in his ancestor's collection. The nomenclature Dougal used wasn't exactly the names currently in use, but as he read, Keegan began to discern which was what. Mariah's bedroom had bright LED bulbs, so the writing was easier to discern.

He just couldn't stay focused while watching for signs of life. He thought she responded when he stroked her palm. He wasn't as certain the reading was reaching her.

Finally, unable to tolerate her stillness any longer, he tucked the precious book away, took off his glasses and boots, and sprawled beside her on the bed.

Maybe she needed the *energy* the Lucys talked about. He had energy to spare, if only he knew how to transfer it. Touching was what he did best.

He dragged her on top of him, with her cheek against his good shoulder. He situated her so she'd be comfortable, then wrapped his arms around her waist to hold her in place. "Breathe, Mariah," he whispered. "Let me know you're alive."

She wiggled and settled in more comfortably, so he had to assume she was in there somewhere.

"I can't read to you like this," he muttered, his body reacting mindlessly to her proximity. "And if you don't wake soon, I'll descend to the lowest dimensions of hell. So if you're in there, let me know."

She seemed to hum in contentment, and the fingers of one hand curled in his shirt. That would have to be signal enough, although he wasn't ready to relax with relief yet.

"I'm looking for ways of sharing my energy, acting as charger for your battery," he told her. "Let me know if I do something right."

He ran his hands down her back, massaging gently. She purred and snuggled closer. Feeling justified, he stroked her round, firm derriere. She dug her fingers deeper, groping his chest. She was in there! He continued to stroke.

Little by little, her breathing expanded and her heart rate escalated. After a while, he dared apply his mouth to hers, breathing into her lips first, until he felt them respond with a pressure that might be a kiss.

"Not exactly Snow White's breath of life, princess," he muttered. "You can do better than that."

And to his relief, she did.

～

MARIAH DRANK IN THE ESSENCE OF MOUNTAIN MAN, THE STRENGTH AND integrity and concern that was pure Keegan. She inhaled his breath, took energy from the muscular arms holding her, the strong heart pounding beneath her breasts. The kiss, when it came, was the electric spark that ignited her engine.

She was still weak, but no longer catatonic as she poured her gratitude and passion into responding to his mouth on hers. He returned the pressure with gentle reassurances, sucking lightly on her lip, planting small pecks on the corners of her mouth, devoting time and thought to her pleasure—giving instead of taking. She was almost giddy from exhilaration.

Being *savored* made her feel special, and knowing the quality of the man favoring her in this way raised far more than her spirits.

But as she gradually gathered all her spun-out electrons and restored them where they belonged, she awoke to physical pressures and all her senses—and panicked.

With effort, she pushed off him and rolled back to the mattress. "You stink. I need to pee. Where's the computer?"

The entire bed rumbled with his laughter. It went on so long and so silently that she feared he was having hysterics. If so, she didn't want to know about it. She punched his arm, kissed his bristly cheek, and ran for the bathroom.

What had she done? Did she want to know? Terrified, she hid behind closed doors while she pulled herself together. She'd had a computer. She'd dived down too many rabbit holes. She needed to stuff that information where only she could find it. How would she do that without a computer? She did *not* want to go through that again. She had nowhere left to run, and if she harmed any more innocents like Keegan. . .

By the time she returned, she was frantic. Keegan, however, was calmly rummaging in her refrigerator for her mineral water and his beer. Looking like a rumpled god, he passed her the chilled bottle and waited, crossing his arms and setting his square jaw dangerously.

She needed water before she could even begin to process any of this. She gulped at the bottle.

"*Zoe de Cervantes*, I presume?" He didn't drink but waited for her to deny it.

She hadn't used that name in so long. . . Mariah—*Zoe*—wildly sought curse words strong enough to cover this moment. He *knew*? Damn, the man was too good at adding two and two and hitting the jackpot. "You're better off not knowing," was the best response she could form. Her brain cells were just recovering.

"I like to know if I'm sleeping with the enemy." He drank from his beer, big gulps as if he were trying hard to swallow more than he could chew.

"I'm not the enemy! And if that's your attitude, you can waltz right on out of here." It nearly killed her to say that, but she had no way of telling that story easily.

She had to focus on retrieving this latest download of nuclear material. Panic didn't help focus.

He pointed his finger at her. "You busted international criminals to bring the trolls to justice. Tell me the rest was incidental."

"Very definitely incidental," she said in a desert-dry tone, mind still racing, trying to remember what she'd done *now*, not then. "But I can't stop the connections when they start happening. The criminal trolls were connected to other criminals who were connected to banks who were. . ."

"And the banks led you to my father's company." He sounded as if he accepted that. He took a normal sip of beer. "I just wanted you to be honest for a change."

Her eyes widened as she absorbed that. "The whole world *hates* me! I destroyed your family. How can you not be angry?"

He shrugged. "I've been told I'm an emotionless robot, but what's done is done. If you didn't mean to hurt my family, where's the point in erupting now?"

"You're hardly a *robot*," she protested in incredulity, but she had more urgent matters to consider than his weird voidness. "Right now, I have to track down whatever I just did and hide it before more *honesty* gets spilled around the world."

Mountain Man wore his stern face. "You'll have some difficulty prying Teddy's laptop out of her hands again. You scared us half to death."

"Not a robot then," she pointed out, taking a deep breath. "I'm sorry. It happens when I'm upset and the connections are strong. I look something up, see three more things I need to follow, and I lose it."

"You lose *yourself*," he guessed, correctly.

She gulped down half the bottle while sorting her memories. *"Teddy's website,"* she said, recovering that lost brain cell. "It's all stored there. I have to take it down before some troll finds it."

Keegan rolled his eyes and slammed his bottle on the counter. "I'll blow up every damned computer in town before I let you near one again."

"That's a strange tactic." She would mock his he-man display, but she had to concentrate. What had she dug out? How dangerous was it?

To distract from her panic, she eyed his dusty clothes. "You might want to shower before you go all macho destructive. What did you find in the cave?"

She reached in the refrigerator for some of Dinah's leftovers. She was ravenous. If the information was safely stored on a private website, it should be safe until she had replenished her energy and could think straight.

"My clothes are at my place," he said in a growling tone. "So I'll just have to stink while you tell me what the hell you thought you were doing, *Zoe*."

She winced, not certain if he was angry because she'd not given her real name or because of what she'd done to his family. One thing was certain, he was not a *robot*.

"That's a little tough to explain," she said honestly. "There are clean jeans and a shirt on the dresser. Tullah said they'd fit you. She found them on special at eBay, and I figured they might come in handy. I'll throw yours into the washer."

"Are you insane, woman, or just pretending you are so you don't have to explain?" he roared in frustration. "You can't shut down every computer in town and go catatonic for hell knows how long and then just fix lunch!"

Oh well, if that was what had him so angry. . . She considered that. "Well, yes, I can. And I am. I'm hungry. You stink. Basics. Easy. The rest. . ." She waved her hand. "Not easy, so it has to wait. And again, whoever told you that you're a robot needs a kick in the posterior."

She itched to get her hands on Teddy's website. She had a vague idea of what she had done, but she had no means of explaining it. But Keegan deserved an explanation, so she needed time to put herself back together. Her mind worked like a computer program, one line after another in logical progression until the goal was achieved. He needed to deal with it and not loom over her like a menacing cloud.

An all-encompassing cloud that had absorbed her, breathed life back into her, whose heart beat with hers. . . She wasn't certain how to fit that into life as she knew it. When she'd fallen into the Void this time, Keegan had been there to catch her. Her mind didn't do fantasy well. This did not compute, but she was immensely grateful for his presence anyway.

He stalked off, apparently afraid he'd say something he shouldn't. Keegan was like that. She ought to be, but she'd spent too many years as an automaton to react humanly now. If anyone was a robot, she was.

She'd shut down computers? Or the internet? She suspected the latter. She'd sucked up the entire band width of the cable system. She would terrify herself even more if she thought about it too hard, so she didn't.

By the time Keegan returned to her front room, Mariah had a table laid with all the leftovers Dinah had sent home with her for the last few days. It still didn't look like enough to feed a man Keegan's size plus her ravenous hunger, but it would have to suffice.

His hair was still damp and curled rakishly on his forehead. The black t-shirt and blue jeans were bland but fit way too well on his narrow hips. She had to force her gaze away while she set two more bottles on the table and took a seat. He glared and yanked out a chair for himself. Damn, but he was the smartest thing that had happened to her in forever, and he had to look good while doing it.

She chewed thoughtfully, still trying to find words. He tore at his bread as if he were ripping meat off bones. She rather enjoyed all that intense focus on her.

"Your Void may serve a purpose," she said conversationally between bites.

He waited. She couldn't decide if that was annoying or useful.

"Mostly, you're this walking black hole, but when you picked me up, you surrounded me with energy. You shielded me in that energy field until I recovered. It took me *days* in the hospital last time to pull myself together. I'm not sure how any of this works. It's not as if there are encyclopedias of the paranormal."

He finished chewing and gulped his beer before replying. "My library is an encyclopedia of the paranormal. You have only to request information on a topic and the librarian will scan whatever you need."

Mariah felt her eyebrows rise to her hairline. "Really?" Then she shook her head. "Nope, not buying that. Your library is full of ancient tomes, and computers are too new. Ancient tomes do not include computers. Even I don't understand what I do enough to write it down."

"I don't know what you do well enough to request the appropriate volumes, but I don't think you invented it. You've just found new uses for your abilities. We are not alone in the universe," he added with a touch of scorn, applying himself to his meal again.

"I suppose it is possible that we have ancestors who flew in the minds of hawks or who could use telepathy to communicate with receptive minds. Maybe they even developed a vocabulary to explain these phenomena. I haven't. What I do involves human essence—that's the only term I know."

"Not ectoplasm?" he asked, still chewing.

She frowned. "Similar, possibly, although ectoplasm seems more corporeal to me. I suppose it isn't or everyone could see it. *Essence* may be what others call the soul, but *soul* is just too spiritual and illusory for what I actually see and do and feel."

His brow drew down to form a V over his nose, but he didn't intervene while she formed her words.

"To me, all living things are connected by this essence. Daisy and all who have gone before her have merely surrendered their corporeal bodies. They are still part of the essence. Trees, flowers—they're *life* and are all there in some form. We live and breathe our ancestors. We're this great living pool of. . . molecules, atoms, electrons, *essence*. In terms of physics—energy can neither be created or destroyed, only transformed."

"You are saying that you *feel* this energy essence, that you know for fact that we are all connected in this way?"

"The same way you feel molecules, I imagine. But it's impossible to convey except in spiritual terms," she continued. "It's easier to believe in the Holy Ghost, angels watching over us, reincarnation and those who died and are waiting to be reborn. . ."

"I comprehend the theory," he said, frowning. "If there were some way of proving what you feel, it would be huge. It may take *me* a lifetime to process, and I'm aware of the difficulty of explaining the inexplicable. Others would call you insane or want to worship you. You could be another Trevor Gabriel guru. But right now, I want to know what this has to do with computers?"

"About as much as the minds of hawks," she said, grateful that he grasped why she told no one. "And more to do with my hatred for trolls."

She thought she detected a curl of amusement on his lips, but he finished off his beer instead. Good reaction.

"Every time one of the trolls asked for my help when they got stuck and didn't give me credit for doing so, I planted what I call a hydra-wormhole. After a while, it became automatic, because they never thanked me for saving their hides, time and again. They got paid the big bucks. I did the heavy work for half the salary. At the start, I got my revenge by using the wormholes for sneaking into their computers and raiding their music, then reading their emails. That was simple hacking. No big deal. I could have emptied their bank accounts, but I didn't. It was just gamesmanship. I could mess with their heads by moving files around or beat them out on projects I shouldn't know about."

"But you were establishing a pattern," he suggested, polishing his plate with the last of his bread.

"Yuppers. When the stuff began going down with Adera, I happened to be working on an operating system update. I was out to torment all trolls by then. I edited the programming so I could manually enter any computer using that O/S. My hydras were multiplying by then. I used them to hunt the information on fraud I gave to Adera. I was only exper- imenting at that point, but then Adera died, and I went a little berserk. I'd never done that before, and it's the part I can't explain except in terms of *essence*."

Keegan held up his hand, apparently asking for time to ponder her rash declaration. She was telling him things that could get her *jailed*. She wasn't certain anyone could prove she'd written any of the holes. But once it was known, they'd most certainly close them. She was practically holding her breath while she waited on Keegan's reaction.

She must have weakened her brain cells to trust a man with her future.

"So, basically, you can hack any computer with that operating system?" he asked without any condemnation, just curiosity.

Itchy with nervousness, she sat back, nursing the rest of her bottled water. "Basically, I can find a path to any computer in existence. It just takes longer if they don't use the faulty O/S. The internet has become as interconnected as human essence. It could become the soul of Artificial Intelligence."

His eyes widened as he took that in. "I'm not sure I want to know more."

"That's good, because it's too tough to explain." Which was her only saving grace. No judge in the world would believe what she did. But *she* knew, and that was worse. She prayed she hadn't unleashed another time bomb. "So just pretend I'm really fast when I hack through webs to get what I want. And let's figure out how to get my information off Teddy's website as soon as possible."

"You are not touching another computer," he said in a voice as stern as God's.

She had to accept that as one of her limitations now. Her career was shot. She didn't exactly *plan* to lose herself to a computer. It just happened.

Could she pray her *essence* had learned its lesson and not downloaded the universe this time? Or that Keegan had stopped her in time?

"I don't need to touch a keyboard," she told him. "I know Teddy's website ID and password. I can give them to you, show you where the data is stored, tell you how to back it up to an external drive. If you have a cloud drive, it would be good to back it up there as well. But once we move the information, I would appreciate being allowed to read the screen as you sort through it."

"What am I likely to find in the data?" he asked in suspicion.

Mariah crumpled her bottle. "Can't say. Essence doesn't think. It *does*. I set a goal and directives and build on them as I go, but what is swept up in the cascade of data bytes is always a crap shoot. I went after the original commune members and their friends, which meant mostly newspapers and books from that era to start with. After that, it got real fuzzy."

"All that for what?" he asked in disgust, scraping back his chair. "You could have killed yourself over nothing!"

"Daisy isn't nothing." With what dignity she could muster, she stood and gathered their dishes. "And it's not as if my life is all that valuable."

He growled, grabbed her waist, and hauled her up against him. When his mouth closed over hers, she melted into him as if they had truly become one physical entity that shared essences.

The man was downright scary.

THEODOSIA

"Are you okay? You're looking. . . not yourself. What happened here this afternoon?" Kurt poured wine and set the glass on the shop table.

Feeling like a limp noodle, Teddy was still trying to figure out what Mariah had done. She shook her head in uncertainty and continued studying her laptop.

The kids were upstairs while her sister ran errands. She couldn't go home yet. But the shop was officially closed for the evening. She pushed a cardboard UPS box in Kurt's direction. "These arrived this afternoon. Sheriff apparently doesn't need them anymore."

He peered inside. "Thalia's crystals? I don't suppose they came with a chemical analysis or anything useful?"

She shook her head again. "Walker just said they weren't needed as evidence. I need a lead box to keep them in. They emanate negative energy. No wonder Mariah and Sam freaked when the dust hit them."

Kurt frowned. "Would a safe do?"

She nodded, then shoved loosened curls from her face. "My lockbox will have to do for now. I'll just hope that along with Harvey's, they don't pollute everything else in there. These red stones are mostly almandine, but there's enough red tourmaline to be valuable."

He dragged out her lockbox, and she used her key and code to open it while Kurt looked for a plastic freezer bag to hold the rocks. They just barely fit in the remaining space. She'd be feeling rich right now if all those stones were good for jewelry. She suspected they were not, unless she meant harm.

Once the box was safely stashed, she turned the computer screen to him while she sipped her wine. "Look at this. Tell me if any of it makes sense."

"What is it?" Taking a seat, he flipped through the pages of old newspaper articles, criminal files, and other documents that had no business being in her computer. His eyebrows raised as hers had.

"Mariah, I think. That's what she dug out this afternoon, after shutting down every computer in town, apparently. I'd have to be more organized to find any pattern to the material, but there are enough familiar names that I think a town meeting may be needed."

Kurt whistled. "Not a town meeting, please. This could be incendiary when it's coupled with what I found in the lodge records. We might need to call in Walker."

Teddy closed her eyes. "That's what I was afraid of. Will he arrest me?"

Her hero chuckled, leaned over, and kissed her. "You have a super-conscience, or a super-ego. Not all about you this time, I promise."

She nearly collapsed in a puddle of relief. "Thank you. I know I wasn't supposed to let Mariah touch computers, but she knows how to fix websites! How can we deny computers to someone with valuable knowledge?"

"Walker will want to talk to her, so I guess we'd better bring in some Lucys to buffer the questioning. But this isn't about Mariah, either. It's about the people she was looking into, if she was researching Daisy. Looking at this, I may have to start believing in evil." He turned the computer back to her. "How do you want to work this?"

"Not in public," Teddy agreed, staring at the screen as if it might explode. "I'm not sure I even want Cass involved."

"So let's have a small dinner party in our place. I'll call on Keegan and Walker. You round up Sam and Mariah." He got up, but leaned over to kiss her again.

Teddy luxuriated in his calm reassurance. She loved that he called the bungalow they shared *our place*. It was a safe place, away from both of their families, a place where they could learn to be a couple together. When he started for the door, she inhaled his scent and held it close. It would be a long evening, she feared. "I'll ask Dinah for carry-out, right?"

He gave her a thumbs-up and departed on his errands. Teddy slammed the laptop closed and headed for her landline.

TWENTY-SIX

They were just cleaning up when someone rapped at the cottage door.

Keegan finished drying a plate and called, "I'll get it."

Just out of the shower and drying her hair, Mariah looked a little panicky. He hated that she had to feel that way in her own home, but she'd done it to herself. All he could do was stand between this mystery woman and the world for as long as he could. Shutting down every computer in town had consequences.

The blond environmental scientist stood outside, looking more worried than Mariah. "We're having dinner at Kurt and Teddy's place. You'll want to come."

He leaned his shoulder against the doorjamb. "That's a very strange invitation."

She nodded nervously. "I know. I'm not entirely certain what it's about. But Teddy insisted you and Mariah need to be there, and that we should make like this is just an innocent dinner party."

"Walker hasn't said anything?"

"No. I'm not even certain Walker knows what this is about. Dinah's providing food, so at least we'll eat well. Maybe Kurt will bring wine.

He's thinking we need a liquor store too." Normality relaxed her edginess a little.

Mariah emerged from the back, still braiding her hair. "Alcohol and Lucys are a very bad mix. What's up?"

"We're going out to dinner." Keegan turned back to Sam. "What time? We have some errands to run."

"At seven, their bungalow, the one behind the shop?"

Keegan waited for Mariah to agree. She didn't look eager to do so, but even hard-core Mariah couldn't turn down eager Sam. She nodded. "Curiosity will kill me otherwise."

Sam grinned and departed. Keegan closed the door, fighting anxiety. Surely Mariah's findings hadn't escaped already. "We'd better download your latest feat fast. I carry an external drive. We'll have to do it from Aaron's place, if the cable is operating again. Are you ready?"

"Give me a minute to finish up." She darted back to the bedroom.

When she emerged, she looked as if she had prepared for war. Gone were the androgynous bulky clothes. In their place was a sleeveless black halter that revealed real cleavage, and jeans that clung to every luscious curve. Her thick braid sported a glittering assortment of crystals and feathers. She wore dreamcatcher earrings dangling to her bare shoulders. Turquoise and coral bands encompassed her brown wrists and adorned her silver buckle. He wanted to fling her back to bed and strip her of all that gear, one shiny piece at a time.

"Indian princess or shaman?" he asked.

"Protective coloration. There are journalists still out there." Barely limping anymore, she took his arm and steered him out the door, locking up behind her.

As if it was possible to disguise Mariah's imposing presence! He'd have to look up old photos of her to see what she thought she was hiding.

The antique shop was closed for the evening, and Aaron was nowhere in sight. They dug Keegan's laptop out of a drawer and got it up and running. He whistled at the size of the files Mariah directed him to. "This could take forever to organize into anything manageable."

"If you give me a computer without internet connection, I can organize it," she said as he hooked up the external drive and began the transfer. "The connections might only be visible to me."

"The mind of Zoe de Cervantes is a mysterious place, got it." He resisted watching while she paced his room, examining everything. Her brown, shapely arms were works of art. He wasn't certain he'd be able to think straight by the time dinner was over. He'd almost rather she hid behind her bulky vests and camp shorts.

He finished copying the material to the disk and the cloud. He grabbed a clean sport shirt from his suitcase and donned a jacket where he could store the drive and the book.

"Is that Lucinda's journal?" she asked, watching him. "I vaguely recall you reading it to me."

"Val had it." He led her out and locked the door. "She mentioned Daisy protecting it. She seems afraid of it, and wants it returned to my library."

"Good for Val," she said. "She may act like a mad woman, but I suspect she knows what she's doing. Did you learn anything valuable yet?"

"Nothing that screams *evil here*, if that's what you mean. The journal author is a very orderly scientist, if one can call anyone from that era a scientist. There is no mention of alchemy so far, at least." They clattered down the stairs and out the back door.

"Alchemy? Surely no one is looking for that book, hoping to turn lead to gold?"

She gave him a long-lashed look that had him stumbling over his feet. The connection between them was so electric, that even Mariah looked briefly startled. She took his arm again but hastily started down the street.

"Alchemy was about transformation of matter, not just lead to gold," he explained, firmly returning to swot mode. "So far, Dougal has not attempted to turn crystals into anything else. He's just studying their properties in meticulous detail, considering he knew nothing of molecular structure. I've flipped through. His mineral collection was limited. I just have the feeling that once he studied the properties, he probably attempted to use them. It just makes sense. And if he had my abilities. . ."

"You'd be rich in diamonds." She dismissed his fear. "If Dougal had paranormal abilities, he was more likely to attempt to accelerate or extend his powers, the way Teddy claims crystals can do. Would his direct descendants have the same abilities?"

They avoided the main street, walking along the back alley until they ran into the obstacle of Teddy's fence. Skirting around Teddy's shop, they hiked down the highway to the bungalow lower down the mountain, hidden by a yard of pine trees.

"You are *not* researching Dougal's genealogy," Keegan told her as they followed the driveway to the house. "And no, we have no evidence that our abilities descend directly. If we wish to completely disregard science and genetics and use your essence theory, then it's more likely we inherit the abilities of whatever essence we absorb at birth."

"Or the soul that possesses the womb," Mariah crowed as they reached the porch. "I like it! So, if we believe essence doesn't travel far, those of us who live and die in weird communities are more likely to be born with weird abilities!"

"That sounds like in-breeding," he grumbled.

The door opened before they could knock. The faces greeting them looked more serious than the occasion should call for. With dread in his heart, Keegan led Mariah in and shut the door.

"Is this an execution squad?" his goddess asked defiantly.

DAMN, DAMN, AND DOUBLE DAMN. MARIAH WANTED TO POUND HER HEAD against a wall. She had never ever meant for this material to fall in anyone's hands but hers, but her essence apparently didn't like secrets. She wanted to crawl under the table and hide while the others sorted through the explosive contents of Teddy's computer. *How* had she unloaded it anywhere besides the website? *Why?*

Was there any chance of preventing her friends from spreading it from here to eternity? She really didn't want to have to hide again. Or blow up more families. Please let there not be anything too dangerous.

Over Dinah's Creole-style dinner, Mariah let the others scan through the mass of information. So far, they were just making connections. If she could actually find Daisy's killer this way, she was almost glad she'd done it. Almost. And Kurt and Sam had added their own information to the stack, making it even more interesting.

She really needed her tablet and phone to make notes, but she was learning to use pen and paper and highlighter. She took Kurt's record of bar invoices and room reservations for the past two years and began a quick cross-match. "Wow, spotting this was clever, for a Null." She added the last just so he didn't get too cocky. "Georgie was hanging with a wealthy crowd way over his plumber's head."

Sam typed Mariah's notes into her tablet. The bungalow didn't have wi-fi, so she had to physically pass it around the table.

"Eat your dinner," Keegan admonished, forking up plump shrimp and savory rice and holding it to Mariah's mouth. "We can't move mountains overnight."

She all but inhaled the jambalaya and kept working, thrilled to be useful for a change, relieved that he didn't hate her. Swallowing, she pushed her paper toward him and forked her own bites. "Every second Sunday night of the month, for the past year, a Caldwell Edison, Robert Gabriel, and Ralph Wainwright stayed at the lodge. Sometimes one or the other came in earlier or stayed later. George Thompson apparently never paid for a room until this month, but he charged the bar tab every so often, just enough to indicate he was a regular, and that he was there at the same time. Georgie is the one who grew up here, so he must have been their inside man. Did he live locally?"

"In Baskerville, half an hour away, so he probably went home at night. He was a bit of a penny-pincher and probably rather drive drunk than pay for a lodge room." Walker had Teddy's laptop next to his plate, skimming over the information Mariah had downloaded earlier.

The chief of police had yet to yell at her, although he wasn't giving off happy vibes. Some of the information she'd accessed shouldn't have been accessible. He had to know she'd hacked.

"His license said Monterey," she recalled. "He must have moved and not reported it."

Sam pushed another list at her. "The journalists pooled their resources and have identified every person in the mural. They want a party and a scoop. I think they brought their own liquor. I left them high-fiving each other and making grandiose plans over nothing. Harvey and a few of the others are encouraging them."

Mariah snorted and scanned down the list. "We already knew the Ingerssons, Peterson, Papa Gabriel and Papa Edison were in the mural, plus Daisy. Gabriel wasn't even an artist. Of the remaining seven—we have three who didn't have red eyes, including Judas, whose eyes we can't see."

"They think Judas is the owner of the gallery where the Ingerssons showed their work," Sam said. "That would be typical irony to paint the money man as Judas. He's dead according to his bio. The other two clear-eyed people are apparently a man and wife who painted landscapes. They're still alive, moderately successful, with half a dozen kids, none of whom look like Daisy's sketch if their social media means anything."

Mariah skimmed down the list. "That leaves four more red eyes—three were successful artists from the looks of it, dead from drugs, alcohol, and one arson. Evil doers come to bad ends? No reported children. *Menendez*, photographer?" Skimming down the list, she frowned. "Which one is a Menendez? None of the people in the mural look like the ones I've met around here."

Keegan stopped eating.

"One of the women, the one with the long brown hair and red eyes," Sam said worriedly.

Mariah cast Keegan a worried glance but when he didn't speak, she asked, "Does anyone happen to have a photo of the mural?"

Sam produced one on her phone. Walker sorted urgently through the material in Teddy's laptop. The phone went around the table, blowing up the image to show a smiling sprite of a Caucasian woman with flowers in her hair—*and red crystals in her earrings*. They really hadn't been visible through the veil of her hair until looked at close up.

"Dolores Menendez," Walker read from Mariah's materials as they studied the image. "Famed photographer, maiden name *Wainwright*, ex-wife of Mateo *Menendez*. . . How the hell did you know to look her up?" Walker glared at Mariah. "Sam just brought me that list."

Mariah shook her head. "I was chasing bunnies, that's all. I had almost half a dozen names to start with. The connections multiply the deeper I dig. I had no way of knowing she was on the mural, but I'm betting there are any number of references to a famed photographer coming out of the Hillvale commune. But this proves the mural is a bust. As we suspected, they're all too old or dead. We still have no connection to Daisy."

"We do," Keegan muttered. "But I promised not to say anything. At the time, I didn't realize there was a connection to the commune. I still don't think it's relevant. Samantha and Valdis are Ingerssons and related to two people in the mural. That doesn't mean they killed Daisy."

"And my. . . *stepfather*. . . is a Menendez. So unless there's more reason to say anything, keep your promise," Sam said.

Feeling a little more confident that the material she'd located this time contained no bombshells, Mariah rolled her eyes, reached across the table, and nabbed the laptop from Walker. She ran a quick search of her documents, pulled up several, then turned the screen around to show the others.

"Everything is online somewhere. There is no privacy and there are no secrets. Harvey told us his grandfather once lived on the commune, and that's how he inherited his crystals. Mateo Menendez was a musician, like Harvey. Dolores was his ex—so Harvey could be her grandson, making him a Wainwright as well as a Menendez. Anyone looking at him can see that his genetics are whiter than mine. Were any of the Menendez family at the lodge on the second Sunday of every month?"

Kurt shook his head. "I would have noticed any receipts anywhere with that name. I want that land they own, and if there's even a suspicion of a hint that they may be ready to sell, I'd be all over it."

"They're talking about it now," Keegan said. "Or so I've heard."

Kurt went still. Mariah waited for dollar signs to spin in his eyes like a slot machine. But he just rubbed his temple and winced. "Figures."

Teddy shook her head at their inquiring looks. "Not now. Daisy first. We're on a roll here. Let's keep going."

"We're not on a roll," Sam said in puzzlement. "We have nothing but names. There's no law against people meeting once a month."

"Daisy carried a sketch in her cart that has a vague resemblance to Trevor Gabriel, the dead guru fraud. We know that, unlike the others, he had half a dozen kids by different mothers," Mariah said, running more searches now that she'd pried Teddy's computer from the police chief. With no internet to slide down, she stuck to sorting pertinent data into folders. She lined up the most recent photos of Gabriel's offspring. "How good are you at identifying faces?"

Everyone looked at Keegan, who grimaced as he studied the images of Trevor Gabriel's sons. "Robert," he concluded. "Robert Gabriel most resembles that sketch, and he's the one meeting with Edison and Wainwright at the lodge."

Silence descended as they digested that information—until Mariah grabbed the laptop again and began filtering more information. "Robert Gabriel has his face all over the city society pages. He's listed on several philanthropic boards, but he doesn't appear to have any real job. Trevor must have left him ten fortunes."

She hit the keyboard and opened another file. "Caldwell Edison's father is also in the mural. He's still alive and a powerful politician. I take it from these files that Caldwell is a wheeler-dealer, negotiating backdoor power plays for his father and others. He would travel in the same circles as Robert. He's recently been accused of sexual harassment, but who hasn't? He appears to be sitting on a fortune, also, although its origins aren't immediately apparent."

She ran a search on the next name. "Ralph Wainwright, Keegan's dodgy pillock of a relation, isn't on the mural. He never lived at the commune, but we have the artwork proving Wainwright visited there, possibly to see Dolores. He's not an artist but a *physicist*," she crowed, digging deeper.

"This is almost more than the mind can manage," Keegan complained. "Wainwright is only a distant cousin. He has to be in his 70s by now." He hesitated and added, "But he's been at our castle, possibly to see the library. I suppose he could have found the crystal journals, at least the one that went missing after the last inventory."

"He's also been accused of misrepresenting research studies in scientific journals and lost his prestigious position at one of the east coast laboratories." Mariah spun through more material, finding the genealogy information. "Here—Dolores Menendez was Ralph's older sister."

Ignoring curses around the table, Mariah continued reading. "Dolores died in a tragic murder-suicide involving drugs and alcohol not long after she left the commune in the 80's. She left one son and one daughter to be raised by her ex, Mateo Menendez, presumably Harvey's grandfather. I love these ancestry places." She shoved the computer at Walker. "I can't imagine Harvey killing Daisy for any reason."

Walker took the computer and opened a different file. "Robert Gabriel is one of Trevor Gabriel's younger sons. He only went to jail once, when he was a teenager, for an elaborate credit card scam that milked hundreds of old people. After his father's death, he must have inherited enough that he didn't need to make further effort."

"Both Dolores Menendez and Trevor Gabriel used crystals," Keegan pointed out. "We have Dolores to connect Wainwright to the commune and thus, the Sunday meetings with the descendants of Edison and Gabriel."

"It all goes back to the commune and crystals somehow, doesn't it?" Sam asked, frowning.

"And if my family is involved," Keegan said, "it may also involve paranormal ability. Hillvale seems to attract the oddly gifted."

Mariah sighed, sat back, and glared at the computer screen. She didn't want to do this, but if they were to get anywhere, all the facts had to be laid on the table. "Would the woman you almost married be called Brianna *Dougal*?" she asked of Keegan.

"Dougal is a common enough name in our town," he responded slowly. "Why?"

"*Ralph Wainwright,* your dodgy cousin, had a daughter, now deceased, who married a Dougal. They had a daughter named Brianna. She's just about the right age."

Keegan growled, shoved back his chair, and stalked out.

TWENTY-SEVEN

Oh damn, she'd done it again. Would she never learn?

Mariah jumped up to go after Keegan, but Kurt rose at the same time, waving her back down. "I'm no good at research," he said, "but I know how to listen. It's not easy knowing your family is working against you."

A Kennedy would be one to know, Mariah admitted. She sat down and swallowed as Kurt hurried out. Her damned nosiness had done nothing but beat up Keegan time after time—the one man who had never done anything more than help her. "I ought to quit now before I destroy anyone else," she muttered.

"If Brianna betrayed him and his family, it's not your fault," Sam said, patting her arm. "And this Wainwright is only an aging, distant relation he can't know well."

Mariah pointed at the computer and stated her greatest fear. "But the files I found may destroy his family, right?" As they had Adera and her family. She felt sick to her stomach. "I only wanted to find Daisy's killer. Why does it have to be so sticky? Can't we just erase all that and forget we ever saw it?"

"As I believe you've pointed out yourself. . ." Walker took back the computer. "Like attracts like. It isn't just the gifted who seek each other out. Criminals seek other criminals. No one asked Edison, Wainwright, and Gabriel to hang out together. We still don't know what they're doing, except that it probably isn't legal and may involve crystals. But if they're behind Daisy's death, then *they* are guilty, not you or Keegan. I'm suspecting they're also behind Thompson's death. This isn't hunting season. His death was no accident, and we have him tied indirectly to this trio. If they're killers, they must be caught."

Knowing it wasn't her fault didn't help. Mariah wanted to use her abilities for *good*, not to cause pain.

She couldn't bear to destroy anyone else—not Keegan or her friends or Hillvale. She sank in her seat, wondering if there were any good way to become a hermit so she'd never come near another computer.

"Just because Brianna is related to Wainwright doesn't mean we know how that links to anything else," Teddy reminded them. "I say we give the list of names to our reporters as a prize scoop and let them run with it."

"I'll just take a little vacation, see if there are any mines in the hills I can hide in," Mariah muttered.

"Don't you dare," Sam protested. "Hillvale is your home. We take care of each other. You've done nothing wrong and have nothing to hide."

Walker snorted and turned the computer around again. "If this blurry image is all your reporters have of you, you're safe."

Mariah didn't even have to look to know he'd brought up the stupid photo all the newspapers had printed. It was one of her at a company picnic with her hair in a knot with a poniard through it, wearing a lumpy blazer and blousy slacks—her standard uniform back then.

"I've always avoided having my picture taken, but people still know me," she insisted. "A reporter recognized me just the other day."

"That was a fluke," Sam insisted. "None of them at the café have."

"They let you wear a dagger to work?" Walker asked cynically, taking the computer back.

"They thought it was a hairpin." Mariah almost smiled at that distraction. "Other women stuck pencils in their topknots. I was just more creative."

"Women might recognize you," Teddy said, reclaiming the screen to study the image. "But if all men ever saw was you looking like this. . . I don't think they'd see the similarity. You barely look female in these clothes."

"That was the point." Keegan would understand why. Mariah's heart cracked a little more fearing this new betrayal would drive him away. "I could hope reporters think all people with brown skin look alike, but then I'd open my mouth, and that would be the end of that."

There were nods of agreement and everyone reached for their wine glasses.

"How are crystals involved in all this?" Teddy demanded, sticking to the subject she knew. "Thompson died in a crystal cave owned by the entire Menendez clan. But as we all know, the crystals are worthless and quite possibly dangerous. So, why?"

Mariah didn't feel like eating anymore, because as long as she was sinking into the lowest pits of hell, it was very possible she had an answer to this. It was right there in that material Walker was rifling through, except he didn't understand the implications.

Knowledge was dangerous. She'd never meant any of the information she'd downloaded to go into anyone's hands but her own. And now they were sitting on a time bomb that could totally take out Keegan's family and more. She just wasn't going there again.

Mariah threw down her napkin and started to rise, but Walker motioned her down.

"Not yet," he insisted. "Keegan and Kurt can do their manly thing. We need to come up with a way of luring killers out of the woodwork. I like Teddy's idea about offering a prize to the reporters for finding connections."

"Understanding what Lucys do is a manly thing," Sam purred, leaning into him. "What do we need to do Fearless Leader?"

Mariah prayed Walker was smarter than she was about consequences because luring killers didn't sound safer than falling down rabbit holes.

～

KURT REACHED KEEGAN BEFORE HE'D PASSED THE CAFÉ.

"What are you going to do?" the resort owner asked, keeping up with Keegan's longer strides.

"Play with rocks," Keegan retorted. "It's all I know to do."

"That makes about as much sense as any of this. Want me to give you some space where you can set up your equipment or whatever you need? If I can help, we can bring down a bottle of whiskey and make a night of it. I have someone covering for me tonight, so I'm allowed to get smashed."

Keegan snorted. "Or I could teach you to smash rocks instead."

"I'd rather smash noses, but rocks might do. I have an unused conference room at the lodge. Long tables but they wouldn't hold up to a lot of smashing." Kurt followed him down the alley to Aaron's back door.

"Tables will work for sorting." Keegan unlocked the door, found the backpacks they'd flung inside earlier, and collected his laptop from the drawer. "I'll pound rocks on the pavement. Why do you want to smash noses?"

"For more reasons than I can count. Unless you wish to hear the resort's financial woes, which are directly related to Hillvale's depressed economy and all that empty land out there, it's best just to let me pound rocks. Do you have any particular goals in rock smashing or just general satisfaction?" Kurt hefted Harvey's pack.

"Both. Do you have a car or are we walking?" Keegan led the way back to the road.

"Car. You don't want to walk that winding road at night when the drunks are out." Kurt led the way to his low-slung Mercedes.

"You could build steps into the hill for pedestrian access between the lodge and town," Keegan suggested. "Then people who drink in town could stumble back on foot."

"Huh, good thought, if I get the liquor license. But that won't put a hole in the mounting debt. I need that Menendez land before Hector gets permission to build a casino up there."

"If they won't widen the road to allow more residential housing, they won't allow casino traffic." Keegan had heard all the arguments bouncing around the café. Journalists were knowledgeable. "You need something like a winery in there."

"That would take years to develop and enormous loans we can't pay." Kurt swung the Mercedes into the lot reserved for his family. "But the Lucys would love it."

"Looks like I'm a Lucy," Keegan grumbled. "Couldn't you find a better name?"

"Want to be a Null?" Kurt led the way down a darkened corridor to a conference room. "Is this close enough to the parking lot so you can smash and tote?"

Keegan observed the long tables and began pulling out his sample boxes. "It's a good start. I don't have all the equipment I need, but I can improvise some of it. I'll need small envelopes for labeling and sending to a lab." He could no longer trust his family lab.

If Brianna had betrayed his family. . . It would be as if their own daughter had done so. The lies, the deceit, the willingness to let his dad and brother go to jail for her depredations. . .

He couldn't handle the rioting emotions demanding release.

He needed to smash rocks.

"Do you have any idea what you want to accomplish?" Kurt asked again.

"Not precisely, but I have a few theories." He was more comfortable with theories than knowing Mariah's damned insidiousness had brought his world crashing down *again*. "It would be good to know if Wainwright has any of my ability, and if any of Gabriel's family might have it too. Because if there's anything in those crystals they know about, I should be able to figure it out. I just don't like that they have the rest of the journals."

Because *Bri* must have given them to her damned dodgy physicist *grandfather*. Why hadn't he seen that?

"It will be nearly a month before the ugly trio meet again, so I can't even search their rooms to see if they have the books on them." Kurt dug into Harvey's backpack and began distributing the sample boxes on the first table.

"Which means I may be re-inventing the wheel here, if they already know what I suspect. How much do you know of quantum physics?" Keegan emptied his pack on a second table.

"I'm an architect. Figure exactly zip."

Keegan nodded understanding. "I'm a geologist, not a physicist, but I follow developments in other fields that might affect mine. Crystals are being used for all sorts of purposes these days, including computers, which has led scientists to theorize they can create crystals that bend space and time and potentially create natural computers."

Kurt snorted. "I think Cass has already done that. Have you seen her place?"

"I have, but apparently you and Walker see things I don't. Looked normal to me."

"Lucky you. Go on. Let's hear how Cass can be a quantum genius." Kurt discarded his suit coat and began organizing the samples by box number.

"The lab Wainwright was fired from has a team of scientists working on what they call time crystals. Even though they are theoretically impossible, several different labs have created working models. The lab Wainwright once called home built a chain of charged particles. A different lab has built an artificial crystal lattice using synthetic diamonds. Both have the potential to fulfill the theory."

"Diamonds, I understand," Kurt said, frowning. "Beyond that, you've lost me.

"I'm not a quantum physicist," Keegan reminded him. "I don't understand the theory either. But I can create synthetic diamonds using some of these rocks. I think the vibrations, or *energy*, in the crystals can be charged in the same way as the ones in the lab. Wainwright may be wary of displaying his paranormal talent, but if he's actually created such a computer, I don't know why he'd hide it. He could regain his reputation by reporting his findings."

Kurt grimaced. "I can't imagine what can be accomplished by bending space and time, although I like the notion of creating a house where you turn the corner and disappear into another dimension."

Keegan laughed. "That may be a way off, unless you believe that's what Cass has done."

"What Lucys do has no basis in science, but I have a feeling that they stay one step ahead of us Nulls, who insist on proving things are possible before we try them."

Keegan thought of Mariah flying with the hawk, mentally calling Cass, and performing witchy searches with her *essence* in computers. "I wonder if there is such a thing as a Lucy who isn't a risk taker."

"You can ask yourself that," Kurt pointed out.

He'd never thought of what he did as taking risks. But he'd never made synthetic diamonds before either. "There may be something to the Lucy's energy theory," Keegan admitted, setting the last sample box on the table. "When we all gather together, it produces an insane energy causing us to do what no sane person would try."

Kurt looked grim. "Tell me about it. You haven't seen anything until you've seen Teddy use crystal energy to plaster a drunken asshole to the floor."

"If my theory pans out, we may just bust this town wide open," Keegan warned as he organized his samples. He could almost feel the rocks vibrating in impatience. "We could have prospectors and scientists and crystal gurus crawling up the walls."

Mariah would despise that worse than anything, he knew.

"You mentioned whiskey?" Keegan asked. It was going to be a long night.

TWENTY-EIGHT

JULY 13: FRIDAY, MORNING

Wondering if Keegan would ever forgive her, Mariah couldn't sleep. The plans Walker and the others had made after Keegan left had made sense at the time, but she really needed his perspective. Or that's what she told herself as she tossed and turned, aching and alone.

By morning, she was telling herself that she ought to get used to it. He really had to return to Scotland to settle his family's situation—one she had caused. She feared his family might be harmed even more before this was over, since two of their murder suspects were relations of his.

She ought to suspect Keegan, as she had at first, but she just couldn't. In this case, she'd rather be wrong than right.

Trolling for information without computers was probably purposeless, but she wasn't touching Teddy's laptop again. If what she recalled from the info dump was correct, their villains were into seriously dangerous territory. She didn't want it touching Hillvale. If they could pin Daisy's death on Edison, Wainwright, or Gabriel, that ought to stop the bastards.

Back to hunting criminals without any clue. . .

She pulled on her usual hiking shorts, vest, and work boots. She left her long black hair unbraided and tied in two pigtails down her front since she wouldn't be serving food today. Feeling as if she was off to

battle trolls, she missed her dagger, but the geek topknot was too identi-
fiable. She really wanted to stay invisible as long as she could.

Sam met her at the café door with a large cup of coffee and a stack of
posters she'd already printed. "The reporters aren't here yet. They
partied half the night according to Dinah. They're probably sleeping it
off in Baskerville."

"They need lives if solving one stupid puzzle requires celebration."
Mariah sipped her coffee and studied the poster. "This ought to really
give them something to chew on."

"Oh, wait until you see what Lance is putting together. He has all
those old portraits he painted of the commune members and anyone else
who crossed his path over the years." Sam leaned in to whisper, "And I
sent Val to explore Daisy's stash for more."

"You are a conniving temptress. Val will eat poor Lance alive."
Someone else's romantic tragedy revived her spirits somewhat. She
refused to ask where Keegan had spent the night.

Because she knew. Damn, if she didn't know exactly what the Mountain Man had done. She loved Cass but couldn't trust the wily old
woman further than a toad could fly. But Keegan—was the most direct,
straight-forward, honest. . . *void*. . . she'd ever known.

Feeling slightly better, Mariah began the task of nailing and tacking
Sam's posters all over town. By the time she'd covered the outer walls,
shops were opening up, and she asked to hang more posters inside.

Explaining only part of what they meant to do took half the morning.
Amber wanted to read her cards to judge the chance of success. Aaron
snorted and told her to hang the poster anywhere she liked, then asked
what she'd done with Keegan.

"Ate him," Mariah responded, checking her ghostcatchers while she
was there, since her knee felt better.

He studied the poster she taped to his counter. "Why don't you just
erect a circus tent?"

"No money," she said cheerfully. "Why don't you wear a turban and
bring your crystal ball?"

He looked serious. "Don't forget I have uses."

Mariah stopped to study the antique dealer. "I don't trust easily," she
admitted. "But it would be awesome if you joined us. Empathy and

psychometry aren't acceptable in court, but if you and Teddy could steer Walker in the right direction, it might speed the process."

He had a long angular face that leant itself to gravity. "I want to find Daisy's killer as much as anyone. I'll be there."

Nulls like the grocer and the ice cream parlor manager didn't ask questions. One more festivity added to the art walk simply meant more business as far as they were concerned.

Tullah took her poster and narrowed her eyes. "Cass know about this?"

"Is there anything Cass doesn't know?" Mariah countered. "It's what she admits to knowing that matters."

Tullah almost cackled as she taped the poster on the back of her register. "I want to see her and Carmel in the same room. If this don't do it, nothing will."

"I hadn't even considered that. Maybe we can persuade Kurt to send his mother back to Hawaii. That kind of explosion—"

"Will make an excellent distraction," Tullah said with her best superior attitude.

"Remind me never to cross you." Mariah marched out, trying to work a catfight into the ugly scenario already playing in her head.

She let it go the instant she entered the meeting hall to see what Lance had done. The hall wasn't huge, space wise. It just had no walls preventing seeing from one end of the building to the other. Lucinda's priceless triptych held the place of honor at the far end of a space made narrow by partitions across the far corners. Lance had started hanging photographs on the partitions, which weren't strong enough for heavy frames.

Normally, track lighting illuminated the triptych. This morning, Lance was rearranging the lighting to focus on the long walls.

Mariah tacked posters on the front door and the reception desk, then wandered in to study the portraits he'd accumulated.

Lance watched her anxiously as he worked from the ladder. "Is this what you wanted?"

"Don't blame this one on me. This is all Walker. He has a wicked evil mind," Mariah protested, stopping before a familiar face. "This painting looks like Keegan's relation from the mural."

The skinny artist nodded nervously. "Trevor Gabriel. Lars captured him better in the mural, just using tempera. Gabriel's features always eluded me. I could never really pin him down."

"Hard to pin slime, so I'd say that's pretty perceptive of you. Lars took him at face value. You saw the lie beneath the pretty features."

Not that Mariah could actually see that in Lance's portrait of a young man with dark curls and a charming smile. She just knew who Gabriel was, and Lance looked reassured at her assessment. She knew what it was like not to have effort recognized, so she always tried to offer acknowledgement of talent and hard work.

"Monty said he was bringing more photos, so I left lots of space." Lance clambered down to remove the ladder to the next fixture.

"The mayor is in on this too? How ducky. What about Kurt?" Mariah asked a little too casually.

Lance's head bobbed on his skinny neck. "He was up all night with that nice Scot, smashing rocks. So Monty said he'd do the photographs. Val found more photos in the bunker. She took them over to Cass." Lance sounded disappointed about that.

"I think we have a real draw here," Mariah said, visiting the next few paintings. "Here's Representative Edison himself and his son, Caldwell, very nice. And I see Susannah let you hang the oil showing everyone at the farm house, including Lucinda's. . . What was Ralph? Her nephew?"

"He was a Wainwright. That's all I remember hearing. He was looking for a journal he thought Lucinda may have taken from the family library. That's right, he called her his aunt. More likely a great-aunt." He stopped to peer at the oil more closely. "Carmel brought him to the farm, I believe. That was back when she liked playing hostess and having parties. She changed after Geoffrey died."

"It had to have been hard on her, running the resort and raising two boys alone." Mariah tried not to sound dismissive of Lance's sister, who had wealth and family and could have just asked for help—and hadn't, because Carmel was a controlling bitch. Not that she was judgmental or anything. "So Carmel knew Gabriel, Edison, *and* Wainwright."

"They were all friends of Lars and Geoffrey. Well, Wainwright wasn't. That's Cass's family, but our world was small back then. Everyone knew each other, one way or another."

Mayor Monty entered, his golden-brown hair falling in his eyes as usual. He carried an enormous box that he held up for inspection. "Who gets to arrange Val's photo collection?"

Mariah and Lance gathered around the box to pick through photos on stiff backing. "Are they labeled?" she asked.

Lance chose one and looked on the back. "Robert Gabriel. So that goes on Trevor's part of the wall, yes?"

The old black-and-white, artistically posed photo of a young man in a field looked vaguely like Daisy's sketch, probably because Robert had Trevor's square jaw. But another thought gripped her. "Dolores Menendez! Are any of these photos ones she took?" Mariah asked eagerly. "Do we need to ask Harvey about her?"

Monty set the box down on a chair. "Val claims some of the early photos from her family album are from Dolores. And Susannah said she'd ask her husband for photos. They may just provide snapshots and put them all on one board. I've never seen so many members of Hillvale working together on a project—but Harvey is going to kill you."

"Did you know he was a Menendez?" Mariah asked accusingly.

"I don't tell people who *you* are," Monty retorted.

"Fair enough." The mayor was a decent sort, for a Null. Grudgingly, she relented as she sorted through photos from the past half a century. "Does Walker think his minions can produce the biographical index in time?"

"Since you apparently provided most of the material—" Monty glared at her, returning her accusation. "It's just a matter of printing one copy and putting a copy on our website for the reporters to peruse."

Mariah smiled in satisfaction. "Let them pursue someone else besides me."

"You'd better see what that man of yours is doing," Monty advised. "He must have spent the night ordering online and paying for special delivery. Mom's pitching a fit about the delivery trucks in the parking lot and the mess in the conference room."

Mariah's heart soared at this confirmation of Keegan's whereabouts. "Oh goody," she said, keeping her cool. "You want me to breathe fire back at her? My pleasure." She started for the door, happy with any excuse to see Mountain Man and tick off Carmel.

"Try not to burn down the lodge," Monty called back. "It's the only income we have right now."

"I'll tell her Lance has her portrait hung in the place of honor, shall I?" she called back.

Monty's shout of alarm did her jaded heart good.

She did so love to wreak havoc. Maybe she was the coyote around here.

KEEGAN HOPPED OFF THE DELIVERY VAN IN THE PARKING LOT, WAVED THANKS at the driver, and aimed for the café. He saw Mariah-*Zoe* before he reached it.

Zoe, who had wreaked devastation on his family. *Zoe*, who had exposed sunny Brianna's relation to her dodgy grandfather. Keegan had spent the night smashing rocks and wishing they were Wainwright's head. Grudgingly, he had come to terms with the correlation between scorned physicist, Bri's greed, and family disaster. That it had been Zoe who had forged those links was a bitter pill, but logically, he had to admit that she had simply uncovered what others had done.

Watching Mariah-who-flies-with-the-hawk come toward him made his unruly heart soar and his brain say *uh-oh*. It would be easier if he could blame her. He had to save his family first and foremost. And it would be wise not to involve Mariah's too-perceptive brilliance in the job ahead of him.

But he couldn't help filling with pleasure at her presence, even when she scowled at him.

"We're building a nuclear bomb. What have you and Kurt accomplished?" she demanded.

"Nuclear bomb? Figurative, I trust?" he asked warily.

She gestured at a colorful poster. "We're having a reception for the original members of the commune and their families, and the public is invited. We have paintings and photographs of as many as we could find. We've added a biography on the dirty dozen to Hillvale's website. Daisy's biography doesn't exist or we'd have all thirteen from the mural. We have an IT guy who says he can display pages from the bio on a screen for the public to read."

He frowned. "And exactly what will this accomplish?"

"We didn't want to wait until Edison and company returned next month, so we're hoping to draw them up here this weekend. And unleash the reporters."

"You're asking them to come *here*?" Keegan tried not to shout, but he might be expiring as they spoke. This was the kind of disaster vengeful Zoe promoted. He grabbed her elbow and began hauling her toward her place. "They may be killers!"

"Don't bully me, Keegan." She yanked her arm from his grip and stopped at Dinah's. "I need food and there isn't any in the house."

"Did you even *read* that material you dumped on Expoleaks and Teddy's website?" he whispered harshly as he followed her inside Dinah's.

"Most of it? No," she said insouciantly. "Who has time?" She continued past the counter, into the kitchen. "Dinah, I'm famished, and I know I haven't worked all day. And I'm broker than broke because of this bum knee. . ."

Keegan waved cash.

Dinah rolled her eyes. "You two go do what you need to do and don't hassle me. I'll send up a box of whatever when it's ready."

Mariah kissed Dinah's cheek, gave Keegan a haughty look, and marched out. She definitely wasn't smiling, and that was his fault.

It was better that way. Since food was imminent, Keegan followed her back out.

"We suspect Edison, Wainwright, and Gabriel are up to their chinny chin chins in a criminal enterprise," she said grimly as they headed up the lane. "We've discovered they own a shady company called EWG. We don't know why they are meeting here, except to assume they don't want anyone to know they're meeting."

Which coincided with that niggling thought he'd ignored the other day—Hillvale was a place for people to hide themselves or what they were doing. No cell reception, or even public cameras, made it far less likely that anyone's presence was recorded.

"I don't suppose you understand quantum physics," he said as they reached her cottage.

She eyed him warily. "Only what I've read in novels. Did you find the secrets of physics in Expoleaks?"

He shook his head as she let him in. "No, I just read a lot in my area of research. And so I've been performing a few experiments on that malleable rock from the canyon."

"Malleable?" She pulled coffee beans out of the freezer to grind. "The rock you turned to a diamond?"

Talking it out with someone who understood diminished his helpless rage. He filled the coffeemaker with water. "The crystals have malleable molecular structures. If any of our unholy triumvirate has my abilities, he will have discovered this. They apparently know about the cave in the canyon. It's possible they've had years to discover the properties of those rocks."

"While this was happening, one assumes Wainwright was also having a nice time selling synthetic diamonds," she said cynically. "Was he looking for another source of artificial gems?"

"I can hope that's all they're doing," he said glumly. "But from what I can tell, Wainwright's knowledge isn't limited to selling diamonds. He's a physicist who may have my abilities and be bankrolling a larger operation."

A knock at the door interrupted this admission. With relief, Keegan answered it. Harvey thrust a fragrant sack at him. "Thanks for nothing, Ace. Walker's been questioning me all morning."

The musician spun on his boot heel, but Mariah yelled, "That was me, Menendez. Keegan didn't say a word. Really, you're not that invisible."

Harvey turned and glared. "I'm *not* my family."

Keegan crossed his arms and leaned his shoulder against the doorjamb. "Sure you are, just as Sam and I are part of our families. That doesn't mean we follow in their footsteps."

"*Your* family isn't on your doorstep. Mine are right down the road, plotting who knows what. Only my grandfather and I got the music genes. The rest inherited *avarice*. You don't think my Uncle Carlos married Susanna out of the generosity of his heart, do you? That's why she's up here alone. Carlos won't come near Cass."

"Maybe you better come inside, cowboy," Mariah said. "You just may be the trigger for our nuclear bomb."

TWENTY-NINE

July 14: Saturday morning

"Do you think we'll ever start drawing enough business for Dinah to actually hire a waitress?" Mariah called from Teddy's kitchen, where she was hiding by making a fresh pot of coffee. "I don't think I can work there anymore."

"Cluck-cluck," Teddy called back. "Wear a sack over your head."

"Would customers be offended if I wore war paint?" Mariah carried two mugs to Teddy's empty shop. It was a good thing Teddy sold her jewelry designs on-line and in real stores because the shop didn't have enough customers to support itself.

"Is that what you're planning on doing tonight? You do realize reporters are already crawling the streets, looking for anyone who resembles the pictures in the gallery?" Teddy strung one of her gems among a line of crystals and admired the effect.

"Why do you think I'm hiding? Although if they're hunting potential killers, maybe they'll not notice a notorious hacker. Can you believe Val produced those photos of the archery contest?" Sipping her coffee, Mariah kept a wary eye on the street outside.

"Doesn't do much good unless we know which of those kids in the contest grew up to become bow hunters. None of them appear to be related to our suspects. They were just friends of Val and Susannah and whoever else happened to be around at the time. I'd hate to believe any of them grew up to kill Daisy."

Mariah grimaced. "I wish Daisy had been more communicative."

She wanted to smack herself in the head the minute she said it. She was the one not communicating what she knew—*because it was dangerous and she wasn't certain it was relevant.* Just exactly the problem Daisy must have had, except Daisy's mind was a confusing place to start with. Mariah's wasn't.

Or shouldn't be. She just wasn't accustomed to wallowing in emotional uncertainty. Computers didn't require deciphering what was right or wrong. She just wrote the code and it worked or it didn't. She didn't have to worry about a hard drive's feelings.

Keegan had held her last night as if she were actually *important* to him. He seemed to have forgiven her for being a walking time bomb, possibly because he was the same. Except he had no compunction about dropping his knowledge upon an unsuspecting world—and she had learned differently.

"I wish I'd known Daisy better," Teddy said. "Do we have more milk? You make this stuff strong enough to walk."

"Amateur." Mariah took the mug and returned to the kitchen. She heard the shop door open while she was adding milk and lingered in the kitchen rather than face reporters or interfere with Teddy's customers.

"Do you have any tourmaline crystals?" a male voice asked.

Mariah stiffened, trying to recall all Teddy and Keegan had told her about the red rocks. Tourmaline was the rare one, she thought, the one that got mixed with the industrial grade garnets and maybe used in the commune's evil-eyed oils. She couldn't remember the uses Teddy had given for it. She simply associated it with *evil.*

"No, sorry," Teddy said cheerfully. "Tourmaline is too expensive for my inventory. I could order what you need if you'd like to leave a deposit."

Yay, Teddy! Mariah was fairly certain Teddy had some of those rocks in her lockbox. Not mentioning them must mean she was suspicious of this customer.

Mariah eased to an angle where she could see the shop doorway.

She caught a glimpse of one of the flowery tourist shirts checking out the merchandise. He wasn't the one talking.

"I heard you just received a whole shipment," the customer argued. "I'll buy all you have."

Teddy had just received the package from the sheriff—the red stones they'd found covering a skeleton. Someone had inside information from the sheriff's office. Mariah didn't like the sound of that. She eyed the paints Teddy's creative sister had left on the kitchen counter. War paint sounded even better than it had earlier. Asking forgiveness from her peaceful Ohlone ancestors, she hastily began braiding her hair.

"How could you hear about my shipments?" Teddy asked, probably in genuine puzzlement. Or maybe fear, since her sister's stalker had been a policeman.

"Word gets around," the customer said, not sounding insouciant so much as threatening.

"Well *word* is wrong. I recently received a package of crude quality almandine. Perhaps your mysterious informant doesn't know one crystal from another," Teddy said curtly. "I will be happy to sell you the almandine, but I don't keep it here. The shop is too small to carry inventory that isn't ready for sale."

Maybe Teddy didn't need her help. Maybe she could keep hiding here. . . or follow these two clods when they left. Mariah grabbed the paint and used her reflection in the kitchen window as a mirror.

"I'll take the almandine," the customer said, in an even more irritated tone than Teddy's. "Here's my number at the lodge. Give me a call when you have it. How long will it take?"

"I can't leave my shop right now. It may be after lunchtime before I can have someone sit in for me."

Teddy sounded cheerful again, but Mariah figured she was seething. Streaking paint across her face, she wished she had Daisy's cloak. And now she really was descending into Daisy-world.

Mariah slipped out the back door and around the alley to the boardwalk. She almost fell over watching the two flowered-shirt thugs climbing into Carmel Kennedy's chauffeured Escalade.

She waited until the Escalade departed, then slipped into the front of Teddy's shop.

Teddy was just emerging from the kitchen and almost dropped her coffee mug. "Oh my grasshoppers, where's the buckskin, Pocahontas?"

"Grasshoppers? I can't wait until Syd takes her kids home so you can talk normal again. Your customers just drove off in Carmel's Escalade. You want to call your boyfriend and ask him who he told about the tourmaline? How dangerous is that stuff?"

"Kurt wouldn't tell anyone, but I'll call and ask about Carmel's *friends*. Although if that's the company she keeps, Kurt might have other problems." Teddy wrinkled her nose. "You'd have to ask Keegan about dangerous properties. He's the one who said there was something wrong with the crystals. These guys asked specifically for tourmaline, but that bag was mostly almandine, a far less precious stone. So we're getting mixed messages."

"What is tourmaline supposed to do?" Mariah asked in frustration.

"As far as I'm aware, *red* tourmaline, or rubellite, is mostly for emotional healing, although there's a lot of blather about heart chakra because of the red tones. Almandine garnets are red, too, and are said to remove unwanted inhibitions. They're fun, but I'm not touching any of the crystals that were on the skeleton, so they're welcome to them." She eyed Mariah's war paint critically. "Do you mean to go around like that all day?"

"I need feathers and buckskin and maybe a bow and some arrows," Mariah said, mostly in jest but thinking a disguise might be a good idea. "Can't we have cartoon characters walking around town?"

"We could, actually." Teddy looked serious. "Re-enactors tend to do better historical research, but for an impromptu costume party—Hillvale has a history of Native Americans, cowboys, spiritualists, miners. . . We could pull off phony stereotypes pretty easily. Amber already has the Gypsy bit almost in hand."

"Go for it." Mariah waved at the landline. "I'll have to make do with leather, but I have the feathers. It will allow me to do something besides lurk in backrooms all day. I want to find out what those bullies were up to."

"Bring bows and we'll have an archery contest," Teddy called after her.

That wasn't a half bad idea, if she wanted to get someone killed.

~

*J*ULY *14: LATER S*ATURDAY *MORNING*

"Keegan, you might want to mosey down to town and rein in your girlfriend." Kurt entered the conference room and assessed the damage left by half a ton of equipment and sample boxes stacked along the walls.

Keegan looked up from his microscope. His *girlfriend?* The casual comment smacked him sideways. Bri had been his girlfriend, until he'd seen her true character. Mariah/Zoe. . . was an untamed force of nature. One did not call a hurricane a girlfriend. He smiled inwardly, remembering her reference to herself as the wind called Mariah. "What has she done now?"

"She's apparently gone off the deep end. She's parading around town wearing war paint. She has Harvey dressed up as a Spanish grandee. And she has Teddy demanding to know who I told about her box of rocks. Am I going to regret working with Lucys?" Kurt paced the room, studying the geological maps Keegan had hastily produced and taped to the walls.

"War paint." Keegan stood and stretched his back. "Sounds more interesting than what I'm doing. Do I need to wear a kilt for this party? And what box of rocks?"

"The ones the sheriff's office was holding until recently. I have them in my safe. Apparently someone knows Teddy got them back and wants to buy them. Selling evil sounds evil. I don't know if it's safe to sort through them." Kurt rubbed his temple as if he had a headache. "But she's right about my mother consorting with some odd fellows. I have Walker looking into them."

Keegan had all but forgotten the red stones. Maybe he ought to smash a few of those and. . .

That's why Brianna had called him a cowardly boffin—because he buried himself in work instead of paying attention to people. Until now, he hadn't cared enough to listen. For better or worse, he cared now.

"All right, if you can check on your mother, I guess I can check on Mariah. Maybe I should start studying women the way I do rocks." Keegan was serious, although he said it lightly. If he meant to have any kind of relationship at all, he should at least attempt to understand Mariah before she turned on him as Bri had.

"If they start talking ghostly possession as the reason for the costumes, I'm outta here." Kurt trudged out.

Why would anyone want those particular rocks? And why now?

Keegan stopped to check his notes on the red tourmaline sample he'd transformed from the canyon's common quartz. The only use he knew for it was to attract particles of dust. Heating or rubbing the stones generated both positive and negative charges, creating an effect similar to—*electronic equipment.*

Damn! They really were working on computer crystals. Why? The secrecy was worrisome. His mind clicked through possibilities as he climbed on the ATV and roared down to Hillvale's parking lot.

Two cowboys, complete with western boots and Stetsons, talked outside the grocery. Cowboy hats and boots weren't unusual, except he'd never noticed them in Hillvale. Amber strolled down the boardwalk, chatting with Samantha. The tarot reader was wearing her usual flouncy skirt with a billowy, off-the-shoulder top and arms full of jangly bracelets. But today, she'd covered her red hair in a turban.

Everything was normal, just a little more off kilter than usual. He checked his watch and saw it was nearly the lunch hour, so the café would be packed. He decided to stop in the meeting hall instead, see how the preparations were going. Mariah had explained Walker's plan last night. He wasn't certain what it would accomplish, but he supposed drawing in as many suspects as possible was better than doing nothing.

The hall was filled with normal, jeans-clad men and women, taking photographs and tapping into electronic devices as they perused the displays Lance was still working on. Teddy's strawberry-blond sister Syd was helping him. Keegan assumed the note-takers were reporters or perhaps art critics, and not tourists.

He found Mariah working with an audio-visual technician and his computerized equipment. Without wi-fi, she should be safe enough, but what the hell had she done to herself?

She always wore her hair in a single braid, so the two down her front looked odd. The headband around her forehead with feathers stuck behind her ears was more hippy costume than anything else. No beads or crystals though. He'd assumed *war paint* had meant cosmetics, but apparently not. Mariah would never stoop to anything so common as lipstick and mascara. She had actual streaks of white and black paint accenting her high cheekbones and hollow cheeks. Damn, if she didn't look hot that way. But she looked like no Native American ever, except for the color of her skin. This was Hillvale artistic irony at work. She could add a rose tattoo and resemble some of the hippies in the paintings.

Her tight suede brown jeans on the other hand. . . needed leather biking boots. She always wore vests, so the denim one wasn't really out of place, although he wasn't entirely certain she was wearing anything under it. It left her muscled brown arms revealed in all their glory.

She looked up as he crossed the room. "I don't suppose you packed a kilt, did you?" she asked, mischief in her eyes.

He liked the mischief even better than the war paint. "No, I did not, although I'm sure Tullah will magically conjure one should I ask. Do I get a clue or is it a surprise?"

She covered her lush lips with a finger and jerked her head in the direction of the reporters watching them. "Hiding in plain sight," she whispered.

He actually understood. Rolling his eyes, he checked out Lance and Syd. Lance was wearing a painter's smock and beret. Syd wore an ankle-length ruffled skirt, a tight-fitting button-up shirt, and her hair stacked high in a vaguely Victorian style—maybe to resemble one of the original spiritualists? "And so you talked everyone else into doing the same?"

"It's fun. It's a party. The tourists are loving it, and I get to be useful." She flicked a button on the AV equipment, bringing up a screen full of writing that drew the attention of several people standing at the reception desk.

It took Keegan a moment to realize the reporters were queuing up behind the desk to use an old-fashioned landline. "In keeping with the Victorian atmosphere?" he asked dryly, nodding at the phone. "The reporters have to call in their stories?"

"Most of them are getting a kick out of it. We have a few grumps, but the smart ones understand we're feeding them new clues every minute." She flicked another switch and a wall-size image of Daisy in her red cloak appeared. Daisy was looking windblown and working on one of her stone statues, her unlined, timeless face a study in concentration. "Val gave us this shot. We've been scanning a lot of good stuff in here." She flipped the switch and an image appeared of Daisy as a plump, much younger woman.

"She wasn't pretty, but she looks very alive," Keegan said, studying the figure dancing through a meadow.

"That's a Dolores Menendez photo of Daisy from Val's album. I think it needs to be framed and hung in City Hall. It makes me happy just looking at it."

A reporter standing nearby, unabashedly listening, took note. "Is that the woman who was murdered? She was one of the original commune members?"

"Yes, you'll see her image on the mural in the café," Mariah said in the tone of a museum docent. "Some of her stone sculptures are still available at Teddy's Treasure Trove. They use crystals found on the grounds of the commune."

"That last part is a stretch," Keegan whispered as the reporter jotted notes. "I've not even found potter's clay there."

She shrugged. "They're not the ones who'll be looking." She nodded at a man in the back corner, studying the illuminated oil painting of the Ingersson kitchen and its odd collection of guests. "The ones who look like that are the ones we're watching."

Still listening, the reporter glanced in that direction and shrugged. "Don't recognize him, but he's probably a goon. You must be expecting some high-level visitors. Want to give me a hint?"

"A goon?" Keegan studied the stranger—clean-cut, wearing a colorful shirt he wouldn't be caught in, and pressed khaki trousers. "Looks like any American tourist to me."

Mariah snorted and let the reporter answer for her.

"He's carrying concealed," the reporter explained. "Don't let the Hawaiian surfer dude shirt fool you. He has an earbud, although I don't know what good it's doing him. It's total air silence out here. Maybe they've hacked your City Hall's wi-fi. Any word on what the prize is for identifying the mural portraits?"

Mariah condescended to answer this question. "Hillvale isn't rich. We're hoping to give you the scoop of the year, since it appears all of you worked together, and there is no one real winner."

Mariah was talking to a reporter, and the reporter didn't recognize her! Keegan blinked in surprise. He'd recognize her from a dot in the distance and wearing a bear suit—she was that distinctive. How could people be so blind?

"Any hint on the scoop?" the reporter asked. "If it involves art, I need to bring the entertainment editor up here. I'm more interested in the recent murders."

"Crime scene news, at the very least," Mariah promised. "If not, then maybe we need to give out artwork as booby prizes."

The reporter snorted and went off to look at what the goon was looking at.

Keegan took Mariah's elbow and dragged her toward the entrance. "What crime besides murder?" he demanded.

"You're the one who mentioned Wainwright and time-space crystals and computers," she said pertly, hurrying toward the door now that he'd steered her in that direction.

"There is no crime in developing new science."

She shot him a dangerous look he never wanted to see on her face again.

"Crystal computers requiring no energy, right?" she asked. And before he could answer, she added, "Have you ever heard of the dark web and cryptocurrency?"

THIRTY

With anyone else, Mariah would be antsy by now. But Keegan with his laptop at her kitchen table actually made her feel—homey. That was probably dangerous for her unstable emotional state, and she focused on their task.

She had no internet, so it didn't hurt if she occasionally punched his keyboard to direct his search for cryptocurrency in her downloads. As she prepared lunch, he was muttering unintelligibly and lining up pebbles from his backpack across the old oak top. She tried not to interrupt, but she needed to return to the gallery soon and keep an eye on the goons.

Gun-toting bodyguards probably had little to do with secretly moving cash over the dark web, but they could be protecting someone who did. She just hadn't seen any of their suspects wandering around town yet.

She looked up in surprise as her front door swung open without warning. Cass and Amber stood on her doorstep. Without waiting for an invitation, Cass strode in. Amber trailed worriedly after her.

"Theodosia and Samantha cannot attend your reception this evening," Cass announced.

Keegan politely rose from his work, looking puzzled. Mariah patted his arm to let him know this wasn't a military invasion.

"I think Sam and Teddy probably have an opinion on that," Mariah said. She owed a great deal to Cass and knew it paid to heed her warnings.

"You have offered an open invitation to evil," Cass said. "Amber confirms my findings. We cannot risk all of us in the battle you have invited. Find some way to persuade your friends to stay with me tonight."

Mariah shivered, processing that prediction.

"Why don't you persuade them?" Keegan asked, coming to her defense.

She adored her warrior for his protective instincts, but this wasn't his battle. "Because Sam and Teddy would react negatively to Cass's commands. They're too new to understand, just as you are. Hillvale survives because there has always been a Lucy to guard it. Try to imagine what we would be if anything happened to Sam and Teddy."

Walker would probably lose it without Sam to bring him back from the abyss. Kurt would release years of stress and tension and explode the entire town, bulldoze it into the ground or worse. Mariah didn't know if Keegan could understand that, but she did. She also knew that this meant the Lucys wouldn't be there to guard her back tonight.

"I don't wish to harm Hillvale," she told Cass. "I'm willing to risk myself but not Sam and Teddy. What about the others? Harvey and Aaron and Tullah and the rest?"

"They are not directly involved. Val is, but I can persuade her. If you'll send them to me, we can form a shielding circle, but that's all we can do." Cass's lined and weary face relaxed at Mariah's cooperation.

"They'll not be happy. You'll have to work to keep them with you," Mariah warned.

"Beware Carmel. She's not what she seems. Those who hide behind crystal evil are beyond my abilities. I can only tell that they are here and they are waiting."

The killers were here? Damn, Walker was too good at grasping criminal motivation.

"Can you tell how many?" Mariah asked, amazed that Cass bothered to offer any information at all. Usually, she chose not to, especially in front of strangers like Keegan.

Cass shook her graying head. "Too many people are tainted. There is no predicting which side they will fall on when the time comes. Trust Lucys and no one else."

"Not even Walker, Kurt, and Lance?" Mariah's mouth dried at the thought of doing this practically alone.

"They will protect family first," Cass warned. "Kurt may despise what Carmel has become, but he will defend her with his dying breath."

"Then we'd better be sure that no one dies," Keegan said in his driest voice. "You have just named the partners of the women you're taking into your home. Perhaps we should send them to you as well."

Cass looked properly appalled. Mariah couldn't tell if Cass was shocked at the thought of Nulls at one of her shielding circles, or at Lance being Val's partner, when they hardly ever spoke to each other— very perceptive was her warrior to notice that. Although the unicorn painting and Lance's artwork sort of gave it all away.

Mariah stepped in to smooth over that bump. "If anything, we would need to send the Kennedys down the mountain, away from whatever happens. Hillvale needs them."

"You and Mr. Ives must decide on that course. Simply assure us that Samantha and Theodosia will join me this evening, and I will depart." Cass held herself regally straight, holding her walking staff without leaning on it. Cass would not beg, but she understood that Mariah wasn't hers to command.

"I will do all in my power to send them to safety," Mariah assured her.

She couldn't harm another friend.

"See that you succeed." Cass marched out. Amber offered an apologetic shrug, whispered, "It's in the cards," then hurried after Cass.

Keegan ran his hand through his unruly curls. "We're talking futuristic computers and currency, and they're talking magic spells?"

Mariah patted his arm again. "Welcome to Hillvale, Mr. Ives."

"YOU REALLY WANT ME TO SELL. . . EVIL. . . TO THE GOONS?" TEDDY whispered when Keegan and Mariah returned to her shop after lunch.

Keegan paced, hating every minute of this. He wanted to sweep everyone out of town and just punch Wainwright's face, but the dodgy pillock hadn't shown said face yet.

The thought gave him an idea, though. If he couldn't send everyone in Hillvale out of town, maybe he could send potential villains to a place where they could cause less harm.

"We do," he agreed aloud, before Mariah could answer. "If the goons are the paranormal police, they'll know what to do with hot rocks. If they're killers, then they can rot in their own hell."

"Paranormal police?" Teddy asked. "You're kidding, right?"

"He's kidding," Mariah said reassuringly. "Our Scot has a conscience bigger than his head. If we're right about what we think is going down, then they might be FBI or CIA collecting evidence. Not that they'll get far figuring out how the stones are used, since they don't have our abilities, but they'll take the evil rocks out of circulation."

Teddy donned the protective gloves Keegan had ordered. "And you can't explain who is doing what with corrupt almandine?" She swiftly sorted through the stones Kurt had brought from his safe.

"You want to explain how you feel emotions?" Keegan asked curtly. He wanted this over. "It has to do with what I can do to the crystals. It's better if you head off to Cass's after you're done here."

Teddy sorted the last few stones, shut the normal ones in her lockbox, and pushed the freezer bag of bad ones across her counter. "I'd certainly rather not see those creeps again. They might be good guys, but I no longer trust anyone carrying guns."

"Cass and Val promised more commune photos, so you and Sam can work through those. The ones they've already sent are fabulous. Maybe they'll have some of your parents as children? Or of your grandparents?" Mariah suggested.

Keegan pulled on the heavy gloves Teddy had taken off so he could handle the freezer bag. "Have Kurt and Monty take the photos you choose down to Baskerville for mounting. If those goons are working with Carmel, it's best to keep them away."

Teddy grimaced. "Does this mean we can't be part of tonight's fun?"

"We'll try to get rid of the goons before the reception. We'll let you know when it's all clear." Mariah stood at the front window, watching for customers heading this way.

Keegan wanted Mariah gone too. He just hadn't found a way to make her leave. She was more creative at making excuses to send people away than he was. She'd already told Samantha that Cass was receiving *messages* for Susannah, and that Cass needed Sam to assist in the séance. Apparently honesty wasn't a Lucy attribute.

Once Teddy had slipped out the back way and Keegan had the stones in hand, he glared at Mariah. "Go play with Lance and the gallery. The goons may recognize you."

"In war paint?" She had touched up the paint with streaks of brown and red and added an abundance of silver and turquoise cuffs to her shapely arms. "Finding a hulk like you in Teddy's place will scare them off. Stay in the kitchen. If they try to cheat, you can come out and shake them down."

"And if they're behind EWG? They're likely to eliminate you as a witness." Keegan grabbed one of the consignment wooden staffs off the wall. He'd tossed a few cabers in his time, but these weak branches would crack with one good blow.

"I'm no loss to the world." She dropped the bag in a drawer.

"There are times when I think you actually believe that, but now is not the time to knock the foolishness out of your head." Laying down the staff, Keegan hugged her. "I'll show you differently later."

He set her aside to retrieve the bag from the drawer and remove a stone with a gloved hand. He snapped it into one of the sample cases in his backpack. He'd yet to don a costume, but he'd pulled a work shirt on over his t-shirt. He'd ask magical Tullah for a hard hat so he could pretend he was a miner.

She watched him worriedly. "I hope the crystals are not affecting you already."

Frowning at that foolishness, he strode back to the window. "Here they come. Will you please leave this to me? I promise, I will not turn into a troll."

She thought about it while his blood pressure rose ten points.

"No, I still think they want to see a female here. You can sit on the stairs right behind this wall and hear everything. Not that either of us can stop speeding bullets, mind you."

Realizing he didn't have time to win this argument, Keegan growled, grabbed her waist, and messed up her war paint with a quick kiss. "Duck if they pull a gun. That counter base is solid."

The flimsy partition behind Mariah wasn't solid, and he had no intention of standing there. Carrying his purloined staff, Keegan yanked open the front door and marched out just as the two colorfully-shirted goons reached for the door. He gave them a steely glare and headed down the boardwalk.

The minute they closed the shop door, Keegan swung on his boot heels and slipped back to the partially open front door. He'd left a wedge in the frame so the door couldn't completely close. He waited on the side without the window. He couldn't see in, but they couldn't see him either.

"Where's the clerk we talked to this morning?" one of the shirts demanded.

"Teddy had to find a costume for tonight's reception. She said you'd left a deposit on these stones." Mariah sounded clipped and professional as she named the balance due.

Keegan clenched the stick in his fists, waiting.

"Will everyone be in costume?" the same man asked.

"No, just the locals. This is a practice run for the big gala next month. Hope you can come back then!"

Keegan heard the register ring. They'd paid cash, of course.

"Are you planning on making natural paints with those stones the way the hippies did?" Mariah asked.

"Paint? That's what they used tourmaline for?" the other man asked. "Pretty pricey paint."

"Teddy did tell you that those stones are almandine, didn't she?" Mariah sounded genuinely worried. "That amount of tourmaline would have cost you enough to buy this shop."

"It's reddish. That's all we need."

Keegan ducked around the corner as the door opened again. They carried the bag of stones toward the parking lot—and the chauffeured Escalade that he'd been told belonged to Carmel Kennedy.

The moment the Escalade drove off, Keegan returned to the shop. Mariah was holding up the bills to the light, presumably looking for the holograph to prove they weren't counterfeit.

"Real," she declared, returning the money to the drawer. "If they have that kind of cash, why would they need drug money?"

"Cryptocurrency isn't all about drugs," he reminded her. "It's simply a way to move funds without the feds or banks knowing about it. Just imagine what politicians could do with unrecorded funds! This, however, was a perfectly legal transaction."

"If selling evil can be called legal," she grumbled. "They didn't even open the bag. Does that mean they can sense what's in it?"

"I think it means the opposite. You'll remember my reaction when I first felt those stones. If they had any paranormal ability, they would have reacted to the bad energy. They took them to the Escalade that belongs to the lodge. Is there some chance that Kurt's mother is a Lucy?" Keegan had yet to meet the woman who owned the majority of the resort.

She wrinkled her nose. "Highly doubtful. Carmel was married to a Null and produced two Nulls. Nulls like money. Harvey says most of his family is Null and affected with *avarice*, as he calls it. I'd wager Carmel is the same. I think *greed* is the evil that lurks in these hills." She locked up the cash drawer and looked at him expectantly. "Now what?"

"Now we lure the villains out of town." Where he could lock Mariah in the bunker, if necessary.

Mariah studied him with suspicion. "I think Teddy is right. I think those stones remove inhibitions. You're not thinking like a scientist right now."

No, he was acting like a man protecting the treasure of his heart and her friends. Maybe the stones had affected him, but Keegan was pretty sure it was Mariah who had shattered his restraint.

MARIAH LOCKED UP TEDDY'S SHOP AFTER MOUNTAIN MAN STOMPED OFF, heading for who-knew-what trouble. How did he propose to find the *villains*? By the time she was out in the street, Keegan was already half way to the gallery.

She hurried after him, but Tullah stopped her outside the thrift store.

"You'll need this to complete your outfit," Tullah said, handing Mariah a bow and a quiver of arrows—real ones.

Appalled at being handed the kind of weapon that had murdered Daisy, Mariah pushed them away. "You do know that I have no idea how to shoot those things?"

"You will need them. The fates will see justice done." Tullah held the weapon commandingly.

Justice, she understood. Still uncomfortable, Mariah hung her crystal staff on her belt so she could gingerly accept the quiver. What the hell did she do with the huge bow? "I hope you didn't acquire them from anyone around here." Like Daisy's killer.

"EBay," Tullah said. "Now go after that man of yours. *He* knows their use."

Mariah saluted with the bow. Tullah was psychic in weirdly unpredictable ways, and she shivered at whatever stray intuition had caused her to look for bows on the internet.

Syd and Lance were still arranging photos when she entered the meeting hall. Mariah automatically checked the ghostcatchers near the ceiling—they were jiggling frantically. *Damn.*

Obviously on a mission, her Scot warrior stalked straight past reporters, Lucys arranging food tables, and tourists picking up pamphlets.

Focus, Mariah. She found a hook on the quiver for hanging the bow and reached for her staff. The energies building in here were peculiar. The crystal in her staff allowed her to feel them more clearly.

She felt a tug from the direction of the north wall. A distinguished man with graying light-colored hair was intently watching Keegan. She glanced down—the stranger's hands were clenched in fists.

The right hand bore a signet ring much like Keegan's.

They'd dragged Robert Gabriel out of hiding. Pulse escalating, Mariah studied Trevor's son, the one meeting with Edison and Wainwright for reasons unknown. What had Keegan said about his ring? It was usually given to the daughters but went to a son if he had paranormal abilities? Would Robert have Keegan's crystal conversion gift?

Of course he did. The question was only—what did he do with it?

She didn't like the way he watched Keegan. Did he recognize him as family? She eased in Gabriel's direction while scanning the rest of the room. She didn't see Caldwell Edison or Ralph Wainwright.

"Ladies and gentlemen." Reaching the podium in front of the triptych curtain, Keegan spoke in his most rounded Oxford accents.

Mariah figured the Brit accent alone caused heads to swerve. His size and movie-star looks would hold their attention.

"We have discovered a secret treasure trove of Ingersson crystals, the famed stones ground into paint and used in the museum pieces found around the world. The pamphlets and website are better at explaining their use in oils and artwork than I am. I'm a mere geologist, but I can recognize and identify the rocks stored on the farm, still in their natural state. This evening may be the one and only time that these rare crystals will be displayed in one place. After that, the rocks will be dispersed to various organizations chosen by the Ingersson heirs. So call your friends and tell them this is the event of a lifetime for art lovers. There's still time to book rooms at the lodge!"

Mariah stared in disbelief as Keegan casually strode out the side exit.

The stranger who had to be Robert Gabriel reached for his phone, realized it wouldn't work, and hustled out.

Appalled, Mariah grasped Keegan's intent. How could he put himself in danger knowing how much he meant to so many people? Including her, in case the beast didn't realize it.

He'd said he wanted to get the villains out of town—he meant to have them follow him! *Crap damn frigging hell.* She'd have to shoot him if the villains didn't.

THIRTY-ONE

Keegan rode the ATV straight up to the farmhouse ruins. He was fairly certain he was running on insanity, but he wasn't born to play cat-and-mouse games. He couldn't cruise the dark web and locate his suspects the way Mariah might. And he damned well didn't want her to risk her soul doing so. He lacked the patience or cleverness to draw suspects into incriminating themselves at a social gathering the way Walker planned. It wasn't as if a killer would conveniently admit to murder.

And he didn't want killers stalking Mariah or her friends.

What he did have was his wits and his knowledge. They'd been enough to help him out of tight situations on six continents. That would have to be enough now. He hoped the bait he'd offered reached the right ears. Even so, it would take time for anyone to find their way up here. While he waited, he needed to choose his battleground the same way his warrior ancestors once had.

Kurt's security guard wandered over to see what was up. Keegan had him radio Walker his position and told the guard to stay out of sight. After obtaining approval from the police chief, the guard returned to the lane to move his car.

Keegan had set up the basics around the bunker door by the time

Mariah hiked up the back trail, still wearing her archery weapons. He had hoped she'd let him be. He'd known she wouldn't.

"I lost my best friend when I gave her too much information," she said ominously. "I am *not* losing you."

That would take a while to wrap his head around—she was protecting *him*? "I don't suppose that's a real bow?" Her declaration had thrown him off balance. He attempted to find firmer ground.

"It is, but I don't know how to use it. Give me a surfboard, and I can knock a man flying. I'd be good with a slingshot too, if we had one." She removed her leather net bag from her waist and opened it.

"Are you planning on spinning string between the rocks, capturing ghosts, and scaring evil-doers to death?" He kept on gathering rocks, rolling boulders, and listening for vehicles.

Mariah punched his arm. "You'd do better moving Daisy's guardians in front of your position. If you keep your back to the bunker door, you only need them in front." She strode off to pick up the foot-high stone statues with crystal eyes.

He didn't bother arguing, which proved his state of insanity. If he could melt rocks into diamonds, why not rely on stone guardians?

"I can't do this if you're here," he warned, which was when he realized he expected her to understand what he was doing. Judging from her lack of complaint, he figured she was a born warrior too. "You're too much of a distraction."

"Get used to it, big boy. Distract is what I do best. Put me to use." She lined the statues in a semi-circle in front of the bunker.

And then she opened the bag she'd left on the ground and pulled out ghostcatchers.

"You think the killers are ghosts?" Keegan asked in disbelief.

"Hardly." She took one of the arrows, twirled it in the ground in front of her barrier of statues, and inserted a long branch into the hole she created. Then she removed her peculiar string and tied a crosspiece on the branch, forming a tall skinny cross, to which she tied one of her feathery, beaded nets. "Spirits—and thus my nets—warn of disturbances in the ether."

"You're crazier than I am." Keegan rolled a boulder to protect his right flank. Mariah dug another hole in front of it.

They had the world's weirdest bunker established by the time they heard the first vehicle roll up the road. Foot-high stone statues with gleaming eyes formed the first barricade. Hip-high boulders, and sticks streaming feathered nets, formed an inner barrier. Keegan topped two of the boulders with a flat-top, table-sized slab of granite. Behind him, he had the manzanita-covered hillock containing the bunker—poor defense but he hoped the enemy didn't know where he was until they came around front.

"Hide," he ordered. "I can't pull this off if they see you here."

"You might, if you'd tell me your plan," she grumbled. She produced a key on a ribbon and unlocked the bunker. "We've left all the Lucys behind. We're on our own."

"Which is the way I wanted it," he retorted. "Here they come. Get in there."

She left the door somewhat ajar. Keegan figured his bulk and the towering bushes would conceal it.

He spread his samples on top of the table rock and faked working with them.

An older man with receding gray hair and a portly build ambled down the rutted drive. He had his suit coat hooked over his shoulder with one hand. Sweat stained his pink dress shirt. Keegan seethed in frustration. This wasn't a physically-fit man capable of bringing down Daisy with a bow, or even one capable of climbing into the canyon to shoot Thompson.

"Thought I might find you here," the stranger said with jolly humor. "You're one of us, aren't you? We could use more of your kind."

"Wainwright," Mariah whispered behind him. "Related to Cass, Lucinda, and you."

How the hell could she identify him? Oh right, she studied computer files and apparently had the memory of one. Narrowing his eyes, Keegan thought he almost recognized the affable gentleman who had visited his family back when he was in primary school. Wainwright was grayer and stouter and looked a little rougher around the edges these days. Bri looked nothing like him, but they apparently had similar souls if Mariah's research was right.

"No idea what you're talking about," Keegan said with equally false cheer, not admitting he recognized Wainwright to see how this played out. "This is private property. Wasn't the security guard out there?"

"Didn't see a soul. You're wearing the same ring as Gabriel. Noticed that right away about both of you. I didn't get the ring. It went to Lucinda's sister and her brood. Were you planning on converting those rocks before you take them down to the reception? They're not really the originals from the commune are they?"

"You might at least introduce yourself," Keegan said, applying pressure to one of the sample pebbles. He'd spent some time practicing this last night.

"Oh, sorry, thought you recognized me. We met once, but that was in another time and place. I'm Ralph Wainwright. Brianna is my granddaughter. I'd hoped you would see reason and work with her. She's a smart girl and can make your fortune."

Behind him, Mariah hissed. Keegan would like to do the same, but he shrugged instead. "I have my own fortune, earned honestly through hard work. Bri apparently chose a different path."

"Not so different," Wainwright objected, stepping over the guardian stones to examine the sample table. "The molecular construction of the gems we created wasn't as genuine as the ones Gabriel creates. Unfortunately, he's something of a loose cannon. I think the rocks are affecting his stability. If he'd read the journals, he'd understand that. You don't have the journals, so you don't know the danger of what you're doing."

Keegan had a pretty damned good idea that turning rocks into gems wasn't healthy.

Wainwright was doing his best to adopt an avuncular tone, but Keegan knew his type well. The world was full of charlatans who sold the modern version of snake oil. These were the greedy people Mariah called soulless. Or lacking *essence*. Bloodsuckers were dangerous to one's pocket, but this one appeared physically harmless.

"You have the journals then? I'd wondered." Keegan held out the artificial diamond he'd just created. "Are these what you need?"

Wainwright's eyes glittered, but he resisted reaching for it. "The market is too wary right now. We had to back out of selling diamonds and use them for experimentation. What we need is the tourmaline. I thought that's what you planned to display tonight."

"No, the feds took that for safekeeping," Keegan lied as blithely as any Lucy. He didn't know if the goons were feds or if safekeeping was their intent. But there was enough truth in his statement for him to stretch it. "You aren't working with them? I should think they'd be funding your line of work."

Wainwright went blank, then suspicious. "The feds? Why would they be interested?"

"Computers that run on synthetic crystals without using energy? Why *wouldn't* the feds be interested? I'm thinking of giving the labs a call, see if they can use my ability. It's pretty freaky, but not any freakier than what they're doing. Warping the space-time continuum? That's huge."

His portly visitor lost his jovial expression. "Don't be ridiculous. Those labs are underfunded. They'll never get their theory off the drawing board. *But we've done it.* We're on the brink of accomplishing the impossible. We only need a little more funding. Can you make rubellite? Gabriel's aren't holding up. The journal says the structure holds the intent of the maker, and Gabriel has lost his focus."

Keegan wanted his hands on those journals so bad his teeth ached with it. The *structure*? The molecular structure of the crystal? *Holds the intent of the maker?* What did that mean?

"Danger!" Mariah whispered urgently.

He glanced past Wainwright. The ghostcatchers danced violently.

"Down!" Keegan shouted. He couldn't reach across the table to force Wainwright to obey. He ducked behind the boulder just as he heard a *thud* followed by Wainwright's groan. *Oh shit.* This was not what he'd planned at all.

That hadn't been a gun shot.

"How good are you at archery?" Mariah whispered. "That has to be Daisy's killer up behind that piece of Bald Rock, halfway up the hill. I saw his bow. Tullah is getting too damned good at predictions."

Crouched behind the boulder, Keegan could see movement behind a broken slab of sandstone. "How did he get there without us seeing him?"

"There's a trail behind him. All the Lucys know it. We need to drive him out so we can check on Wainwright. The old boy dodged at your yell and threw the shooter off. He may still be alive, but he's visible."

"All right, hand me the bow. Do I make war cries or is that your department?" He placed himself in front of the bunker door so she couldn't go around him.

"My Nana was Ohlone. If they have a war cry, I don't know it. I can do better—echo effect." She passed him the quiver and bow through the opening. He notched the arrow and tried to look for a good shot without having to stand. Without warning, she hooted. The sound bounced off the bluff and resounded through the valley.

Startled, the archer jerked around to look behind him, just enough for Keegan to catch a glimpse of a khaki shirt . It had been a long time since he'd pulled a bow and this one was unfamiliar. . .

With no chance to think, he simply acted. Drawing the bow until his shoulder muscles strained and the string brushed his ear, he squinted to narrow his focus—and let the arrow fly.

The ensuing cry of pain indicated he'd hit flesh. Whether it was sufficient to stop someone determined to kill. . .

A hawk screeched and swooped low. Waving his arms, the archer tumbled from his hiding place. With the man fully visible, Keegan pulled his bow again. He released the arrow the instant his mark scrambled for escape. This time, he had a clear view but had the wind and a moving target working against him. He couldn't tell how hard he'd hit, but the archer collapsed on the rocks.

"Are you still with me?" he demanded, lowering the bow but terrified to look behind him and find Mariah lost to a hawk again.

"I'm good," she said. "The hawk was just providence working, not me. I think you got him. Can I come out now? That has to be Daisy's killer, and I want to rip his eyes out."

"Or maybe that was Daisy trying to rip his eyes out," he said in relief. Verifying that his target wasn't moving, Keegan leaned inside the doorway and kissed her. "No eye ripping. Give me a minute more. And thank you for listening."

"You did what none of us could, Big Boy. I'll try to listen more often."

He snorted in disbelief. Standing to circle around his boulder barricade, he located Wainwright on the ground between Daisy's statues and the rock table. An arrow stuck out of his left shoulder, but the old man was still breathing.

"Gabriel is cracking," Wainwright muttered through his pain.

Keegan threw a glance up the hill. Did that mean he'd just shot his distant cousin? Horror rippled through him. If Gabriel hadn't used crystals for wrong—could he be saved? He had to climb up there and find out.

Apparently Wainwright felt the same. "Our line will die out if you don't carry it on. Don't let him get you too."

"The crystals are more likely to *get* me than Gabriel is," Keegan warned. "I need those journals you and Bri stole. Tell me where they are, or I'll just let you die here the way you and your fiendish friends did poor Daisy."

"I didn't know anything about the old lady," Wainwright protested. "I told you, Gabriel is cracking. We only kept him on because he spent his summers here, knows everyone and everything."

Interesting point, but not the one he wanted addressed. "The journals," Keegan demanded again.

"In my briefcase, in my office in Sacramento." Wainwright was looking more gray.

Somehow, he'd have to reach that office before anyone else did. Checking the archer now attempting to escape, Keegan fought a snarl. "Mariah, wait until I'm up the hill before you come out. There's a security guard on the road who can call Walker."

She peered from behind the partially open door. "Harvey is up on top. He can't do more than smack people with a stick, but he has your back. If we're lucky, Aaron or someone else is stationed on the road by now. I'll send a signal."

Lucys! Keegan didn't know whether to be happy or furious at their interference. He didn't want anyone hurt in this battle he'd chosen for himself. But he acknowledged her warning with a nod and headed out, praying his quarry didn't have a gun.

THIRTY-TWO

The spirits that inhabited the valley had been stirred by the violent encounter between Keegan and the archer. The ghostcatchers swung warily, but not with the agitation of earlier. Mariah had no idea why spirits lingered here. She just knew the spirits of those who had gone before them clung to this land.

She crawled out of her safe abode and scanned the hillside. Keegan strode up the mountain as if he were a boulder rolling uphill. She held her breath as the man he approached reached under his shirt.

Whatever Keegan did or said had the injured man collapsing.

"Thank you, Daisy," she whispered, stopping to wipe her nets clean. She didn't know if Daisy's stone guardians had kept them safe or not, but she felt connected to Daisy here.

She continued around the barricade to Wainwright. Because she was angry and scared, she sent her bits of ectoplasm into the ether by slapping his wounded shoulder as she tested the arrow. It was lodged firmly. "I'm no medic. I probably need to leave this for the professionals."

He winced at her rough handling. "Where the hell did you come from?"

"We're working on corporeal transitioning," she said maliciously.

He rightfully ignored that riposte. "You're the worthless illegal Keegan prefers to Brianna?" he asked in what sounded like incredulity.

"I'm the relatively wealthy, totally legal Californian with a degree from Stanford who told him about cryptocurrency and how it might work with your synthetic gems and computers. Want to call me more names?" So much for concealing her identity.

But in Hillvale, she didn't have to put up with sexist, racist crap. Obligated to no employer, she could stand tall and punch back with impunity. She rather enjoyed his wince as he shut up. She could see where people might get off on power trips.

Not wanting to be that kind of troll, she turned her attention away from her selfish whims. Up the hill, Keegan had his knee in the back of the man he'd brought down. She whistled and waved her staff to signal others it was safe to come out.

Harvey's crystal glinted in acknowledgement above Keegan. From the road, Aaron and Walker sauntered down. Hillvale was becoming really good at predicting trouble—although she and Keegan had left a pretty clear trail.

"I meant no insult." Finding another angle to work, Wainwright whimpered while trying to sit up. "You would benefit from asking Keegan to join us. We have the future in our hands."

A whole new world of computing beckoned if what Keegan had told her was true. Bending space and time and creating energy with crystals. . . Every household could have a computer.

And this clod's only goal was to make *money* with Keegan's ability. Avarice instead of thinking of how the earth and humankind could be improved. She'd seen greed at work. She wanted no part of it. She waved her staff as peremptorily as Cass at the men approaching.

"Ralph Wainwright," she called. "Probably guilty of money-laundering and fraud. The real killer is up there with Keegan."

Walker jogged toward Keegan. Aaron joined her out of curiosity—or perhaps he picked up vibrations from the stones he ran his hand over, ones Wainwright may have touched.

"Ralph here has Keegan's journals in a briefcase in his office in Sacramento." She kept her voice down so Walker wouldn't hear. "Is there any way we can retrieve them before the feds seal the place?"

With his long thin face and goatee, solemn Aaron looked as if he belonged on the apostle mural. He raised his dark eyebrows, glanced down at the groaning man holding his shoulder, and nodded. "I'll go down to get help. We'll figure it out while you're dealing with the law. Tell Keegan I have the ATV, and he'll have to ride with Walker. That should slow them all down."

"We're pretty sure there's still a third one involved," Mariah warned. "Maybe in addition to whoever is working with Carmel. I don't think this is over. Be careful."

Aaron watched the men up the hill and nodded thoughtfully. "Keegan has an interesting family. I'll let Cass know you're all right." He jogged back toward the road.

"You can't just break into my office," Wainwright complained after Aaron left. "And I'm not a money launderer. I'm a scientist."

"You don't deny you're financing cryptocurrency with fake gems and dealing with killers?" She offered him a bottle of water from her bag.

He leaned against a boulder and sipped, grimacing in pain. "Gabriel is unstable. I don't know what he's done. All I'm doing is building a better future. Brianna understands. She helped me set up the funding, but now that she no longer has access to Keegan's firm, we're having difficulty. Converting the malleable crystals seems best. Learning there might still be some here was a blessing. If Keegan would only work with me. . ."

The ATV roared off, and Wainwright sent a worried glance in the direction of the road.

"Who told you there were malleable crystals here—Gabriel?" If so, she hoped that gray-haired man they were carrying down the hill was Gabriel.

"Gabriel is an arse. Thompson was the one who knew where to find this bunker and the crystal crevasse. Gabriel just wanted to make more pretty crystals like his father's. He never applied himself to learning anything other than how to use them for his own purposes. I warned. . ." He shut up, looking puzzled that he'd revealed so much.

She needed to keep him talking. The cops wouldn't understand Gabriel's paranormal uses for crystals. She tried another angle. "Why would George Thompson try to break into Daisy's bunker?"

Mariah wanted answers before Walker warned Wainwright he had a right to remain silent.

The old man closed his eyes and leaned heavily against the boulder. "Gabriel was obsessed with his mother, convinced she was keeping him from some truth only she knew. He warned us she had ways of stopping us from collecting the crystals, that she probably had a supply hidden here. He pointed out those little stone men she made as proof." Wainwright nodded at the figurine Mariah hadn't realized she'd picked up.

She gripped the stones tighter, studying the little warrior, appalled at what Wainwright seemed to be saying. *Those little stone men she made—*Daisy? Peace-loving, crazy, talented Daisy? Mother of a killer?

Daisy had carried the sketch in her cart because *Robert Gabriel was her son?*

The whole appalling story unraveled in Mariah's head just as if Daisy were here to tell it. Unlovely, socially impaired Daisy, playing with her stones and crystals in a commune filled with handsome, talented young men. The pot, the mushrooms, the LSD, and free love. Handsome Trevor from the mural, the man who talked dozens of old ladies out of their fortunes, who used crystal power to mesmerize the vulnerable—Daisy wouldn't have resisted his charm.

"Gabriel might have been *born* unstable," Mariah murmured, horrified. Remembering the photo of a plump young Daisy dancing in the field—Daisy had been happy about the child. Daisy had not been competent enough to raise one. No one knew about the danger of drugs to fetuses back then. And if that fetus had an erratic Lucy heritage from both parents. . .

"I don't know anything about that," Wainwright said. "Gabriel told charming stories of his childhood summers playing with the other children here. He complained bitterly about spending his winters in the mansions of his wealthy stepmothers. So maybe he *was* cracked from birth."

Preferring sunshine and freedom with a mother who loved him to the wealthy prisons of adults who didn't care didn't seem cracked to Mariah, but it may have created a fissure in a vulnerable child.

Susannah and Val must have known Robert as children. But she and Keegan hadn't confided in them. The Ingerssons had no reason to mention Trevor Gabriel's son spending summers here, if they even knew his parentage. He could have been one of the many children in the photograph of the archery contest.

She watched Walker and Keegan carry the injured man down the hill, in the direction of the road and the police chief's car. She could hear the ATV returning, probably with Brenda, the nurse.

Information just wants to be free had been her mantra for years—until it had hit her upside the head, destroyed her life and that of countless others, and deposited her here.

She no longer knew how to be honest or what should be made known and what shouldn't. She looked at the big man returning for her and swallowed hard.

She didn't want Daisy's peace-loving image ruined by revealing that she had had an unstable child by a criminal who had defrauded hundreds of vulnerable women. Trevor had taken advantage of an innocent. Mariah wanted to rage at the selfish ways of men, but Keegan had made her realize they weren't all like that. She couldn't be equally selfish by deciding who got to know what.

She had to trust someone, and that was Keegan.

~

July 14: Saturday evening

Keegan slammed the hardhat on his head and paced up and down Mariah's front room. "If Robert Gabriel is the son of Trevor, the charlatan, and your Daisy, then he knew about the Hillvale crystals. Since Robert wears his father's signet ring, he must have inherited his paranormal ability. If Wainwright claims Robert was helping them with the crystals, then his ability must be similar to mine. If making gems broke his mind so much that he killed his mother in a bout of paranoia, I don't think I want to touch rocks anymore."

What the hell would he do with himself if he couldn't hunt minerals?

"I only told *you* as a warning," Mariah said, refastening her braid after their shower. "All our talents have limitations and dangers. Now that you know yours, you'll have to find a way to work with it, just as I must."

"You stuffed your talent under a rock and hid." He glared at her. "Not helpful. I need those books."

"Aaron will find them," Mariah said reassuringly. "With his

psychometry, he might learn a thing or three while he's there. He, at least, has learned to deal with his talent."

Keegan lifted the hardhat to run his hand over his still-damp hair. He couldn't stop fretting over all the dangling threads left undone and unanswered. He was relieved that they now had evidence of his family's innocence, but he didn't think Mariah grasped the next step. "Wainwright's confession could clear my family's name, but if he hires a lawyer. . ."

He watched Mariah grimace as she grasped the implication. She would have to testify—in court, under oath, under her real name. He *hated* this.

"I caused your family's problems. I'll fix them," she said flatly. "But right now, we need the rest of the story. I'll hope Gabriel is confessing to Thompson's murder as well as Daisy's. I'd hate for there to be more than one killer around. But Edison is not innocent. He's been meeting with the others for a reason. We need to find out what he wanted out of cryptocurrency."

"We can guess that—unrecorded funds for his father's political campaigns. And probably bribery or worse." Keegan scowled and donned the tool belt he wore when rock hunting. "But your reporters have left town. They're all down the mountain, calling in Gabriel's story, or what they know of it. Your element of surprise is gone. Edison will have run."

She shrugged and finished clasping a silver cuff on her upper arm. "We can hope Edison is arrogant enough to believe he's safe. The reporters will be back for free food and drink. So I guess we just give them the party we promised."

Keegan wanted to pour himself into kissing her rather than think of a party on top of this afternoon's stress. He felt drained from repeating his story to Walker and again to the sheriff. He needed a corner of quiet to process all they'd learned. "I'm glad Wainwright spilled his guts to you. That helped tremendously."

A frown formed between her eyes. "It was a little weird. I thought people only did that in mystery books when they're about to kill their victim. If he'd lawyered up instead of talking, we'd still know nothing. It's not as if paranormal gems and cryptocurrency are the kinds of fraud and theft the law understands."

"Maybe he felt guilty for pinning the fraud on my father. Who knows the way the criminal mind works? Let's go. I hope there's lots of food. I'm about to eat my arm." Keegan put a hand at the small of her back and nudged her toward the door before she could fiddle with her bands again.

Keegan admired the sway of her full hips in the tight suede pants as she sauntered out ahead of him. If he could just think about sex, he might make it through this evening.

It was early yet. The meeting hall held mostly locals milling around the food tables. Mariah squeezed his arm and nodded at a group of gray heads by the refreshment table. "I think the couple in tie-dyed shirts are the married artists from the mural, the ones without the red eyes, the Morrisons."

He ambled in that direction for a better look. "Is that Bradford Edison with them, the elderly politician?"

"Shit, yes." She hung back, scanning the crowd. "I don't see his son. And that looks like a Menendez hanging with them. I've seen some of them around but never been introduced."

"The only Menendez in the mural was Dolores." Keegan studied the distinguished man with gray at his temples and the brown skin of a weathered native. "And she was a Wainwright. Could this be Susannah's husband, Carlos, or one of his relations?"

"Maybe. Where's Harvey? He was supposed to drag his whole family here, not just Carlos." She released his arm to swing around and scan the room. "The dirtbag is hiding." She marched off toward a coven of women still setting up the refreshment table.

That left Keegan alone when Caldwell Edison entered with a stunning ash-blonde on his arm. About the same age as her escort, she had a familiar square-jawed face and held herself as if accustomed to peons scraping and bowing. From all he'd heard, Keegan assumed he'd just had his first glimpse of Carmel Kennedy.

The couple strolled directly toward the older generation congregating in the back corner.

A stunned hush fell over the meeting hall. Mariah turned from her conference with the women, apparently to see why. Keegan loved the way her thick-lashed eyes widened at sight of Carmel. He could almost see the wheels grinding behind them. She sent one of the younger women off. He hoped it was in pursuit of the errant Harvey, because one of the goons had just slipped in.

So, maybe they still had unfinished business here.

Keegan idled over to the AV presentation and flipped it on. The speakers burst into life with a soaring orchestral production. As if the music introduced them, Sam's mother and the man who must be her husband strolled in—which meant the older man standing with Edison wasn't Carlos, but one of his family. This had all the earmarks of a planned meeting.

Keegan couldn't make himself small, so he simply sauntered over to the refreshment table and began filling a plate. He didn't want to meet the evening on an empty stomach.

The slides streaming across the far wall didn't appear to interest the older generation. A few of the locals who hadn't been around earlier wandered over to admire the flashing images taken by commune members half a century ago, interspersed with the biographies Mariah had compiled.

To his relief, Mariah joined him and began filling her own plate. "They're plotting. How can we find out what?"

"Without planting electronic equipment or developing super hearing? I have no suggestions. They'll shut up if we intrude. We need Samantha or Kurt or someone they consider family and harmless."

She narrowed her eyes and studied the hall's occupants. "Speaking of harmless, where's Dinah?"

"Hiding, like Harvey, I suspect." Keegan scanned the room. "Tullah is either talking to herself or there is someone in that closet in the back corner."

Mariah snorted. "Or both. We need to make an announcement thanking Dinah for her hard work and saying there is a donation jar at the reception desk to defray the expenses of this event. We set the official opening as 7:30, right? Is it almost time?"

He checked his watch. "It is. Do we have an official speaker?"

"The mayor, if he was here. Do you think he actually went into town with Kurt? Or is he hiding too?" Mariah washed down Dinah's quiche with bottled water.

"Why do I have the perilous feeling that this battle is being orchestrated by our elders?" Frustrated, Keegan continued plowing through Dinah's delectable dishes.

"Well, if no one else shows up, I'll have to step up to the podium. I know most of the reporters are gone, but I really don't want to put myself on display." Mariah eased closer to the chatting group at the end of the tables while she eyed the forbidden dessert tray.

"Everyone went to a great deal of trouble to put this together in a day for us. We ought to get something out of it." Keegan fretted, not wanting to put Mariah on display either.

The audio-visual presentation abruptly cut off and a more dramatic orchestration rose from the speakers. The gallery lighting dimmed. At the same time, balls of light floated down from the ceiling.

Mariah hissed. "Cass."

But it wasn't Cass entering through the open double doors at the front of the hall. It was Valerie Ingersson, aka Valdis, goddess of death. Keegan recalled her operatic keening over Daisy's body and shivered. "Where's Lance?" he whispered.

"Damn." Mariah searched the dimming room. "In back, guarding the triptych. I can only see his shadow."

"I don't like this, but we need to separate. You head for Val. I'm putting myself between Lance and the crazies." He set down his plate, kissed her, and eased his way into the milling audience.

Weird choice but Mariah supposed men had to stick together—and the position would give Keegan a better view of the room and reassure Dinah in her closet.

Which meant she was on her own now, with potential killers, vultures, and a coven of unpredictable witches. Oh, joy.

THIRTY-THREE

The crowd separated to let the drama queen pass. Wearing an elaborate black lace mantilla over her hair and face, Val dragged a long black train of ruffles, probably from a vintage role in *Hello, Dolly*. She'd prepared for this—with Cass's help, for sure.

Mariah fell in behind her, keeping to one side. It was dark enough in the center of the hall that she didn't worry about being recognized, unless reporters were looking for computer engineer Zoe de Cervantes as a caricature of a back-to-nature hippy.

She could see Keegan in his miner's hat easing along the wall toward the podium. The track lighting on the artwork had gone out, but it was still daytime outside. Sunshine filtered through cracks in the wall and the open front doors. Cass's damned weird light balls added to the illusion.

It was intuition, pure and simple, that made Mariah turn and look behind her.

While the audience watched Val and her spectral form drifting toward the back of the hall and the podium, Cass and her cadre were slipping through the entrance. Mariah nearly expired of relief, followed by a rush of terror. What did it mean that Cass had dared bring Sam and Teddy here?

She hated not being in on the plot.

Helplessly, Mariah continued after Val. She eased to one side, placing herself between the podium and the older generation watching the performance. Keegan took a position behind the podium, near Lance and the talking closet. Mariah could see Dinah's full pink skirt peeking from behind Tullah's statuesque form—not far from one of the goons who had bought Teddy's gems. Dinah feared the law. If she thought the sunglasses and a gun meant the feds, no wonder she was hiding. Maybe she had a point.

When Val reached the podium, the music abruptly halted. Waiting for one operatic moment, until she was certain all attention was on her, Val burst into a heart-wrenching rendition of *Amazing Grace* that filled the entire hall to the rafters. By the time she finished, half the audience was in tears, and Sam and Teddy had taken up positions in the center front, facing the podium.

Cass was barely an arm's length behind Mariah, which meant Cass was in Carmel's direct line of sight. The silence was deafening as Val began to speak.

"Kris Kristofferson once famously wrote 'Freedom is just another word for nothing left to lose.' I am free. I have lost everything and everyone I have ever loved. I have lost myself. All I have left to lose is a meaningless plot of dirt and rocks that once housed a vibrant, loving community, a community that lost its soul to greed and ambition."

Mariah had goose bumps just hearing the anguish Val poured into her speech.

The crowd murmured. Mariah tried to keep an eye on the wealthy, powerful clique to her side, the ones to whom Val was really addressing this speech. Poor Lance stood like a frozen shadow in the background. No one stepped forward to interrupt. Most of the audience thought Val as mad as Daisy had been. But Val had hidden depths and a simmering anger begging to emerge. Mariah recognized the symptoms well.

"Before I let one more person die for that land," Val continued, "I will set it free as well." Playing the audience like a pro, she waited until the crowd quieted.

Mariah had a feeling this was Cass's work, and the real reason she'd wanted Sam to stay behind.

"In memory of Daisy," Val continued, "in memory of the family we once were, in memory of the brilliance that died for dirt, my niece and I give the Ingersson property in its entirety to the town of Hillvale for the betterment of the community, for the education of artists and musicians, in perpetuity. Samantha and I reserve the right to choose the first board of governors, who will then choose their replacements when the time comes. There will be no politics, no filthy lucre, nothing but love and hard work involved in this land. The town will make of it what it will."

Mariah heard a male curse nearby, but she didn't recognize the voice. Someone wasn't happy with Val's decision, though.

"This is *your* work, you old hag." A female cry followed the curse.

That voice, Mariah recognized—Carmel.

Still attuned to Val at the podium, Cass didn't acknowledge the insult —or the truth. Of course Cass was behind Val's decision. The consequences might destroy any hope of the Kennedys expanding the resort.

Val turned toward Cass and the gathering of elders. Cass's floating balls of light framed a halo over Val as she raised her voice.

"Bradford Edison, you were once a friend of my father's. You know the tragic circumstances of his death. I do not blame you for not helping him when he needed it. He was lost to his addictions, to the greed and ambition that consumed him. No one could have saved him."

The older gentleman who had once worn a bear claw for a mural and played folk music for the commune stepped toward the podium as if wanting to speak. As a life-time performer and politician, Bradford Edison was accustomed to commanding attention.

His son caught his arm and held him back, while whispering urgently to Carmel. Caldwell Edison appeared intent on dragging his father from the hall, but the old man refused and shook him off. If any of that crowd carried a gun—Mariah couldn't stop bullets. She swallowed hard and prayed Val would use common sense.

The death goddess wasn't known for common sense.

Trust Lucys and no one else, Cass had said. Lucys were stirring this dangerous pot. Mariah had to trust that they knew what they were doing, because it certainly looked as if the pot was about to boil over.

"But the evil that pollutes this land continues to poison it," Val said in a ringing voice. "Until we learn to work for the good of all and not just the wealthy few, we will never know harmony."

"That's socialism, Val." Caldwell Edison gave up on persuading his father to leave. Brushing off Carmel's restraining hand, he took a step toward the podium. "Every man has an equal chance to get ahead in this country. Some are just better at it than others."

"Oh right, like a kid from the slum has the same exact opportunities as the trust fund set," a voice cried from the back.

Intent on his own purpose, Caldwell ignored the cry. "You're preventing the town from succeeding, with this hare-brained scheme of yours, Val."

Before Mariah could intervene, Cass caught her arm and dug her long nails into bare skin in warning.

Val pointed her finger at Caldwell, broke out in an operatic song in Italian, then flung back her veil.

The lights came on.

The audience gasped as Val stood there in all her ruined beauty. Cameras flashed. Mariah glanced over her shoulder—the reporters were returning. One of them had probably been the heckler. They would eventually recognize the local actress who had once achieved stardom. Val had come out of hiding.

"You, Caldwell, haven't changed," Val declared. "You still think *men* are created equal, and that women don't figure into the equation, you poor pathetic soul. Now I understand why you destroyed me—not out of jealousy, but because a *woman* had the fame and power you craved."

Cass muttered under her breath and didn't release Mariah from her grip.

"That's a lie!" Carmel cried. "Caldwell would never lift a hand against a woman. You're the jealous creature here, denying everyone else the happiness you lost."

"Old bones," Mariah murmured, trying to tug away from Cass. The older woman's nails dug in tighter, and then Cass nodded in a signal that stirred Sam from her post near Val.

As loud voices broke out in argument, Sam carried Mariah's canvas sack of ghostcatchers over to her. "They're wriggling like crazy," Sam whispered.

"Demand truth," Cass told Mariah. "Take what your grandmother taught you and apply it now."

What her Nana had taught her? To weave nets to catch ectoplasm and fling it across the veil? Stunned by the senseless command at a time like this, Mariah retrieved a wriggling net from the sack's interior. This one looked as if it came from the café.

Instinctively wiping the threads of ectoplasmic energy to calm the net, she recalled doing this at the farmhouse only a few hours earlier.

When Wainwright had confessed.

Keegan had said Harvey thought their abilities were what they made of them.

If she didn't fling essence through the veil. . .

Shooting Cass a startled glance, Mariah stepped between Caldwell and Val, raised her hand, and slapped the politician's tight-assed son with invisible plasma. "Let the truth be free," she said in glee.

She had no idea what she was doing, but she loved the freedom of being herself.

"Why you—" Caldwell raised his fist.

Keegan was there so swiftly that he may as well have flown. He collared Caldwell, lifting his shoes from the floor. "Careful," he warned.

"Who cut Val?" Mariah demanded, testing her insane theory.

"It was an accident," Caldwell roared, wriggling to be set down. "The bitch lied and schemed and then she walked out, leaving me looking like a fool. No one does that to me."

In front, Val began to hum the "Battle Hymn of the Republic."

Mariah almost snickered. *His truth is marching on,* indeed. "That doesn't sound like an accident," she said, keeping accusation from her voice. Here's where she applied what she'd learned from dealing with trolls—give them an opportunity and let them hang themselves.

Caldwell's father seemed prepared to intervene, but Keegan's glare would have turned a lesser person to stone.

"I was angry. I was drunk. It just happened. That was a long time ago," Caldwell shouted. "It has nothing to do with her destroying our lives now!"

Wow, this ectoplasmic truth-telling took interesting turns.

"Oh, well, if we're talking lives, do you know who killed George Thompson?" Mariah wasn't entirely certain where that question came from—the ether? Maybe the spirits had a need for justice too.

"That little rodent?" Caldwell asked in surprise. "Rats die. George was an incompetent blackmailing piece of shit. No one would have missed him."

He looked startled and fearful at the words falling from his mouth.

Even Carmel gasped. "What are you doing?" she whispered to no one in particular.

"Extracting the truth," Cass said. "You really have an appalling taste in men. That's what happens to people who break promises."

"I didn't break any promises," Carmel hissed. "I just found a way around them."

Cass snorted and pointed at Caldwell. "That cockroach?"

Keegan sent them both a look of impatience. "Mariah, ask if he knew about the crystal cave."

Shocked that she may have just discovered another killer, Mariah saluted her Scot's wisdom. "So Thompson was blackmailing you. He was a rat. Did you send Gabriel to take him out?"

Caldwell shot her a murderous look. Really, if looks could kill, she'd have been dead long ago. She had shed her shield of invisibility, but surrounded by friends, she still felt impervious to this troll.

"Gabriel was only interested in himself, even as a kid," Caldwell complained. "He learned a lazy sport like archery to please the girls. I won awards for sharpshooting. I should have been in the military but Pops needed me."

Huh, even if ectoplasm demanded veracity, Caldwell was good at evasive tactics.

"Crystals," Keegan repeated, rattling his victim to shake out the truth.

Caldwell attempted to shrug him off, but Keegan was twice the man he was, in so many ways.

"So if lazy Gabriel wouldn't take out blackmailing Thompson, you must have told Thompson you'd meet him at the crystal cave?" Mariah asked. This wasn't exactly an internet search, but with practice. . . she might learn to question better.

"If Thompson hadn't shot at you two, no one would have *known* about the cave," Caldwell shouted. "He blew everything! He couldn't even get into the damned bunker after Gabriel took out the old witch. The world is better off without stupid trash."

Pow. The truth was out, and it hurt. It hurt like hell that harmless Daisy had died for no good reason at all. There had never been anything of value in that bunker.

The foolish reason for Daisy's death would have crushed her—except Mariah realized that Daisy's murder had revealed the explosive power of ectoplasmic truth. Even in death, Daisy helped. Mariah fought back tears with wonder in this astonishing gift.

"*You* killed Thompson with your sharpshooting," Mariah concluded.

"Oh, God," Carmel murmured, falling back into the arms of the elder Menendez.

Caldwell attempted to use the moment to break free. Keegan put one brawny arm under Caldwell's chin and bent his neck to the breaking point. His prisoner quit struggling.

"Tell me again you're a nerd," Mariah whispered.

Keegan flashed a gleaming white-toothed smile in return.

"Did you intend to tell us we have valuable crystal in that canyon you wanted to buy for next to nothing?" the distinguished Menendez demanded of the weeping woman in his arms.

"As I told Hector, it's not valuable," Keegan explained, letting Caldwell's toes touch the floor again. "Not in the way you mean. The rocks are valuable only to science. It may be a century or more before we understand what you have. And by then, we may have found bigger and better pockets of it."

The older Menendez still looked suspicious as he dumped Carmel into the hands of Bradford Edison. "Thank you. It's nice to hear an honest man for a change."

He turned to Carlos and Susannah. "I'll wait until the crazy dust settles before I call for a vote. Are you coming with me or do you want to watch the drama?"

Susannah gazed longingly at her daughter before taking her husband's arm. "I'm sorry, Sam. This is the reason I left. I can't handle the madness."

Sam nodded. "I understand, and you shouldn't have to." She glanced over her mother's shoulder. "I'll be fine here."

"Walker," Keegan murmured to Mariah, following Sam's glance. "If you have any more questions, make them quick."

"So you cut Val because she ditched you and killed Thompson because he blackmailed you," Mariah said to see if the truth spell had worn off yet. Caldwell merely rubbed his stretched neck in confusion. "What did you know of the tourmaline?"

He scowled. "That's Wainwright's department. When our source of synthetic diamonds was cut off because of that damned hacker—"

Her infamous info dump had stopped a murderous crook! For the first time since the Expoleaks screw-up, Mariah took pride in her accomplishment. It had only been another form of truth-telling, after all.

"Wainwright knew about Gabriel and the cave crystals," Caldwell said. "I just made the financial connections, invested funds from the diamonds, rolled them into profitable ventures. Now the old goat is talking about running computers on weird crystals. I understand money, not computers."

"Ask about his investments," Sam whispered, clinging to Walker's arm.

Mariah figured the chief was behind that question, so she obliged. "Cryptocurrency requires reliable assets, and all you had were questionable diamonds. From the looks of it, the only investors you could find were on the dark web, drug and porn dealers and greedy dictators looking to hide ill-gotten gains. . . That sound right?"

Caldwell slumped, looking tired. "It's just money. Once we have the crystal computers, we won't need all that expensive electricity to run the databanks, and we can go large. We weren't selling drugs, just moving money. That's how banks work."

"That's why the feds regulate banks," Walker said crisply. "You have the right to remain silent. . ."

The goon in Dinah's corner approached, flashing a badge. "We'll need to take in Mrs. Kennedy as an investor and possible witness. I have men with warrants ready."

Carmel glared at the federal agent accusingly, then wept. "I thought you were helping me!"

Kurt Kennedy stepped out of the shadows. "Mother, listen to the man and remain silent for a change. We'll call your lawyer."

Carmel attacked her son with a tirade of profanity that even shook Mariah.

Teddy slipped from her position by the podium to take Kurt's arm. He hugged her to his side and stalwartly withstood the abuse. Teddy had found a rock of a man who didn't bend in the wind, but protected his own no matter the circumstances. Mariah had to quit judging him as a useless Null.

Mayor Monty simply shook his head and walked off to join his uncle Lance.

Bradford Edison gave both Carmel and his son a look of disbelief and walked away. Keegan released Caldwell Edison into custody of the federal agents. The powerful arm he'd used to confine a killer circled Mariah's shoulders instead. She gratefully leaned into him, still shaken by the truths she'd unleashed.

The elder Menendez's gaze searched the room—probably for the missing Harvey, Mariah figured.

Cameras flashed. Startled from her reverie by reporters shoving microphones into her face, Mariah cursed. She should have disappeared faster.

Weirdly, Val broke into an old sixties' song about the sounds of silence. The song rose in an eerie condemnation of a society that never spoke up, never protested.

Silence. Decades of silence. Val talking without speaking. Edison hearing without listening. Cass. . . Carmel. . . Lance. . . All with untold stories, burying the secrets under their carpets, never protesting the crimes committed here, never speaking in defense of the injured. How many had known about Daisy and Trevor and their son? What if Robert had been raised by normal parents, as Sam had? How had it helped to keep all those secrets buried?

And what about the larger secrets, like the ones she'd uncovered with her hacking? The corrupt corporate theft, the criminals operating behind politicians. . .

"Can you confirm that you are Zoe Cervantes?" one of the reporters shouted.

"Did you uncover the material on EWG?" another called. "Is this another Expoleaks?"

She'd included the EWG material in the biographies flashing across the screen. Someone had paid attention.

Mariah turned to Keegan. He kissed her, accepting whatever she chose to do. "I'm here for you," he murmured against her mouth. "If you want to leave, say so."

He had been there for his father and brother, going half way around the world in search of truth. He meant what he said, and her heart filled with joy for the first time in a long time. He knew her reputation and didn't care.

She was free at last. In relief, she turned back to the cameras. "I am Zoe Ascension de Cervantes. The truth is stranger than fiction. Do your own research. Tonight, we celebrate Hillvale and the beauty that was born here. Music, maestro!"

Someone flipped on the AV equipment again, and the recorded orchestra sprang to life while images of laughing children and beautiful artwork filled the wall.

Under Cass's imperceptible direction, the locals began crowding the food tables, shoving aside the reporters, breaking up the gathering of elders, giving Keegan room to block Mariah from microphones and cameras.

"Side door?" he suggested.

Deciding the reporters had all they needed for now, she nodded. "We'll have the vortex and the stars to ourselves. Let's spend this night together in peace before the world crashes down on us."

Outside the side exit, Harvey played his guitar. "Numero Uno could not come," he said apologetically. "Numero Dos acts in his place."

Presumably, the elder, distinguished Menendez, may they some day learn his name. The Menendez land was safe for another day.

Harvey blocked a reporter trying the exit, letting them escape down the street. Neither Mariah nor *Zoe* had any interest in investigating Menendez secrets.

THIRTY-FOUR

Keegan wrapped his arms around Mariah—*Zoe*. She'd spent this past week reclaiming her life, one small slice at a time. He had to adjust accordingly. "I want you to come with me. My home is as private as Hillvale. My family and everyone will love you."

Wearing her hair free in a rippling river down her back, *Zoe* gazed up at him with an adoration he'd never get used to—as if a nerdy rock hound could really be her hero. She kissed him with mind-bending sensuality, before abruptly pushing away.

"And I want to go with you," she said with regret. "Just not this time. I need to stand my ground and fight my battles here, not hide in Scotland. I want you to go home, see what's there for you, then come back because that's what you want, not because of me. Maybe you belong there as much as I need to be here."

He snorted. "Give me credit for knowing my mind. I have traveled the world. A *place* can never be my home. But you can," he insisted, as he had every day this past week. "I know this happened fast, but you're the only woman who has ever made me want to settle down. I won't rush you. I just want you to trust that I'm always here for you."

She snuggled into him. "Amazingly, despite all prior experience, I believe you. And because I think you are the most amazing man in my universe, I want you to be happy, which means you need to be positive about leaving your home. We have frightening talents we don't fully understand. I know I must learn here, where my essence joins with that of my ancestors. You need to be certain that you can go anywhere."

The word *love* didn't come easy for either of them. Since he'd never previously experienced this roller coaster of upheaval, Keegan feared declaring his riotous feelings might be premature. If Zoe didn't reciprocate them, he didn't want to scare her off. But his heart felt as if it might explode if he said nothing.

"The only place I want to go is with you," he admitted, searching her face for reaction. "I need to see my family and return these books to the library. I need to be certain there aren't any more journals we can use. I want them scanned so we can have them here. And I need to speak with our librarian about a computerized library. I want you to meet everyone," he said, hiding his anguish.

She stroked his clenched jaw. "You're such a dumb ox, you'll force me to admit you've burrowed into my non-existent heart, and that I want to be with you too. How can I not love the genius who created my magic mouse?"

"That was no genius," he said in deprecation. "Teddy chose the stone to help you focus. I just formed it into a solid round form that fit a thumb roller. I don't know for certain that it will prevent you from disappearing on an electron highway. . . ."

He stopped his nerdy explanation when what she'd said fully sank in.

She was looking at him in amusement. Mariah-Zoe, amused. He loved it, and he loved her, and she was giving him the opportunity to admit it. Really, she should smack him more often.

"I love you even when you're yanking my chains," he said in relief. "And I love that you trust me enough to yank them. And I want you even more with every moment that passes, so this is scary territory. But mouse or not, I *still* think you need to keep a journal on a non-internet computer and let someone else build the library website."

She was covering his face with kisses as he spoke, making it difficult to think even after she stopped to answer his fears. "I promise not to experiment with the internet until you return, even with my magic mouse restraining me. But that means you have to hurry back. Walker gets impatient when I pull a truth out of his bad guys, and I can't back it up with real evidence. The feds think I know more than I do, and they're gnawing at my door. If I could just show them. . ."

Knowing the pressure she was under, he kissed her fervently for her promise, then dragged her for the door. "*No*. Let them do their own research, just as you told the journalists. Give them direction and stay out of it."

"Yes, Oh Wise One. Besides, Gabriel and Company are spilling secrets on each other so fast, they don't really need me. Carmel hasn't been very cooperative as a witness, but Kurt and Monty are working on her."

"It's a wonder they're still talking to Walker after he brought in the feds and let her hire them as bodyguards." Keegan hugged her close as they stepped outside.

"They appreciate that the chief was just keeping their mother safe from her own dangerous impulses." She squeezed his hand. "Speaking of feds. . . Now that I'm no longer hiding, my lawyer thinks telling the feds that there's a fault in the Macro Computer operating system, and offering to show them where, will get everyone off my back, but it means my best research channel will dry up."

He kissed her again. "Please do and I'll thank you a thousand times over. I'm terrified I'll lose you down one of those rabbit holes."

"Now that I have more interesting channels for ferreting out the truth. . ." Mariah laughed as he squeezed her warningly. "Okay, I'll wait until you bring back journals that will tell me my ectoplasmic limitations."

"The books take some study," he warned. "I'm still trying to figure out the ancient phrases in the ones Wainwright had. No wonder Gabriel ignored them, if he read them at all."

"None of this will help me with the Lucys and Nulls and all that damned land out there," she complained. "Teddy and Kurt will be at each other's throats shortly. Cass and Carmel have turned the town into a war zone. And we won't even mention whatever dance Val and Lance are performing."

He grunted agreement as they stepped out of her cottage, only to see Sam and Walker leaving theirs. "At least those two seem to stay together despite the conflict."

Sam hailed them. "Walker's mom is sending us a feng shui expert to sort us all out," she said it with a strained smile while Walker rolled his eyes.

Okay, maybe there were still a few obstacles in the way.

"You'd do better with a *legal* expert to sort out that farm you and Val dumped on the town." Mariah squeezed Keegan's hand, so he kept his mouth shut. "Monty is losing his mind trying to placate everyone while sorting through all the unreasonable development ideas being dumped on his desk."

Keegan took that to mean he shouldn't mention his discussion with the Menendez family about the crystal cavern. He had too many people to talk to anyway before he got anyone's hopes up.

"Have you heard what Kurt told Teddy about the fight between Cass and Carmel?" Sam asked, keeping her voice down. "You've been so busy with the lawyers and feds, I can't keep up."

"About the day of the triptych and why it was significant enough for Lucinda to paint it? I'm amazed Cass explained." Mariah released Keegan's hand to fall in step with Sam.

"Only because Kurt pried it out of his mother, and Teddy took the information to Cass for confirmation," Sam said. "It's all about communication."

And bringing secrets into the open, Keegan understood. "I'm surprised that Cass would blackmail Carmel for the benefit of Kurt and Monty. It seems very un-Cass-like."

Sam glanced at him in disbelief. "You think Cass did it for *Nulls*? She was just getting even with Carmel for exploiting the town and to stop Carmel from turning Hillvale into a glitzy resort, just as she prevented Kurt and Monty from doing."

"They are talking Lucy language, are they not?" Keegan asked Walker over their heads.

"No, they're talking female," Walker responded. "They don't want to say that Cass knows where all the bodies are buried, knew Carmel had been involved in her husband's criminal depredations, and that she told Carmel she had evidence to send her to jail if she didn't hand half the resort over to the control of her sons."

"Monty and Kurt *didn't* inherit the resort?" Keegan asked. "I hadn't heard that part."

"They didn't inherit the *voting* rights of the corporation that controls the resort. Carmel had to sign those over. If Lucinda's triptych is to be believed, that was the day the town turned around," Walker explained.

"And that's why I have to stay," Mariah said, leaning into Keegan. "If Carmel is attempting to gather her own forces to buy the surrounding land, she'll be in control again. Cass believes that means Carmel broke her promise, and she's now free to reveal everything she knows."

"But to do so would be harmful?" Keegan suggested, grasping how small towns work.

"This is the fine line we walk," Mariah explained with a frown. "Just as you wouldn't want your father put in jail, neither will the Kennedys want Carmel locked up. And a division between the Kennedys and Cass will tear Teddy and the rest of the town in two, just when we're finally getting our acts together. Maybe Lucys can't achieve world peace, but it's our responsibility to make our little corner better. If you have people on your side of the pond who know how to do that, feel free to send them."

"I'll think on that." He hugged her shoulders, then held out his hand to Walker. "Look after the crazies while I'm gone. I promised to Skype to Teddy's computer, but someone may need to keep Mariah's hands off the keyboard while we're talking."

Walker's handshake was fervent to seal that promise.

"That doesn't make for very private conversation," Sam protested, wrinkling her nose.

"I'm practicing," Mariah said, wearing her mysterious face. "We'll see about that."

"No essence through the cable wires," Keegan warned threateningly. "No talking inside my head. I will be back here in person in no time."

"In time for the wedding, we hope," Sam said, waving the sapphire on her left hand.

Mariah exclaimed in excitement and hugged her friend. Keegan shook Walker's hand, again, while realizing he needed to hunt through the family jewels for just the right piece to bring back with him—in case the universe finally swung his way.

"We can make Hillvale the place to come to for weddings!" Mariah-Zoe cried.

"Better than murders," Walker muttered.

"There's always domestic crime," Keegan reminded him with a chuckle.

Mariah smacked his arm. "Love conquers all." She took off running down the hill—where Teddy and Kurt were just emerging from their love nest looking as if they'd resolved an argument in time-honored style.

"Love eradicates evil," Sam cried jubilantly, running after her.

Left with no choice, Keegan pursued his love, flinging Mariah-Zoe over his shoulder and carrying her into the café to the cheers of the breakfast crowd.

Looking starry-eyed, Kurt and Teddy followed them in.

Sam and Walker found a more private place to stop first.

HILLVALE CHARACTER LIST

MARIAH—CREATES GHOSTCATCHERS AND WORKS AT DINAH'S CAFE

Keegan Ives—Scots geologist and mineralogist

Theodosia (Teddy) Devine-Baker—empathic jeweler

Sydony (Syd) Devine-Baker Bennet—Teddy's sister, mother of **Mia** and **Jeb**

Kurtis Dominic Kennedy—architect; part owner and full-time manager of Redwood Resort

Montgomery Kennedy—Hillvale's mayor, part owner of the Redwood Resort

Carmel Kennedy—mother of Kurt and Monty; also part owner of Redwood Resort

Lance Brooks—Carmel's brother; artist who lives at resort

Samantha (Sam) Moon—environmental scientist

Chen Ling Walker—Hillvale's new police chief

Cassandra Tolliver—mother's family once owned all of Hillvale

Dinah—cook and owner of the café; originally from New Orleans

Crazy Daisy—homeless but creates marvelous sculptures of twigs and stone.

Valerie Ingersson (Valdis)—eerily correct harbinger of death; Sam's aunt on maternal side;

Susannah Ingersson Menendez—Val's sister, Sam's mother, lives in Malaysia

Carlos Menendez—Susannah Ingersson's second husband; Sam's stepfather

Amber—non-native; bangle-wearing Tarot reader

Tullah—owns thrift store; tall African-American psychic medium

Harvey—musician friend of Monty's; carves energy-oriented walking sticks;

Aaron Townsend—goateed owner of antique store who practices psychometry

Xavier Black—former contract lawyer and addict; now rents out housing

Lucinda Malcolm—famed early 20th century artist who once visited Hillvale; deceased

Brianna—Keegan's ex-girlfriend

Ralph Wainwright—relation of Lucy Wainwright aka Lucinda Malcolm;

George Thompson—local plumber who once lived in commune

Trevor Gabriel—Keegan's great-uncle in café mural

Robert Gabriel—son of Trevor

Bradford Edison—musician in café mural. Now conservative politician

Caldwell Edison—Bradford's son

CRYSTAL MAGIC SERIES

Other books in this series —

Sapphire Nights
Book 1 of the Crystal Magic Series

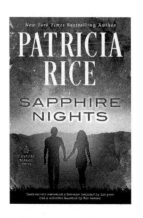

A lawman haunted by his past . . . a scientist haunted by her future.

Samantha Moon arrives in Hillvale— population 325 lives and countless ghosts—in a fog as thick as the one circling the aging mountain town. Bereft of friends and family, money and memory, all she has to her name is a stray cat . . . but that's apparently enough for the people of Hillvale to take her in.

L.A. investigator Chen Ling Walker's problem is too many memories. He's come to bury his tragic past in this remote California town, where his father vanished years before. Ever watchful, Walker sees how Sam's arrival disturbs the deceptive peace of Hillvale. Old bones lead to new death, stirring ancient fears and feuds.

Sam will need Walker's help to uncover the truth of who she is and face the burden that brings. But how can he accept a reality that stretches beyond the borders of what he knows -- one that contains spirits, psychics, and imaginary voices—the weirdness that ruined his life before?

And if they survive what lies ahead, will they find any way to make a future together?

~

Topaz Dreams
Book 2 of the Crystal Magic Series

An empathic woman searching for safety - An architect yearning for dreams - And the ghost house that endangers them both

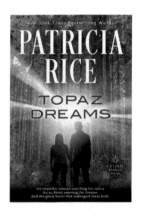

Teddy Devine-Baker arrives in her childhood home of Hillvale with a box of crystals and an attitude. Her empathic gift has ruined one relationship and most of her jewelry business, leaving her determined to learn more about a talent she's never properly respected. Unfortunately, her empathy fails to work on tall, dark, handsome Kurt Kennedy, the aloof architect who warmed her heart as a child.

Although his family owns most of Hillvale, Kurt avoids the eccentrics inhabiting the ghost town. . . until irrepressible Teddy waltzes in and lays claim to a jinxed and unrentable house that belongs to him. Now he's being dragged into the emotional whirlwind he's spent years training himself not to feel. Kurt's plans for rebuilding the house -- not to mention his future -- will go up in flames if he heeds the intriguing redhead who claims to *sense* ghosts.

But when they find an actual skeleton in the attic, the two must work together to uncover a killer . . . assuming Teddy can apply her empathy and break down Kurt's emotional barriers. If she can't, she may wind up with only the family ghost for company and a murderer on the loose.

ABOUT THE AUTHOR

With several million books in print and *New York Times* and *USA Today's* bestseller lists under her belt, former CPA Patricia Rice is one of romance's hottest authors. Her emotionally-charged contemporary and historical romances have won numerous awards, including the *RT Book Reviews* Reviewers Choice and Career Achievement Awards. Her books have been honored as Romance Writers of America RITA® finalists in the historical, regency and contemporary categories.

A firm believer in happily-ever-after, Patricia Rice is married to her high school sweetheart and has two children. A native of Kentucky and New York, a past resident of North Carolina and Missouri, she currently resides in Southern California, and now does accounting only for herself.

ALSO BY PATRICIA RICE

Mystic Warrior

Mysteries:

Family Genius Series

Evil Genius

Undercover Genius

Cyber Genius

Twin Genius

Twisted Genius

Tales of Love and Mystery

Blue Clouds

Garden of Dreams

Nobody's Angel

Volcano

California Girl

ABOUT BOOK VIEW CAFÉ

Book View Café Publishing Cooperative (BVC) is an author-owned cooperative of over fifty professional writers, publishing in a variety of genres including fantasy, romance, mystery, and science fiction. Since its debut in 2008, BVC has gained a reputation for producing high-quality ebooks. BVC's ebooks are DRM-free and are distributed around the world. The cooperative is now bringing that same quality to its print editions.

BVC authors include New York Times and USA Today bestsellers as well as winners and nominees of many prestigious awards, including:

Agatha Award
Campbell Award
Hugo Award
Lambda Award
Locus Award
Nebula Award
Nicholl Fellowship
PEN/Malamud Award
Philip K. Dick Award
RITA Award

Made in the USA
Lexington, KY
08 August 2018